REDEMPTION

THE EMERGENCE: BOOK 2

SETH M. BAKER

The Emergence Series
Reaction: The Emergence, Book 1
Redemption: The Emergence, Book 2
Reunion: The Emergence, Book 3

Copyright © 2013 by Seth M. Baker
All rights reserved.
ISBN-13: 978-1-938830-07-5
ISBN: 1-938830-07-5
Cover design by Deranged Doctor Design
Published by Dark Hollow Press, 2013
www.sethmbaker.com

REDEMPTION

Prologue

Three Months Post-Emergence

Everything was coming together, despite the setbacks. From one end of the labyrinthine ship to the other, acetylene flames and soldering irons sparked and smoked, forging strong bonds that could withstand deep-water pressure. Nimble fingers controlled by dexterous minds entered the refactored assembly code. The administrator had learned from his mistakes, and his operation would be stronger for it. Something still bothered him, but he would figure it out soon enough.

Through smoky lenses, he saw Marshall stepping through the bulkhead door. Marshall wore no goggles; his eyes had gone black early on, and he seemed to revel in other's reactions to his condition. Even the administrator, Marshall's old pal, found those eyes unsettling, and he required everyone else on his payroll to utilize the safety gear he provided. Like strength, uniqueness should not be flaunted. Carry a big stick, keep your fucking mouth shut, and keep your eyes shielded. Only, now he had to do exactly the opposite: talk, talk, and talk some more, all the while making plenty of eye contact and stroking the netherparts of meaning in order to convince his allies that his goals were actually their goals.

"You really should take a vacation," the administrator said to

Marshall, who responded with a broad smile. Running a hand through his long hair, Marshall shook his head. "Spend some time with your family."

"And miss out on all this?" Marshall gestured to the work going on all around them. "It's so ... elegant. Besides, I'll have plenty of time to spend with them once everything's done. We're already looking at villas. This is going to be my last Mid-Atlantic winter. Good riddance to this snowy cold bullshit. I had high hopes for global warming, and that turned out to be a honey wagon."

"The Norwegians have a saying: there's no such thing as bad weather, just bad clothes. A new winter wardrobe might be cheaper than Central American property."

"What can I say? Spend a few years in the desert, and you start to appreciate the heat."

A notification appeared in the bottom right corner of the administrator's field of vision. He focused on it, and a box expanded to display a message: *Ready for testing*. He blinked, and the message receded, the scene of industrious activity he had been enjoying replaced it. The administrator still felt he was forgetting something important. He supposed it had something to do with the culmination of Abdullah's current project.

As if reading his mind, Marshall asked about the upcoming experiment. "You think they'll be like they were last time?"

"I have no reason to think otherwise."

2006

The heat drained the administrator like a transfusion, and Alyssa's persistence did nothing to steady him. A man's wife should support him, not make him falter. Yet, he could tell from her look that she was about to start again in three, two, one ...

"It's been over a year now," Alyssa said. She held Kaylee against her chest as they walked. She had dressed the child in a white linen wrap to protect her from that damn relentless sun.

Presently, they stood in the shade of a column outside the entrance to the Republican Palace. Watchful soldiers, nervous bureaucrats, and bearded contractors scurried in and out of the main entrance.

"I just need some more time. Abdullah, my engineer, says the bridge contract is, like, three steps away from being approved. This one's going to be huge for the big H."

"These guys." Alyssa rolled her eyes. "They tell you anything just to avoid saying they don't know what the hell's going on."

"It's a bad time right now. The coalition wasn't expecting the level of resistance they're seeing."

"I don't give a sparrow's fart about the capital C coalition. I care about our little coalition, about you, Kaylee, and me. Do you really think this is a safe place to raise your daughter?"

"She was born here. This is kind of her country now, too. The Green Zone has more security personnel per capita than any other place on Earth. Is it dangerous? Yes. But we're civilians, and I'm here to help."

"Help? Help? Look around you, dear. You're helping them build a bridge that our pals blasted to powder last year. You're helping to build a school our allies cluster-bombed during Ramadan. You see the pattern here?"

"And everything will be much better for it. Remember when you broke your collarbone playing racquetball, and the doctor said the fused bone would be stronger than it was in the first place? Or the way your dad used to rebuild cars, how he would totally disassemble them, even the sections that were working, and put them all back together? In the end, all these things ended up stronger because they were broken and rebuilt."

"The same doesn't apply to broken promises," Alyssa said.

Kaylee squirmed beneath the wrap, then began to whimper. In the distance, beyond the concrete walls and across the Tigris, a garbled voice beckoned the faithful to pull out their prayer mats, aim for Mecca, and prostrate themselves. For such a religious group, these people were brutal. The administrator had a theory that a direct relationship existed between the strength of a group's religious belief and their propensity to commit heinous violence. If he ever wanted to pursue a doctorate, he had his thesis.

"And you're not even listening to me," Alyssa said. "That's great, just great. I try to tell you why our family is falling apart, and you're daydreaming about ... about ... what?"

"The road to the airport. I know I told you—"

"Promised me. Continue, please." She patted Kaylee, who nuzzled her chubby cheeks into the soft skin of her mother's tanned neck.

"Right. Promised you we'd leave after a year, after Kaylee was older, but the road to the airport ... well, you know what it's like. I'm—I'm hoping things will settle down." As if on cue, small arms fire crackled in the distance.

"And in the meantime, you keep finding new opportunities. Right now, you're chasing two rabbits. One is your family. The other is your very lucrative government services career. The difference is if you let this rabbit return to its warren," she placed a hand over her heart, "it'll still be waiting for you when you've caught the other."

"Alyssa, it's so dangerous," he said, clasping his hands in front of him. He didn't want to watch his daughter grow up on Skype, but neither did he want her to take her first steps while bombs fell and men died only blocks away.

"Please. Convoys make the trip every day. It's not 2004 anymore. I'd rather spend an hour scared out of my wits on the airport road than wake up every day with this needling, gnawing sense of dread." She gave him a moment to answer, and when no words came, she said, "I've already made arrangements. I just need to specify the day."

Tears welled up in the administrator's eyes. He took Kaylee, who reached for him and beamed, showing off her four new teeth. He wrapped his arms around her warm little body and held her close. He wanted to keep her here with him, in the place she was born, but his wife was right. The correct decision was never an easy decision.

"Well, I guess I need to help you pack."

Three Months Post-Emergence

In a closed holding tank the size of a basketball court, the administrator, Marshall, and eight of his guys watched Abdullah make a final inspection of the machine. Half the men held long metal shafts tipped with wire hoops like those used by dog catchers, only these had been augmented with electrification. The other four held .50-caliber Browning M2s, just in case capture wasn't an option.

At first glance, the machine looked like a miniature techno-Stonehenge, but instead of megaliths, this apparatus consisted of aluminum posts as thick as baseball bats, supported by tripods and topped by lead glass bulbs. Eight of these posts were arranged in a circle. In this particular design iteration, Abdullah had simplified the wiring; the improved controller design eliminated the need for about half the external equipment. Everything else was shielded and shrouded in flexible tubes. At this rate, their systems would be wireless and remote-controlled by this coming summer.

If he didn't know better, the administrator would've thought the entire setup could've been mistaken for the decorations of some cultish religion. Raëlians, or Scientologists, maybe. But this altar would make his people stronger than any religion could ever hope to. In the States, they'd had religion for almost four hundred years, and look where it had gotten them: most citizens were spineless, passive desk jockeys, not the noble gentlemen-farmer-poet-citizens envisioned by the founders.

Everyone but Marshall wore goggles and nanofiber safety jumpsuits. The concern about endocrine disruption was only that—a concern—but the administrator didn't want his people coming down with mystery illnesses in a month, a year, or even a decade. He needed them healthy and strong for the long-term.

The delayed-onset ocular darkening was bad enough, even if it was only temporary.

Abdullah strolled toward the administrator, pushing a cart laden with various pieces of equipment and trailing a power cord. The administrator recognized the equipment immediately: very expensive variations on the detection system that damn Brunmeier boy had created. Abdullah gave the administrator a nod, then returned to his control station, which was nothing more than a tablet and an aluminum case the size of a two-speaker guitar amp. He connected the plugs for the detection systems to the ship's main power drop. The administrator half expected the lights to flicker under the power draw, but experience had taught him this wouldn't occur until the main event began.

With the guys at the ready and the equipment plugged in, Abdullah looked to the administrator. He nodded and gave Abdullah a thumbs-up. After some initial misunderstandings, this had become a running joke between them. Abdullah now knew that the administrator's skyward-pointing thumb did not signify rectal insertions, as it did in his home country. Abdullah smiled in response, nodded, and typed something on the tablet. The glass spheres began to glow blue, the overhead lights dimmed, and a flickering orb of searing white light appeared in the center of the circle and began to grow.

"Alive this time, if possible," the administrator said.

2006

The next morning, the administrator rode with his family in a luggage-laden Humvee situated in the middle of a Bravo company convoy. He had secured one week's personal leave with his supervisor, which he hoped would be enough time to fly home with his family and help them get settled before returning to Iraq. Holding Kaylee in his lap, she placed her little hands against the bulletproof glass.

"Baby girl, this is the last time you'll see this, so I want you to remember it. There's a butcher shop where we get steaks and chickens and goats. That's a mosque. People pray there. Over there is a market where you used to be able to buy shoes, purses, jackets, and books."

They hit a bump. The Humvee lurched. Alyssa gasped, while Kaylee giggled. The administrator closed his eyes and waited for the explosion that would tear them apart.

Nothing happened.

He expected trucks and vans to appear from the side streets, block their convoy's progress, and open fire, but again, nothing happened. At the checkpoints, he braced himself for suicide bombers to throw themselves against their Humvee, mutter some religious nonsense, and press the button that would put them on the express train to paradise. During take-off, he sat there stiffly, waiting for surface-to-air missiles to assail their ship.

Nothing happened.

The only thing that did happen was Kaylee spit up on the administrator's blazer just before they reached cruising altitude. By this point, the administrator was so relieved he just laughed and daubed it up with a napkin.

For the administrator, the next few days were a blur of apartment hunting, social events, and, once they found a nice two-bedroom in Dupont Circle, lovemaking, at least when Kaylee was asleep.

The day before his return flight, the administrator, Alyssa, and Kaylee took the Metro to the zoo. Alyssa had covered her hair with a beautiful green and turquoise *hijab*. She wasn't interested in modesty or religion, only the *hijab's* ability to protect her pale Nordic ears and neck from sunburn. The administrator had dressed Kaylee in a pink jumper with black buttons and shiny black patent leather shoes. While he dressed himself, he had reached for the bulletproof vest, but laughed at himself and left it on the bed.

The happy family visited the big cats first, followed by the lumbering rhinos, then the elephants, who trumpeted water into the air from their trunks. Kaylee squealed with delight when the administrator held her up to the thick glass of the monkey house, but by early afternoon she was whiny and refused to ride in her stroller. Alyssa gave in and carried her as the administrator dragged the folded-up stroller behind them.

While they stood on the platform waiting for the next train, the administrator's gaze darted across the crowd. His heart began to pound. Something felt off, but he attributed it to spending the past three years in a war zone. Alyssa must have noticed his discomfort, because she moved closer to him, placed a hand on his forearm, and whispered in his ear, "I love you."

At that moment, screams began to echo off the subway's concrete walls. A man's voice cried, "He's got a gun!"

A rifle shot exploded. Sparks showered down from a light on the ceiling. Kaylee began to wail. The administrator put himself in front of her and Alyssa. He guided them backwards, away from the confused mass of people and toward the exit. He scanned the room, locking eyes with a white man who held a hunting rifle. The man smiled as he cocked the rifle, aimed it at the administrator, and fired.

The administrator writhed on the floor before his brain registered the throb in his stomach and back. He felt himself draining out. Whiteness clouded his vision, sleep threatened to take him, but he could see the shooter's wild gaze as he cocked the lever again. The spent shell casing clattered on the floor. Fighting to stay conscious, he turned his head toward Alyssa and Kaylee. Alyssa was backing away, her brown eyes wide. Kaylee shrieked.

He looked from the shooter and back to the crowd. They were ... watching the shooter, frozen. Just standing there. The shooter's grinning, demented gaze was now fixed on Alyssa. His every step was deliberate, considered, and patient. His movements gave them time, yet all those able-bodied people just stood there, dumb as ruminants.

"Help," the administrator said. The word came out a garbled croak. "Someone. Help." A plea. A simple plea.

No one moved to help.

The shooter was less than ten feet away.

"Kaylee," the administrator said. The shooter raised his rifle and began to speak. The words were English, but they meant nothing except time, more time. He was giving the crowd every opportunity to stop him. Alyssa turned her back to the shooter, putting her body between the rifle and Kaylee.

The rifle fired again.

Alyssa and Kaylee fell to the floor. Blood drained from a red hole that blossomed on his wife's right shoulder blade. Kaylee's crying stopped. One more spent casing clattered onto the platform's brown, hexagonal tile. The shooter started to turn the rifle on himself, but before he did so, the side of his head exploded in a red spray. The last thing the administrator saw was a long-haired young man in a security guard's uniform tucking a pistol into his waistband and swinging his boot into the belly of the shooter's corpse.

2006

When the administrator opened his eyes, he saw a familiar-looking long-haired man clad in the uniform of a security guard. "Hathaway" was embroidered on his nametag in red thread. The man held something pink and black in his hand. As the administrator's mind tried to register what was so familiar about the object, dread filled his heart. He strained to look around, but the tubes in his throat, neck, chest, and arms kept his gaze forward. A priest stood up from a chair at the foot of his bed, his thinning gray hair slicked back over a cadaverous skull. He placed a reassuring hand on the administrator's chest.

"I'm sorry, my son. They're with the Lord now."

The administrator choked on his feeding tube and tried to swat at the priest, but the pain overwhelmed him, and he sunk back into his pillow. The priest nodded to Hathaway, who leaned over the side of the administrator's bed.

"I'm deeply sorry for your loss. I started running as soon as I heard the shots. By the time I arrived ... I know it's not much, but I had a friend make this for you." He gently placed an object, a doll, on the administrator's chest. It felt like Kaylee. Same size. Same weight. Same dress she had been wearing that day. The head was soft cloth filled with rice, as was the body. At first, the administrator wanted to say this was sick, morbid, but when he felt its weight against him, felt the familiar cotton weave, he wrapped the doll in a weak embrace, and for a brief moment, he was comforted.

Hathaway stood and started to leave, but the administrator grunted and looked at the chair. Nodding, Hathaway sat back down and gazed out the window with steely eyes. The strength of this man's presence gave the administrator comfort, far more than the collared huckster at the foot of his bed could ever hope to. His country could use far more like the former and far fewer like the latter. Strength alone would make them great again, but not today. Today was a day no man should have to endure. The administrator pressed the button for the morphine drip and waited for the opiates to do their work.

Three Months Post-Emergence

The swirling, crackling orb expanded. In less than ten seconds, the orb's outer edges had reached the outer perimeter of the circle. The steel beneath the administrator's feet rumbled. The lights around them darkened. A brilliant blue-white light filled the room. Something large and spindly rocketed out of the portal just before the orb blinked out and everything went pitch black.

"Shit," the administrator said. As soon as the word left his mouth, a man shrieked like a fox crying out in the night. Every hair on the administrator's body stood up and he pulled off the goggles.

Four blue-white electric arcs flickered, revealing the outline of a subluminal the size of a buffalo. Another man screamed. Two .50-calibers opened up. In the strobe effect created by the firing, the administrator saw the creature stumble, regain its footing, then pounce. Equipment clattered to the floor. A man's screams turned to gurgles. The electric hoops sparked like a severed power line as they sought the creature. One .50-caliber resumed firing. When it finished, the only sounds were of something sizzling and a man wheezing.

"Get us some fucking light, right the fuck now," Hathaway said. Two powerful handheld lamps illuminated the scene. Three soldiers were dead. One had been eviscerated, his body torn open from neck to groin. Bullet holes riddled the other two. Shit. Poor firing discipline had killed more of his guys than that fucking mindless beast. The communicator had said it should be able to calm them down as soon as they came through, but the administrator could see how well *that* had worked out. Those fucking devious, lying *Takun*. They just told him what they wanted him to hear. People, and now these creatures, had a habit of doing that. Maybe they had picked up the habit from associating with humans. But if the communicator was right, if it really could start controlling them when they first arrived, rather than after a couple weeks, then the administrator's life would be so much easier, and all this trouble would be worth it.

Fighting down the sick feeling in his stomach, the administrator stepped forward for a better look. Though no two creatures were alike, this one was especially remarkable. It had a well-defined head, and a hundred black spines covered its back. He had been reading a lot about porcupines, *erethizon dorsatum*, lately, but ... no, that didn't have anything to do with it. Surely not.

"Where's Abdullah?" the administrator said. One of the soldiers aimed his lamps at the control area. A headless, legless torso bled out onto the digital control surface. Abdullah's head lay nearly ten meters away.

The administrator's stomach curdled. He thought he was

going to cry. But not here, not now. He placed one hand over his mouth and rested his elbow in the other. They needed to see strength, but when he turned to leave, he nearly tripped over Abdullah's leg.

"Fuck. Hathaway, get a crew to clean this shit up. Usual procedures." As he turned the wheel on the bulkhead door, he cast one more look at his engineer's grisly remains. What a waste.

His footsteps echoed through the long corridor. This shit still gave him the heebie jeebies, but all the computer models said this was the best possible course of action.

Poor Abdullah. The administrator smiled and choked back a sob as he thought of all those *halal* cookouts the little Iraqi had hosted, both over there and back here. His death was yet another sacrifice to regain the strength that never should've been lost ... and for a country that wasn't even his own.

By the time the administrator stood among the spartan furnishings of his own quarters, his vision was blurry with tears and his throat ached from a hundred suppressed wails. So many lives lost. He sat down on the bed, scooped an infant-sized pink-and-black doll up in his arms, and held it close as he began to pace the steel floor. As he did so, he looked at the calendar and realized what had been bothering him. How could he have forgotten? He had thought about her, them, every day for the past eighteen years. He had even marked it during his planning session last Sunday. There it was, written in red, right on his calendar: her initials set inside a little heart, with two sets of dates. He squeezed the doll, taking comfort in its familiar weight and contours, and thought of her smile at the monkey house.

Kaylee would've turned twenty today.

1

Washington, DC
Winter, Three Months Post-Emergence

"Your father is alive ... and working with Maximilian Ross," Jones said, his oversized black eye looking like a tadpole egg ready to burst. Amadeus' fists clenched. The scant trace of pity he felt drained away and was replaced with something new, something slimy, something he liked. He stood a bit straighter as he looked down at Jones' withered and contorted body, which was strapped to the electric wheelchair. Overhead, fluorescent lights pulsed. Through the ducts a chorus of machinery hummed to life. "And I'll tell you the same thing I told you back in September," said Jones. "He's alive, but I have no idea where he is."

"He's dead," Amadeus said, trying—but failing—to keep his voice level and even as his knees went weak. He didn't know why he had come here. "He's dead *because* of Ross."

Amadeus looked over to Gravity, who was leaning against the wall, a sport coat thrown over his shoulder. Gravity shrugged. "Why do you insist on getting my hopes up? Are you just trying to fuck with me?"

"Because, my boy, it's true. Look at me. At this point I've got nothing to lose. I say this as a peace offering. I'm sorry I had to lie to you. I'm sorry I tried to kill you. What else can I do? You've come back here hoping I'll throw up my hands and admit I'm making a sick joke at your expense, but that's not the case. Your father is alive, and he's collaborating with everybody's second-favorite villain—behind yours truly, of course. Like you, I too was used, manipulated, and tricked. But I'm just a confederate. Plus, I always liked your father, no matter how misguided his research became."

"What are you trying to do, Ziggy Stardust?" Gravity said.

"Comparing me to Bowie is anything but insulting. At least I'm not as bad off as poor Amadeus here. Excited kipium does that to a fellow, though."

Amadeus pushed his sunglasses up on his nose. Since his eyes had gone black back in October, Amadeus had been careful to always wear sunglasses in public, even though the blackness had almost faded. Most people assumed he just wanted some privacy and some relief from the incessant flashing of a thousand cameras.

"But I still have to ask: do you make a habit of mocking those with legitimate neurological conditions?" Jones arched one eyebrow, causing the pale, sallow skin on the right side of his forehead to wrinkle.

"Normally no, but I'll make an exception for you," Gravity said.

"I am exceptional."

Amadeus looked from Jones to Gravity and back. He wondered why Jones would tell him this, what his motivations were. But if what he was saying were true, if his father was alive …

"If he's alive, then where is he?" Amadeus said.

"How many times do I have to tell you? I. Do. Not. Know."

"So *how* do you know he's alive?" Gravity asked.

"That doesn't matter. And besides, if I told you everything I knew, if I went all in, what would I get out of it? I'm not about to throw away all of my bargaining chips."

"Bargaining?" Amadeus said. "You think this is about bargaining? You're going to die here, Jones. You'll never see the sun again. You'll rot away—that is, if someone doesn't kill you first."

"Are you threatening me, Amadeus?"

"I wouldn't do anything you haven't done to me," Amadeus said.

"Ah, I suppose that's a fair point. No good deed ..."

"Jones, you don't seem to understand," Amadeus said, putting his hands on his temples and shaking his head. "You are *the* villain, public enemy number one. In his last speech, the president mentioned you by name."

"I'm flattered."

"You shouldn't be. Your own daughter won't even say your name. The world needed a villain, someone to blame for the Emergence. And capturing you, that's the win. Do you understand that? Or has the tumor destroyed your logic centers?" Amadeus clenched his fists. For a moment, he imagined striking Jones, his fists pummeling the man's face; he could see the way his head would bounce off the back of his wheelchair. Keeping his hands to his sides, Amadeus said, "Until someone captures or kills Ross, you're the one."

"Jones," Gravity said, "Amadeus is right. You are in no position to bargain. Tell us what else you know, and we'll see about getting you some proper medical treatment and perhaps a cell with a window."

"Gravity, Gravity. The old war dog. Always after a new enemy. But I'm not your enemy."

"You tried to kill me, Jones," Amadeus said.

"If only it were that simple. I want to see my daughter."

"She won't see you," Amadeus said.

"Then I'm done talking. Leave me." Jones folded his hands in his lap and bowed his head like a sick man praying for recovery.

"We'll decide when you're done talking," Amadeus said, but

Jones wouldn't look up. Amadeus started to reach out and shake him, but Gravity placed a hand on his shoulder.

"Don't touch the prisoner," Gravity said. "We'll come back. He'll tire of this."

"I'm not coming back. I don't even know why we came in the first place."

But, as the guard escorted him and Gravity away from Jones' cell, Amadeus knew exactly why he had come: he wanted to believe what Jones was saying. He had to believe him.

When the alarm buzzed the following morning, Amadeus mashed the snooze button and nuzzled into the smooth skin in the crook of Lilly's neck. She awoke and grabbed his cock, which led to sleepy intercourse. After he finished, and just before he drifted off to sleep, Amadeus decided he should ask Lilly to marry him. When the alarm went off again, Lilly stretched and pulled the plug from the wall. He had something to do, but sleep ...

Incessant knocks finally roused him from the hotel bed. Grey winter light filtered through the window. A sense of urgency propelled him to pull on his pants and shirt. He peered through the door at a little man in a bellhop uniform. The man smiled, said, "Good morning," and scurried off. Back in the room, Amadeus wrapped a purple-and-black paisley tie around his neck as his hotel phone began to ring. He watched as Lilly pulled a thick black sweater over her head and a billowing gray skirt over her pale thighs.

"Don't let yourself get distracted doing cleavage signatures today," she said. She gave him that inviting half-smile.

Amadeus licked his lips and wished he had a little more time. He pressed the receiver to his ear.

"The wolves await," Gravity's voice said on the other end of the line.

"Fifteen minutes," Amadeus said.

Twenty minutes later, Amadeus wanted it to end, and it hadn't even started. Despite the cold outside, the congressional hearing chambers had begun to feel like an oven despite the cold outside, and they were only fifteen minutes in. He loosened his tie as he examined the committee members and observers. Politicians wrapped in somber, well-cut suits sat shoulder-to-shoulder with uniformed military leaders bedecked with glinting brass buttons and colorful insignias. Grassal Delgado, Claudius Owens, and Lilly Jones sat with Amadeus at the table. Before each of them sat printed copies of their testimonies. Though absent from the inquiry, the president remained one of Amadeus' most vocal supporters. Gravity had assured Amadeus this would soften the blow of the committee's questions, but something in the room felt off.

Amadeus loosened his tie, straightened his papers, and pushed the sunglasses up on his nose. He'd been having some trouble with his eyes, but this morning he had another problem: a condom still clung to his cock, the result of sleepy wake-up sex with Lilly followed by a mad dash to make the hearing on time.

A paunchy, pale aide with an early bald spot blooming in his black hair distributed full copies of his testimony. The aide moved with awkward, tentative steps, and Amadeus felt pity for him, though he wasn't sure why. When all the copies were distributed, the aide slunk away to a table behind a senator Amadeus recognized. Gravity saw Amadeus watching the aide, and across the bottom of his yellow legal pad, Gravity wrote:

The suits and the brass are the grasping tentacles of the same beast, but this kid is the ink-spitting head of this diseased political cephalopod. Not necessarily in control of his tentacles, but he probably knows what they're grappling.

A silver-haired politician cleared his throat and nodded to Amadeus, who walked to the front of the room. There he placed his hand on an old leather Bible held by a man whose shirt bulged against his girth. While Amadeus swore to give the committee a true rendering of events, he couldn't help but notice the tiny yellow spot on the man's otherwise lurid red tie. Looking down, he also noticed a tiny patch of semen that had seeped through the front of his own trousers.

After the oath, Amadeus took his seat and addressed the panel.

"You've all read my advance testimony. Even though I was in the middle of the events of the Emergence, you must understand that many details remain unclear to me. I wasn't even aware of the, um, nature of my father's research until events propelled me to become so.

"My house was invaded by armed gunmen. My father stayed behind so that Grassal Delgado and I could escape. I soon learned I was wanted for murder. At my father's request, I sought shelter with Holden Jones, an old friend of my father's and a man I thought I could trust. I—"

"Yes, Mr. Brunmeier." Every head in the room turned toward the voice that had interrupted Amadeus. Senator Amanda Payne clicked an ink pen then said, "We know your story well enough. We're not here to hear it again. The purpose of our hearing today is to ensure we have the tools to protect our citizens."

Amadeus regarded her with a look that bordered on, but didn't quite reach, contempt. She held his gaze. Evenly matched, Amadeus thought. Senator Payne was head of the Committee on Emergence Response and Oversight as well as the Committee on Morality and Government. According to Gravity, she'd gained the latter position through a potent mix of private blackmail and public prayer.

"That matter being your bill to privatize significant parts of our domestic subluminal defenses," Amadeus said. He adjusted his sunglasses. "So that you can ensure the river of government gravy keeps flowing to your biggest campaign contributors."

"That's enough, Mr. Brunmeier. The senator's point is valid;

the threat remains," a new voice said. "An enemy wounded is not an enemy destroyed." The voice belonged to a middle-aged woman in an Army blue service uniform. Three silver stars adorned her shoulders. She scanned the room with triangular eyes the color of midnight. Lieutenant General Janette Nguyen.

"This is true," Amadeus said, "but the US has more firepower than any country in history. What we need is a more effective use of our domestic intelligence."

"And as we saw last summer, private enterprise can do that better than government can ever hope to," a man's voice said. Amadeus recognized the voice before he saw its source: Roland Jessup, founder of Securaux, one of the companies who had made it their business to kill subluminals. Amadeus looked over to catch Grassal's eye. Grassal gave him a wink that looked more like a tic.

"I suppose you are referring to your own enterprise, Mr. Jessup?"

"I am. My enterprise saved hundreds of lives during the Emergence because we were able to deploy quickly."

Amadeus said, "I'm pretty sure that another private military operation, acting at the behest of a wealthy misanthrope, was the driving force behind the Emergence."

"Mr. Brunmeier, if you're suggesting that *all* private military corporations are like the one we suspect carried out these attacks, then I'm afraid your judgment is clouded," General Nguyen said. "I've served with some honorable individuals employed by PMCs. A vast majority of them are ex-military. As you can see, the heads of several of these companies are here today." She extended her hand to a group of six men sitting in a section reserved for industry members interested in the senator's bill. They wore well-cut suits, buzzed hair, and hawkish expressions.

"General Nguyen," Amadeus said, "I'm sure many of them are honorable. I'll even admit they can serve vital and useful roles in combat operations. However, I believe this is a matter of intelligence, rather than combat. I don't see the benefit in doling out billions of dollars in contracts to professional goon squads."

"Though I take issue with your terminology, I tend to agree," General Nguyen said. "According to a report commissioned by Senators Graythorpe and Fielding, our own investigative forces were too busy chasing low-level drug dealers and wannabe-jihadists, while our so-called 'homeland defenses' are scattered all over the globe."

"Exactly," Amadeus said. He took a deep breath and tried to wrap things up. "I don't consider myself an expert in anything except maybe geovisual analytics, but the president wanted me here to provide my expert opinion, so I'll provide it. I believe that the Emergence was such a bizarre and unexpected series of events that even the most well-organized of security forces would've been caught with their hands on their—"

"Your opinions *are* of questionable validity, Mr. Brunmeier," Amanda Payne said. "Seeing as you're the son of the man responsible for the Emergence."

"Unleashing these creatures was never my father's intention, Senator." Heat rose under Amadeus' collar. "It's also true that I was able to limit the damage because of his contingency planning. I know you're disappointed this wasn't the apocalypse you were hoping for—"

"So says the man who fornicates with the delinquent daughter of one of Maximilian Ross' collaborators."

"That's enough, Senator Payne," a man's voice said. Amadeus found its source: Senator Graythorpe, a thin, youngish man with a mane of silver hair combed flat back over his head.

Amadeus bit his lip and fought the urge to yell expletives. The heat around his collar rose to his cheeks. A glance at Lilly confirmed that she was enjoying herself, though whether at the senator's expense or his own, Amadeus wasn't sure.

"Thank you, Senator Graythorpe," General Nguyen said. "Senator Payne, your line of questioning is irrelevant to the issue at hand."

Amadeus nodded his thanks to the general, then sat back in his chair and crossed his arms. As he did so, he felt the condom slide off. He shifted, hoping its payload remained intact.

"I think it's quite relevant," Amanda Payne said. "This man's family is an enemy of the state. He's voicing his opposition to this bill because ... because he's up to something. Consider this: when his father was murdered by this so-called goon squad, why didn't he go to the police in the first place? How do we know he didn't murder his father, sell the technology, and play the hero in a bid for, for—"

Gravity cut her off. "Conjecture and paranoid delusions of conspiracy may play well to your base, Senator, but they are a waste of everyone else's time. You're on the record for calling the Emergence both the beginning of the rapture, then an act of divine retribution for the lechery of Babylon. You can believe what you want, but your apocalyptogasmic beliefs have no role in public policy. Perhaps you should stick to interpreting Revelation for the Sunday prophecy brunch crowd."

A few chuckles of laughter escaped from members of the committee, including General Nguyen. The senator from South Carolina scowled.

"Your words, Senator, not mine," Gravity said.

"Mock The Word all you want, but we'll see where it gets you," Payne said. "There will be judgment for each of you."

With that, Congresswoman Payne stood up and stormed out of the committee chambers, followed by two male aides.

"While our bill's co-sponsor might have taken her accusations too far, I think that you, Mr. Owens, do have a certain checkered past to answer for," Roland Jessup said. He stood from his chair and began handing out a stack of manila folders. When Roland reached Amadeus' table, he said, "I thought you should know more about the man you've put so much faith and trust in." He handed identical folders to Amadeus, Lilly, Grassal, and Gravity. Amadeus peered inside and saw a stack of government reports.

"Irrelevant," General Nguyen said.

"Seconded," Gravity said.

General Nguyen continued. "Now is not the time to introduce new information or to call into question past actions of those here to testify. I should remind you this is Congresswoman Payne's call for public comments on her bill. Since she's decided to excuse herself, I move that we end this farce for today. In fact, I'll go on record saying that this bill was rotten from the start and would do little to provide for the common defense." A murmur of approval rumbled through the chambers; no politician with a sense of self-preservation wanted to spend unnecessary time scrutinizing Amadeus Brunmeier or contradicting General Janette Nguyen.

"I move to adjourn this farce of a meeting," Senator Graythorpe said.

"Seconded," said another senator. Amadeus thought it was Senator Fielding, but he wasn't sure. A murmur of assent followed.

With a nod of appreciation to the general, Amadeus stood up and collected his papers. As he walked out of the hearing chambers, he felt the condom tumbling down his leg and onto the floor. Amadeus heard a stifled laugh from Grassal but didn't permit himself to look back.

2

Amadeus seethed. One hand rested on the folder Roland Jessup had given him, the other on his lap, clenching and unclenching like a bellows. The folder's contents swam and squirmed in Amadeus' mind like an eel. Gravity sat straight-backed in the booth across from him. Untouched mugs of beer sat in front of them. Music Lilly would call "jazz for people who don't like jazz" leaked from the pub's hidden stereo.

Amadeus scrutinized Gravity's bespoke suit, his well-manicured nails, the wrinkled skin around his eyes, and the overall look of Gravity's brain container; he wondered what other secrets that head held and what those eyes had seen. Amadeus decided he didn't want to know. The photographs, newspaper clippings, internal reviews, reprimands, and a couple declassified documents contained within the folder had told him enough about the sins and follies of Claudius Owens: White phosphorous purchased from Russian gangsters and deployed on a village in rural Pakistan (an unknown number of civilians killed). A picture of a young, bearded Owens in desert camouflage standing in a poppy field with one foot on a dead Afghani's chest, with several live Afghanis bound and kneeling behind him. A report detailing how he was nearly stripped of his US citizenship due to destabilization efforts in Sub-Saharan Africa. A formal reprimand from a one-star general that included a handwritten note at the end ("Your methods disgust me. The Geneva Convention exists for a reason ... but good work anyway.")

Amadeus slid the folder across the table. "According to this file, you've been right on the border of being a war criminal for decades." He searched Gravity's face for some hint, some crack in the leather, but found none.

"I still like to go to the range now and again, but I hung up my grenades twenty years ago, " Gravity said. "I know I did some awful things, so to restore my karma, I spent a decade building things: wells in Waziristan, sewers in Somali slums, and even a hospital in China's Hunan province. But that prick wouldn't include any of that, would he? You can rest assured that I am a different man."

"Still. What am I to make of all this?"

"I deny nothing, but Satan's in the specifics. Yes, I did secure a supply of white phosphorous and use it on a village. Yes, four civilians died. But the report fails to mention the village was hiding a well-trained group of Taliban—they were dug in deep, and from there they had been launching shoot-and-scoot attacks on our company for weeks. I lost three soldiers because of them, two boys and a girl, all of them not much older than you. After I got what I needed, I sent our translator in to deliver a message: women and children should leave the village because it was going to cook. The barbarians beheaded the translator. Many women and children did leave. They knew we weren't fucking around. We watched them leave, making sure none of the fighters left with them. Most of them hadn't heard of the Geneva conventions, but they'd damn sure heard of napalm. After we did our thing, the military went in. You know what they found?" Gravity paused. "Five thousand rounds of .30-caliber ammunition, a bunch of rockets, and four toasted invalids the villagers had left behind. The tactic worked; the province quieted down, and no one fucked with the company for months. For me, however, that was the turning point. I was thirty-three at the time."

"What did you do?" Amadeus said.

"What could I do? The soldiers loved me, the brass hated me, the locals were terrified. I later learned they used the incident as a recruiting tool. I singlehandedly recruited at least a thousand men into the resistance. Amadeus, have you ever heard of Whac-A-Mole?"

Amadeus shook his head.

"It's a carnival game. Four rows and columns of holes. When the moles peek their little plastic heads out, you whack them with a rubber hammer, scoring points for each mole whacked. The problem is ..."

"For each one you whack, two or three more pop up."

"Right. And we spent over a decade playing that game. The difference was the moles had assault rifles and religious zeal."

"So what did you do?"

"You want the short version or the long version?"

"For now, the short version."

"My life was chaos, so I went on a walkabout. Along the way, I got hooked on opium in western China, spent a year at an Indian ashram, and sired a bunch of dark-skinned babies in a Hmong village in northern Thailand. I couldn't just let my spawn grow up in poverty, so I returned to Afghanistan for some drug-running. By the time you were born, the wars were winding down and I was in rehab. When I got out, I started making deals. I can't go into specifics, but let's just say I started making a lot of money for a lot of agencies, and that's made me a valuable man."

Amadeus stared at Gravity as if he were a man from another planet. "I, uh," he said. He wanted to ask Gravity a thousand questions, but he couldn't find the place to start.

"Your mouth is hanging open, kid." Amadeus took a swallow of his beer. "Look, that file in front of you, Jessup compiled it that way for a reason, but I don't know what his reasons are."

"The day of my speech, he tried to recruit me."

"I can understand why. It'd be damn good PR for his little operation, but I suspect a significantly better offer might be coming your way, provided your goal is still the same."

"It is," Amadeus said. The past two months had been a warm, boozy blur of sex with Lilly, public adulation, and nightmares. He had also enjoyed the irresponsible freedom that comes with being both unemployed and heir to patent royalties, but Amadeus had wallowed in victory long enough.

"Now that you've had my dirty laundry piled on top of you, you've got a decision to make: you want to help me wash that laundry, or do you want to get the hell out of the Laundromat all together?"

Amadeus liked Gravity, but he liked him better when he was the mysterious guy who showed up, saved his ass, helped him save the world, and told him to spend two months "publicly enjoying himself in a lecherous manner" while he was off pulling curtain cables or whatever the hell it was Claudius Owens did for a living. Yet Amadeus knew his own work wasn't done. He needed somebody he could trust. He could trust Grassal and Lilly, but like him they were just kids, outsiders to the military-industrial-subluminal complex. He needed people who knew the intricacies of this corrupt system and had seen its machinations from the inside. More importantly, he needed people in his life who had trusted him and defended him when everyone else called him a murderer.

Amadeus made his decision: everyone else could go fuck themselves, with the exception of Lilly, Grassal, and a couple others. Drug-smuggling, civilian-murdering war criminal or not, Gravity was a man he needed because Gravity got things done, and Amadeus needed to find his father and punch his smiling, lying face.

"Pass the detergent. And what was that about a better offer?"

The following day, after pulling a grumbling Grassal away from the archives of the National Cryptologic Museum, Amadeus accompanied Gravity to Janette Nguyen's office in the Defense Intelligence Analysis Center. Amadeus had been playing with Lilly, but when a lieutenant general and head of the DIA summoned, you pulled on your trousers and did your duty.

A United States map hung on the wall. Red pins dotted several locations on the East and West Coasts. A legend at the bottom read: "Known remaining ID infestations." In a discreet corner of the walnut-paneled office, a little gold Buddha sat in a red shrine, flanked by burned-down incense sticks. The general slid aside a panel to reveal a dorm room refrigerator, from which she removed four frosty bottles of beer.

"Owens, thanks for bringing them over. Yesterday's inquiry was a farce. I wish I didn't have to participate in these sideshows, but even the head of the DIA is accountable to whatever clowns our fellow voters elevate to ringmaster. But clowns or not, this privatization business bothers me, and I appreciate that you gave the senator and her legislation the respect they deserve."

"Thank you, General. I've had good counsel," Amadeus said, nodding to Gravity.

"Call me Janette, A.B. You don't mind if I call you A.B., do you, Amadeus? Your name is kind of a mouthful."

"That's fine," Amadeus said. He did in fact mind, but the general terrified him, and he wouldn't protest if she wanted to call him *conejito.*

"Now, down to business. First, just to make sure, you all have TS clearances, right?" Amadeus looked over to Grassal and shrugged. Gravity nodded. "If you didn't before, you do now. Congratulations. Moving on. Owens, your past is questionable, but you did bring us Jones. Nevertheless, I need to ask you something: whose payroll have you been on for the past seven years?"

"Until recently, a single wire transfer from Concrete International Associates fattened my bank account. I also occasionally receive retainer payments from various individuals. Tommy Brunmeier, for example. I'd be happy to submit a full list of these if you like."

"Something about your employer's acronym seems familiar," Janette said, frowning. "But I suppose you're just the kind of jackal they're looking for."

"Hey now," Grassal said, speaking up for the first time. "It's people like him that saved my life, and Amadeus' too. This guy is first-class. If it wasn't for Gravity, the world would be overrun with subluminals." Grassal took a long swallow of beer then suppressed a burp. The lieutenant general raised her eyebrows and waited on Grassal to continue. Grassal sunk down in his chair. "That's all I wanted to say."

"Jackals are part of the game," Gravity said.

"And so are the crows, black and cunning, living off the largesse of the government's slaughter," Janette said. "Granted, crows do serve a purpose, such as cleaning up the carrion more honorable agencies would rather not touch."

"I'll just assume that's not a peck at the ebony shade of my skin," Gravity said.

"From one person of color to another, please shut the fuck up," Janette said.

Gravity stage-whispered to Amadeus, "I like her." To Janette, he said, "In a strictly professional sense, of course."

"The feeling is mutual, even with your dubious background. Since all the, ahem, pleasantries are out of the way, here's the word." She took a step toward the map and pointed to the red pins. "We have eradicated almost all the subluminals near major population centers, but apparently that turd wrangler Ross thought it would be funny to scatter about two hundred subluminals across the Southwestern desert. Alone, these critters are no worse than a mountain lion on meth, but in packs they're damn dangerous, so I sent some guys out to eradicate them. Everything's going swell, until one day I get this fucking thorn stuck in my ass cheek. You know what this thorn is? It's a report that says, 'Hey Janette, some dude in North Carolina is charging five bucks a head to see a caged subluminal.'"

"Another example of Ross' sense of humor?" Amadeus said.

"Ross has nothing to do with it. Word is some Piedmont carny managed to capture or purchase one of those stinking beasts, but I can't spare a squad to send for some quixotic search-and-destroy mission. Besides that, Payne is scrutinizing my every move and chomping at the proverbial bit to call me out for ineptitude. Imagine the fallout if members of the best trained and equipped military in the word couldn't track down a troupe of hillbilly neckbeards in bozo makeup. The job's not even that important, but it would be terribly embarrassing if it was poorly executed."

"Deniability, misdirection, and back-room deals. Right up my alley," Gravity said.

"Killing demons. It's been awhile. Sounds like a nice change of pace," Amadeus said. He would rather not be separated from Lilly for so long, but he could feel himself growing dull and soft from all the sex, booze, and easy days. "But why us?"

"On the day he brought me Jones, Owens here offered his services to me. I didn't need them at the time, but now I do. Owens also mentioned you two are looking for gainful employment, so I thought I would extend an offer to you and Mr. Delgado. You three comprise a surprisingly effective team, and you appear to have loyalty to something other than your own bank account—not that your bank account is irrelevant. My offer includes a respectable salary, expense account, benefits, and access to various properties around the city."

Amadeus and Grassal made eye contact. Amadeus nodded. The prospect excited him, but he thought Grassal looked distracted.

"Amadeus," Janette continued, "I understand you have a mission of your own, someone you'd like to find."

"Um ..."

"Don't play coy. I have transcripts of all your conversations with Jones. I know that Jones said your father is alive and working with Maximilian Ross. If this turns out to be true, and we have reasons to believe it is—"

"What reasons?" Hope rose in his heart. Even Grassal smiled, belying the foul demeanor he had exhibited since Amadeus and Gravity had picked him up.

"My sources tell me the Stamford police were either lazy, stupid, corrupt, or some combination of all three."

"I could've told you that," Grassal said. The general ignored this and continued.

"The first officer who arrived on the scene stated that a man with FBI credentials told him they had already removed the body for national security reasons. When the officer tried to argue with him, this supposed agent showed him digital images of a body that looked like your father. Apparently, this was enough for the local fuzz, and the rest is history."

Amadeus had never been so happy to hear about police ineptitude.

"Stamford cops are all idiot dicks anyway," Grassal said.

"You're still mad about that time they smashed your bong, aren't you?" Amadeus said. "What was that, like ten years ago?" Grassal gave him a "shut the fuck up" look. Gravity and Janette exchanged a smile.

"Amadeus, if what Jones says is true, then technically your father is an enemy combatant. You know what that means?"

"He's pretty much a target dummy for Predator drones," Amadeus said.

"Holden Jones helped replace the Predators with something better, but close enough. However, I can prevent this. I *have* been preventing this by keeping a lid on those transcripts."

"I see," Amadeus said. He gazed at the little red altar. "If that's the case, I don't see that I have much choice in the matter of your offer."

"No, no, no. It's not like that. Even if you don't want to help me, I'll still ensure he's protected. He's brilliant, and whether they're research scientists or tacticians, we're generally willing to ignore the indiscretions of brilliant men. Owens here is a fine example of that."

"Flattery will get you everywhere, but I already said I'd work for you," Gravity said.

"My point is this: if you work with us, you'll have resources at your disposal that may help you find your father, including access to Holden Jones. You'll receive a *very* long leash. Understand?"

"I understand," Amadeus said. He still had some questions for his lover's father. "I'm in."

"Delgado?" Janette said. "We can always use information security professionals, especially those of your caliber."

Grassal nodded at the compliment, then scratched at his place where his prosthetic met his stump, just below the knee.

"Your face is practically a question mark, Delgado. What's on your mind?"

"What's with the Scrabble tiles?" Grassal said. The general had begun twirling one over her knuckles since she mentioned Amadeus' father.

"I was born in San Francisco but grew up in Little Saigon. My parents didn't know much English, so when we started school, we didn't either. Delgado, maybe you know what that's like. The other kids gave us hell, called us all kinds of names, and even though we didn't know the words, we understood what they meant. This motivated us to learn, to push each other. We used to use these tiles to practice our spelling. We would stay up late in the night, challenging each other to come up with a ten-point word, or a sentence worth thirty-four points." She flipped a tile up in the air like a coin and caught it, never taking her gaze from Grassal. She gestured around the room. "These tiles remind me of where I'm from and how hard I had to work to get here."

"I can relate to some of that," Grassal said.

"Good. I'm happy to have another newish American on my team."

"But I have to pass on your offer."

"What?" Amadeus said. Janette arched one eyebrow. Gravity's expression remained neutral.

"Look. In the past six months I've been shot, shot at, dismembered, and locked in a bunker with a couple who fornicate with the frequency of rabbits and the vocalizations of coyotes. I figure it's time to find my own path. It's not like I did anything that important anyway. You understand, don't you, Amadeus?"

This was new, Amadeus thought. He had assumed Grassal would stick with him, and he knew Grassal could use the money. Amadeus took a moment to collect his thoughts and figure out the best approach. Surprisingly, everyone seemed to be waiting on him. "When I fell, who helped me get back on my feet? Who pushed me on when I wanted to give up? Who saved both our lives with his wicked hacking skills?"

"Information security professional skills," Grassal said, a half-smile on his lips.

"Whatever. Grassal, you know damn well I would've failed without your help. Is it about Lucretia?" Grassal's reaction told Amadeus he was closer. "Or is it Zella?" Amadeus held Grassal's gaze while he took a victorious swig of beer.

"That's part of the problem," Grassal said. "I can't decide. But that's not all of it." Amadeus nodded for Grassal to continue, but Grassal shook his head and said, "Later. Let's just say that I need to rebuild my life."

"If he can't do it, that's fine," Janette said, "but I'll have to revoke his clearance, and he won't be able to hear what I'm about to tell the two of you."

"I'll leave," Grassal said. He guzzled the remaining half of his beer and got to his feet.

"Then go," Amadeus said. "Go on. Shoo."

"I'm going."

"I mean, if that's what you want."

"Amadeus, you're angry with me."

"Maybe, but it'll pass. Just go work your shit out. I know you never asked to play in this game, but I'm glad you did. So go do what you need to do."

Grassal nodded at everyone before turning toward the door. A photograph on the wall caught his attention. He moved in to examine it, shuddered, and then left the room without another word. Amadeus walked over for a closer look. The picture showed a small mountain of half-burned demon corpses piled in a mass grave.

"This is from the cleanup?" Amadeus asked. The general nodded. No one spoke for a long time. Gravity swirled the beer in his glass. Both seemed to be waiting for Amadeus to say something. Finally, he did.

"He'll find something productive to do. Now, what was it you wanted to tell us?"

Janette sat down behind her desk, started up an old carbon-fiber-encased laptop, and put her feet on the desk while the software loaded. For some reason, Amadeus had the urge to slouch down in his chair. Outside the window, something caught his eye: on a patch of brown grass behind the building, a quartet of men and women in military uniforms were tossing a Frisbee around.

"I'm sorry Grassal left," Janette said. "We really could've used him, but this isn't a small thing to ask, and this particular lifestyle isn't for everyone. Anyway, here's your job: word is, our circus demon is part of a traveling carnival operation. In a twenty-four-hour period, they roll up into a town, put up flyers, build an Internet buzz, do their show, then move on, deleting any trace they were ever there. As for the actual show, some reports indicate they let people throw rocks and bottles at the creature. Others say it's more like a zoo exhibit. One eyewitness wrote that the creature telepathically addressed the crowd, but this was probably just some parlor trick. Whatever they're doing, I need you two to find the creature and put it out of its misery."

Amadeus bit his tongue and suppressed a shudder. He hadn't mentioned the voice he had heard to anyone, and as far as he knew, neither had Grassal. Maybe it was just as well Grassal had left. This was one secret he had no intention of sharing yet. As he felt his own expression ready to betray him, Amadeus said the first thing that came to his mind.

"That's so humane of you, General." He nodded to the picture on the wall.

"By ending its suffering, I'll be doing it a favor."

"Where do we start?" Gravity said.

"I was getting to that. Do either of you have an external drive with two-factor authentication?"

"If you tell me I have to go collect thumbprints and blood samples, I'm going to walk," Amadeus said. Gravity chuckled at this.

"The only thumbprints you'll need are your own." She stuck her hand out, and Amadeus removed a round plastic drive the size of a quarter from his pocket. She took it, made a few precise pecks on the laptop's keyboard, swiped the drive over a close-range data transmitter, and returned it to Amadeus. "There you go. I've copied over everything you need to know about the job, including your first lead. There's an acrobat in Portland who apparently used to work for this troupe. He's Chinese, but his English should be good enough, and he's going to know more than we do. One more thing: I put a digital watermark on that file. If it leaks, I'll know exactly who leaked it, and I will not hesitate to turn your intestines into streamers for Tet. Understand?"

Both Amadeus and Gravity nodded.

"One more thing, A.B.," Janette said. "Would you like to have one of our doctors take a look at your eyes? You've been wearing those sunglasses for over a month now."

"The black is fading already," Amadeus said. He took off his sunglasses and revealed to her eyes laced with spidery black threads. "Thanks, though."

When they stood to leave, Gravity said, "General Nguyen, you wear no ring, but I have to ask: are you married?"

"Owens, I'll pretend you're just asking a courteous, professional question so I will answer you accordingly: I am in a polyandrous marriage. One husband is the Agency, and the other is the Army. Needless to say, my bed is quite full."

3

Grassal signed himself out of the Pentagon and took the shuttle to the Anacostia Metro Station. While waiting for the train, he used his phone to book a ticket for the first flight to San Francisco, which cost him about a quarter of his remaining savings. At the airport, he resolved his romantic indecisiveness with a coin toss. By the time the sun was lowering over the bay, he was sharing a spicy squid salad with Lucretia and watching the workers who were still busy welding, painting, and fitting the Golden Gate Bridge back together.

When he had shown up at her door, she'd been surprised. When he explained that he wanted to be with her and her alone (the implication being not with Amadeus or her sister Zella), Lucretia had beamed and took his hands in hers. Now, Grassal listened as she talked about the Interstellar Sisters' newest album, the spring tour they were planning, and the finer points of the differences between the harmonic and melodic minor scales. Grassal liked listening to her, even if his own musical education had ended with the alto saxophone in the eighth grade.

After dinner, they bundled up and left Lucretia's vast studio apartment, laughing and cuddling in the foggy night. Both acknowledged the smiles of people who recognized them but chose not to bother them. Later, even though their evening had been a good one, Grassal found himself stretched out to sleep not in a warm bed, but on a divan chair, covered in a blanket of synthetic bear fur. The night grew dark, the steam radiators left pockets of air in the room unwarmed, and Grassal found himself assaulted by a twitch that started in his hand and spread up his arm. After an hour of tossing and turning, Grassal's jaw began working like a ruminant's to chew something that simply wasn't there. When he couldn't stop it, he went to the kitchen and made coffee, hoping his problem could be solved by a strong cup. The apartment smelled like burned charcoal and sliced cucumbers. He cracked a window and turned on the ceiling fan, but the smell remained.

A quart-sized jar of pickled gherkins sat on the plywood table, and a streetlight's yellow glow glinted off its glass. Grassal picked up the jar, shook it, and watched dill and caraway seeds swirl in the brine. Even though the coffee had been finished for some time, Grassal still held the jar in front of his face. His back tingled, like someone was dragging a hundred tiny electrified wires from his tailbone up his spine to the base of his neck. He became aware of several bright white lines floating above his head like jellyfish tentacles, but when he tried to focus on them, they disappeared.

Lucretia padded into the room, wiping sleep from her eyes. "You okay there? You sleepwalking?"

Grassal growled in response. Lucretia stepped back toward the wall and cursed under her breath. Grassal didn't move to acknowledge her, and he said nothing that would indicate he even realized she was there. She said his name again, and in a single, fluid motion Grassal flung the pickle jar at Lucretia's head.

Lucretia ducked. The pickle jar shattered against the wall, spraying acrid juice and broken glass around the cramped kitchen. Lucretia screamed, staggered, and grabbed a dish-drying rack to steady herself. Silverware and plates clattered onto the tile floor. Lucretia backed against the wall, her eyes darting from Grassal to various objects around the room. Grassal started to move toward her. She stomped her foot, shaking the walls of the little cubicle apartment, grabbed a chair, and commanded him to stop. He stood still and straight, except for his fingers. Separately, but with both hands, he touched each of his fingertips to the tip of his thumb. Forefinger on thumb. Middle finger on thumb. Ring finger on thumb. Pinkie on thumb. Repeat. Sixteenth notes at one hundred fifty beats per minute, like a saxophone player practicing scales with their fingers, or a schizoid stuck in an endless thought loop.

"What the fuck is wrong with you?" she said as she held the chair before her like a lion tamer.

Grassal growled again.

"Are you a goddamned grizzly? Grassal, honey, it's me, Lucretia." She waved her hands in front of his face, but her voice had no effect on him. Like talking to a houseplant. "If you're fucking with me, please stop. You're scaring the skirts off me." She wore a paisley skirt with little aluminum beads that dangled from the hem.

"Grr." Grassal's eyes were fixed on some distant, invisible point. His head and body were corpse-rigid and piano-wire tight. Lucretia took another step back and cried out as she stepped on a piece of glass. Blood seeped from inside the arch of her foot. Grassal's body convulsed and then returned to rigidity. Except for the drumming fingers. Back and forth. Up and down the scale.

"You see what you've done?" Lucretia said, pointing to her foot. Blood mixed with the pickle juice to make a Christmas-colored lake. "You have any idea how much this stings? Come on, Grassal, please, help me. Calm down."

Grassal said nothing.

"Fuck you, then. I'm calling Zella." She picked up her phone, dialed the other half of the Interstellar Sisters. As Lucretia simultaneously watched Grassal's face and related the events to her sister, something in his expression lifted like bay fog burned off by the morning sun. He began to gaze around the room, shaking his head like someone trying to remove water from their ears. He then rubbed his hands across his chest and down his pants legs, wiping the sweat from his palms.

"Lucretia? What happened?" Grassal said. He breathed in the smell of vinegar and felt only confusion. The burned charcoal smell was gone. The tendons in his arm felt tight. He caught Lucretia's gaze and saw panic on her face. His heart skipped a beat. He lurched, adjusted his footing, slipped on a pickle, and fell on his ass. He braced his fall with his hands. His right hand landed on a glass shard that sliced open his palm. When he clenched his fist, blood streamed out. Lucretia only stared at him. Grassal could hear Zella's tinny, furious voice coming from the phone. Nearby, a wall clock ticked away the minutes.

Grassal began to weep and his vision blurred. He hated not knowing what was happening. Lucretia looked down at him, muttered something into the phone. She then passed the phone to Grassal, holding it between two fingers like someone disposing of soiled underwear. Grassal put the phone to his ear and said, "Hello?"

"I don't care who you are, who you *think* you are, or how awesome everyone *imagines* you are. You stay away from Lucretia and me, you elephantine, psychopathic beaner. Leave our apartment. Right now."

"Zella, Lu, oh my God I am so sorry. I had no idea. I mean, Lucretia, you should hear this too. It's like I blacked out then the next thing I know I've hurt Lu. I'm sorry, I'm sorry, I'm sorry. I have no idea what happened." Grassal heard a click, and then a recorded voice informed him the other party was no longer on the line.

"Leave, Grassal. Just leave," Lucretia said. Grassal's shoulders sunk further. The phone slipped from his fingers and blood poured from his hand onto the uneven floor. Lucretia's and Grassal's blood drained to a low spot on the kitchen floor, where it mingled with the brine, forming a strange potion.

After wrapping his hand in a T-shirt, Grassal gathered his few possessions and walked out into the cold San Francisco night.

Grassal left Lucretia's apartment and stumbled down the hill. He passed colorful Victorian row houses painted bright like the Catrinas his mother used to drag out of storage for *Día de los Muerto*. The white scallop cornices set on a marigold background of a house on the corner reminded him of the teeth set in their grinning skeletal faces. As he walked down the hill and the sun rose over his head, the heavy straps of his backpack dug into his shoulders. He knew he deserved the pain. He deserved much, much worse, but this would work for now. He had tried to hurt, even kill Lucretia. The thought brought on a wave of vertigo. Grassal grabbed a lamppost to steady himself against a knee-buckling sob. When his vision cleared, he gazed into a house's picture window full of purple and white orchids and wished they would wilt and die.

Late morning found Grassal sitting on a curb in the Mission District. Despite the smells of fresh tortillas, bacon, and coffee wafting from the diner across the street, food was the last thing on his mind. Holding his big head in his hands, he spit into the street and tried to figure out why he had tried to hurt Lucretia. He'd never been a sleepwalker, but even if he was, sleepwalking wasn't supposed to exhaust every muscle in your body and leave you feeling as thin as a shed snakeskin.

A pair of shoes scuffed on the pavement in front of him, and after a moment another pair joined the first. Grassal ignored them. He preferred to keep gazing at the crumpled papers and cigarette butts caught among the road dust and pebbles against the curb.

"Grassal Delgado?" a man's voice said. Grassal ignored them. The inflection rose in that lilting West Coast way that Grassal found grating. He spit. "Aren't you Grassal Delgado?" Grassal still refused to respond. They would go away soon enough. "We think you're really awesome."

"Fuck off," Grassal said. "I'm not Delgado."

"Jesus. Try to give a guy a compliment." The feet departed, and Grassal was left to his solitude as a bay wind rustled the nylon shell of his jacket. Being recognized was a problem; he needed to do something about that.

An hour later, Grassal sat cross-legged on a piece of plastic in an alley filled with shadows. He found his disguise by first rubbing his hands across the ground, then smearing the resulting dirt and grit on his face. He reasoned that no nationally known hero of the Emergence would be covered in filth and huddling with rats. Any resemblance he might have to Grassal Delgado was purely coincidental. Satisfied that he wouldn't be bothered by any more star-struck hero-worshipers, he settled in for a long, chilly afternoon of rumination. He liked being out of sight, in the shadows. From his place in the shadows, he had helped Amadeus save thousands of lives.

When he thought of Amadeus, Grassal shook his head at his own willingness to abandon a perfectly good offer of employment in favor of following his cock. Yes, he cared for Lucretia, but leaving everything he knew had brought him to this point. Love was important, but stability was better. He had survived the past two months on the fruits of public gratitude. Complimentary hotel rooms and meals at restaurants throughout the city. Unlimited free Metro rides for life. A promotional—and complimentary—prosthetic leg. The best was the five thousand dollars granted to him by the Professional Association of Hispanic Information Security Professionals.

He didn't deserve any of it.

His mother had been right, all those years ago; he was no good, a hindrance to everyone, an idiot who ruined people's lives. He considered going to the liquor store, but that was what she would want him to do, and even at this point he wouldn't give her the satisfaction. Besmeared and sullen, Grassal pulled himself to his feet. His haunches had begun to ache from so much sitting. He decided to wander again in the hopes he would exhaust himself.

By the afternoon, Grassal had ended up at a park on the waterfront. Along the way he passed through Fisherman's Wharf, stopping briefly to sit beneath the claws of the crab statue where he had arranged for Amadeus to meet him. Despite the light January drizzle, the market was packed with visitors. Grassal walked right down the middle of a Chinese tour group. He knew he looked like some creature that had just crawled out of the bay. Grassal derived a perverse pleasure from the looks of disgust, dismay, and embarrassment that appeared on their faces as they pressed against each other to part for him, lest his condition be contagious.

His wandering led him to a park on the edge of the bay. Feeling the burn from the distance he'd walked, he found a bench on which to rest and watch the gulls fight over scraps of bread. An hour passed, then two. When red streaked the sky, he heard derisive laughter in front of him. Two young white men dressed like recruits on leave regarded him with haughty looks. One had blond hair; the other's was chalkboard black. Grassal returned his gaze to the ground. He heard one of them spit.

"You looking at something, hobo?" the blond one said. Grassal ignored him. He was sure they would leave; he just needed to wait them out. "I said, what are you looking at? You like what you see?" Grassal shook his head. The smells of burned plastic and ammonia mingled with the bay's dead-fish-and-salt aroma. The tips of his fingers began to drum against his palms. He became aware of a tingling current pulsing up and down the length of his body.

"Go away," Grassal said. "Please." White light crept in from the edges of his vision. Grassal found himself on his feet, fingers drumming, heart slamming against the wall of his chest. Grassal's last conscious thought was that he never should've left the shadows. He began to mutter a string of random, unaccented syllables.

"And leave you all alone on this bench?" The blond man cracked his knuckles. "Listen to that weird shit he's saying. I think this is our bench, and I think people like you need a lesson in respecting—"

The heel of Grassal's hand struck the man's jaw. His head snapped back and he staggered. The black-haired man tried to kick Grassal in the side. Without turning his head from the blond man, Grassal caught the kick and twisted. Something snapped, and the black-haired man fell to the grass. The blond man landed a haymaker on the side of Grassal's head. Grassal took the blow as if he were a statue.

Without the give he was expecting, the blond man lost his balance. Grassal attacked. Grabbing a fistful of his olive green T-shirt, Grassal began to deliver rhythmic punches to the man's face as if he were striking a timpani during an overture. Punch two three four. Punch two three four. The blond man landed some blows to Grassal's side and face to no effect, but each of Grassal's blows resulted in a pulpy thumping sound, and soon the blond man gave up and squirmed out of his shirt. Bloodied and staggering, he helped his buddy to his feet. Together they limped away, leaving Grassal muttering and punching the air.

4

Lilly Jones regarded Amadeus with a bemused look. After accepting the general's offer, Amadeus had made a beeline for her hotel room, stopping only to pick up carryout and two bottles of moderately priced merlot. Amadeus thought an evening in would bookend their capitol-city sojourn nicely. Tomorrow morning, he would have his discussion with Jones, and in the afternoon, they were off to Portland. Yet, when he told her about his upcoming travel plans, he hadn't expected her to be so ... relieved. They now lay in bed, naked and spooning, both spent. Two half-eaten Thai curries sat on the table atop scattered pages of a handwritten manuscript.

"So your vacation is over, and you're off to find more trouble?"

"Well, yes." He had been vague in his description of their mission, mentioning that he had a security clearance. He chose not to mention tomorrow's visit to Jones.

"And you didn't think that maybe, just maybe, I might be interested in playing James Bond with you?" She rolled over and faced him, leaning on her elbow. Her eyes absorbed the dim light from the bathroom and reflected it all back toward Amadeus.

"I'm sorry, Lilly. It's just that you seem pretty wrapped up in this book. And I didn't solicit the offer—it came to me. Gift horses and mouths, and all that. I think this could be the next step in helping me find my father."

"I wouldn't want to join that boys' club, anyway."

"My boss' name is Janette."

"Whatever. And Grassal?"

"Grassal decided to take a different path. I suspect he's trying to rebuild things with Lucretia."

"Well, that's good for him. Besides, I have some things I need to do back in Colorado."

"Like what?"

She placed a hand on his chest and shook her head. Her touch was warm and reassuring, and he tried to impress the sensation on his memory. Some part of him expected it would be awhile before he felt it again.

"Ami, you're not the only one who gets to have his little secrets. Suffice it to say that I could generate significant amounts of capital with only minor estate liquidations."

Icy rain streaked the windows of the taxi that took him to Jones' holding facility in the basement of an unmarked building across the river in Virginia. Upon arrival, Amadeus gave the driver his new agency card, then wrote a generous tip on his receipt. Inside, he nodded to the uniformed woman at the desk and showed her his clearance badge. She waved her hand dismissively.

"Mr. Brunmeier, a pleasure to see you. We're expecting you. Just sign in here." She had him place his thumb on a scanner. "And go on down." She pressed a button on her desk phone and told someone Amadeus was coming.

Amadeus walked downstairs and through the now-familiar hallway, escorted by a steely-faced guard about his age. The guard started to talk, but decided against it. Amadeus gave him a nod, as if to confirm the guard had made the right decision. They reached Jones' cell. The guard opened the door for Amadeus and said he needed only to press the call button when he was ready to leave.

Inside, Holden Jones' dim cell smelled of piss and floor cleaner, but Jones didn't seem to mind. When he saw Amadeus, he smiled like a child receiving a birthday gift.

"Where is my father?" Amadeus said.

"No pleasantries for an old friend? Amadeus, my boy, you disappoint me. It's been so long since you last honored me with your company. And last time," Jones said, a sly smile creeping across his face, "you had your attack dog with you. Where is he now?"

"Gravity isn't here."

Jones looked him over then smiled.

"I see that. I do still have one functioning eye," Jones said, rubbing his palms together like someone applying hand lotion. "And with that little eye, I spy a Stamford guy who appears well-sated by the warm cornucopia of my daughter's loins." Amadeus' mouth dropped and tried to work out a retort, but Jones waved a dismissive hand at him and continued before he had a chance to do so. "Don't look so confounded, my boy. Even someone like me gets his hands on a tabloid every now and then. Tell me, how is my dear daughter? I do wish she'd come by for a visit."

"Lilly is fine, but she won't see you. Please, Jones, answer my question."

"I don't know where that magnificent bastard is. Truly, I don't. Just that he's alive and working with you-know-who. But give me some news about my daughter, just a little morsel, and I promise it'll be worth your time."

"Fine. She's going back to Colorado."

"That's funny. Why would she go back to the bunker? I thought she was enjoying the cosmopolitan life."

Amadeus crossed his arms.

"Aw, come on, Amadeus, just a little more."

Amadeus put both hands to his temples. "God, Jones. Why am I telling you this? I think she intends to start selling off parts from the Pachyderm."

"It's also funny you should mention my little project. I assume you're curious as to why I would bother to help you learn to fly the damn thing, only to send it and you spiraling into the black waters of Raquette Lake."

"The thought has crossed my mind. I assume it was because Ross asked you to do so."

"Maximilian Ross had nothing to do with it."

"You're lying, Jones. Lilly said she caught you talking to him."

"No, she only saw me talking to *someone*, but she never figured out who. And at this point in my life, I can receive no benefits from lying. Look at me, Amadeus. I'm a broken and condemned man who can only gain benefits for himself by either revealing or withholding information. And right now, I feel like generating some goodwill between us. You are, according to the papers, quite good to my daughter, and I'd like to reward you for this."

"Are you going to tell me the truth, or are you going to open your mouth and let it roll out?"

"Amadeus, my boy—"

"Don't fucking 'my boy' me, you unctuous prick. I ... I ..."

"Whoa. Whoa. Whoa. Easy now, Amadeus. Let's back up and try using our brains for a minute. You say I tried to kill you, but why would I wreck a multi-million dollar machine in the process? There were plenty of other times I could've revealed your location to henchmen or the police and saved the Pachyderm from waterlogged ruin."

"How do I know you didn't?" Amadeus said, remembering the sight of Laroux's bullet-riddled body.

"Fair point. I suppose you don't, but I didn't. Amadeus, I wouldn't have crashed you when I did if I didn't think you would survive. I knew damn well you were hovering above that lake and that you were smart enough to survive a water landing. As many times as you crashed in the simulator ..." Jones smiled at his own reminiscence. "Besides, if I killed you, it would've hurt Lilly."

"You weren't trying to kill me?" Amadeus said, speaking before he could stop himself.

"Have you been doing nothing the past three months except fucking my daughter and smoking that DC green? Yes, that's what I'm telling you, but let me make myself clear: I had to make it *look* like I tried to kill you in order to protect Lilly. And before you ask why ... oh, what the hell. Since we're having a confession party, and I don't expect to live much longer, I might as well spill it: I have absolutely no interest in subluminals, apocalypses, or the Vedic cycles. I'm a family man and an opportunistic engineer. All I'm interested in is securing Lilly's future and licensing the rights to manufacture Pachyderms."

"Manufacturing—"

"Yes. I had an arrangement set up, but my buyer, that stupid son of a bitch, blabbed about the details. Those details included information on my test pilot, and somehow that information reached the people who wanted you dead. At first, there were hints from my buyer, suggestions that I turn over your location. I never did. But no sooner had Lilly left for Prague than the broker called. He said, 'Kill Brunmeier, or this deal won't be the only thing you lose.' The threat to Lilly was implicit, Amadeus. What choice did I have?"

Amadeus folded his arms over his chest and walked around behind Jones. Jones rotated his wheelchair, following Amadeus' movements.

"All this was over a manufacturing contract? You sold me out for a bag of silver?"

"And my daughter's safety, Amadeus."

"That's what you assume, you evil prick."

"Her safety is not something I can just leave to chance! Don't you want Lilly to be safe?"

"Of course I do. But you," Amadeus pointed a finger at Jones, "you betrayed me. Who was the buyer? Who was the broker?"

"Not Ross."

"Not Ross?"

Jones sighed. "Amadeus, I'd really rather not say. In this cell, we are without the ability to speak *sub rosa,* and I've already given you so much, all for a little first-hand news of my daughter. If you could get me out of here—"

"Not even I could do that," Amadeus said.

"Then I guess you'll never know."

"Shit, Jones. Shit." Amadeus ran a trembling hand through his loam-brown hair. "I'm going out of town, so it'll be awhile, but I'll try to arrange something for when I get back."

"When you do, will you bring Lilly? I'd like to see her once more."

"Jones, the odds are slim to none, but I'll ask."

During the four-hour flight from Washington to Portland, Amadeus and Gravity abandoned the executive comforts of the front of the 767 for the austere privacy provided by the nearly empty environs of economy class. Until now, Amadeus had said nothing about his meeting with Jones, and Gravity hadn't asked, but once they were settled into their new, stiff seats, Gravity said, "Well? How's our pal?"

"He finally admitted it."

"Admitted what?"

Amadeus told Gravity about his conversation with Jones, omitting nothing.

"Blackmail, industrial intrigue, indirect pleas of sympathy. I expected nothing less. So, new questions loom over us: Who was the buyer? More importantly, who was the broker? Was he from the same group who wanted you dead, and presumably placed the demon gates? Was Ross involved?"

"We only have Jones' word that he wasn't."

"Actually, I'm inclined to believe as much." Amadeus arched a single, quizzical eyebrow. Gravity continued, "If Ross was truly a crazy misanthrope, he'd probably be all about some revenge killings. Revenge, however, doesn't seem to be a factor; if it was, his goons would've already murdered you in a public and gruesome way, just to make a point. But now that you no longer pose a threat to anyone's plans, you're just ignored because it's easier for everyone."

Amadeus liked this theory. "But Ross announced his intentions on international television to millions of people."

"Did he? Truly? Think about that, and we'll come back to it. In the meantime, let's back up and sort out this broker-buyer business. Who would be most interested in buying experimental aircraft like the Pachyderm?"

"The same people who sell Cessnas?"

"Think harder, Amadeus. Who developed the Internet?"

"Um, I'm not sure how that's relevant, but if I had to guess, I'd put my money on highly intelligent cats."

Gravity permitted himself a chortle. "The goal of early computer networking was to permit the exchange of data between Department of Defense computers. Once the process started back in the sixties, network technologies followed the standard pattern of technological adoption: first the military gets it, then research institutions and corporations, and finally consumers."

"You think the military wants to buy Pachyderms?"

"They'll buy them from a defense contractor, but yes."

"So why would the military want me dead?"

"They don't, and neither do the defense contractors who want to manufacture Pachyderms. It's this broker Jones mentioned. Somehow the broker learned about your involvement from the defense contractor, and this broker ... hmm." Gravity stroked his chin and took a sip of bourbon. "If I were a gambling man, and I'm not, I would put money on a strong connection between our broker and whoever set up our demon gates."

Amadeus took a moment to let this sink in. Turning this over in his mind, he found it satisfactory, but one question continued to bother him. "Was Ross the broker?"

"Do you think your father would work for Ross if Ross was actively trying to kill you?"

"No, but maybe he didn't know, or maybe he was a captive, working with a gun to his head, though even then, I ... don't think he would. I think he would fight." Saying it out loud lifted a weight from his chest.

"Then let's imagine another scenario," Gravity said, "one in which Ross didn't place the demon gates. He might be a wealthy son of a bitch, but he's a tech guy, not an operations guy. Even with his resources, I'm not sure even he could have pulled this off. First, his kooky story reeks of hucksterism and mumbo jumbo, and he knows it. Second, the general and I talked about the logistics of not only building the gates but distributing them around the world. They're actually not that hard to set up. Just one or two guys can do it. Manufacturing is a bit more involved, as is sourcing the kipium, but it's all doable. The real challenge would be keeping everything secret. I mean, how could you execute a project like this and not have *a single goddamned leak?* Even with tight compartmentalization, at least three or four people would have to know about the whole scheme, not to mention the hundred or so you'd need to set everything up."

"What if the people setting up the gates were told they were actually doing something else, like putting together communications gear?"

"Unless they're mental defectives, they'll know exactly what they're setting up. However, once you have the parts, you don't need an engineer to construct a demon gate, just a grunt who's able to follow instructions and has a good incentive to keep his mouth shut."

"I'm sure Ross has grunts," Amadeus said.

"Federal agents have interviewed and interrogated everyone who has ever been involved with Tivooki Systems in any capacity, from the sys admins to the janitors, as well as their friends and families. Every one of them said the same thing: 'We work for an Internet company.' And they all had the digital alibis to prove it. Nothing."

A flight attendant pushed a cart down the aisle and offered them drinks. Both requested coffee. Amadeus continued, "If they weren't technical contractors or people associated with Tivooki ..."

"I hate to say it, but as a former military man, you'd find plenty of compliant grunts in the military. One well-disciplined company could have pulled this off, assuming they had air support."

"Everything I read said Ross has spent his career bitching about the military-industrial complex, and even if that was a really, really long con, how would he get access to that many soldiers?"

"He wouldn't, and if he tried, Washington would've heard about it. That's because Ross isn't behind the Emergence, and I don't think any of our regular military are either. They're mostly grunts and jarheads, but I guarantee you none of them over the rank of sergeant would wreak this kind of havoc on their home country. It's one thing to do a false flag operation, like the Gulf of Tonkin incident, but this thing with the subluminals and demon gates is in a class by itself. I think we're looking at a paramilitary outfit or a private military corporation. Between the Narco Wars and a hundred small-scale conflicts in Africa, you wouldn't have any trouble finding experienced soldiers."

"Would they do this?"

"Is there a fat paycheck involved?"

"Good point." Amadeus closed his eyes and tried to re-remember events from this point of view. Because his father was working with Ross, according to Jones, Amadeus truly wanted to believe that Ross wasn't the villainous mastermind behind the conspiracy, because he didn't want to be the child of a villainous mastermind's henchman. But if Ross wasn't behind everything ... "Why would Ross want people to believe he did this?"

"A confidence trick," Gravity said. "The world needs a villain, and Ross knows it. Ross martyred himself and his reputation to induce collective action ... and your father helped him do it."

A gray drizzle greeted Amadeus and Gravity when they left Portland International Airport. A yellow light rail car carried them past dense housing developments intermingled with green space. When the train followed the road, cyclists pedaled alongside it like pilot fish swimming with whale sharks. The train would stop, and some cyclists would get on, rolling their bikes in front of them, while others would ride right off the train and onto the street. When they quit the train downtown, Amadeus heard more birds than traffic.

"Where are the cars?" Amadeus said. The streets were busy, bustling with people on bicycles and electric scooters. A couple taxi vans drove over windswept streets.

"Elsewhere," Gravity said. "When I was young, we used to call this the People's Republic of Portland. This city was the most progressive—or leftist, depending on who you asked—city in the country. The people of Portland wanted to make a walkable, livable city. They were tired of traffic, pollution, and noise, so they taxed the shit out of that which caused those things."

"You sound nostalgic."

"Perhaps. When I was younger, I lived in Seattle for a while. I used to come down here on the Zephyr Line and visit with this girl named Wendy Kowalski. Good times, then." Gravity said nothing further, and Amadeus decided he didn't really want to know the details.

"Excuse me, fella," Gravity said, catching the eye of a youngish man with spiky, blood-red hair. "Where's the square?" The man pulled his arm free and looked Gravity up and down.

"I think I'm looking at him," Red Hair said. "And his emaciated sidekick." Gravity raised one eyebrow.

"My friend," Gravity said to him, "we're just looking for Pioneer Courthouse Square. I haven't been here since you were suckling milk from the fountain of your mother's breast, and I'm asking a simple question in the hopes of refreshing my memory."

"And I'm giving you a simple answer—fuck off." The man spat, then lifted his chin and trotted on down the street. Gravity shook his head as he watched him walk away. The man slapped a street sign before turning a corner. Gravity smiled. Amadeus looked from Gravity to the man and back to Gravity. Confused, Amadeus started to speak but Gravity cut him off.

"By judging his manner rather than his actions, you missed an important detail: he answered my question." Unsure, Amadeus looked at Gravity, who nodded down the street. "Take a look at the sign he slapped. Note the brown background and white arrows." Amadeus squinted to make out the letters. When he finally did, he smiled and saw: "Pioneer Courthouse Square, 0.2 km."

"You underestimate the curious nature of Cascadians," Gravity said. "That pioneer-prospector-frontiersman-adventurer personality came out here, bred with itself, and, in my lay opinion, created a new class of humans. Not better, not worse, but decidedly different. He was just fucking with us."

They followed the sign's directions and reached Pioneer Square less than ten minutes later. If buildings hadn't blocked their view, they would've been able to see the square from where they stood when Gravity had questioned the man. No wonder he gave them attitude, Amadeus thought. He thought they were morons.

A group of people stood on the corner of the square, dressed proudly in the stained fabrics of yesteryear, as if they had conspired to and succeeded in liberating all the clothing from the back room of a low-rent thrift store. In their hands, they held signs bearing apocalyptic messages: "Heed the Messengers." "Renounce This World." "The End is Now!" "Prepare. Prepare." "Ban Signs Now!" Their faces were rapturous, happy, and a little vacant. Amadeus pulled a baseball cap farther down over his face; he didn't want the sign people recognizing him. On the edge of their group, a middle-aged white man stood as rigid as the hundred-and-fifty-year-old gas lamps that lined the perimeter of the square. The rhythmic way the man drummed his fingers on his palms reminded Amadeus of a boy with autism he used to know, but Amadeus decided that boy's face had shown more emotion than this guy's.

About fifty yards distant from the sign people, on the edge of the amphitheater, Gravity stopped and said, "Now we wait for the show to begin."

"I thought we were supposed to be tracking down this acrobat."

"We are. You didn't read the files? He's expected to—"

"He's a street performer?"

"You really didn't read the files, did you?"

"I started to." Amadeus had abandoned the files when he found no mention of how this mission might relate to finding his father. Changing the subject, Amadeus said, "So the plan is to stand around in the rain and wait until some street bum may or may not do a half-ass juggling routine for spare tourist quarters?"

"Basically. You have anything better to do?"

"Can we at least wait in a coffee shop?"

"I'd hate to miss his entrance, but I suppose that's fine. We can keep an eye out for him." They found a window booth at a crowded coffee shop overlooking the square. Amadeus ordered cups at the counter for both of them.

"He has a name, you know," Gravity said.

Amadeus nodded.

"Right. Of course he knew the acrobat had a name, but it started with an "X" and Amadeus wasn't sure how to pronounce it. "And that name is?"

"Wen Xiang."

"Just testing you.

"Think of it like 'Wind Song.' That was his carny name."

"Wind Song, right," Amadeus said. He slumped back in his seat, trying to make sense of the atonal jazz playing on the café's sound system. He noticed Gravity bobbing his head to the beat. For a moment, Amadeus felt terribly inexperienced. He still couldn't believe the salary the general was paying him, but he reminded himself of everything he had done, and the feeling subsided.

Draining their coffees, they watched the clouds swirl in silence. Time passed. The sign people remained, though they seemed to lose their vigor as the afternoon waned. While they waited, Amadeus reviewed the file that he should've reviewed earlier. Wen Xiang had been in the United States for nearly a decade, and spent most of that time with an outfit named Captain Carl's Magnificent Mobile Extravaganza. Wen had sent what he thought would be an anonymous e-mail to the FBI, saying that the boss of his troupe was keeping a subluminal as a pet. Wen had stated this was a dangerous activity, and he disliked said activity enough to leave the troupe and set out on his own.

When the hands of the unnumbered clock on the wall announced the time at just past four o'clock, sixteen hundred hours, Gravity nodded to the square. Amadeus looked around and saw nothing.

"What?"

"There he is," Gravity said. "Pulling the wagon. Let's go."

They selected an observation point set at a respectable distance from the coming spectacle and watched Wen Xiang set up his props: two hoops on metal stands. Both were a little less than a meter wide, one chest high, the other waist high. Kitchen knives and barbed wire covered the outer rings of the hoops. A little hose ran up each of the stands, around the rings, and into a small tank on the wagon. After he set up the rings, Wen placed a bucket on the wagon. On the bucket was scrawled the word "Tips." He fiddled with the tank then set the hoops in a row, the shorter set back a few meters. He held a lighter to one hoop, then the other, and each emitted a small *whoosh* as the gas ignited. With the hoops aflame, the performance began.

He started by burning a small piece of paper, just to demonstrate the danger. Next, Wen the acrobat took about fifteen steps away from the hoop, bowed, and ran toward the flaming hoops. When he was only steps away, he stuck his arms out in front of his body and dove through the hoop, landed on his hands, did two somersaults, and sprang through the second hoop. As he passed through each hoop, the flames licked at his body but caused no perceptible damage. A couple people clapped, and Wen took a bow. He then backed about twenty yards away from the lower hoop, spread his arms, and took off in a run. This time he completed a series of somersaults, then used a handspring to send him feet first through the lower hoop. He cartwheeled between the hoops, then dove headfirst through the higher hoop, landing with another string of cartwheels to greater applause. Wen repeated this exhibition of feline grace three more times. Each time he added a new element: more tumbling, longer and longer series of somersaults, and even a feigned mistake where he grabbed the short hoop and pulled it down to his feet. He bowed as blue and orange flames licked up around him.

Three people placed crumpled bills into Wen's bucket, but when the time to pay came, the rest of the crowd began to ignore Wen, as if his performance was as mundane as a traffic light. While Wen took down his props, Amadeus and Gravity approached him. Amadeus caught Wen's eye and conspicuously placed a large bill in his bucket. Wen Xiang smiled and gave them a nod. His face was wide and smooth, his nose pert.

Patient, their hands in their pockets, Amadeus and Gravity

waited for Wen to tear down.

"That was a hell of a show," Gravity said.

"Thank you."

"I used to know a girl who was into gymnastics, but she wasn't anywhere near as good as you are."

"Thank you."

"Where did you learn to do that?" Amadeus said.

"Thank you?"

"No, I mean, we've already said you're good, but I want to know how you learned to do that. How long have you been doing acrobatics?" Amadeus said.

"No English," Wen said, fussing over his hoops as he tried to reattach a knife that had come loose. The lingering heat thwarted his attempts, so he put on gloves and reattached the knife with a length of wire. Amadeus looked at Gravity, who raised one eyebrow.

"You don't speak English, huh? But Wen, we know you've been in the states here for nearly a decade," Gravity said.

"You immigration?" Wen asked. His body shivered a little, like he'd just taken a shot of strong liquor. He looked around.

"No, we're not immigration," Amadeus said, removing his glasses. "We want to talk to you about your former employer."

"No have former employer. I am self-employed man," Wen said. He finished disassembling the hoops, and his wagon was loaded and ready to roll. All three knew if Wen wanted to run, Amadeus and Gravity would never catch him. But Wen stayed.

"As you should be—you're quite skilled at your chosen occupation," Gravity said. "Your skill is like someone who has spent years and years jumping through hoops for half-drunk crowds of Southeastern yokels. You've clearly put in your ten thousand hours. But I know you didn't get that good doing these afternoon shows in Pioneer Courthouse Square."

"No understand."

"Wen, help us out here. Look at me," Amadeus said, lifting his ball cap and pulling down his fake beard. "Do I look familiar?" Wen shook his head. "Not at all? Think about the recent news, especially as it relates to the subluminals." A tiny flash of recognition lit up Wen's face, then it was gone. Wen shrugged.

"Help us, Wen, and we'll help you. We just want to talk for a little bit. We'll buy you dinner at any restaurant you want."

"My English very bad. And my children is sick."

"I'll pay you one hundred dollars an hour for your time," Gravity said. "And get you whatever medicine you want."

"Too much work, no time," Wen said. He dropped his voice. "One hundred dollars no is good. Two hundred. And immigration problems, you help with. You are government people?"

"Sort of," Gravity said. "But not bad government. Good government. We're not police or immigration. And if you have visa problems, we can help. I have a cousin at INS."

Wen smiled. "Okay, we talk. Only talk. Two hundred an hour. We talk acrobatics, old life in China. We go to good restaurant. Okay?"

"Okay," Gravity said. "We talk acrobatics."

5

Wen selected a sleek fusion restaurant with modern décor, a celebrity chef, and a menu that didn't list prices, one of those places where the quality of the furnishings dictates the price. A lone cellist sat in a corner playing Bach. Wen ordered first.

"I'd like the sirloin, please. Medium rare. For the sides, seasonal vegetables steamed and drizzled with olive oil and salt. Is that local salt?"

"Collected from around Puget Sound," the waitress said. Her short hair was slicked back with pomade. "Sustainable, organic, kosher, and blessed by one of our druid chefs."

"That sounds absolutely fabulous," Wen said. Amadeus and Gravity ordered ostrich pasta and eggplant lasagna, respectively. Gravity scowled at the waitress when she asked if he would prefer a senior portion.

"Your English has improved considerably," Gravity said when the waitress left.

"It's part of my act. If I'm on the job, I stay in character."

"But you are Chinese? From China?" Amadeus said.

"From China, yes, but my people are Tujia, not Han. My mother, aunt, and I came to America when I was a small boy. On a container ship. In a container. With ten other people."

"Jesus," Gravity said.

"We barely survived. When we arrived at the port, our

container was put on a truck. We didn't see the light of day until Omaha, where my uncle signed for the crate. When he opened the door, he threw up because of the smell. We had planned for the trip—brought barrels with lids for toilets and lots of water and food—but one person had died a couple days before. They stank. Obviously. Because dead people fucking stink. But you're not here to hear my story. You're here because of that creature. Right?"

"That's right," Amadeus said. "I mean, who is keeping it? How did they catch it? And why would anyone want such a thing? Let's face it: they're nasty creatures. Then there's care and feeding. What did Captain Carl feed it, anyway?"

"Mostly roadkill," Wen said. "But that was just to keep expenses low. It would eat hay if it was soaked in ammonia."

Their food arrived, and Wen started eating immediately, both elbows on the table, hunched over his plate. Amadeus picked at his food; he thought the ostrich was bland and, as he watched Wen devour his food, Amadeus wished he had ordered the ribeye as well. He added red pepper flakes to his pasta. They ate in silence. When Wen finished eating, he continued his tale, even though Amadeus and Gravity were still working on their dishes.

"I don't know how you found me or knew who I was, but I understand why you would be interested in my former employer ... Amadeus Brunmeier." Amadeus raised a loam-brown eyebrow. So Wen Xiang had recognized him after all. "Being the world-famous creator of the Gate Crasher, I suppose you would be interested in this matter. You know the name of the troupe I formerly toured with?"

"Captain Carl's Mobile Extravaganza?" Amadeus said.

"Captain Carl's *Magnificent* Mobile Extravaganza. I assume you want to find Captain Carl, ask him about his pet subluminal, and then kill it?"

"Most likely, yes," Amadeus said.

"I'm not sure that's the best choice, at least in this particular situation," Wen said. Amadeus started to protest, but Gravity stopped him and asked Wen to continue. "Thank you, Mr. ..."

"Just call me Gravity. Before you tell us why we shouldn't exterminate this creature, can you tell us how it came to be in Carl's possession?"

"Gravity, okay, sure. You Yankees with your fucking nicknames. Whatever. So a couple days after the gates came down, we were camped at an RV park in South Bend, Indiana. Sitting around outside, most of the troupe just killing time, drinking whiskey. Nearly all our shows had been cancelled because people were worried about the monsters. We listened to all the reports, heard about everything happening, but we just made jokes about them. We were so far outside the mainstream anyway; it didn't seem real. Sure, we'd been through Huntington, West Virginia once, years before, but it looked like every other post-industrial dump and didn't really stand out in our minds. Despite the joking, we hated to hear of people getting hurt, but we just didn't have any connection to it. It didn't affect us.

"But late that night we heard a woman scream, somewhere not far away. Captain Carl had this fucking cowboy revolver. He always talked about it but he'd never used it. I guess he thought this was his chance. He got the revolver from his trailer and asked a few of us to come along. This being a circus, me and three other guys armed ourselves with whips, swords, and some other sharp props and then followed the screams to their source."

Wen paused, took a sip of water, and looked down at his hands.

"We found a monster the size of a chimpanzee eating this poor woman alive. It was tearing into her stomach, pulling out her intestines. 'Kill the thing,' I said. But instead of just putting a bullet through that monster's head, Captain Carl walks over to the woman and the monster. The monster ignores him and just keeps on eating. He looks down at the woman, says 'I'm sorry, ma'am,' and shoots her between the eyes. I guess he was doing her a favor, I don't know. It was awful. But then he says if we can capture the monster alive, we all get a five-thousand-dollar bonus. Heat of battle, thrill of the hunt, pursuit of greenbacks, whatever, we started attacking it. I threw one of my rings around its neck and, along with the sword swallower and the contortionist, I pinned it to the ground. It fought like hell, but the strong man hit it over the head and it stopped struggling. Captain Carl gave us a round of applause then bent down to examine it. When he bent down, he put his hand on the monster's face. At that moment, it opened its eyes and bit off one of his fingers. He pulled his hand back, shaking it, spraying blood everywhere, and put his foot down on the monster's neck. There we were: a half-eaten dead woman, knocked-out subluminal, a nine-fingered, screaming Captain Carl, and four carnies who had just become five thousand dollars richer."

"What happened after that?" Amadeus said.

"We put the monster in the bear cage. The bear never used it anyway. At first, the bear went crazy, but later she took to the creature, even started sleeping in the cage with it. But that night, after we'd captured the monster, we packed up our stuff and got the hell out of there."

"Tell me more about this Captain Carl," Gravity said.

"What do you know about him?" Wen said.

"I know he's the founder and manager of your former troupe. Studied theater at a state school, supposedly had an excellent voice, but somehow ended up in prison for armed robbery. After prison is when he started the troupe, supposedly kept his nose clean ever since. I'm not sure what it means that this guy chose an occupation in a field that mostly died out before he was born. His tax returns show he's made a profit for the past ten of sixteen years."

A noise from outside made them all turn their heads. A group of people, the same sign carriers from the Square, was marching down the street, chanting something indiscernible. Bicycle bells jingled as cyclists swerved around the crowd.

"Hmm," Wen said, returning his level gaze to Gravity. "He always talked about the troupe losing money, but somehow he always paid us well. I knew about the armed robbery. He told people that right off the bat. He said he'd already paid his debt to society, but he still wanted to give something back. He said one of his happiest moments in prison was when a traveling ventriloquist performed for the inmates."

"So why did you leave?" Amadeus said.

"Why did I leave? I had my reasons. I kept thinking about what we had done to that poor woman, and I couldn't take it. I mean, that woman was probably somebody's wife, somebody's mother, and we killed her. Come payday, I took my check and my bonus and left the troupe and, to clear my conscience, made a call to the FBI, which brings us to now. But it wasn't just that. Let's just say having a subluminal in the troupe didn't make me want to stay. Especially when it started talking."

Amadeus shuddered and shook his head. "No," he said. "It ... it's not possible. Those *things* don't talk. They're animals. Beasts."

The voice at the bunker—that had been a stress hallucination, nothing more. Grassal had claimed to hear it too only because he didn't want Amadeus to feel alone in his craziness. He was a pal like that. Wen, however, was lying, or maybe just fucking with them like the red-haired guy had. Amadeus thought about the picture of subluminal corpses on the wall in General Nguyen's office.

"You don't believe me? That's fine," Wen said. "It don't mean anything to me. You asked me why I left, and I told you. Thanks for lunch." He dabbed the corners of his mouth with a cloth napkin and pushed his chair back from the table.

"Wen, hold on," Gravity said. "It's not that we don't believe you. It's just that to suggest these things can talk, or at least this one can, well, that has a lot of implications, none of them good."

"You're damn right," Wen said, remaining at the table.

"Okay, let's pretend that these things do communicate. How did they talk? I mean, how did they learn English?" Amadeus asked.

"They don't speak, not as we speak. It's telepathy. We interpret their messages in our first language. I heard them in Xiang Chinese. The sword swallower said it spoke Turkish. Carl said it was English. Also, the words come fast and sudden, too, like a thunderstorm filling a dry creek bed."

Amadeus felt sick. Wen had just described Amadeus' own experience in the bunker.

"How do you know you're not anthropomorphizing?" Gravity asked.

"What?" Wen said. "My English is good, but come on."

"Projecting your own thoughts and beliefs onto it. Giving it human characteristics where there are none, like cat owners who say they fulfill the orders of furry dictators who shit in boxes."

"It ... it said it understood what I had gone through, how I had made a long, difficult journey to come here only to be shunned and sometimes reviled. It said it was learning about this world. In my mind, I told the creature it understood nothing of me or this world. At that, it growled at me, told me we were both immigrants, but it was forced to make the journey by circumstances beyond its control. Just like me and my mother."

Amadeus had stopped eating. The food, as fine as it was, had turned dry and chalky in his mouth. With one thumb and forefinger, Amadeus twisted the cloth napkin in his lap and wished it were made of paper.

Maybe Wen was just insane. Maybe that was why he left the troupe. They kicked him out for being crazy. Nevertheless, General Nguyen's intelligence indicated the troupe possessed a captive subliminal. Insane or not, Wen's story corroborated their own intelligence. They had to find Captain Carl and his subliminal, if only to confirm the creature was just a mindless beast.

"Have you told anyone else about this?" Amadeus said.

"No one would believe me. You don't."

"I don't *want* to believe you," Amadeus said.

"I can understand why," Wen said. "Your actions helped to kill many of them, Amadeus."

"Subluminals kill humans. They are predators," Amadeus said. "They attacked us first. We have a right, a duty to fight back and defend ourselves. We can't *not* kill these ... things."

"The subluminals are here because of your father," Wen said. "I don't know how your father's demon gates worked, but I doubt the subluminals wanted to come here."

"God damn it! They can't *want* anything because they cannot think." He slammed a hand down on the table for emphasis and drew glares from displeased diners. Gravity placed a hand on Amadeus' arm, and Amadeus hung his head.

"I'm sorry, Wen. This is a, um, stressful time for me. I meant no offense to you. Thank you for speaking with us."

Amadeus stood up from the table, stumbling and nearly falling into Gravity as he did so. He needed to find a quiet place to collect himself, away from the glares and stares of those around him.

"Don't you want to find Captain Carl?" Wen said. Amadeus looked up and saw the acrobat was smiling at him.

"Well, yeah. Of course. Where is he?"

"I don't know," Wen said, his voice almost singsong. Amadeus scowled. Everyone was fucking with him today. Even the wrinkles around Gravity's eyes were bunched up in a grinless smile. "But I'll tell you how to find him. A couple days before a show, he sends people into town with posters and flyers. News spreads by word of mouth. Before he had the demon, he would send performers to a central location and have them do free performances. Now, though, he simply has people go to public places and hand out flyers the day of the show. And almost all his shows sell out."

"Then it shouldn't be hard to find him," Amadeus said.

"We could set up some kind of as-it-happens keyword monitoring alert for online media," Gravity said. "I'm sure there's plenty of chatter when the flyers go out."

Wen shook his head. "It won't be that easy. Carl's smart. He knows if people like you found him, he'll be out of business."

"He can't keep information off the Internet," Amadeus said.

"No, but he can pay a company to post a hundred pieces of false information for every piece of accurate information."

"That explains why our intelligence up to this point is about as accurate as a North Korean news broadcast," Gravity said.

Wen smiled at this, then continued. "It gets weirder. A lot of the good information gets removed by the very people who post it. Remember how I said the creature communicated with me? I think it does the same thing with the audience. It makes people believe they're part of something so special it shouldn't be shared. Yes, when they first hear about it, people post info like, 'I'm going to see a demon tonight, hahaha,' but that's all *before* the show. Afterwards, for whatever reason, they go back and remove what they posted. They feel compelled to keep it secret. It's not mind control, but I'm not sure what else to call it."

Amadeus shook his head and checked himself before he spoke. "Is there anything else you can tell us that'll make it easier to find him?"

Wen sucked air through his teeth and looked up at the ceiling.

"This time of year, he'll probably be in the Southeast, as it's still somewhat warmish. You might try along the Gulf Coast, or maybe rural Georgia. In the winter, they usually take it easy and live off the harvest of all the fall festivals, though they might've decided to hit it hard and work for an early retirement. I think Carl knows he won't have his little attraction forever."

6

The next thing Grassal knew, the sky had grown black-orange and he was shivering. He felt trampled earth beneath him. Every fiber of every muscle in his big body ached. A rough wool blanket covered him, and two full plastic water bottles lay in the grass by his head. He remembered sitting on a bench, being approached by the two men, and then nothing. No, not nothing. A snippet of memory showed him pummeling the blond man's bleeding, terrified face. His stomach soured further with the fear he had killed the man, but no corpses lay before him, and he wasn't in jail, so he supposed they had escaped. Not only that, but someone had covered him against the cool night air. The blanket smelled clean, like it had just come out of the laundry. When he checked the water bottles, he found the seals unbroken.

Grassal began to cry. He didn't deserve this. He had done ugly, violent things, yet the universe had still seen fit to provide him with these acts of kindness. Someone must've seen his prosthetic and assumed he was a veteran. No one ever recognized him, not like they recognized Amadeus.

Through bleary eyes he looked out across the bay, toward the Golden Gate Bridge. The ice-blue lights of welding arcs flickered like fireflies. A whirring grinder sent a luminescent shower of orange sparks from the primary support down into the chilly waters of the bay. Above the city's midnight noise, Grassal was certain he could hear the steelworkers calling out to each other in satisfied and happy voices.

Rebuilding. What choice did they have? You fall down, you get back up. But Grassal didn't think he could get back up on his own. He needed help, and not the strait-jacket-and-Thorazine kind he suspected he would receive as an uninsured patient, heroic subluminal chew toy or not. From his bag, he retrieved his phone and dialed the girl who had put him back together once before. If Lilly Jones couldn't help him, no one could. Despite the hour, he decided to call her. Lilly answered on the first ring. She sounded awake.

"Amadeus told me you went off on your own path. I assume you're calling me at five in the morning to tell me how good everything's going for you?"

"If only. I kind of need your help." He heard the desperation in his voice. Silence hung on the line, and for a moment Grassal was sure she was about to refuse him.

"Come on out. I just got back to the bunker last night."

"You're in Colorado?"

"I have some business to attend to here. You can help me pack."

"Pack?"

"You heard me. I'll give you the details later. What's your ETA?"

"I'm in San Francisco now. I'll catch the next train."

"Then I'll see you soon."

Grassal slept for most of the trip. When he arrived in Denver, he headed straight for the pair of life-sized sandstone bears that flanked the entrance to The Grizzly. Something about the grizzlies appealed to Grassal. He liked that they were solid, ancient, and unlikely to offer any surprises ... just the opposite of kipium. Fucking kipium. Grassal wished he had never heard of the stuff. He wondered how one little element could cause so much trouble, but then he thought of uranium and felt foolish.

At a table beneath a stuffed elk's head, Grassal gazed at The Grizzly's menu, a multi-ethnic selection of food porn: venison hot pots, rare elk steaks swimming in goat cheese, Rocky Mountain oysters, several preparations of squid, and a hundred other offerings that serenaded his stomach with their siren songs. Lilly would arrive soon, and Grassal thought that after the drive down from Leadville, she might appreciate a warm dish. Maybe this would allow him to put off explaining what he had done to Lucretia. But even if he could delay it, he'd have to tell her eventually, and then what would she do? Lock him in the Panic Room until this blew over? He hated the idea but had to admit it sounded sensible.

Choosing to ignore the cost, he ordered venison hot pot. The broth had just begun to boil when Lilly strode through the threshold and scanned the room. Grassal waved, and her eyes glimmered when they fixed on his.

"Grassal! You look ..." She looked him up and down then brushed back her shoulder-length hair. "Like hell. Did you really order hot pot for me?" Grassal nodded. "I'll pay. I got it."

Grassal put out both hands and tried to protest. "You can't. You're already—"

"Shush, boy, before I change my mind."

A twinge of shame twisted in Grassal's stomach. Lilly had her own bunker and, like Amadeus, probably received royalties from her father's patents. He had nothing more than his wits, a few thousand bucks, and twenty boxes of computer parts in a New Jersey storage building. He was sure Lilly was well aware of this fact.

"Thanks for letting me come up. I'm really in a bad place."

"I guessed that when I talked to you. You're lucky I'm in Colorado. I was just packing some things up, and I could use the company."

"Packing?"

"I'm going to stay in Washington for a while."

"To be closer to Amadeus?"

"That's one reason. There are other factors." Her expression darkened, but Grassal chose to press on.

"What else?"

"I have to sell the bunker."

"Damn."

"I hate that place anyway."

"Why?"

"Why do I hate it? It's not obvious?"

"No, I know why you hate it. Why are you selling it?"

"Grassal, there are currently seven lawsuits pending against my father's estate. Sympathy for me is the only reason the feds haven't seized the place like they used to do in big drug cases."

"And it's up to you, his daughter, to sort it all out. That's rotten." A server set a plate piled high with chunks of raw venison on their table. "Are you sure it's not a problem that I'm here? I mean, you're obviously busy."

"I will make time for you, no matter how fucked up you think you are." A lump formed in Grassal's throat. He didn't deserve this.

"I hope Amadeus won't think—"

"Would you stop with this whiny shit? It doesn't become you. If it were a problem, I would simply tell you to go sleep on a park bench." Grassal worked his mouth but no sounds came out. "Yes, I know San Francisco wasn't kind to you. Some blogger posted a photo he snapped of you during your recent adventure in homelessness."

Grassal felt his face flush.

"I just don't want things to get weird."

"Just don't do anything sexy or psychotic, and we'll be fine."

Lilly dumped the venison, along with sliced onions and oyster mushrooms, into the boiling broth. While the meat cooked, Grassal told her everything except the part about assaulting the blond man. Lilly nodded while he spoke. The more he told her, the lighter his heart grew.

"Have you called Lucretia to apologize?"

"She's blocked my calls. I don't blame her; I did throw a jar of pickles at her head. This is entirely my fault. I think we were arguing, but I'm telling you, I don't remember doing it. That's what scares me. All I remember is the aftermath."

"Use my phone." She slid an ancient dumbphone across the table. Grassal thought of Tommy Brunmeier's obsession with dead technology and felt another knot trying to form in his throat. Even if Tommy was alive somewhere, he still felt dead to Grassal. "She won't recognize the number. Just tell her you're sorry for what happened, and that you're getting help."

"I can't."

Lilly crossed her arms. "Grassal Delgado, you are one of the strongest people I know, but right now, you are acting like a bitch."

"I need more time to heal, or at least level off. Lilly, I ... I didn't tell you everything." Lilly raised one eyebrow and waited. As Grassal explained how he had assaulted the blond man, her already-pale face went chalk white.

"You still sure you want me staying with you?"

She spoke immediately. "For the hundredth time, yes. Now stop asking and enjoy the deer."

Lilly piloted her orange hearse over snaking mountain passes. Outside, scrub pines clung to snow-covered peaks. Warm air billowed from the vents and onto Grassal's face. Grassal attempted to fight the altitude sickness with limited success. Nevertheless, Lilly's company had lifted his spirits.

"Do you think you're the only one?" Lilly asked, flexing her gloved hands on the steering wheel.

"The only what? Genius in a sea of morons?"

"Infected. Because of your leg. Maybe something got into your bloodstream and is making you act ... strangely." Something about the way Lilly said *infected* bothered him.

"Please don't use that word," Grassal said.

"What? Infected?"

"Right. It sounds contagious."

"Are you contagious?" They neared the entrance to the compound.

"I don't think so, but there's no way to know."

"You're not contagious, but you're right, maybe we do need another word." Lilly muttered to herself for a moment before saying anything. "Affected? No. That's not right. Altered? Um, no … Afflicted. That's it. You're afflicted with something we don't understand yet. Does that work for you?"

Grassal nodded and commented on the lack of snow on her driveway.

"I used my father's money to install a heated driveway before the legal assaults started. I was tired of having near-death experiences every time a snowstorm blew through." Grassal chuckled, and Lilly continued, "According to my real estate agent, it's already paid for itself in the increased potential selling price. Everybody wants a bunker, but nobody wants to go off-road to get to it."

They reached the end of the drive, and Lilly pressed a button. The rock slid away, and they drove down the tunnel and into the Jones compound. The hangar was as he remembered it, full of tarp-covered parts and contraptions, only now an office—complete with a treadmill desk, recliner, bookshelf, Tiffany lamp, and oriental rug—occupied the corner closest to the living quarters. Stacks of paper were piled on nearly every flat surface. Grassal stretched after he stepped out of the hearse and failed to suppress a yawn. "I think I need to sleep for awhile and get used to the altitude."

"*Mi casa su casa.* There's a couch out here, you can hit one of the bedrooms, or you can take the lift down there." Grassal felt the edges of his mouth involuntarily curl downward, but he recovered himself.

"You couldn't pay me to step into that elevator."

"Can't blame you. I've only gone down there a couple times

since ... then. It makes me nervous," Lilly said as she feigned a tic and Grassal laughed. They locked eyes and nodded goodnight to each other.

The smell of roasting chicken woke Grassal several hours later. He pulled himself from bed, padded past the empty kitchen and its olfactory temptations, and found Lilly at her desk. She was cleaning a pistol, only it didn't look like most pistols. Its shape was funny, with a box magazine and a long wooden handle. Grassal thought it looked like something out of an old war movie. She looked up at him, and he nodded at it. She handed it to him.

"My mother's grandfather was an officer in the Second World War. He brought it back from Germany. It's a Mauser C96. I've got a shoulder stock for it around here somewhere."

"Funny how both you and Amadeus have these heirloom weapons lying around."

"The difference is I actually know how to use mine." They exchanged a smile, and her expression darkened. "Grassal, all joking aside, I learned something important today: you're not alone," Lilly said.

"I know. I see you right in front of me," Grassal said, but he knew what she meant, and had suspected as much since he first realized something was wrong with him.

"Despite our boy's ingenious invention, plenty of those things emerged and ran amok. And in each place they did, I've found second and a few firsthand accounts of people with symptoms similar to yours." Lilly paused then began ticking city names off on her fingers. "New York, Huntington, San Francisco, Newcastle, Mar del Plata, Montevideo, Bangkok, and Phnom Penh. All these places had confirmed operational demon gates, and all of them except Bangkok are giving me similar reports from the past few weeks."

"Why not Bangkok?"

"At first I thought it was censorship. The Communications Authority of Thailand blocks sites that host porn and content unflattering to the king. It's not a stretch to say that a bunch of inter-dimensional creatures turning your people into violent psychotics would make your country look bad. But so far there's nothing."

"Why didn't we hear about any of this before?"

"The symptoms just started manifesting in the past couple of weeks, and there's not really a media narrative around it yet. But the government knows something's up. Apparently, based on the informal recommendations of a doctor named Marjorie Marx from the Centers for Disease Control, TSA agents are asking travelers to report if they've had any contact with, and I quote, 'otherworldly invading entities.'"

"Marjorie Marx. I'm sure that plan is about as effective as asking a terrorist if he is a terrorist."

"The thing is, it's kind of a 'gotcha' situation. There's actually a registry of afflicted. Every hospital that treated injuries during the Emergence had to report the type of injury and whether the patient had contact with the creatures. I'm sure they could cross-reference that with passport information."

"That's fucked up."

"All in the name of public health. At least, I think that's the justification."

"I don't like it. I think this is going to do more harm than good. What's next? Are they going to make the afflicted sew yellow stars onto their sleeves?"

"Come on, Grassal. This is different. The people who are afflicted need help. You included."

"I know. It's just that, well, if I've learned anything over the past few months, it's that good-intentioned acts usually have unintended consequences."

"That's the risk anyone takes by doing the right thing. We are directly affected by this, we're in a position to do something about it, and we have a *responsibility* to do something about it. I mean, what if somebody kills their kid, or starts attacking the elderly? I know you're not a violent person, but from what you've told me ... I want to show you an article I saw this morning." She turned her attention back to her computer for a moment then showed him a headline: "Crazed citizens pummel pedestrians in Queens."

Grassal narrowed his eyes as he read. The article described how a group of four muttering people marched in lock-step down a busy street and attacked anyone who stepped in their way. A witness said the marchers were subdued only after a team of people in hazmat suits showed up and used shock batons and animal control poles to herd them into a box truck.

"Jesus," Grassal said. Lilly gave him a searching look.

"Do you still think we should ignore this? What's next?"

"I guess we need to find out what the CDC knows and whether or not there's any known treatment."

While she worked, Grassal paced the floor of the hangar, trying to untangle everything in his mind and develop a list of people who might be able to help him.

"The CDC's not saying anything, either in official statements or on their website. I'm sending them a message now." After she finished, she stretched her arms over her head. "We'll figure this out, Grassal. We sorted out the mess that was Tommy Brunmeier's files, did we not?"

"We did."

"This is no different. We just need to figure out some unknowns, then we can figure out what to do about your, ahem, affliction."

Grassal smiled and snapped his fingers. Lilly raised an eyebrow and said, "What do you intend to do?"

"I'm going to go right to the source," Grassal said. "I'm going to call Marjorie Marx."

7

That evening, in the room of a midrange franchise hotel, University of Connecticut valedictorian Amadeus Brunmeier began to scrape the rust from the skills that made him valedictorian in the first place: rule creation and parameter definition that would make relationships between data visually comprehensible. For his senior project, Amadeus had mined public health statistics to demonstrate a positive correlation between an experimental hydraulic fracturing process, aquifer contamination, and adrenal tumors in diabetic children. Professor Swann had confirmed his findings and passed the results to the EPA, who determined that in this case this correlation did suggest causation. Amadeus' project had improved the health of hundreds of children, resulted in three class-action lawsuits, and was the primary reason he, and not Jessica Kwan, Brandon Turner, or Deshawn Campbell, had received the honor. Not that Amadeus had wanted to be valedictorian; he just wanted to investigate the lead Regina, his rare-book girl, had dropped in his lap about the same time he needed to select a final research topic. Now he needed to figure out how to use these skills to find Captain Carl and his pet subluminal.

Amadeus stretched his flexscreen computer out until it covered the lacquered pine table. He logged in to the mobile version of the GeoVer development platform. The interface was simultaneously familiar and alien to him; he had used GeoVer only once since he had graduated, and that was to develop a triangulation routine that would monitor for mentions of his father. After only an hour, he realized the data were too scattered to be both reliable and valid, so he had abandoned that project. This project, however, should yield better results.

Amadeus set up a search-and-match routine that would provide him with geographically concentrated, multi-source mentions of a keyword set, along with the time frame in which the mentions occurred—in short, a geo-spatial-temporal-thematic analysis of a massive data set. A positive correlation among these sources should give them the location. These sources would include public Internet chatter, of course, but he could also benefit from local radio and video signals. There were other ways to increase the size of his dataset. If he could incorporate some signals interception software into GeoVer ...

Amadeus knocked on the door that connected his room to Gravity's. A moment later, Gravity opened the door, his eyebrows arched.

"Have you ever heard of Carnivore?" Amadeus asked.

"Carnivore? As in the 'eats flesh of animals' sense, or in the 'antiquated signals intelligence software' sense?"

"The latter. I know Carnivore's about six generations out of date, but I ..."

"What are you saying, kid? I've been around for a while, but I didn't retire twenty years ago. You think we'd benefit from a little professional network monitoring?"

"Yes. I've got something in mind that should match chatter to a location, but so we don't waste our time, I'd like to get data from as many sources as possible."

"You do remember you're on the payroll from the Defense Intelligence Agency, don't you, Amadeus? Traffic analysis is old hat for these cats."

"Of course I remember."

"But you're not yet thinking about the resources at your disposal."

"What kind of resources?"

"Besides technical tools, your best resources are the people in this agency and others who can give you tools ... or favors. I suppose it helps if you've actually met some of these people, which you haven't." Gravity paused and stroked his chin. "In that case, I think you need the latter. With all that NSA crap a few years back, it's not as easy as it used to be, but I've got a gal who might be able to get you what you need." Before Amadeus could say another word, Gravity removed a phone from his pocket and dialed a number from memory.

"Kimberly?" Gravity's voice was high and sweet. "Hi, it's Owens." A long silence. "I know, I know. That was wrong of me. But remember Qatar? Uh, yeah. Like that. Uh huh? Well, okay, fine, you always did like to hear me beg, so here it is: I need a favor. Yes, pretty please, with sugar on top ... are you kids still using Yama's Eye?"

Eight hours and as many cups of coffee later, morning light filtered in through the window, and Amadeus still hadn't gotten the motherfucker working. Everything in GeoVer was functioning as it should, but his results lacked reliability. More confounding, he was getting strange errors from Yama's Eye, the program Gravity's pal Kim had given him access to. The program wasn't returning any data, but every once in a while GeoVer would dump his user files into a backup folder. Each time this occurred, Amadeus had to manually move the files back to their original location. Then there were the repeated ping sweeps against his GeoVer server, but Amadeus had decided that was just a fluke. Maybe it was an automated routine in GeoVer's own network security package.

Bleary-eyed and woozy, Amadeus stood up and considered ordering room service. Gravity had done so earlier, before retiring to his room. Now the thought of food was the only thing that prevented Amadeus from flopping onto the bed and allowing sleep to take him away from filters and variables and charts and terabytes of noise. He initiated an automated rescan of all previous matches before picking up the phone and ordering oatmeal, scrambled eggs, and a thermos of coffee. In the fifteen minutes that passed, Amadeus performed some of the body-weight exercise routine he had started and abandoned during his junior year at UConn.

He had almost finished his breakfast when the computer chimed, alerting him to a high-confidence correlation. Amadeus sipped coffee and reexamined the results: seventeen keyword matches among six sources clustered in Athens, Georgia. Shoveling scrambled eggs into his mouth, he verified the results had originated on the University of Georgia campus. One result was a geotagged image of a broad-faced woman in a purple dress holding a sign that read, "Beware Satan's harbinger! Counter Beelzebub wherever he appears." The caption on the photo read, "Not sure if fundie protestor or publicity stunt." Amadeus wasn't sure either. The photo had been posted almost four hours ago, but if they moved, maybe they'd be able to find out. He picked up the room phone, dialed Gravity, and said, "We're going to Georgia."

Two airports, three naps, and eight more cups of coffee later, Amadeus looked out the window of a rented flat panel van at Athens' red brick downtown and the University of Georgia campus. A flexscreen spread across his lap indicated the source of the correlation—a lawn in front of a residence hall—was only a few blocks away now. He supposed they would start their search there; it seemed as good a place as any. When they reached the lawn, the woman from the photo was still there. She gesticulated before a semicircle of onlookers. Her sign leaned against a nearby water fountain.

She was dressed in old clothes frayed from too many washings. Her ashy, wrinkled skin was parched like a drained lake. In person, Amadeus thought she looked like a nursing home escapee. Perhaps she was. When he stepped out of the van, her eyes locked with his. Recognition flickered on her face like a spark. She poked the air with a knobby finger.

"You! Son of the demon-bringer," she said. Amadeus expected her to hiss. "I suppose you're here to see more of the old man's handiwork?"

Amadeus' throat constricted as he said, "I'd rather see my old man, but that's not happening, now is it?"

Her expression softened. "My apologies. I get a little carried away sometimes."

"We're here to kill it," Gravity said. "We are the bringers of justice."

She cocked her head and raised an eyebrow. "That's good. That's good. The world needs justice, but this is out of your hands now. Pandora's box has been opened, and we must live with its vile contents."

"It was here? Last night?"

"They set up their Babylonian amusement in a vacant lot at the end of the street. My goal was to warn the indecisive away, and I did some good, but still the creature's corruption spread. I can feel it."

"Any idea where they might've gone next?"

She shook her head. "After the last glassy-eyed gawker left, they pulled up stakes and got out of town. They knew they weren't welcome."

"What do you mean by 'glassy-eyed?'" Gravity asked.

"When people entered the amusement, they were laughing and enjoying themselves as young people having an evening out are wont to do. But when they left, their mood was subdued and their eyes furtive, like they had seen something they weren't quite prepared to see. Today, no one speaks of it, as if the night's activities brought them great shame. To revel in the sight of such a beast, it's unnatural."

Amadeus and Gravity exchanged a glance.

"Just out of curiosity," Amadeus said, "are you aware that a picture of you with a protest sign is circulating online?"

"Of course I am. I put it there."

As afternoon turned into evening and another Southern winter day grew dark, Amadeus and Gravity nursed coffees in the booth of a little café off Lumpkin Street. Grayscale photos of famous visitors and antique cars covered the walls. They waited. For what, Amadeus wasn't sure. Another blip on his flexscreen. Chance? Fortune? Luck? Amadeus checked again that no new data had appeared. He was disappointed and decided to pass the time by broaching a topic that had been bothering him like a toothache.

"Gravity, tell me about your family."

"As in, the family to which I was born, sired by a uniformed stranger?"

"Them, maybe later. I'm thinking more about the family you started."

"Tasanee and I met by chance." Gravity took a sip of his coffee. "I never intended to stay, but three years later, I was father to four beautiful children. We had twin boys, another boy, and a little girl. It was too good to last."

"What do you mean?"

"My past caught up with me. I was blackmailed. I could stay with my family but be extradited for war crimes within the year, or return to the states to work for the concrete company ... alone. The bastards made me sign a seven-year contract. My contract ended just after the business with your father began, and I couldn't exactly leave you hanging."

Amadeus' gut twisted as understanding dawned on him.

"I've been keeping you from your family," Amadeus said. "If it wasn't for what's happening now, you'd be with them?"

Gravity nodded then said, "Soon. Of all the things I can pull off, expediting immigration paperwork isn't one of them. Tasanee has said she'd like the kids to go to an American high school, and they're almost old enough. I've spent some time researching neighborhoods and school districts in northern Virginia and Maryland. For what it's worth, the pre-arranged payments provided by your father's contract with me should allow me to put them in a nice, private Catholic school."

Amadeus tried to wrap his brain around what he was hearing but failed to do so. As he formulated another line of questioning about Gravity's future plans, his flexscreen chimed, alerting him to new matches in his application. They exchanged a glance, which Amadeus interpreted as an agreement to continue this discussion later.

On the map, three data points had appeared at Athens Ben Epps Airport, along with ten more just over a hundred kilometers south, in the town of Milledgeville. According to the origination information, all the data was sourced from text message data that included the keywords he had defined. His subroutine was finally returning results from Yama's Eye. Gravity pointed to the blips at the airport.

"Either Captain Carl has some fans coming in from out of town, or we've got company," Gravity said. "What do these messages say?"

Amadeus extracted their contents and was rewarded with a garbled string of ASCII characters.

"Yama's Eye noted the match during the original transmission, but in the—I don't know—nanosecond after interception, the message became garbled. We've got nothing."

"The good old self-destructing message," Gravity said.

"Pretty much."

Now that he could do so, Amadeus expanded the time frame to include the last week. The data created a path marked by text messages and recently deleted social media mentions: Charlotte to Spartansburg, Greenville, and Greenwood, then on to Athens and now Milledgeville. Unlike the messages from the airport, these were neither self-destructing nor scrambled. Amadeus opened a few of them, just to confirm he was getting the results he had hoped for.

"I'm going to see the demon tonight. Want to go?" and "Some circus guy has a subluminal," and "Carl's mobile subluminal extravaganza ... I just heard about it an hour ago. Headed over there now." This last message was time stamped two hours ago, which suggested to Amadeus that the exhibition was already underway and possibly over.

"Think we have what we need?"Amadeus asked. Gravity nodded. "What about the people at the airport?"

"Nothing we can do except hope that we find this perverse menagerie before they do."

"And if we don't?"

"Then may God help Captain Carl."

8

On the road to Milledgeville, in the minutes before carsickness made it impossible, Amadeus examined his application and realized he had made a serious mistake. In addition to remote backups, GeoVer permitted users to share data definitions, program parameters, and query results on a GeoVer community forum. By default, sharing was disabled and results were private. Amadeus, however, had overridden the default value in the function he wrote to add the Yama's Eye data to his own. As a result, details of each hit were posted to the community forums, potentially alerting anyone else who was interested in Captain Carl's location. He debated telling Gravity but decided to wait. In the meantime, he fixed the function call and focused on the road ahead, hoping to quell his rising nausea. If only Grassal had been able to help him with the coding, none of this would've happened.

"When we arrive," Gravity said, "we'll have missed the show, but perhaps some humint could be beneficial."

"Humint?"

"Apologies. I forget that you're new at this. Human intelligence. You'd be surprised by the information people will reveal, especially when they don't intend to," Gravity said. For the first time in an hour, he turned control of the van over to the navigation system, took his eyes off the road, and gave Amadeus a significant look. With a sinking feeling, Amadeus realized he had to confess. Like a contrite child, he hung his head before he spoke.

"Gravity, I think it's my fault those people showed up at the airport. I'm a shitty coder, and an error in my script basically broadcasted my search query results."

"Shit happens. We fix it, we go on."

"That doesn't make me feel better."

"Your feelings don't matter, Amadeus. Only your actions matter. So suck it up and put your social face on."

Milledgeville was really two towns: one the old town, where reconstruction-era brick buildings housed restaurants that looked out on tree-lined streets; the other, the new, where big-box franchises grew like jimson weeds along an eight-lane highway. Gravity directed the van to stop on the old town's main drag. They stepped out, and the van drove itself away in search of parking. Couples and groups dressed in light jackets or flannel shirts strolled along the sidewalk. Music poured from the competing speakers of bars, restaurants, and cafés.

"Where do you want to start?" Amadeus asked. He had donned yellow-tinted glasses. His eyes had almost cleared up, but they still contained enough black to appear abnormal, even in the dim light of the evening.

"According to your data, your intercepts originated here." Gravity passed to Amadeus a slip of paper on which he had scrawled two intersecting streets.

"This is the street, and," Amadeus looked at the map on his flexscreen, "the intersection's just a couple blocks up ahead."

"That's why we're here."

Their destination was a community information kiosk located beneath a wooden picnic shelter set in the middle of a small park. Affixed to the kiosk were notices advertising weight loss supplements, revivals, church potlucks, yoga classes, and a small engine repair service. None mentioned Captain Carl or his mobile extravaganza. The ground was clear of any flyers or debris, but Amadeus thought he might have some luck in the trashcan, so he started to remove the lid.

"Wait," Gravity said. He sniffed the air and scanned the area with darting eyes.

"What?"

"What do you see?"

"Nothing, just—"

"Exactly. It's too quiet. Something's not right. Get back to the strip. Stay where people can see you."

"Thank you, mother."

Gravity pulled the van's key fob from his pocket and tossed it to Amadeus, who caught it. "If I don't contact you within the hour, leave."

Amadeus hesitated.

"Go, Amadeus. Trust me."

Amadeus wanted to protest, to stay with Gravity, but he knew he wouldn't be much use in a fight, despite the smattering of training he had received. Instead, he stuck his hands in his pockets and made his way back, trying and failing not to feel like he was the one and only kid rejected from the kickball team. Just before he rounded the corner that would take him to the strip, he glanced back to see Gravity fading into the shadows of the park, silenced pistol in hand. Amadeus' abdomen muscles tightened and he wished he had a weapon of his own.

After some internal debate, Amadeus decided he would be better off indoors so, after looking around to be sure he wasn't being followed, he ducked into the first establishment he came to, a crowded sports bar. Inside, University of Georgia jerseys and pennants decorated the wall. Men played pool on red-felt tables beneath wall-sized flexscreens that broadcasted basketball highlights. As the door closed behind him, a few people looked him over before returning to their conversations, games, or drinks. Although he hated bars, this one offered an excellent view of the street, so Amadeus ordered a draft beer and took a stool at the counter in front of the window. The beer glass chilled his fingers as he focused his attention on the conversations around him.

Topics included speculation on the Bulldogs' upcoming bowl performance; a couple's argument about money, followed by its subsequent resolution where the woman agreed to take care of everything; good-natured shit talking at the pool table, which made Amadeus miss Grassal; and tales from a recent hunting expedition to western North Carolina.

While listening to detailed instructions on how to rebuild a carburetor, delicate fingers settled on his forearm. The only thing that prevented him from jumping out of his chair was the ironic grin worn by the woman who had touched him: late twenties, white, with wavy black hair pulled back in a bun and secured with two replica camouflage arrows.

"Amadeus Brunmeier, my goodness. That's so weird. I was just thinking about you for some reason, and here you are. It's a pleasure to meet you," she said, positioning her hand for an affable shake. Her voice was just loud enough for him to hear, but not loud enough to carry, despite their proximity to glass. Amadeus arched one eyebrow then accepted her handshake. Her grip was firm, but there was something else there, too. He wondered if this was going to be a signature request.

"You as well. Can I help you with anything?" he asked as his eyes traced the low neckline of her shirt.

"No, you've already helped everyone plenty, but I think I can help you." Amadeus pushed a vision of a barroom bathroom quickie out of his mind. He'd done that once with Regina, and once was enough. Besides, he didn't expect Lilly would appreciate it. The vision passed, but it left behind a warmth in his cheeks. Maybe bars weren't so bad after all.

"How so?"

"The people with the subluminal. You're looking for it."

"Um, no I'm not." He wondered if this was some kind of trap.

"Right. Then I guess you're not interested in knowing where they set up tonight, huh?"

Amadeus sighed. "Okay, fine, I'm here looking for the creature with my, um, team, all of whom happen to be outside."

"Uh huh. Well, my father heard they were set up down at Baldwin State Forest. It's been a couple hours since I talked to him, but he said he was going to call the police. I wouldn't be surprised if half the town showed up with deer rifles to run them off."

"Shit," Amadeus said. "Miss, thanks, but I've got to go." Amadeus gave her a nod and turned to leave.

"Before you do, could you—"

"No, I'm sorry, it's really not a good time—" She grabbed his hand, but Amadeus didn't stop, and she was pulled along with him.

"Is this guy bothering you, miss?" a beefy goateed guy said. He wore a shirt that read "Staff."

"No, I wasn't bothering her, and she wasn't bothering me. Everybody's cool."

The woman had released her grip and now stood with her hands on her hips. "I don't think I like your attitude, Mr. Brunmeier."

"I'm sorry. Tell me, what can I do to make it up to you?"

"Molly," a new voice said. Amadeus turned to see a man even bigger than the bouncer approaching.

"Is this guy giving you a hard time?" the big guy said.

"Looks that way to me," the bouncer said.

"Oh come on," Amadeus said. "We were just ... she wanted to tell me something. Miss, I'm very sorry. Did you want me to, um, sign something for you, or what?" Amadeus' eyes dropped to the milky, exposed skin of her chest. She saw his gaze and her brown eyes widened.

"You think I want you to sign my chest! I've seen you do it on videos, but I never thought ... you pig. I just wanted to ask if you'd call my brother ... who's sick with leukemia."

"I'll call him, still, if you want."

"I don't want him talking to no pervert."

"Jesus," Amadeus said, shaking his head. "My God."

"Watch it now," the big guy said. He had moved closer to the woman, who had moved closer to the bouncer. Now the three of them stood before him, and Amadeus couldn't help but think of last week's inquiry, and how well he had done there by going on the offensive. He squared his shoulders and faced the two men.

"Watch what?" Amadeus said, crossing his arms and cocking his head to the side.

"Your blasphemous mouth," the big guy said, "unless you want to get it bashed in. Pervert."

Amadeus realized he had nothing to gain by escalating this further. "Okay, okay, I meant no offense. I'm leaving now. Excuse me." Amadeus turned, but before he did, he muttered the phrase "degenerate redneck" under his breath. He had almost made it to the door when a hand gripped his shirt and pulled him backwards. He turned to see the big guy's fist coming toward his face.

Amadeus dodged by dropping to one knee, then countered with an uppercut to the man's groin. The big guy dropped.

"It's Amadeus Brunmeier! He just assaulted that guy!" a random voice said.

Two pairs of hands lifted Amadeus up off the ground. This time it was the bouncer and another female staff member of equal size. Amadeus struggled for a moment but gave up when he saw that both were chuckling to themselves. As they carried him through the crowd, he thought he would be okay, but when they opened the door they heaved him out onto the sidewalk like a spent keg. Amadeus landed on his shoulder, hit his head, and came to rest sprawled in a heap. Just before the door closed, he heard a cheer go up through the bar.

Amadeus hated bars.

He managed to stay conscious, but he wasn't ready to walk just yet. Instead, he found a comfortable tree nearby to lean against. The night had cooled, and he could see his breath. He knew he was beyond defenseless. If anyone wanted to carry the fight outside, or if the danger Gravity perceived was real, he would be at their mercy. At least, he thought with some degree of pride, he had pulled off a surprisingly graceful dodge-and-counter. Maybe he wasn't entirely useless as a fighter, just inexperienced. He wondered how he would handle himself if he had another match with Davy. Amadeus expected he would do just fine against that frog-faced bastard.

Several minutes later, Amadeus saw Gravity moving toward him at a rate somewhere between a fast walk and a jog. When Gravity got closer, Amadeus saw blood splattered on the man's tailored white shirt. They made eye contact. Gravity's expression was as neutral as stone as he extended a hand and helped Amadeus to his feet. Gravity kept moving and told Amadeus to follow him.

Amadeus, still woozy, struggled to keep pace. "What's going on? Was there anyone ..."

"Keys," was all Gravity said.

Amadeus passed him the keys. "They were definitely here. A girl told me where they were set up."

When the van arrived, Gravity motioned for Amadeus to get in the driver's seat. He did so, and Gravity climbed in the side door. "Drive," Gravity said. As Amadeus drove away, Gravity kept checking the mirrors. He still hadn't said anything. Amadeus wanted to tell him about his barroom victory, but something about the man's manner told him now wasn't the time.

When they reached the new town and the highway expanded to eight lanes, Gravity told Amadeus to find a place to pull off. Amadeus did so, settling the van on the vacant end of an Übermart parking lot. Gravity handed Amadeus a phone and its now-separate coin-sized battery. Amadeus' eyes flashed to the blood on Gravity's shirt.

Gravity gave him a mirthless smile. "There was a man who wanted to talk to you. I convinced him it was in his best interest to talk to me instead. Turns out he was among the crew who arrived by air. They managed to get here to Milledgeville before us and, fortune of fortunes, they know where Captain Carl is spending the night."

"Where?"

"We didn't get that far. Negotiations broke down."

"Then ..."

"Then I realized I had enough information. We've got Yama's Eye, and it's perfect for something like this. Just figure out who he's been calling, plug their numbers in, and we should be able to pinpoint their location."

"What if he warns them?"

"That won't be a concern, at least for a few hours."

Amadeus suddenly felt much worse about the flippancy with which he had recently conducted himself. "For what it's worth, a woman recognized me and told me where Captain Carl set up his show." He decided not to tell the rest of the story just now.

"That's not surprising. I had half-hoped someone would tell you something. Assuming even one-tenth of the town was chattering about the Mobile Extravaganza, I knew you'd be just below the surface of their awareness, the memory of you like a batter on deck waiting to step up to the plate."

"I was bait? For intelligence gathering?"

"Sort of. But you weren't in any danger—unless you brought it on yourself."

"Nothing I couldn't handle." Amadeus turned the phone over in his hand. It was a common model, light and thin as a credit card.

Amadeus closed his eyes and visualized the process for plugging in phone numbers to Yama's Eye, then integrating the output in GeoVer. His only concern was being reverse-traced when he turned the phone on. If anyone was paying attention, it wouldn't take long. However, he could just also copy the data to an emulator and ditch the phone ...

"I've got it," Amadeus said. Gravity nodded, but his attention was elsewhere. "I've figured out how to get the information off the phone and—" Amadeus stopped.

Gravity examined his hands and hung his head. "Sometimes, I hate the person I've become. You're a good man, Amadeus. Stay that way."

A good man. Maybe he was. He patted Gravity's forearm before he began to transfer the data.

Fifteen minutes later, GeoVer and Yama's Eye gave him the output he had hoped for: four blips on a map of central Georgia. The blips had congregated at an RV park called River's End.

"They've already arrived," Amadeus said.

"It doesn't matter. If they kill the creature, and I suspect they intend to, then our job is still done. But we can benefit from finding out who, exactly, was tracking us."

Outside Milledgeville, stars dotted the sky like a monochrome print splattered with acid. Only a faint orange glow in the distance interfered with the starscape. Amadeus assumed it was the lights from the next town. A low, full moon cast long shadows dissipated by the van's cold blue headlights. Amadeus tapped his fingers on the steering wheel, drumming along with music he heard in his mind. The van's instruments bathed their faces with soft red-orange light.

A pair of headlights appeared in the rearview mirror, tiny at first, then growing closer and flashing red and blue. Police. Amadeus eased off the accelerator even though he wasn't speeding. The lights bounced all over the interior of their car. The sirens crescendoed into a wildcat's howl. As fast as they had begun, the lights and the sound and the fury blew past them with a tidal roar. The three police cruisers moved so fast the van rocked back and forth from the rush of wind in their wake. The red glow in the distance grew brighter, larger, and pulsed like embers. A spotlight illuminated rising ribbons of smoke.

"Do you think ...?" Amadeus asked.

"Yes."

"What have they done? What have *we* done? That's a ... I mean ... people take vacations there. There could be families. People just camping."

"Calm down, Amadeus. We don't know anything yet. For all we know it could be a bonfire."

"With police rushing in like that?"

"Maybe they're strict about their burning laws."

"Where are the fire trucks?"

"Just keep going."

A row of police cars sat below the painted timber sign for the park, blocking the entrance. A digital sign's output read, "Emergency vehicles only." Four uniformed police officers stood around in a group. Amadeus slowed the van to a crawl as he approached. The officers waved him on, but Amadeus only slowed. In the distance behind them, streams of water arced in the night. The smell of burnt plastic filled the van's cabin.

"Pull over," Gravity said. "I'll talk to them. If anything happens ... no, nothing's going to happen."

Amadeus brought the van to rest on the road's rough, dusty shoulder. As soon as he stopped, he saw two officers creeping toward the van. Each had his hand on the butt of his pistol. Gravity got out, keeping his hands conspicuously away from his body.

"Evening, officers," Gravity said, closing the door behind him. Gravity kept talking but Amadeus couldn't hear him. Amadeus wanted to get out but thought maybe he didn't want to be recognized. Not here, not yet. His fingers drummed as he waited, checking for the unseen in his mirrors. A few minutes passed, then Gravity opened the door and slid back into his seat, shaking his head.

"It's no good," Gravity said. "Somebody high up is working on this, and they're trying to keep a lid on it. Go ahead and drive, Amadeus."

"We can't just go. We've got to find out what's going on."

"A propane tank exploded. That's what these local police think. They're saying no one was hurt."

"Do you believe that?"

"Do you need to ask?" Gravity said. Amadeus shook his head and Gravity continued, "According to your map, the park sits up against a lake, and the highway crosses the lake just up ahead."

"What do you have in mind?"

"I hope you brought your swimsuit."

With the headlights off, Amadeus parked on the boat ramp at the base of the bridge. The campground lay less than a hundred meters away across the water, situated in the middle of a pine grove. To remain under the cover of darkness, he would have to wade up to the campground's floating dock. He could walk along the shore for the first fifty meters, but emergency lights and the glow of the fire illuminated everything close to the camp. From there he would have to push through the thick branches of the binocular-blocking longleaf pine in order to see anything.

"It's not cold by New England standards, but it's cold enough for the water to leach the heat out of your body. Once you're out of the water, you'll have about fifteen minutes until you'll need to change into dry clothes. Don't stay any longer than you have to. Hypothermia is a motherfucker. Good?"

Amadeus nodded and stepped out into the night. In his hand he held a night vision lens for the camera on his phone. He doubted he would need it. The campground was lit up like a music festival. Gravity rolled down the window and spoke to him before he set out.

"Just jump right in. Anything else and you're prolonging the pain."

"Words to live by," Amadeus said.

He followed the contours of the lake shore, passing around the private boat docks on this side. He expected to see people standing outside, watching the blaze, but the shore was lonely. The lake water was low, and the previously submerged areas were still muddy. His shoes squished and farted as he walked through the mud. He stepped in a puddle and the icy water seeped into his shoe, between his toes. He involuntarily inhaled, air hissing through his teeth. A shiver ran up his body.

Finally the muddy shore ended and he had to enter the water. He tried to remain silent but failed. His heart skipped two beats and a moan escaped his mouth, followed by a rush of energy, and he pushed farther into the water, first up to his knees, then up to his waist. His stomach clenched and his already-small penis shrank even more. Forcing himself down, he lowered his body into the water, keeping only his head above water.

With emergency lights shining not only toward the blaze but onto the lake beyond, Amadeus had to drift through a small sliver of shadow, the only darkness around the edge of the lake. He passed through the sliver, scrambled up the bank and into a stand of pine trees, then darted across a vacant parking spot for an RV. As he took cover behind a utility box, frigid water dripped from his clothes.

From his obscured vantage point, he saw only fragments of the entire scene: people in hazmat suits, masks, and respirators carried burnt and broken things. Soldiers stood around a Jeep, holding rifles. Corkscrewing flames rose above the treetops, trying to lick the stars. Streams of water from fire trucks mated with the fire, rushing steam clouds their progeny. He wanted to move closer, to see what fueled the fire, but he couldn't see any cover. His gaze drifted upwards, into the bristling pines, where evenly spaced branches begged to be climbed.

Once he selected a suitable tree, one of the tallest in the park, Amadeus pulled himself up into its dense maze of limbs. The exertion felt good and warmed his blood, but twice his body tried to betray him with its grip-loosening shivers. Time was short. His body temperature was dropping, and he still needed to cross the lake again. Up the tree he moved, as quietly as he could, the ground moving farther away, the smoke growing denser, the curtain of pine boughs gradually becoming thinner. Finally, twenty meters above the ground, he pushed a branch away and had a clear view of the happenings on the ground. He pulled his fleece jacket over his face to filter the choking air.

Below, the burned-out shells of four camping trailers were arranged like the smoking skeletons of Conestoga wagons around a tour-bus-sized RV. Flames still danced over the half-melted shell of the RV, oblivious to the streams of water that sought to quell them. Above a rear wheel well the remnants of a blackened vaudevillian logo proclaimed: "Cap---Ca---Mobi---vaganza."

With his feet planted and an arm thrown over one branch, Amadeus pulled out his phone with his free hand and began to record some video, watching the scene through the little six-centimeter screen. He zoomed in on a cluster of people in hazmat suits. They were examining a pile of something that at first glance appeared to be charred logs. Amadeus blinked, and his brain registered first an arm, then the open-mouthed face of a burnt corpse.

Amadeus vomited into the pine boughs. After he wiped his mouth, he counted at least eight humans—eight innocent individuals—and the body of a creature with six legs and a three-pronged tail. The subluminal. Amadeus shivered and for a moment he forgot why he had climbed the tree. The cold was doing its work. He needed to finish this up and get back to the van.

A wide sweep of the area with the phone captured most of the scene and showed the fire was limited to the cluster of RVs. The rest of the park, with its paved streets, manicured hedges, and facilities building, was thankfully unoccupied. Behind the building sat a hippopotamus-sized silver cylinder tank with a blue top. The propane tank, intact and unexploded.

He wanted to believe this wasn't murder, just a recreational accident, but RVs didn't just burst into flame. He especially had trouble believing it when his eyes settled on two familiar faces his brain wasn't presently able to connect with any particular memories. Amadeus zoomed in and recorded a clear, undeniable image of their faces, then panned the camera back to the flames and the bodies, making the association as clear as tropical water.

His body shuddered against the cold, and Amadeus decided he had what he needed. Down the tree. Back into the cold. Shivering. Chattering teeth. In waist-deep, halfway across, he stumbled, and his head went under. Out of the water, back onto the muddy shore. For a moment he forgot where he was going. He had to focus, to keep moving, even if moving was difficult and he went the wrong way. Away from the lake and its frigid water. Amadeus decided he wanted to rest. Maybe if he just sat down for a minute, he would remember where he was going and who those men were. He had just seen something awful, but what was so awful? The bodies, that's right. And the men. He had brought them. They killed the people, and it was Amadeus' fault.

Amadeus sat down on a dry dock. He watched traffic crossing the nearby bridge. His teeth knocked together. The orange glow from the campsite had faded since he arrived. How long ago had that been? He stood back up. Movement, he needed to move. He couldn't stop. Where was he going? Back, to the bridge, that was right. But sitting here, resting, that felt good.

A few minutes passed. Amadeus had his arms wrapped around himself, rocking back and forth, shivering, teeth chattering, when he felt himself being picked up for the second time that day. A familiar face, dark, wizened, and kind, looked him over, but Amadeus couldn't quite remember who the face belonged to. A professor, perhaps.

Amadeus just shook his head and pulled away. He didn't want to talk to any of his professors right now. The man sighed, bent down, and threw Amadeus over his shoulder.

"Come on now."

"You're carrying me," Amadeus said. "I guess that's okay."

"Hypothermia. That's why you're spacey. Let's get you into some warm clothes." The man placed something on Amadeus' head. Amadeus reached up and felt a soft fur-lined hat.

"I did something bad. Academic dishonesty. My friend is a programmer, a really good one. He helped me write a script for my last project. It was the health one—"

"It's okay, Amadeus. That doesn't matter now. What matters is getting you warm."

Something about the man's voice brought Amadeus back. "I'm not in Connecticut, am I?"

"No," the man said. Amadeus closed his eyes. The worst of the shivering had subsided, and now he needed only to wait. The man would help him. But Amadeus needed to tell him something. What was it? The dead people, that was it.

"They killed them ... Claudius, they killed them. That's right. Your name is Claudius Gravity Owens," Amadeus said. "I'd go by Gravity, too, if my name was Claudius." Amadeus remembered why he was wet. "They killed them with fire." Gravity carried Amadeus through the mud and back to the van. Amadeus said, "I have video. Proof. Why? Why would they kill them all? Wen will be so sad."

"Don't worry about Wen right now," Gravity said. They rounded a corner and he saw the van shrouded in the steam of exhaust. Gravity slid open the side door.

"Get in and take off your clothes," Gravity said.

"But it's so cold ..."

"Do you want to die, Amadeus?" Amadeus shook his head. "Then take off your damn clothes. They're soaked and sucking the heat right out of you. There's a blanket under the seat." Without giving him a choice, Gravity pushed Amadeus into the van and slid the door closed. Amadeus did as he was told, peeling the wet clothes from his body. Air from the heating vents warmed his naked skin. Gravity climbed into the front. Amadeus dug his phone from the pile of wet clothes and handed it to Gravity. Gravity reached back, pulled the blanket from under the passenger seat, and threw it onto Amadeus just before spinning the van's tires on gravel and pulling back onto the highway.

Back at the hotel, with Amadeus still shivering and wrapped in a blanket, Gravity filled the bathtub with warm water and helped Amadeus step in. He checked his watch and said he'd be back in fifteen minutes.

With steam rising around him, his body floating in hot water, Amadeus finally stopped shivering. As his body warmed up, the memory of everything he had seen came back to him. The charred corpses. The hazmat suits and the soldiers, both business-like and efficient. And the face of an individual he had seen twice before: the black-eyed man.

9

Two days after witnessing the smoking remains of the Mobile Extravaganza, Amadeus set out for a fact-finding meeting with Jones. On the way to the holding center, he debated calling Lilly and asking if she wanted to talk to her father during his visit, but he decided against it. Instead, Amadeus picked up carryout food from a Mexican restaurant and took it with him to the holding facility. He decided this would be an appropriate goodwill gesture. Upon arrival, he and his food were searched, and then a guard escorted him through the concrete bowels of the complex, passing cells filled with suspected terrorists, subversives, double agents, and other accused-but-untried individuals. The guard pressed a button outside Jones' door and informed him he had a visitor.

"He brought you food, you slimy fuck," the guard said into the speaker. To Amadeus, he said, "I'd rather feed him rusty nails on dry toast, but suit yourself." Amadeus passed through the threshold and the steel door shut behind him. Jones was slumped forward in his wheelchair with his hands folded in his lap. Only the leather strap around his chest prevented him from toppling forward. His skin had grown more sallow since Amadeus' last visit.

"My boy, I don't know how much more of this I can take. These people exhaust me. Since you last darkened my door, they've taken away all my reading materials, and now they won't even permit me a pencil and paper. They're trying to take away my right to use my mind."

Amadeus hoisted the bag. "It's not *Crime and Punishment,* but I brought some *carne asada* for you." Jones arched an eyebrow and, for the first time since he had entered the room, regarded Amadeus with something other than cultivated detachment. His face was like that of a parched man being offered a canteen.

"It'll be a fantastic change from the partially hydrogenated squid products they slide through the slot." Jones rolled his chair to the table on which Amadeus had set the food and began to eat. While he did so, Amadeus collected his thoughts and planned his approach for getting his questions answered.

"Jones, I've got to start with the bad news. Lilly refused to talk to you, and the officials responsible for your containment have denied all my requests to get you outside. I'm working on it, but today it's not possible."

"I didn't expect much," Jones said as he scooped up refried beans with a tortilla chip.

"But maybe I can be more persuasive with both your captors and your daughter if you're forthcoming with me."

"Thank you for the food," Jones said, turning his chair so that his back faced Amadeus.

"Holden, please, that was poorly worded. I'm sorry. Don't shut down on me. I need your help. I really do. I need to know everything you know. We both got fucked on this deal, and if you want to get unfucked, if you don't want to die in here, you'll talk to me. I really can work on getting you more privileges, maybe even a better plea bargain."

Jones ate his *carne asada* in silence and ignored the pleading tones in Amadeus' voice. Amadeus waited a few moments then continued.

"For Lilly's sake, please. Talk to me."

"I did it all for Lilly's sake, and look where it got me."

Amadeus looked down at his hands. This was the moment. "I understand why you did it, and I ... I ... I forgive you." Despite his other intentions, Amadeus realized that he meant it.

Jones turned around to face Amadeus. "You forgive me? You, golden boy of the Eastern Seaboard, deign to extend your forgiveness to me, the crippled criminal mastermind? Oh yes, you privileged little cunt, I know exactly what you think of me. Amadeus, my boy, here's my response to you: go fuck yourself with a nanosteel rod. Am I making myself clear?"

Amadeus smiled, nonplussed, and continued his previous task. "In your position, you couldn't have done anything else. I recognize that. I think I can make Lilly understand that. She might even forgive you ... but you have to help me. How do you know my father is alive? Who was the broker?" Amadeus spread his hands in a gesture of benevolent magnanimity. "You have nothing to lose, Jones, nothing—everything to gain."

Jones' eyelids quavered then he closed his eyes and hung his head. When he finally spoke, his voice was breathy and tremulous. Amadeus stepped closer to hear better. "Between this tumor, a thousand would-be citizen-assassins waiting for me outside, and the slop they pass off as food in here, I suppose I'm already a dead man. I will help you, if only for her sake."

"Thank you, Jones. Thank you," Amadeus said. "First, what else do you know about my father's current status?"

"We'll get to that. I need to give you a more complete version of the story. But understand every word I speak is one more molecule of wax that will be applied to the seal on my death warrant."

"What do you mean?"

"I mean, in plain old, red-blooded, American English, that what I'm about to tell you will get me killed. But nobody ever said redemption came cheap."

"Jones, you're in the basement of a federal lockup. Only a handful of people have access to you, and every one of them wants to see you alive, if only to find out what you know."

"You underestimate your nemesis, Amadeus Brunmeier. But if you haven't learned your lesson by now, you never will." Jones stretched, spreading wide his old basketball player's arms. Amadeus watched, impressed by the range of motion and agility Jones still possessed.

"I had a small deal set up with the buyer, and everything was set to go, provided I demonstrated proof-of-concept and showed the Pachyderm could withstand real-world abuse. The loss of our first test pilot was a tragedy that set everything back six months. Then you showed up—"

"And you had a convenient test pilot no one would miss should something go wrong."

"It wasn't like that at all," Jones said, but his tone wasn't chastising, only clarifying. "I provided you aid and succor because of Tommy. You could've hid at the compound indefinitely, and the world would've been none the wiser. But we both saw an opportunity, Amadeus. I needed a test pilot. You needed transportation that would keep you literally under the radar. The problems started when you left for New York. I told my buyer I had a test flight underway. The buyer pressed me for my pilot's identity, and I let it slip. By the time you were done crop dusting with that farmer, the broker had contacted me."

"His name?"

"This is ... this is going to cost me, Amadeus. You should know that."

"His name, Jones. What was his name?"

"Pearl Sundajos. He went by the name Pearl Sundajos. He called me three times. He spoke with educated, unaccented American English. Each time, he used a voice modulator."

"To conceal his identity, so you couldn't record it then run the voiceprint through a database."

"Correct. The first time he called, he made these wild promises, talked about upping the order from five to a hundred and paying me a fifteen percent royalty on each Pachyderm sold. This was the stuff of an inventor's wet dreams, so of course I assumed he was full of shit. But, while we spoke, he told me to check my bank account. I did, and saw he had made a five-million-dollar deposit. That's when he wanted to know about you. I denied knowing you. I obfuscated, wheedled, and dodged the question. He called me on it all, but I persisted. That's when he told me to kill you, or I would see my own daughter murdered. Sure, I could've hid Lilly on some desert island and maybe kept the initial deposit, but we both know how that would have worked out. Besides, I'd be a fool to turn my back on a deal like this, old friendships or not. So, yes, I did it for the money. Principled and poor, or compromised and cash-flushed; I chose the latter.

"I thought, 'I'm trapped. Damage control, Holden.' So I told him the Pachyderm didn't have embedded GPS tracking or remote shut-off, as it was only a prototype, and for some reason he believed this. By the end of that call, Sundajos knew you were going to New York, and I realized I was lost.

"The second call came when you were in Prague. Pearl demanded to know the whereabouts of your father. I told him he was dead, killed in the attack on your house. He accused me of hiding him as I hid you. I never told him where you were, but by this point I don't think that was necessary. I'm pretty sure there was an intercept on all my communications. Every time you contacted me, your signal gave them your location.

"The third call was the worst. Sundajos sent video and pictures of all the times they could've had her killed but didn't. He said these images would have a different outcome if you weren't dead within forty-eight hours, and I didn't doubt the man was anything but sincere. That's when I crashed you into the lake, locked Lilly in the bunker, for her own safety—you understand—and arranged my own transportation to LA ... which eventually landed me here."

"Damn," Amadeus said. "And you think Sundajos was involved with the Emergence?"

"There's not a doubt in my mind. New York? I attributed that to coincidence, but then there were more. That, however, is a story for another day. I'm tired, Amadeus. All this truth-telling, it's supposed to be cathartic, but I just find it tedious. I miss my hangar, my contractors, and most of all, my daughter. I hope this is how she remembers me, as a man who made the right choice in the end. And I hope you find Tommy. Parents should be with their children. But you need to understand that it might be a long time until you see him again. Your father hasn't contacted you because to do so would be to risk giving himself away. If your father was anything less than hyper-paranoid and secretive, he would've been killed long ago. These people have resources, connections, and tentacles in every Washington barrel o' pork."

Amadeus said nothing because to do so would've revealed the constriction in his throat. Jones had been more than helpful. Amadeus kicked himself for believing the worst about the man. Not that Jones was innocent, but he wasn't a monster either. Just a confederate. Amadeus wondered if Jones should even be here. He would sort this out later. Leaving Jones with a nod of gratitude, Amadeus pressed the buzzer and allowed the guard to escort him out of the building and into the biting winter morning.

In an attempt to make sense of everything he had just learned, Amadeus spent the rest of the day wandering around the National Mall. He strolled through the Smithsonian Natural History Museum. In the gift shop, he bought an Ethiopian opal set in a silver ring. The stone's bright reds, blues, yellows, and greens reminded Amadeus of a brain scan, and he thought Lilly would like it.

A group of school children recognized him, and he spent half an hour answering questions and scrawling his name on wide-ruled notebooks. Just after dark, he bought a hot dog and was debating how to spend his evening when his phone rang.

"Is there anything you need to tell me?" Gravity said. He sounded furious.

"What do you mean?"

"Jones is dead." Amadeus dropped his hot dog and chili splattered on the sidewalk. His knees began to shake. "You visited this morning. The guard said he checked on him after lunch and he was slumped over in his chair. It looks like poison, or maybe a complication of his disease."

"Oh no," Amadeus said. He staggered over to a wooden bench looking out onto the Mall. "I brought him Mexican food."

"I know. You understand how this looks, right?" His voice carried the hint of an accusation.

"Me? Kill Jones? No. Of course not. I wouldn't even know how. Why would I kill him? Where would I get poison?" Pigeons picked at the hot dog bun. Amadeus reached in his pocket, found the receipt for his hot dog, tore off a scrap, and popped it into his mouth like a painkiller.

"Are you eating paper?" Gravity said.

"No."

"Amadeus, keep your composure. Sit down. Let's talk this through." Amadeus closed his eyes and replayed parts of his conversations with Jones.

"I don't want to, Gravity. This is ... and Lilly. Someone must've heard what Jones told me. When I talked to him, Jones sounded resigned to dying in that cell." Amadeus touched the scar on his cheek and considered possible alternative explanations. "After what happened with my father. Have you seen the body?"

"I haven't, but General Nguyen has. She was the one who told me."

"Not a ruse, then. What does she say?"

"She says she can keep the wolves at bay, though this is bound to leak soon."

"She knows I brought him food?"

"I don't know. I'll tell her. If it's still there, we can have it analyzed. That could clear you of any suspicion. But Amadeus, before we go any further, you've got to be straight with me. Did you kill Jones?"

"No. I did not kill Holden Jones."

"That's good. That's good."

"Jones told me everything he knew: why he betrayed me, who he worked for."

"Tell me more," Gravity said, "but not right now."

"Is there any way we can keep this quiet? I have to tell Lilly. In person."

"She's in Colorado?"

"Yes."

"I'll see what I can do, but if you want to tell her, you'll have to do it fast. Get there, and get back. People will want to talk to you."

"Do you think I'm being set up?"

"Let's see. The day you happened to bring in food for the prisoner, the prisoner dies of what looks like poisoning. I'd say so."

"Fuck." Amadeus ran his hand through his hair.

"If it makes you feel any better, even if you were accused, no jury in the world would convict you, and even if they did, you'd get off without serious punishment. It's you, and it's Jones. People die in custody all the time. It happens. No big deal."

"No big deal? A man is dead."

"People die all the time."

10

At Dulles International, Amadeus bought a ticket for the next flight to Denver, paying with the credit card Gravity had given him. The girl at the desk recognized him but, to Amadeus' relief, only wished him a good day. Amadeus had no idea how much credit was available on the card, but he had already used it to make several thousand dollars' worth of purchases, and none had ever been declined, even the wine he had bought for Lilly. With a backpack slung over his shoulder and two hours until boarding, he made his way to airport security. As he waited, he whispered the name to himself: Pearl Sundajos.

Lines a hundred people long snaked back from the entrance to the Trusted Flyers secure area. Security personnel in bug-eyed respirator masks manned backscatter scanners, computers, and metal detectors. A flexscreen on the wall showed thermal images of everyone in the line. Two uniformed officers marched up and down the lines with tail-wagging German shepherds, letting the dogs sniff passengers and parcels. A digital sign above the entrance told him the wait was approximately an hour for Trusted Flyers, four hours for everyone else. Printed signs read "Safe and Secure Skies Depend on You! Please inform airport personnel if you have had any contact with otherworldly invading entities (OIEs) or if you are experiencing any of the following: fever, sweating, chills, hallucinations, temporary palsies or paralysis, or unexplainable anger or rage."

Resigned to his fate, Amadeus wished he still had the Pachyderm and joined what he hoped would be the shortest line. As of two weeks ago, he was a Trusted Flyer, but he certainly didn't feel trusted.

Sunglasses and a hat shielded his face, which he buried in a long article about elephant poaching he had opened on his flexscreen. But he couldn't focus on the magazine. He kept thinking about Jones' death and how he would break the news to Lilly, assuming he was the first to do so. Only a week before, Amadeus knew he would've rejoiced over the engineer's death, but Amadeus' view had changed. In the end, he realized, Jones had helped him again ... and this was probably what got him killed.

Amadeus reached the screening area. Ahead of him, a screener with a goatee and a too-tight shirt was leading an old man with a cane to a windowless room nearby. Amadeus emptied his pockets and placed his phone, loose change, and scraps of paper in a plastic basket. He removed his belt, hat, and sunglasses and placed them on the scanner, smoothing out his mussed hair with his hand. He handed his passport and boarding pass to the stony-faced screener. The screener scrutinized his documents, then Amadeus, then the documents again.

"Step forward please, Mr. Brunmeier." Amadeus stepped forward into a gray plastic scanner shaped like a doorframe. "Any direct contact with OIEs?" the screener said, his voice bored and automatic. The question struck him as funny, and Amadeus suppressed a laugh. "Any of the following symptoms?" The screener repeated the list like a mantra. Amadeus said no to them all. "Any contact with foreign individuals or live animals?" Amadeus shook his head. "Is your bag your own? Have you been in possession of it since you arrived? Has anyone asked you to carry anything? Are you carrying any illegal substances?" At that moment, Amadeus wanted two things: the Pachyderm and a free pass to smack the screener across the face. As he questioned Amadeus, the screener watched a digital readout in his hand.

"According to my instruments, you're lying about something, Mr. Brunmeier," the screener said. "Wait here." The screener carried Amadeus' passport and boarding pass back to a gray-haired man sitting at a high desk. The overseer scrutinized Amadeus as the screener spoke to him in a low voice. Other screeners were now looking in this direction, and their gaze drew that of the passengers.

"Mr. Brunmeier, please follow me," the screener said.

"What is this? I have a flight to catch."

"Come with me."

"What gives you the right—" The screener grabbed his arm and started to lead him. Amadeus knocked his hand away. "Don't you touch me, you overpaid, under-bathed toad." The screener glared at him.

"You're not making things any easier on yourself. I could call that assault of a federal employee if I wanted to, but I don't want to. I like what you did, but any of us could be a threat. You want to catch your flight, you'll follow me." Amadeus shook his head and followed the screener. The eyes of the waiting passengers and screeners followed them out. A woman yelled something about them arresting the Gate Crasher guy. Some people in line started to hiss and boo the screeners and security personnel. Amadeus turned and gave them an appreciative smile. The screener led Amadeus past the overseer's desk and into a room at the end of the hallway. The room was white and sterile and filled with other detained passengers who sat on steel benches. A pasty blue curtain was set up beside an examination table covered in unrolled paper.

"Wait here," the screener said, handing Amadeus back his passport and boarding pass.

"What the hell is this?" Amadeus said. The screener just smiled at him as he left the room and closed the door behind him. Amadeus tried the door. It was locked. He looked around. Cameras were mounted on the ceiling at both ends of the room. Several people sat in a row of rigid plastic chairs. At the end, a woman was rocking back and forth, her arms wrapped around her. Her grey-streaked hair was piled on her head. Amadeus thought she looked like a professor. The old man with the cane was among the detained. Amadeus approached him.

"Sir, excuse me, do you know what this is?"

"This is a perversion of liberty," the old man said. His hands trembled. "I'm on my way to my sister's funeral. I'm in line, minding my own business, and they pull me out. No reason I can see. But real polite like, with their, 'Sir, please come with me.' And I've been in here since then."

"I read the Gestapo was polite, too."

"You don't have to tell me. My grandfather, rest his soul, had the numbers tattooed on his forearm. He was the only one in his family to survive. For years, I heard, 'Eat your food, Lem. Don't waste anything, Lem.' People don't think anything like that could happen here, but this is how it starts."

"What can we do?" Amadeus said, shrugging.

"Nothing. I can't, anyway. My time here is almost done. But you," the old man wagged a finger at Amadeus, "you're a young man. Got your whole life ahead of you. I tell you, when I was young, people wouldn't stand for such treatment. But then that nine eleven came. That's when things got even worse. People became more fearful, scared of each other, of the world, of themselves, of their own power, and they traded their liberty for security. At least we got the right to marry who we want."

"Shut the hell up," said a slightly overweight middle-aged man. "It's bad enough we're in here. Do we really have to sit here and listen to this bleeding heart history lesson?"

"Hey, fuck you," Amadeus said. The woman began to mumble something.

"You say 'fuck you' to me?" the man said. He started to get to his feet. Amadeus nodded at the old man and walked toward the other man, keeping his gaze level, his voice low and even. He used the same stance he had used when he faced down the big guy in Georgia.

"You do not want to tangle with me, dough boy. I promise you that." Amadeus felt adrenaline surging through his stomach to his head and back down to his feet. He liked the feel of his own power. Amadeus held the man's gaze until the man looked down at his feet and started breathing through his teeth, air hissing in and out like the air coming from the vents in the room. The old man was smiling. Without saying a word, Amadeus took the seat beside the old man, who patted his leg. The woman was still muttering. Her sounds made him shudder.

"Has she been doing that long?" Amadeus said.

"No, she was just sitting still when I came in," the old man said. Suddenly the woman stood up and threw her lime green handbag across the room. It bounced off the door and landed at Amadeus' feet.

The woman's voice crescendoed. She had lost her left hand just above the wrist and wore no prosthetic. The fingers on one hand drummed against each thumb, like someone calculating figures. A man in a suit at the end told her to sit down. This didn't even register. She kept up her chant, her volume just below a yell. Amadeus picked up her purse and took it over to her. He tried to hand it to her but she ignored him, so he set it in her chair. Her eyes were bloodshot, the sclera the color of polished copper, almost like that of a hepatitis sufferer, but brighter. Her breaths came in rapid, shallow, dog-like pants.

As Amadeus returned to his seat, two uniformed officers came in, pushed past Amadeus, and approached the woman. They tried, unsuccessfully, to talk to her. When this failed, one of them reached for her arm. When he did, she swung her left arm, hit him in the throat with her forearm, and resumed her pose. He doubled over, gasping, hands covering his neck. The other officer pulled a baton from his belt and, wary, approached her. The people nearest her slid out of their chairs and crept to the front of the room. Amadeus stood as well. Everyone's eyes were on the woman and the officer. He was curious and more than a little concerned for the woman. He wanted to wait and see what happened, but in the open door he saw his chance. The old man noticed Amadeus creeping toward the door and winked at him. Amadeus took that as his cue.

When he stepped outside, he saw four more officers running toward the room.

"Hurry! They need your help," Amadeus said. "A woman attacked a policeman. She's freaking out and the guy needs help." One of them nodded to him as he passed. None made any move to stop him. Amadeus patted his jacket pocket, reassuring himself that he still had his boarding pass and passport. This was a big airport. It had two other security entrances, and he would have just enough time to make it through. On his way to another gate, he called Gravity, who answered on the first ring.

"I'm having some trouble at Dulles. Security has decided I'm a terrorist. They detained me, but I managed to slip out."

"Shit, Amadeus. I know a couple good gals there. I'll make some calls."

"Great. And Gravity, they held me in a room with some other people," Amadeus said. He went on to tell Gravity about the woman without the left hand. "I don't know why, but I think this might be something worth looking into."

"Give Lilly my condolences," Gravity said. "We'll get this sorted out. For now, sit tight for about five minutes." Four minutes later, he received a text from Gravity that read only, "Gate Three."

"Thanks," Amadeus said aloud. He found a line. At first, this line moved at the same glacial speed as the others, but after a few minutes, the screeners stopped pulling people aside. Fewer bags were searched. More and more people streamed through, Amadeus included. The woman at the x-ray machine simply looked at Amadeus' passport, smiled at him, and wished him a good flight. Amadeus strode into the secure area and boarded his plane with ten minutes to spare. For a rare moment in his life, but the second time that day, Amadeus felt like a powerful man.

11

Grassal deployed a black hat vulnerability scanner against every CDC resource he could find. All their software was up to date and their authentication security policies were effective. Even if he had access to a room full of quantum supercomputers, he estimated a brute-force password guessing attack would take at least three months before it returned a match that may or may not have the necessary permissions to gain access to their database and e-mail servers. A port scan over the full range of CDC IP addresses showed all unnecessary ports were locked down.

In short, all avenues led to dead ends.

At first, Grassal had enjoyed the challenge, but after nine hours, two cans of hyper-caffeinated cola, and one severe wrist cramp, he tossed the keyboard across the room. In desperation, he called the CDC's technology office and attempted to recover a lost password by impersonating one Dr. Eli Rosecranz. When Grassal couldn't name Dr. Rosecranz's alma mater, the tech support guy threatened to call the FBI. Grassal racked his brain to make sure he hadn't forgotten anything, but at this point in his efforts, trying to remember more access techniques was like trying to recall the middle of a dream.

To stretch his aching thighs and relieve a persistent phantom itch, Grassal left the data center and went into the hangar, squinted against the morning sun's rays, plopped down into the recliner, and fell asleep. He awoke to the clacking of a keyboard and the smell of coffee. Grassal yawned, and Lilly turned and gave him a smile.

"You were talking in your sleep."

"What did I say?"

"Something about tech support hell. How's it going?"

"They're locked down tighter than, than … they have great security. I think it's a lost cause. I couldn't even get in to find an internal phone directory, let alone e-mails or anything about the registry."

"I meant, how are you feeling? You look like hell."

"About like I look. I just need some caffeine and breakfast then I'll get back to it."

"Are you sure that's a good idea?"

"What else would we do?"

"If we can't get in to find out what they know, maybe we can pressure them into talking. There's a looming public health emergency, and the very organization in charge of managing public health has its head stuck up its own ass. Like you said yesterday, there's Annie Brunmeier. Hell, you wouldn't even necessarily need to talk to her. You've got the credibility that comes with celebrity. But we can trust her. If we had some actual information, something that amounted to verifiable evidence of a new threat to public health, we could embarrass the CDC into taking action before things get any worse. I'm just afraid they'll take the *wrong* action."

"Then we'll have to stay on top of them and make sure they do the right thing."

They spent the morning collecting and compiling injury reports, blog posts, social media updates, articles, snippets of hearsay, and even a few videos related to the strange behavior of individuals and crowds since the Emergence. Grassal thought they needed more hard data. He downloaded and defined the parameters for a program that would automatically collect information from official and user-generated media. He specified keywords like "demon, psychotic, Emergence, psychosis, madness, mania, infection, catatonic, violent," and several others. The program ran for an hour and returned several thousand results.

While they waited, Grassal scanned the news. The subcommittee chaired by Senator Amanda Payne continued to push for the bill that would authorize approved private security companies to provide services related to subluminals and the Emergence cleanup efforts. Even now, creatures remained. An independent commission's findings stated that the military was overtaxed and oriented primarily toward the defense of US interests abroad, rather than providing for the common defense of the country that finances it. Apocalyptic furor had died down, though the Jesus' Church Southern Independent Baptists continued their three-month-long gathering in Kentucky's Daniel Boone National Forest, despite the deaths of three participants due to hypothermia. A team of biologists had recently announced that the subluminals were indeed carbon-based and composed entirely of Earthly materials.

By evening, they had manually filtered the thousands of sources down to about five hundred, which they organized, categorized, and geotagged. Grassal wrote a simple script that used reports of afflicted behavior to estimate the number of afflicted in any given geographic area. Using primarily official sources, Lilly calculated the number of demons per region then compared that with the population density. By combining this with the output of Grassal's script, they were able to come up with the number of afflicted per person in each of the eight regions. Every city had a similar number of afflicted per subluminal per person per square kilometer—.015—except one: Bangkok, Thailand.

"It's like I said, but it doesn't make sense," Lilly said. She looked down at the one-page distillation of their research entitled "Subluminals in BKK." "Local hospitals reported just as many if not more injuries per capita as every other city, but there's nothing about Thai people spacing out. Just a few foreigners."

Grassal remembered a news roundup he had scanned then dismissed as pure hokum. He had dismissed it because the site was poorly designed, and it claimed that people were being treated for maladies of a spiritual nature. But maybe there was something to these reports. On the screen, he typed *Thailand, news, treatment*. The roundup appeared on the flexscreen that stretched across the data center's back wall. The author was a Bangkok-based Welsh travel blogger who called himself "The World's Eye." Grassal watched Lilly's eyes dart across the text and her brow furrow.

"This website emits the florid aroma of bullshit," she said. She clicked the link to the temple's treatment website. The browser returned a 404 error. "See? It's all bunk. Is there anything else online about this treatment facility?" Grassal did a quick search then shook his head. "False hope. This guy should be ashamed of himself."

"I don't really see why ..." Grassal said, trailing off.

"The writing's awful. Look how he loaded up the article with keywords." The writer's phrasing did make for some awkward reading. "Trying to appear in the top search results."

"It doesn't look like he's selling anything; he just casually mentioned it, along with a couple more articles about the government's plan to keep several subluminals in the king's personal menagerie."

Lilly crossed her arms and shook her head. "He's a hack. He just threw that in there to get page views. Check his stats." Grassal did so. Since the World's Eye had posted the entry, his traffic had increased by a factor of twelve, giving him almost a million page views over the past four days.

"Isn't this what we're looking for? A reason why almost nobody in Bangkok's afflicted? I'm going to contact him. I think we could almost call it a lead." Grassal narrowed his eyes and tried to make some sense of her reaction. He felt his face break into a grin and he prodded her.

"You're jealous, aren't you?"

"What? Jealous of some expat sex pest with onion breath?"

"Sex pest?"

"Jesus, Grassal. He's in Thailand for women. Why else would he live there?"

"Beaches and curry? Maybe he has a professional interest in elephant training." Lilly's face was red, and she stood with her hands on her hips. Grassal put his hands in front of him and made a placating gesture. "If it's about the web traffic ..."

"This hack has had a million people read his work," Lilly said. He had hit a nerve. Grassal thought fast and decided on a tactic that he supposed would calm her down.

"But he's been at it for a while. You've only just started working on your book. It's a lot of time, and you don't need to focus on traffic-building right now. I'm sure that if you actually set up a blog, the traffic will come pouring in on the strength of your name alone. Just post an article about your father. That should bring you at least half a million hits."

"I don't want to write about him, not now, and even if I did, all the traffic would be rubberneckers visiting for the look-at-this-poor-daughter-of-a-monster factor."

"And then they'll stay because your writing is so engaging, acerbic, and entertaining. You're good, Lilly, and it's not fair to yourself to compare your professional standing with this guy."

"Professional standing. I like that. You know what, Grassal?" Lilly uncrossed her arms, strode to where Grassal sat, and gave him a kiss on the cheek. "That's really sweet of you to say. You're a good friend." She kissed him on the other cheek. Grassal felt his face flush. "You can deal with the sex pest. I'm going to get Annie Brunmeier on the phone and tell her about all this."

Lilly dialed Annie, who answered on the first ring. Lilly put her on speakerphone. "Hey girl and boy, I hope everything's good with you," Annie said. "What's up?" Lilly told her about their Thailand lead and their affliction hypothesis.

"This should occupy the news cycle for a while."

"Annie, I have it too," Grassal said.

"I'm so sorry. I guess you would. I forgot … It's just that you were shot and *then* dismembered; it's hard to keep up with all your injuries."

"I know. I take them for the team."

"Some less-reputable conspiracy theorists have postulated a connection between the Emergence and the, um, afflicted," Annie said.

"That's the problem," Lilly said. "Nobody with any credibility has the stones to say what's really going on. They either don't have solid proof, or they're scared of the backlash. Accusing victims of violence of more violence isn't exactly a popular position. But you've got both the reputation and the stones to float this hypothesis. People trust you."

"Thanks, Lilly," Annie said. "I'm glad when you think of credibility and testicular fortitude, you think of me."

"Only because it's true," Lilly said. "The courage and the clout parts, anyway."

"Lilly and I spent a couple days putting together some pretty solid information. If this Thailand thing turns out to have any merit, we'll need to figure out how to do that here."

"How can you make sure people who needed treatment actually received it?"

"They're denying it, but we think the CDC has a registry of afflicted," Lilly said.

"The problem is that a registry implies rounding people up," Grassal said. "And that won't be necessary. Speaking as someone who is afflicted, I can tell you that I'd sign up for just about any experimental treatment offered if I thought it would help. Right now, though, nobody's even admitting that this is a condition, let alone offering treatments."

"It's risky. I'm not sure which would be worse: false

information—or false hope."

"I promise you, our data is solid," Grassal said. "But there's a tiny problem. I'm afraid of being on an airplane full of strangers, especially for such a long flight. I don't really like to fly anyway, and if something happened ..." He didn't need to mention he'd probably be executed by an air marshal if he entered his afflicted state.

"Why Grassal, if I didn't know better, I'd say you're using me to get a ride on the *Times'* charter jet. I'm sure we can figure out a way to strap you down." Her voice was playful. For this, Grassal was glad.

"If it means helping myself and a hundred others like me, then maybe I am."

"Do I get an exclusive?"

"Who else?"

Satisfied that their plan was worth pursuing further, Grassal encrypted and sent the following message to the blogger who had written about the treatment clinics.

Dear World's Eye,
I saw your recent entry on the treatment clinic in Ayutthaya. I'm interested in learning more about this clinic. Can you tell me more?
G.D.

The response came back two hours later.

Dear G.D.,
I learned about this from a friend of mine. She says that Thai people are already disinclined to be affected by bad blood because of their religious traditions, but nevertheless a clinic and rehab center has been set up for those who have had contact with subluminals. Who are you, and what is your interest in this?
Sincerely,

Lewis Braxton

Dear Lewis,
Fascinating. My interest is personal and, I suppose you could say, professional. My colleague and I are researching the Emergence, and according to our data Thai people typically don't become "afflicted" (the term we use for those who were attacked by the creatures and now display strange and sometimes violent symptoms). We'd like very much to learn more about this clinic/rehab center. Please contact me if you can tell me more.
Grassal Delgado

The rest of the day passed without a response from Lewis. Grassal attributed this silence to the time difference. Just before he shut down his computer for the day, a new message appeared in his inbox. The sender's e-mail was a random string of characters, but the subject was entitled "Holden Jones" and contained two attachments: three pictures and an audio recording. After running a scan and determining the message and attached files were clean, Grassal opened them.

The first image showed the naked, withered body of Holden Jones stretched out on a steel slab; every rib and joint was visible under a layer of thin, pallid skin. Black stitching held his eyes and mouth shut. Grassal's first instinct was to turn away and give the poor man's body some privacy and respect, but he knew he couldn't do that. Instead, he enhanced the image and looked for evidence of doctoring, but as far as he could tell, everything was authentic. The second image was a scan of the coroner's report. The time of death was yesterday afternoon. The cause of death was asphyxiation due to exposure to an unknown substance. The final image was a time-stamped surveillance still of Amadeus handing a bag of carryout food to Jones. According to the time stamp, the image was taken early this morning.

The audio recording was short, only a few seconds long.

Grassal pressed play and gasped when he heard the contents.

"You're going to die here, Jones. You'll never see the sun again. You'll rot away—that is, if someone doesn't kill you first."

"Are you threatening me, Amadeus?"

"I wouldn't do anything you haven't done to me," Amadeus said.

"Ah, I suppose that's a fair point. No good deed ..."

Grassal played it again, and a third time. Just like the photo, this was undoctored, but Grassal knew as well as anybody that this could've been taken entirely out of context ... but the vitriol in Amadeus' voice, the naked hatred. Grassal knew the voice, but he wasn't sure he recognized the speaker. Not anymore.

He checked the news aggregator. So far, Jones' death remained unreported. That was a blessing. The sender's e-mail address had been anonymized, but even then Grassal thought it safe to assume that the sender would've used a free public e-mail account. Nevertheless, he replied to the e-mail:

Who are you? What do you want? Why did you send me these?

That sent, he put his head down on the desk and tried to make a decision. Should he be the one to tell Lilly that her father was murdered? And if so, should he tell her that someone wanted her to think Amadeus had killed her father? *Had* Amadeus murdered her father? Grassal wanted to sleep on this decision, but he knew this would be out within a matter of hours. He was surprised neither of their phones was ringing.

The sound of sandal-clad feet padding across the concrete floor, followed by a gasp and a whimper, simplified his decision-making process. Grassal cursed himself for leaving the images up on the screen. She shouldn't have to see these. It would be better just to tell her, but by the time Grassal turned around to face her, Lilly's eyes were welling with tears, her lips set like a thin rose quartz seam. She leaned in close to the computer and examined the photo of her dead father, followed by the others. She sighed when she saw Amadeus.

"There's a recording. It sounds awful, but we don't know the whole context." He pressed play and watched as Lilly's face darkened. "I think someone is trying to set up Amadeus. Amadeus wouldn't do something like this." I don't think, he almost added.

"Play it again."

Grassal did. Lilly listened, nodded once then walked out of the room, sobbing as she went. Grassal decided to give her time and space. He needed another opinion, so he contacted Gravity by video chat. A grainy image appeared of Gravity eating lo mein from a takeout box. Grassal skipped pleasantries and asked if this was true.

"I wish I could tell you this was false information, but that would be incorrect. Jones is indeed deceased. Amadeus is on his way now. He wanted to tell Lilly in person."

"And, what? You're sitting around eating Chinese food?"

"Would you prefer I ate a salad?" Grassal shook his head, and Gravity continued.

"What else can I do, Grassal? Do you want me to call Lilly and speak with her?"

Grassal considered the dramatic potential of such a conversation but decided he couldn't do that to either of them. He still liked Gravity and wanted to keep the peace between him and Lilly. "That's probably a real bad idea. Terrible, in fact. She doesn't think so highly of you right now. I'll keep her calm. But tell me the truth: did you or Amadeus have anything to do with his murder?"

"No. Hell no. I wouldn't want him killed. He's not some mercenary or hired gun. The man was a regular Von Braun. To kill him would've done a great disservice to the world of applied science."

"What about Amadeus? Do you think someone put him up to this?"

"I don't think so, but the puzzle pieces are still on the floor, and I don't have a full picture to which to refer. Amadeus isn't a killer. You and I know that. Let's be honest—he's kind of a weenie. But from what I gather, Jones had been revealing more and more to him, pretty much answering all his questions."

"Lilly thinks he did it."

"Lilly thinks wrong. Would you take down a message for me? Handwriting, if you don't mind, since yours is so excellent? I'd like to give her my condolences, but it might be better if they came from me via you."

"Sure, I excel at clerical tasks. Go ahead," Grassal said as he scrounged for pen and paper. Gravity took his time speaking, weighing each word, and Grassal had plenty of time to write out the following message:

Lilly,

Your father made invaluable contributions to the world of aeronautics and, with his recent contrite loquaciousness, to our current operations. Even if his allegiance was questionable, his loss will be sincerely felt by all of us. But you must recognize that your father played a dangerous game. Nevertheless, he is still the man who cared for you, and for whom you cared. I extend to you my sincerest sympathies.

Grassal has told me that you believe Amadeus guilty of your father's murder. I don't believe Amadeus is capable of such a crime, but at present, I have no evidence to the contrary, so I will leave you only with this:

The labyrinth will continue to twist and turn, taking us deeper into ever-darkening places where the only light is that which we bring into it. The danger is that, in our search for light, we recoil at shadows of our own making, when in fact the darkest shadows prove to be our greatest allies.

Your Friend,

Claudius Owens (a.k.a. Gravity)

Whether or not this would provide comfort to Lilly, Grassal wasn't sure, but it was better than nothing. Gravity signed off with a nod, and after rereading the note a couple times, Grassal busied himself by reviewing the report he and Lilly had compiled. He knew he could probably continue searching, but they had already discarded seventy percent of what they had found, and what was that quote on perfection? He looked it up: "Perfection is achieved not when there is nothing else to add, but nothing else to take away." They had collected almost all the pieces to this peculiar puzzle he and Lilly had decided to work on, but the most important piece, the one that promised hope of a treatment, still remained unknown.

Just before midnight, he left the data center for the night and heard clinking glass in the kitchen. He decided that now was as good a time as any to pass Gravity's message along. In the kitchen, Lilly sat at the table with a mason jar full of clear liquid in front of her. Her eyelids were heavy, and dark circles ringed her eyes. On the table sat a photograph.

"Join me?" she said. Grassal sat down beside her. She offered him the jar, but Grassal shook his head, pulled a glass down from the shelf, and poured himself half a drink. He nodded at the photograph, and Lilly passed it to him. A much-younger and more able-bodied version of Jones stood on a beach with a young woman who looked like Lilly and a little girl with pumpkin-colored hair. Jones held the girl above his head. They all looked so happy. Grassal smiled at this and returned it to her.

"My mother left a year after this photo was taken. For about a decade, she sent Christmas and birthday cards, but the cards stopped. Sometimes I think about tracking her down, but ... fuck her. She didn't want a relationship with me—with us—and the feeling is mutual."

"Here's to scumbag parents," Grassal said. Lilly rewarded him with a half-smile. "From them, we learn what not to do." They clinked glasses and drank.

Grassal nodded. The liquor burned and then warmed his stomach. He pulled Gravity's message from his pocket and placed it on the table. Lilly read it, scowled, and let the scrap of paper fall to the floor.

"This doesn't change anything about your friend."

"I think you're jumping to conclusions. It's looks bad, but—"

"Grassal, there's a recording of Amadeus telling my father that he should kill him. Amadeus is somehow able to bring him food, and a few hours later my father is dead. He might've been a profiteering traitor, but still. This is too ... Amadeus had a motive. It all fits. Aren't you a fan of Occam's Razor?"

"I've begun to question my devotion to this concept. I think there's more to it than this."

"I wish, I wish, I wish that I could say I agreed with you, but I don't. Amadeus did this. He's not right in his mind, Grassal. Did you not listen to his voice? He sounds *sinister*." She took a long swallow from the jar and winced.

"Are you sure that's a good idea?"

"Let me mourn in my own way, please. Nothing is more appropriate for a dark mood than moonshine."

"Why would Amadeus murder your father? To me, it looks like he's bringing him food, trying to talk to him, and somebody set him up."

"Amadeus has changed. He's not the same neurotic little boy from Connecticut he used to be. I think it's partly because of what happened to him, what he had to do, but it's also because of Gravity, that shady motherfucker. He's been drip-feeding militaristic poison into his ear for months. I think he manipulated stupid Amadeus into doing what the government doesn't want to: kill public enemy *numero uno*. Come on, Grassal. He's on their payroll. Then he has the nerve to send me this note. Fuck him, and—" Grassal looked at her, and she stopped herself. "I'm sorry. I know he's your best friend and all, and it can't be easy for you to hear me trashing him. Sure, maybe there is a small, tiny, miniscule possibility that Amadeus didn't do it. But there's too much evidence against him, and none for him. It's all just really heavy, and it's not the way I expected things to play out. Look, I'm glad you're here, but for now ... I'd appreciate some solitude."

Grassal squeezed her hand and left her to the kitchen and her jar.

12

Late in the evening, Amadeus landed in Denver, hired a car, and drove up snow-plowed mountain passes to Leadville and beyond, noting with interest the melted snow on the recently paved driveway that led to the Jones compound. Lilly Jones' compound, as of today. At the rock entrance, the same entrance that had pinned the head of a giant demon, Amadeus stepped out into biting, icy wind to enter the access code. It still worked. The door opened and he drove in.

The tunnel ended and Amadeus parked under the high ceilings of the hangar. Snow covered the skylights and, even with the dimmed overhead sodium lights, darkness enveloped the hangar. Before Amadeus got out, Grassal and Lilly emerged from the living area. They stood side by side. Grassal raised one hand in a half-hearted greeting. Lilly watched him, her smooth, pale face unreadable.

"Grassal, what are you doing here?" Amadeus said.

"Good to see you too," Grassal said. "Been a while."

"I thought you were with the Interstellar Sisters."

"I was, but—"

"He had a problem," Lilly said. "And he came to me for help. Since you were doing other things."

Amadeus tried to say something but his voice croaked. This was going to be far, far worse than he expected.

"Lilly ... I ... there's something I have to tell you," Amadeus said.

"Did you do it?" Lilly said. "Did you kill him?"

"Lilly, I went to see him. I brought him some *carne asada*. He was starting to open up, to tell me things that will help me find my father."

"Answer me, Amadeus. Did you kill him?"

"No." Amadeus shook his head and held her gaze.

"But you were the last person to see him. And you took him food. And a couple hours later, he was dead. Poisoned."

"I came out here to tell you," Amadeus said. "It's a—just—I didn't kill him. It was a horrible coincidence. Lilly, he was helping me. He told me why he betrayed me."

"What did he say? About me?"

"He said that he loved you, and that he was confessing so you would know he had done the right thing." Amadeus glanced over at Grassal and noticed his eyes were glazed over, like he had just awoken from sleep.

"I want you to hear something," Lilly said. From her pocket, she pulled a phone and typed on the screen.

A recording began. Amadeus recognized it instantly. Heat rose to his cheeks as Amadeus heard himself say, "You're going to die here, Jones. You'll never see the sun again. You'll rot away —that is, if someone doesn't kill you first."

She paused the recording and played it again. The sound of every syllable from his mouth felt like a wasp's sting.

"Where did you get that?" Amadeus said. She played the recording again.

"It's not important," Lilly said.

Grassal looked down at his feet.

"That's from a long time ago. And it's out of context. I promise I never wanted to kill your father."

"Your promises don't mean much," she snapped. "Not anymore. All this time, you were talking to my father, and you never even told me. Hell, you never even called me."

Grassal moaned. They both looked over at him before Amadeus continued.

"You told me you didn't want anything to do with him, so I didn't tell you I was talking to him."

"For fuck's sake, Amadeus. You just said he was coming around, if not apologizing then at least trying to atone. And you didn't even tell me. Yes, it might not be much, given what he did, but it's a step in the right direction, and I would've been so happy to know that, even if I still cursed his name for selling you out. But you say you're worried about *upsetting* me? What do I look like, a fucking orchid?"

"A lily, actually," Amadeus said. The words escaped his mouth before he had chance to stop them.

"And you're making bad jokes. My father is dead, you might've killed him, and you're joking? Oh fuck you." She reached down, pulled off one of her black canvas shoes, and threw it at Amadeus' head. He ducked and the shoe bounced off a propeller-less Cessna 172 engine. Lilly's ears and nose were flushed geranium red. Her chest rose and fell like ocean waves in a tsunami.

"Lilly. Look at me." Amadeus took a step forward. Lilly flinched. "Whoa. I am sorry. So sorry. About your father, what happened to him. About not telling you. But I swear on—on whatever is swear-upon-able—I did not kill your father." Lilly shook her head, her brick-red hair whipping back and forth like a whirling dervish's skirt.

"I wish I could believe you, Amadeus, but ever since you arrived, my life has spiraled downhill. I grew to love you because I got to know you, and ... and it was all so thrilling. What you had done, the man you became. And you and Gravity, I really thought you were both fighting the good fight. Things went bad with my father, but I hoped he would eventually do the right thing.

"And when he finally did, you ... murdered him! I might be disgusted with him, I might not want to talk to him, but he's still my father, and you assassinated him, you and your fascist pals. And for what? He and only he told you that *your* father was alive. And it's your father who's the real goddamned traitor."

Lilly shook the phone at Amadeus.

"I'm so sick of all this, this conspiracy and double-crossing and intrigue and patriarchal power struggle, the lies and alliances and tricks. *Pantallas*, screens behind screens, one ruse on top of another, all so one shadowy organization can figure how to ass-rape another shadowy organization. It's like the Hatfields and McCoys, only with suits and better teeth. It all makes me ill. Except you, Grassal. You have a good heart. You might be afflicted, but at least you're not corrupted."

"Afflicted?" Amadeus said. "Is he all right?" Lilly shook her head but didn't otherwise acknowledge Amadeus' question. Grassal was oblivious to their mention of him. He was rocking back and forth and drumming his fingers. His eyes were the color of a blood orange. Whispers as loud as the winter wind escaped his mouth.

"You had a good heart, too. But it's corrupted. All that power, all that attention went to your head. And now you think you can do whatever you want, kill whoever you want, so long as they're the bad guy. Oh, how I fucking despise you right now. Get the fuck out of my bunker. Now!"

"Lilly, he's sick." She turned her back on Amadeus and took a step backwards. Amadeus looked back at Grassal. The airport, Amadeus thought. Grassal was like the woman in the airport, even starting to mutter nonsense. "And I've seen this before. It could be dangerous. For you."

"Leave, Amadeus."

"No. I'm not leaving him, not here with you, not while he's like that." Amadeus took careful, measured steps toward Grassal.

His lips were moving as he mouthed nonsense words. The veins on his neck and his forehead bulged as they pumped blue, afflicted blood through his big body. Amadeus placed a hand on his shoulder. Grassal punched Amadeus in the chest, knocking the wind from his body. He gasped for breath. When air finally returned to his lungs, he spoke to Grassal in soothing tones. He touched his friend again, this time with more care and gentleness. The muscles in Grassal's shoulder were rigid and rock-hard. Amadeus squeezed his friend's bicep and felt tight, tensed muscle.

"Grassal, brother, can you hear me?" Amadeus said, trying to calm Grassal, trying to calm himself. "Lilly, we've got to do something."

"You've done enough."

"God damn it," Amadeus said. He felt anger rising in his stomach like an uncoiling cobra. "I didn't kill your father."

"I've made my decision. Leave. Right now."

"Ahh," Grassal said. His breathing was fast and shallow. He occasionally moaned.

"He was fine before you arrived," Lilly said, still turned away from him. "Get out of my sight. For my sake and for Grassal's. He might want to see you again, but I don't."

Amadeus' pulse pounded in his head, and his heart was a redlining engine. Lilly had turned on him, and poor Grassal was about to explode from whatever had afflicted him. Psychotic paralysis. Like the handless woman at the airport. And like her, Grassal had lost an appendage. United by severed limbs. Amadeus felt he was on the verge of something.

"Why are you still here?"

"A woman at the airport. She was like him. She had lost her hand. Maybe because of a subluminal. I couldn't ask her ... because she was acting just like this."

"Grassal said this has happened to him before. Stay until you get him under control, then leave. I don't want to see you anymore." Lilly walked away, out of the hangar and back into the living quarters, slamming a door and leaving Amadeus alone with Grassal.

"Lilly," Amadeus said, calling after her, unsure if she could even hear him, "I will make this right. I'll show you I didn't do this. You'll ... see, you'll believe me." His voice croaked as he finished. He looked to Grassal. "And as for you. I don't want to do this, but it's for your own good. If you can hear me, please don't hurt me. This is to keep everyone safe."

Amadeus found some duct tape and with great care looped it around Grassal's wrists, arms, legs, and ankles. Amadeus pulled a couch from against the wall, behind where Grassal stood. With legs taped, Grassal could fall, and Amadeus decided it would be better if he were lying down. Amadeus wrapped the rest of the roll around Grassal then lowered him onto the couch.

Despised by Lilly, invisible to Grassal, Amadeus sat on the floor and began to cry. When he had exhausted his tears, he used his phone to record some video of his friend. He zoomed in on the eyes to reveal the bulging veins in the sclera, which carried tiny black specks, the blood flowing like swollen rivers filled with post-storm detritus. Amadeus recorded Grassal's rapid, shallow breathing then placed the phone against his chest to record his pulse. The audio readout on the phone showed his pulse at about one hundred fifty beats per minute. Too fast. He had heard somewhere that people with certain diseases have peculiar smells. He sniffed the air a couple times and tried to focus on what he smelled, but it amounted to nothing but the usual shaved metal and machine oil smell of the hangar. He leaned closer, just over Grassal's face, and sniffed.

"Argh!" Grassal said. His body began to thrash and flop like a hooked fish dropped on deck. Amadeus involuntarily scuttled backwards.

"Grassal, buddy, it's me, Amadeus, your old friend," Amadeus said. This made his thrashing worse. Grassal's head craned back and forth, and he tried to bite the tape binding his body. "I can't let you go, not right now. I'm sorry, Grassal. You've got to understand, I'm worried about Lilly. About you. About everything."

Grassal stopped moving and stared straight at the ceiling. His fists were clenched and his breathing began to slow. Amadeus backed away, furious that the subluminals were still doing damage *ex post facto*.

With one eye on his friend, Amadeus sat down at Lilly's writing desk. Upon the desk sat a pile of yellow legal pads, covered in Lilly's flowing handwriting. Her writing reminded Amadeus of festival lights strung across a street. He grabbed a blank sheet of paper and composed a message he hoped she would read in good faith and consider. His own handwriting looked like the work of a child holding his pencil in the wrong hand. He rarely wrote anything by hand. As he wrote, explaining what had happened to her father, and what her father had told him, Amadeus grew introspective and realized she was right: he had changed, and not necessarily for the better. He wrote out a quick conclusion in which he begged for forgiveness and promised to make things right with her. For a moment, he entertained the idea of leaving the opal ring on her desk but decided against it.

On the couch, Grassal appeared to be sleeping. Amadeus decided Grassal would be fine if he left. And as he assumed manual control of the rental car, Amadeus thought that maybe he himself would be fine, too.

Amadeus was sobbing and slamming his hands against the faux-leather steering wheel by the time he left the compound. Only the demands of driving over icy mountain roads kept him from completely losing himself. On the radio, he found a station with loud, distorted music, singers growling about epochs, angst, and self-mutilation. This helped.

Every few minutes, his navigation system's pleasant female voice would inform him that road conditions were poor and remind him to observe a safe speed. The heads-up display on the windshield projected green vectors onto the road ahead of him, as well as suggested speeds. He drove well over these speeds. A tiny part of him, hidden these past months, began to gather strength. You're no good, it said. You hurt everyone around you. Who do you think you are? Amadeus pushed the voice from his mind and found some paper, a receipt for watery coffee purchased at Denver International Airport. He tore off half the receipt, crumbled it into a ball between his fingers, and popped it into his mouth. On the radio, the announcer said something about a riot in New York City.

Grassal was broken. Lilly hated him. He didn't even know *who* his father was, let alone where. Amadeus wondered what would happen if he went over an embankment into a snowy ravine. Would he die quickly? How would he pass through the guard rail? Most likely he'd just bounce off and have to deal with the rental car agency, a fate worse than death. Escape wouldn't be so easy. And it wouldn't solve anything. Sure, Lilly might mourn for him, and maybe she would be sorry, but that wouldn't matter to Amadeus, not if he was dead. Perhaps he could buy a small trailer in the desert, far from anyone, and spend his days reading, thinking, and hiding from the world. But that, too, wouldn't work. The world would find him and demand his return.

He chewed, swallowed, and regurgitated these thoughts as he drove onto the interstate and slightly better driving conditions. There he drove even faster through salty slush, sending up icy gray rooster tails, passing cars on the right and on the left. He even passed a state police cruiser. When he blew past the cruiser, Amadeus saw a look of befuddlement on the officer's face, but, inexplicably, the officer chose not to pull him over. Amadeus realized he wouldn't be lucky enough to have any harm befall him. Not tonight.

Out of habit, he checked his mirrors. No giant subluminals were chasing him. The only demons around were the ones gnawing on his heart. Amadeus knew he couldn't run anymore, couldn't react anymore. He had to prove to Lilly that he hadn't murdered her father. He had to find his own father. And he needed to find a way to save his best friend from whatever was ailing him. Because, Amadeus now knew, he wasn't the only one. Hundreds, maybe thousands of people were going through the same thing. He hadn't acted fast enough, hadn't found the answers until the demon gates were already in place. Too many had come through. He had prevented some of the damage, but not nearly enough. This was his fault. Jones' death was his fault. Everything was his fault.

"Stop," Amadeus said aloud. "Just stop." And, much to his surprise, it worked. He focused on the sensation of the wheel in his hand, the way his body curved against the seat, and the way his breath flowed in and out of his nose. This focus gave him just enough clarity to realize that the grind of his thought pattern wasn't going to help anyone. Jones' death wasn't his fault. The Emergence wasn't his fault. The afflicted weren't his responsibility. He didn't kill anyone, unless subluminals counted as people, and they definitely weren't people.

His only fault was being too passive to react sooner. No more. He was tired of running. He was tired of hiding behind Gravity's skirts. He was tired of letting things happen. When Amadeus thought back on his life, he knew that building the Gate Crasher was just about the best thing he had ever done, and he knew he had only done it because he had decided to take action, to stand up and do something about the shitstorm into which he had been thrust, umbrella-less and naked.

Now he saw another storm approaching, its roiling clouds crackling with lightning, threatening a million-volt strike. He was tired of being soaked and left out in the rain. He began to formulate a plan that would simultaneously place him in the middle of the storm and provide protection from the lightning that had already killed Jones.

By the time his flight landed on the snowy runway at Dulles International, Amadeus had a plan of action so bold, so exciting, he had to keep himself from running out of the gate. If the broker and the buyer were involved in the commercial defense establishment, and if someone were able to record his conversations at a supposedly secure holding facility, then someone in Washington would have the answers he needed. Amadeus just needed to find them. To find them, he would just follow the money, wherever it might lead.

When Amadeus left the Farragut North Metro stop, five centimeters of snow crunched underfoot. A parade passed by, though he couldn't remember any holidays happening today. The marchers were mostly Asian. Some people held sparklers. Others carried red flags emblazoned with gold Chinese characters. Under the power of four humans, a dragon puppet the size of a class B subluminal snaked its way through the crowd.

Amadeus checked his phone for holidays and learned that tomorrow was the Chinese New Year, and that tonight marked the end of the Year of the Rabbit and the beginning of the Year of the Dragon. Amadeus smiled as he thought of the way Grassal used to call him *conejito,* little rabbit. He didn't feel like a little rabbit, not anymore.

He wrapped his black scarf tightly around his neck and shoved his hands deep into his coat pockets. As he trudged his way toward the Cathedral of St. Matthew, he turned the opal ring over in the fingers of his right hand. On his way to the cathedral, he saw a small crowd of people marching in lock step, muttering nonsense words in unison. They sounded like the woman at the airport, like Grassal. Only two wore jackets. The remaining eleven looked as if they had just walked out of their houses.

Before going inside, he dusted away the snow that had collected on his hair and jacket. White flecks swirled in the lights that shone on the red sandstone of the cathedral.

Gravity and General Janette Nguyen sat beside each other on a pew. Amadeus almost didn't recognize them. The general wore a thick brown turtleneck, black pants, and a mild expression. Gravity was dressed in a dark gray worsted wool suit and had his head down in prayer. Amadeus sat beside Gravity. Janette glanced over at Amadeus, put a finger over her lips, nodded to Gravity, then returned her attention to the Heinlein novel she held in her hands. After about ten minutes, Gravity raised his head and nodded, acknowledging him for the first time, and whispered, "Outside."

"Just when I was starting to warm up," Amadeus said. They gathered themselves and returned to the street. Outside, four workers in yellow biohazard suits were loading the last of the group of people—an obese man with a wide scar down the side of his bloated cheek—into a mobile medical truck. The obese man was unresisting but rigid, and it took all four of the workers to wrangle him into the truck.

"This could get real bad," Janette said, indicating they should keep walking. By the time they reached Connecticut Avenue, Amadeus was covered in a layer of thin, puffy snow that reminded him of fuzzy white mold.

"Lilly?" Gravity asked as he removed a cigarette from a gold pack retrieved from his pocket.

"She thinks I killed him. Somebody sent photos of his corpse and a recording of my conversation with Jones to Grassal, and Grassal let her see them. And something's wrong with Grassal —the same thing that's wrong with those people. What have you heard this?"

Janette said, "Word is, people who were bitten by subluminals or exposed to their bodily fluids have begun to exhibit strange behavior. Their bodies seize up, they begin muttering to themselves, and occasionally they attack people close to them."

"Sounds about right. I had to leave Grassal bound in duct tape."

"That's the best thing you could've done for him," Janette said.

They reached DuPont Circle. Snow danced in the wind that whipped around their feet, and Amadeus pulled his coat tight against the cold. Winter had driven most non-celebrating people inside, but Amadeus glanced back over his shoulder anyway. The street was clear.

"Does the name Pearl Sundajos mean anything to either of you?"

"Pearl Sundajos," Janette repeated.

"Is that a Filipino pop star?" Gravity said. Amadeus narrowed his eyes and shook his head. "Joking. Go on."

"Right. Anyway, before he died, before he was murdered, Jones confessed some things to me." Amadeus summarized his last two conversations with Jones for Gravity and Janette. "We need to find out who Sundajos is, *where* he is, and what he wants. All I know is that he's an insider, an operator. The man gets access to a high-security federal lockup, and he was apparently on good enough terms with a defense company to know the details of the deals they were making."

"Which company?" Janette asked.

"I ... damn it. Jones didn't tell me, and I didn't think to ask him." Gravity shook his head. "But I can tell you that it's a company that wanted to license the rights to manufacture Pachyderms."

"Do you think Sundajos is associated with Maximilian Ross?" Janette asked.

"No," Amadeus said. "I don't think Ross is the man he portrayed himself to be." He took off his scarf and tried to rewrap it around himself, but a gust of wind blew it from his hand. "Maybe Ross knows something we don't."

"Amadeus is right," Gravity said, bending over to pick up Amadeus' scarf. "The working theory is that, after the first demon attack, Ross used some kind of predictive model to determine which public persona would generate the most fear and outrage. Ross' purpose was to compel our forces to go on the attack."

"That's ... absolutely brilliant."

"I wouldn't call it brilliant," Amadeus said. "To perpetuate his ruse, he destroyed his reputation, ruined his business, and got two of his partners killed." Amadeus' stomach twisted when he thought of Vesely Gustavius' mangled corpse and Quinton Laroux's bullet-ridden body sprawled on a cloaking tarp.

"The day after New York, I had two divisions ready to go, just in case more of these creatures showed up. But you know what? The authorizations came way too late," Janette said. "These fucking politicians are all chomping at the bit to have our boys go kill brown people in warm climates, but when inter-dimensional hell bears crawl out of their invisible caves, all they want to do is make speeches and find someone to blame."

Amadeus was shivering. Tears had dried on the corner of his lids. He, Gravity, and Janette were covered in a white fur of snow. The storm had grown stronger.

"Okay. Ross doesn't matter right now. Nobody knows where he—" Amadeus shot a knowing look to Gravity and Gravity nodded, indicating he trusted General Janette Nguyen "—or my father are, so we have one primary target to locate: Pearl Sundajos. My father is going to have to wait. If we find Pearl Sundajos, I'm pretty sure we'll find the group behind the demon gates. And since Pearl Sundajos appears to have defense industry connections, we have a place to start."

"Tell me more, young grasshopper," Gravity said. He lit another cigarette. The smoke mixed with his breath and clouded him in a spectral white shroud.

"Remember those kids delivering the printed testimonies and coffee at the hearing? We start with them. At UConn, I knew a couple political science majors who spent their summers interning in Washington. They said they had the run of the office because, almost invariably, the politicians they interned for assumed they were incompetent, ignorant, or both."

"You're saying we make friends with the coffee jockeys?" Janette said.

"If anybody knows what's going on, it's the interns," Gravity said.

"I'll narrow down who Jones' buyer was," Janette said. "Only a handful of companies would be able to handle an order like that."

"Excellent," Gravity said. "Amadeus, where would you like to start?"

"With Senator Amanda Payne," Amadeus said. "She's on the Subcommittee on Defense Contracting Oversight, so she'd know about any deal over five million dollars, which would include Jones' Pachyderm deal. For all we know, maybe she connected our broker Sundajos with Jones. Plus, she's pushing this subluminal defense privatization bill. I don't think she's involved with the demon gates, but I think if we dug around ..." Gravity smiled. Amadeus thought he looked almost proud.

"We might just uncover some skeletons," Gravity said. "I've trained you well. You work on the interns. Tell them I can guarantee them profitable employment within the district, and, provided they're not perverts or foreign agents, the General here can fast-track a security clearance for them. Does that work for you, General?"

She inclined her head and smiled. "I've left the lion's den to join a pack of foxes. But even foxes need a den." She gave Amadeus a business card. "This has the current address and passcode for our movable HQ. Be inconspicuous when going in. Got it?"

Amadeus nodded as the clock struck midnight. A cheer rose from the crowd nearby, and fireworks lit up the sky, thundering and bursting and flashing through the snow that blew all around them.

The Year of the Dragon had begun.

13

Grassal awoke bound in duct tape. He tried to remember what had happened. Amadeus had showed up to break the news about Lilly's father. As they argued, all the colors in the hangar had grown bright and vivid, despite the darkness, and then Grassal had lost consciousness. Now, his tongue was thick, his mouth felt full of cotton, and his stomach rumbled. He felt worse than after the last episodes, and he was afraid he had hurt someone. He cried out for Lilly, bellowing at first, but then softer and softer. For a moment he thought she might've decided to leave him here, and he knew he wouldn't blame her if she did. However, when she came out looking well rested and fresh, he breathed a sigh of relief and felt gratitude wash over him.

She regarded his predicament with a mixture of delight and sympathy. "He tried to help, in his own stupid way. Let's get you out of there." As she leaned over him to peel the duct tape off, Grassal heard the sing-song ring of the video chat. Lilly looked at him, unsure whether to focus on him or the ring.

"Please get that," Grassal said. She hurried down the hall and returned bearing a tablet that showed the face of a man in his mid-thirties with purple hair and thick-rimmed, green glasses. When he saw Grassal, he nodded his head as if in confirmation, though of what, Grassal couldn't imagine. In the corner above

Lewis' head, Grassal saw the video image of himself, looking like a silver mummy with excellent skin. Lilly set the tablet on a chair so that the screen was level with Grassal's position on the couch. Lewis' face broke into a wide smile, revealing yellowed teeth.

"Grassal Delgado? No shit?"

"No shit."

"I expected this was some kind of prank. I'm Lewis Braxton. Did I catch you at a bad time?"

Grassal gave Lewis a wan smile and said, "No, it's a great time. I usually sleep like this."

"I can call back." Lewis' eyebrows were arched, his expression bemused.

"No, really, it's good. Look, I'm really excited to hear about this treatment. From your post, I gather there's an actual clinic set up."

"Are you ... " Lewis trailed off, the expression on his face suggesting he was afraid he might cause offense. Grassal smiled. Lilly sat at the desk with a pen in hand, ready to take notes.

"Yes."

"Thus the reason for the duct tape?"

"You're perceptive," Grassal said.

"I do my best. About the clinic. I've visited there, and it's not what you'd expect. It's as much a meditation retreat as a clinic. Whatever it is, Dr. Kongsampong appears to have an effective treatment."

"Kongsampong?" Grassal said. He wanted to practice his pronunciation well before he met the doctor.

"Right."

"How do you know it's effective?"

"First off, he had a nice-sized *farang* control group."

"*Farang?*"

"Sorry. I've been here too long. *Farang* is the Thai word for foreigner. Foreigners have shown the worst symptoms. Thais have symptoms too, but nothing like what happened to

Westerners, both here and in other places. So anyway, the doctor manages to get about a hundred patients, including twenty *farang* from the US and Europe. First, he found a correlation that indicated a strong, positive relationship between long-term meditation practice and significantly milder affliction symptoms. Next, he demonstrated that with the right combination of drugs and mental practice, the effects were almost entirely eliminated."

A smile spread across Grassal's face, and for a moment he allowed his heart to sing a song of hope.

"Can I meet this Dr. Kongsampong? I'd really like to see his clinic."

"That depends, Mr. Delgado."

Grassal raised an eyebrow. "Oh, come on. What does this depend on?"

"Introductions and access."

"To whom?"

"I need to think about that."

"Fine. You think, and I'll make travel arrangements."

"We'll chat soon, then. Cheers," Lewis said just before he ended the call. Lilly hummed to herself as she cut Grassal free of the duct tape. She seemed pleased by the prospect of travel.

"Are you sure you want to make a deal with this sex pest? You did see him, right? He looks like, I don't know, kind of a creeper. And God knows what he wants from us."

"At this point, I don't care what he's like. He probably just wants to interview somebody famous so he can raise the prestige of his crappy little website. As for us ... I don't want to get my hopes up, but if this is what it seems, we may have found a cure."

With the moon overhead, they boarded the charter jet at a small public airport west of Denver. The jet's interior was shabby, with worn maroon carpet, tattered leather seats, and the faint smell of stale tobacco smoke.

Annie greeted them with hugs and handshakes while the pilot stood away at a respectable distance.

"Where's Mark?" Grassal asked.

"At home. You know how he is; he doesn't like to leave the county, let alone the country."

When takeoff pushed him back in his seat, Grassal gripped the armrest and looked over at Lilly. She gave him a troubled smile. Grassal had never imagined she'd be afraid of flying. Once airborne, Grassal and Lilly presented their findings to Annie. She nodded as she read, occasionally furrowing her brow and running her finger over one passage or another.

"This sucks," she said in conclusion.

"What's wrong?" Grassal asked. Her declaration had stung, and he realized his voice sounded hurt. Annie softened her tone.

"It's just that you've got this really compelling data, and you make a solid case. But I don't care. The reader doesn't care. What do they have to care about? Numbers? No. These are sick people, but this just gives me information. There's no interpretation."

"Information should be all we need," Lilly said. "That's the whole reason we're on this flight, to get information. With the right information, we can pressure the people at the CDC to share what they know and do something to help these people."

"You have a laudable goal, and you're on the right track, but right now, this will probably be read by one or two people and thrown aside. Understand that government agencies are like teenagers. They're disorganized, stubborn, and hate being told what to do. However, as with teenagers, it's possible to shame them into action. To do that, though, you need to be able to apply public pressure, and public pressure is created with a compelling story. Ideally, that narrative would have either a happy ending or the promise of one." Annie put a finger to her lips. "Let me think."

The droning engines filled the silence, and nearly three hours passed before Annie spoke again. During that time, Grassal allowed himself to slip into a light sleep. Annie's sudden proclamation pulled him from a dream about hornets.

"I've found the story. It's a good one, involving willful ignorance and incompetence by public officials. All we need now is the ending."

"What's the story?"

"In a nutshell, you have two brave, independent researchers who proved definitively that the recent spate of strange violence is a direct result of subluminal attacks. Ignored and dismissed by the very bureaucrats who are supposed to manage such things, these heroes proceeded to find a solution on their own. They return to those bureaucrats not only with the answers, but with an olive branch. They're willing to give them a chance to save their reputations and possibly their careers by taking action on the information presented to them."

"It's bold, direct, powerful, and still allows us to walk the high road," Grassal said.

"Assuming this Dr. what's-his-name is actually offering a cure," Lilly said. "And not just some hokey religious mumbo jumbo."

"Hokey religions and ancient weapons ..." Grassal said, waiting for one of them to catch the reference, or even finish the quote. Neither did, and he missed Amadeus.

"We'll find out soon enough," Annie said.

They landed at sundown, which left Grassal feeling disoriented. Stepping off the plane into warm, humid air in the middle of January didn't help matters. They hired a taxi at the airport to take them downtown. During their ride, Grassal gazed out the window at the tightly packed buildings, traffic circles overflowing with tropical flowers, and everywhere, pictures of a benevolent-looking man framed in ornate gold. Lilly informed Grassal the man was the king of Thailand. Motorcycles and scooters zoomed past either side of the taxi.

When the taxi let them out at the hotel, the air was a heady mix of flowers, car exhaust, and sewage. Water circulated through an obelisk-shaped fountain.

The hotel lobby was furnished with black leather couches, teak paneling, and shiny onyx surfaces, upon which sat vases overflowing with fresh-cut white orchids. Their top-floor room overlooked a city awash in neon light.

"An expense account is a beautiful thing," Annie said. "But getting old is a motherfucker. Why don't you kids go out and have some fun? There's a good strip of drinking establishments two blocks away. I've got a per diem," she said as she handed Grassal an envelope. He opened it to find several crisp orange bills.

"We can't take your money," Grassal said. "I have my own, or I will as soon as I get to an ATM." Grassal's bank account was almost empty. When he tried to return the envelope to her, she grabbed the envelope, smacked him on the head with it, and stuffed it in his shirt pocket.

"It's cool, really. That would buy a few nice meals in New York City, but here, it's like I just won the damn lottery. And they're giving me twice that, every day. Besides, you two are setting me up with what I expect will be yet another prize-winning story. With friends like you, it's almost not fair to all those poor Columbia-trained journalists I work with."

"Do you feel up to it?" Lilly asked Grassal.

"Good. Great, actually. First-class. There's no way I'd be able to sleep now, especially not with actual, honest-to-God Thai food waiting just outside the door." He felt his stomach rumble. Lilly raised her eyebrows.

"We'd better hurry," she said. Before they left, Grassal sent a message to Lewis and asked if they could meet tomorrow afternoon. Outside, they bought pad thai from a food cart vendor and ate in the courtyard of a red-roofed temple. Incense smoke billowed from altars nestled in alcoves along the outer wall. Floodlights illuminated gold spires that pierced the sky like jousting lances.

By the time they finished, Lewis had responded, instructing them to meet him under the clock at the train station at nine the next morning.

Grassal woke before dawn and roused his companions. Lilly and Annie were ready and out as soon as the coffee was made. Despite being the cool part of the day, Grassal's body was drenched in sweat by the time the *tuk tuk* dropped them off at Hua Lamphong Station. Grassal decided during the ride that *tuk tuks* were even more terrifying than Amadeus had described them. At the station, young men offered Grassal taxi rides, lodging, and/or girls, despite the fact that Grassal was already with two women. An old woman sold bags of jackfruit, papaya and fried cakes from a basket. Grassal bought enough for everyone, and as he received his change, Lilly grabbed his shirtsleeve and pointed. Grassal's eyes followed her finger and saw what she was pointing at: a white man with purple hair leaned on the doorframe of the station, smoking a cigarette.

"That's our boy," Grassal said. He looked up, and his eyes settled on the wrought-iron clock. "Right where he said he'd be, and five minutes early."

"My kind of guy," Annie said.

They crossed the station. Lewis ground out his cigarette on the concrete floor and waved before he looked up or made eye contact with them.

"Glad to see you're free and untied. This must be Lilly and Annie." He shook hands with them both. "Ya'll ready to take a ride?" Lewis said, adjusting the leather messenger bag that hung over his shoulder.

"I thought that might be what we were doing," Grassal said.

"Meeting in the train station didn't make it obvious?"

Two hours later, the train pulled into Ayutthaya station. Lewis hailed a cab and spoke to the driver in what Grassal guessed was fluent Thai. The driver laughed at something

Lewis said, motioned for everyone to climb in, and then drove them down long, straight roads that ran between rice paddies.

Just when Grassal thought his body was going to lock up from so much sitting, the driver turned off the road, passed through a gate flanked by two mythical guard statues, and approached what Grassal guessed was a temple. It looked like the place he and Lilly had eaten the night before, only the main building was long, like a community hall, and flanked on both sides by smaller buildings. In the distance, several people in white gowns meditated in the shade of a palm tree. Grassal looked closer and counted at least two amputees. He suspected there were more, but from this angle it was hard to tell.

When he stepped out, the first thing Grassal noticed besides the heat was the lack of machine noise. All he heard was the chirping of birds, the rustling of the wind, and a droning chant from one of the smaller buildings. Two monks dressed in saffron robes walked out from a building. Lewis bowed and addressed them in Thai. After he finished, they looked at each other then scurried off into the main building. One looked over his shoulder and called out something to Lewis.

"He says he'll bring the doctor out."

Grassal looked around and was delighted to see green bananas growing from the wide-leafed plants that had been planted in orderly rows. He pointed this out to Lilly, who only nodded and wiped the sweat from her brow. She looked pastier than usual.

"Problem?" Grassal asked.

"It's just ... no, I'm okay. It's kind of warm. And all the oxygen. I'm to that thin mountain air."

Ten minutes later, an older Thai man supported himself with a gold-topped cane as he descended the stairs of the temple. He wore a white coat and a loose orange-and-blue plaid sarong around his waist. One of the monks who had greeted them ran out and offered the man his arm. The man shooed him away with a swipe of his cane. When the man reached the bottom,

Lewis spoke to him, then turned to Grassal and said, "I will translate for the doctor, and it's easier and faster if I speak in the first person. This is Dr. Kasem Kongsampong."

Dr. Kongsampong eyed Grassal with suspicion as he spoke, giving space between phrases to allow Lewis time to fill in the gaps. Dr. Kongsampong, speaking through Lewis, said, "You say you have come all the way from America to learn what we do here, but what is your real purpose?"

"I'm trying to find a way to help those afflicted by the subluminals," Grassal said. As Grassal spoke, Lewis translated almost simultaneously. Annie nodded, clearly impressed. She made a note in her steno book.

"How much money will you make from this?"

"None," Grassal said.

"What? You're American and you don't want to be rich?" the doctor said. He was smiling now. "I thought all Americans wanted to be rich."

"I've never had much money. I'm used to it. I promise you that I only want to learn what you're doing here and, if possible, to share it." Grassal gestured to Annie and said, "She is a writer with a large audience. We believe that we can compel the government to offer treatment for free to those who need it."

The doctor scratched his chin. "What else would you like to tell me? Surely you are motivated by some self-interest?" The doctor nodded to Grassal's leg and gave him a sly smile. Grassal cursed himself for wearing shorts.

"Yes. I have this problem, too."

"To heal others, you must first heal yourself. How stable are you?"

"I don't know. Not very. It's only been a couple days since my last, um, attack."

"Then your time is short. You could get worse, so I will be expeditious. The saliva of the creatures contains something similar to prions, basically infectious proteins. Prions are normally responsible for various forms of encephalitis. At first I thought that the victims were suffering from a ..." Lewis paused here and asked the doctor a question for clarification. "... transmissible spongiform encephalopathy. This hypothesis was mostly incorrect."

"Mostly?" Lilly said.

"Well, they weren't prions, and this wasn't encephalitis. How do I know this?" Dr. Kongsampong pulled a pack of cigarettes from his pocket and lit one. Rather than blow the smoke out, he allowed it to roll out of his mouth as he spoke. "Because meditation has no effect on traditional encephalitis."

Grassal scratched his head, trying to make sense of this.

"During the Emergence, I was working at Bumrungrad Hospital in Bangkok," the doctor continued. "When we admitted people, our staff asked about the patients' religious practices. We had a fair mix of practicing and non-practicing Buddhists, as well as Muslims, Christians, and nonbelievers. I decided to track the long-term health of people who were injured during the Emergence. Among those injured in subluminal attacks, I found a strong relationship between people with a regular meditation practice and people with lowered susceptibility to post-attack behaviors."

Annie's pencil danced over the page, and Grassal wondered why she wasn't recording this.

"With this observation in mind, I developed a hypothesis based on what you might call heretical ideas. You see, about a decade ago, an associate of mine named Daree Suttani developed a technique for meditators she called 'fast-tracking.' This involved attaching a tiny electrical device to the cerebral cortex, then administering a drug preparation. The technique worked wonderfully. After the treatment, a novice could meditate for only ten minutes and experience effects similar to those enjoyed by a trained monk who had practiced for a decade, so long as the patient continued to take the drugs. Brain scans showed that the treatment even changed the prefrontal cortex. Unfortunately, two of her patients died during the trials."

"That doesn't sound like a very good technique," Grassal said. Dr. Kongsampong narrowed his eyes at Grassal, then flicked his cigarette ashes. Lewis brushed a strand of purple hair from his face and turned his head away from the smoke.

"The Suttani Technique was very good. Nearly perfect, I think. Her work was sabotaged. She learned too late that the preparations were tainted. We suspected Pattani separatists, but nobody ever found out for sure. Nevertheless, she was barred from conducting further trials. Five years later, professionally ruined and consumed with guilt, she killed herself."

Here the doctor paused then excused himself and left the room. When he returned, he was composed, but his eyes were red and moist.

"Your hypothesis was that Suttani's technique would benefit the afflicted because of what you observed at the hospital," Grassal said.

"Exactly. And my hypothesis was correct. It worked. Even among *farang* unfamiliar with any practice at all," Dr. Kongsampong said in nearly unaccented English.

A smile spread across Grassal's face.

"Come with us," Lilly said. "Back to the United States. So you can train other doctors in the ... the ..."

"Suttani Technique. But it would not be necessary."

Grassal arched an eyebrow. He wanted to protest, to say of course it was necessary, but he nodded and asked the doctor to elaborate. The doctor did, reverting to Thai.

"The technique is so simple that any country doctor could implement it, and any pharmacist could provide the necessary drugs."

"Well, that's great," Grassal said.

"However, your country doctors won't be doing it, nor will anyone else in the United States."

"What?" Grassal and Lilly said simultaneously.

"Your AMA called Suttani's work 'quackery of the highest

degree.' After the deaths, they even barred her from attending a UN conference on public health. Even though they knew the truth about the tainted drugs and could find no fault with the data, they backed the calls to suspend her license. They could not accept that someone like her, or like me, from a developing country, could develop such a potentially powerful treatment for mental health. A colleague later told me certain pharmaceutical companies were especially interested in preventing this treatment. So, the AMA refused to help Suttani when she needed it most, and I think it eventually took her life."

Grassal looked at Dr. Kongsampong and ran a finger across his chin stubble. Grassal knew he was missing something. If the doctor hadn't wanted to help them, he wouldn't have agreed to meet with them or to explain what exactly the treatment entailed. He tried a different angle.

"I believe the AMA was wrong. What you're doing here is the right thing to do. Lilly and I have the data to back this up. You've helped the victims of the afflicted when doctors in my country have not." Grassal watched the doctor's face and saw that his words were having the desired effect. "Your work alone should be enough to vindicate Suttani, but together we can do even better."

"Tell me more," the doctor said.

"It's now possible to show that her treatment is effective and safe. I believe that we can convince policymakers at the Centers for Disease Control to implement this treatment on a large scale."

"The CDC? They're no different than the AMA. They all have dinner together. Same same."

"True, they are the epitome of the medical establishment," Annie said, "but they also believe in good medicine, good policy, and we now have the ability to demonstrate that implementation of the Suttani Technique represents both."

Grassal said, "If you'll tell us how to replicate the Suttani Technique, we will see to it that it is used to treat the afflicted in our country."

"And if it's used in the United States," Lilly said, "then every other country with afflicted will follow suit."

"It is no good, I think," the doctor said. He had finished his cigarette, and now his brow was furrowed.

"What are the side effects?" Grassal asked. The doctor spent a moment contemplating the question before he provided an answer.

"Provided the patient maintains the regimen, there are no significant side effects."

"And if he stops taking the drugs?" Annie said. "What then?"

"So far I haven't had anyone stop. But in Suttani's studies, she found that individuals reverted to a mental state equal to or slightly worse than they had experienced before the treatment."

Grassal watched Lilly and Annie exchange a look, but before they could say anything, Grassal put a hand on his chest.

"I'll volunteer to be the first American recipient of the Suttani Technique. I believe in your treatment, and, Annie, I'll go on the record saying as much. Between her and me," Grassal said, pointing to Annie, "we have the ability to influence large numbers of people. We can see your Suttani vindicated by the very establishment that rejected her."

"*My* Suttani," the doctor said. A smile spread over his wide face like a banner unfurling. "Was it that obvious?"

"I'm a romantic too, Doctor," Grassal said.

"What about the side effects?" Lilly said. "What if something happens and the patient runs out of drugs?"

"The drugs are common. Any pharmacist can prepare them. So long as there are pharmacies, Mister Grassal will be fine."

"Are you sure, Mister Grassal?" Annie said, a half-smile on her lips.

"My mind is made up. I'm going to do it."

"Then come with me," the doctor said.

Twenty minutes later, Grassal was lying face down on an operating table. Lilly had opted to pass on observing the procedure, choosing instead to talk with a monk, but Annie and Lewis stood along the wall some distance away from the table where Grassal was strapped down. A nurse who smelled of jasmine was shaving the back of his head with a straight razor. The doctor had donned gloves and a surgical mask. He held a pencil-sized syringe filled with a viscous yellow liquid. Light glinted off the needle. Grassal shuddered then looked away. The nurse rubbed something gooey onto his skin before stepping back and crossing her hands in front of her.

"What is that?" Grassal nodded, looking at the needle.

"The machine. Actually, it is several thousand nanomachines arranged in a helix half a centimeter long. I will inject this just below the base of your skull. Please try not to cough." Grassal shuddered again. Hospitals. He hated hospitals. At least this place, with its murals, dark teak paneling, and incense smell didn't have that antiseptic, piss-and-disinfectant, cancer-and-death smell.

The doctor gave Grassal a reassuring pat on the back. "The needle's not that big. But if you coughed, it could puncture your cerebellum. So please don't cough."

While the doctor spoke, Grassal felt a pinch on the back of his neck, followed by a sensation of cold that spread from his neck forward. His body stiffened, and within half a minute he was unable to move. He tried to speak but only groans escaped his mouth. Wide-eyed, he looked around the room and caught Annie's eye. She was biting her lip. The nurse returned and covered his mouth and nose with a plastic mask. Grassal made his eyes shake back and forth, as if shaking his head. The doctor gave him a broad smile and turned a valve on a metal tank.

"I recognize this is a distressing sensation, but it only means my machines are doing their job. You'll receive your first dose later in the evening. Until then, sweet dreams, Mr. Grassal."

Minutes after regaining consciousness, Grassal choked down five pills of various colors and sizes. A narrow-lipped monk with glimmering black eyes sat across from him, and, with Lewis translating, began trying to teach Grassal the basics of Vipassana meditation. The doctor sat cross-legged on the floor nearby, making notes on a clipboard and occasionally speaking something to the monk that Lewis chose not to translate.

"The goal is to focus on the breath. That's all. Why the breath? Because this is the first step to deep awareness of your body." The monk then closed his eyes and began to breathe. Grassal watched him, and in his mind ticked away the passing minutes. Eventually, the monk opened his eyes.

"When your mind wanders, and when your thoughts depart from your breath, simply bring them back gently, as if you were herding an infant. Because right now, you have the mind of a newborn within this practice. Now you try. For your first time, try only a minute."

Grassal closed his eyes and breathed. At first he focused on the air going into and out of his lungs. Then he thought about the carpet under his feet. He listened to the hum of a fan. He wondered what the people looking at him were thinking. Finally, he became aware of a phantom itch. He flexed the muscles in his thigh. Sometimes that helped. This time, however, it didn't, so he flexed again, and in doing so upset the bindings that attached his prosthetic to his stump. He fidgeted and moved his body. He needed to see, so he opened his eyes—

The monk shook his head like a disappointed parent then said, "One minute. That's all you needed. The easiest thing in the world. And you couldn't do it."

"But ..." Grassal said. "How long did I sit?"

"Twenty seconds passed before you moved. I cannot read your mind, but I expect you had maybe five seconds of silence. Try again."

This time, Grassal made it a full forty-five seconds before he began to fidget, but this time he caught himself and managed to sit the remaining fifteen seconds. This earned him a nod from the monk. After standing up to stretch, Grassal returned to the floor, crossed his legs, and started a five-minute session. When the session ended, Grassal experienced a feeling of well-being he hadn't known since Amadeus' graduation day.

The following evening, when Dr. Kongsampong was satisfied that Grassal wasn't showing any adverse reactions to the preparation, he gave them a memory card loaded with data and sent them on their way. Before they left, everyone exchanged handshakes.

"I'm sorry about what happened to Ms. Suttani. I promise we'll do everything we can to make it right," Grassal said.

"I know you will," the doctor said, speaking without a translator. "That's why I agreed to talk to you in the first place."

14

They took the next train back to Bangkok and were in the air within the hour. Even though the time in DC was five in the morning, Grassal called Dr. Marx at her office. The receptionist answered, his voice weary, either from an early morning or a late night. Grassal asked to speak with the doctor.

"She's not taking any calls. This is her prime working time," he said. "And you—you sound familiar. Please wait while I ruminate." Grassal heard coffee being slurped. While he waited, he checked the CDC directory and learned Dr. Marx's administrative assistant was named Chuck Ansell. "You're that Delgado guy, right? I should've known. And why is your connection so bad? All I can hear is this whooshing sound."

Grassal smiled. He couldn't have asked for a better in.

"You're Chuck Ansell, right?"

"That's right," Chuck said.

"Well, Chuck, my connection is bad because I'm ten thousand feet over the Pacific, on my way back from a little clinic where I learned how to help the afflicted."

"Have you been reading Tolkien?" he said. "Because that sounds like a whimsical tale of fantasy. Not that there is any kind of affliction."

"Come on, Chuck. Both you and I know this is a real thing. But what you don't know is how to treat the symptoms. I do. It's not a cure, but it's pretty close. Now, are you sure the doctor is too busy? Because I'd hate to think that the CDC is willfully ignoring the opportunity to effectively control a disease that threatens both public health and security."

"Fine. Just, fine, you ruthless bastard. But you must understand that if she fires me, I will personally track you down and say insulting things about your gender identity. And this is a fate you do not want." Chuck emitted a long sigh. "I'm transferring you now."

Grassal laughed. He had won, and it felt good to win. He was making something happen, and as far as he could tell, doing a pretty good job of it. While he waited, he glanced first at the blackness out the window, then at Lilly, who had fallen asleep, and Annie, who stared at the seat ahead of her with an intensity Grassal found unsettling.

The phone clicked and a harried female voice came on the line.

"This is Marx. Is it true?" Dr. Marx said. "That you have a treatment?" The voice was as precise as a surgeon's incision.

"That depends. According to the official word—"

"Oh, cut the shit, Mr. Delgado. You and I both know what's happening. Officially, we have to deny it. There's enough crazy going around as it is. But, yeah, this situation is problematic. And I know you've got it, too, so don't bother lying."

Grassal smiled as she spoke. She was everything he had hoped she would be. When Dr. Marx spoke, Grassal heard the voice of someone who would get things done.

"Well, speak up, Delgado. What did you find, and why did you go looking for it?"

"You see, I wished there was something I could do, so I did something about it." He told her about collecting and analyzing the data, meeting Lewis Braxton, traveling to the clinic, and finally about letting the doctor perform the procedure on him.

"Big deal. People go to Thailand all the time for spiritual experiences and dubious medical procedures."

"But I haven't gotten to the good part yet, Dr. Marx. You see, Dr. Kongsampong has hard data on both his work and that of a doctor named Suttani. Both kept meticulous records, and I have the procedural data that will allow us to replicate their results."

"Suttani. Why does that sound familiar?"

Grassal chose not to answer that. She would remember soon enough.

"Do you want to do the right thing, or not?" Grassal said, hearing only silence from her end of the line. "Because if not, well ... you know Annie Brunmeier from the *Times of America*? She saw the clinic, the data from the trials, and even the procedure. It'd be awfully embarrassing if the public learned you ignored an effective procedure that was practically dropped in your lap."

"Mr. Delgado. I appreciate your initiative, but your respect for rank is lacking."

"I respect leaders when they actually lead. This is why I contacted you. You're a leader." Flattery was good, but he knew he was being transparent, so Grassal decided to push it further. "Your work on cleaning up the chicken industry was great and long-overdue. But that was almost a decade ago. What have you done since then?" Silence on the line. "You know this is the right thing to do. It's the only thing to do. Will you do the right thing, Dr.?"

The doctor sucked in a breath through her teeth, then sighed. Eventually, she said, "Charles was right. You are a ruthless bastard. How can I contact Kongsampong?"

Grassal told her, then said, "I have the documentation for the procedure. Everything you need to know. It's on a memory card. Provided our plane doesn't crash and you have access to a nano-manufacturing lab ..." Grassal trailed off, allowing the implicated insult to sink in.

"I'm neither a political assassin nor a pioneer medicine woman, Mr. Delgado. How long do you need to get here?"

Grassal asked the pilot for an ETA, listened to his response, then said, "I'll see you in four hours."

By early afternoon, Annie and the pilot were on their way back to New York while Lilly and Grassal shivered in the back of a cab. They conversed in low, uneven voices.

"You really think it's going to be this easy? Just walk in, say, 'Here's the treatment. Let's treat people,' and then see what happens?" Lilly asked. "This feels off. I'm uneasy."

"I'm not," Grassal said. In fact, he was exhilarated by the possibility of being known as the man who returned from the sweltering tropics with a treatment for the poor, afflicted Americans.

"Dr. Marx wants to help. I believe that. You saw what I found on her. She's not just some petty bureaucrat. She's actually serious about public health."

"I know, but still, Grassal. I just get a feeling this could go really, really wrong."

"And I feel like it's going to go really, really right."

They reached the CDC's downtown offices. Lilly paid the cab fare, despite Grassal's protests. They entered the office building and rode an elevator that opened to a waiting room. There, a receptionist's desk and a set of glass double doors led to a hallway flanked with offices. Grassal scrutinized the electronic access system. He saw a magnetic card reader on the wall, right beside a multifunction biometric reader. The chubby man behind the desk had jet-black hair and pointy sideburns that dropped just below his ears. Grassal gave him a wide smile and wondered if he was dealing with an Elvis Presley impersonator.

"Chuck?" The man nodded then extended a tablet to them.

"Signature and prints, please," Chuck said.

"Do we have to?" Grassal said. "It's just that, for now, I think it's better if no one knows we're here. Except you and the doctor, of course."

"It's policy."

Grassal looked at Lilly, who had one hand over her mouth, as if trying to stifle a sneeze ... or a laugh. The receptionist's chubby face had gone red in the cheeks, giving him a cherubic look.

"Surely you can make an exception for us?"

"Nope. Not gonna happen. I've been making exceptions all day for you. You should be thanking me."

"Thank you very much," Grassal said, deepening his voice for the right effect.

"You're welcome. Without me, you wouldn't be here. Chew on that for a bit." Lilly blew out a puff of breath then put her hands on her hips.

"I think both you boys could do with a little less chewing and a little more walking."

Grassal and Chuck scowled at her, but Grassal had to admit she had a point. He had put on a few pounds. At least his shoulders were still wider than his hips, unlike the receptionist, who had a dumpy look about him that suggested years of sedentary life. For a moment Grassal almost felt sorry for him, but then Chuck spoke, and his tiny spring of sympathy ran dry.

"Oh, shoot. I am so sorry, but I just remembered that I'm also required to scan and log identification documents for all unscheduled visitors. And looking down this list here," Chuck tut-tutted, "I don't see you on today's agenda. Sorry. Any state or federal identification documents will work."

Grassal fumed and considered for a moment what would happen if he gave up and went to a private hospital. Sure, they might be able to provide the treatment, but what if they decided to charge so much that people couldn't afford it? No, Grassal thought. If the treatment wasn't available to everyone who needed it, then he had failed.

Just seconds after he had made up his mind to pass over his Connecticut driver's license to Chuck, Lilly put a hand on his arm. "Just do what the man asks." She leaned in close and whispered in his ear, "When you make the small feel powerful at no cost to yourself, everyone wins. We'll get our revenge later."

Chuck arched his eyebrows as he scanned the fronts and backs of their identification cards. "I forgot that I'll need to hold these while you're with—"

An opaque glass door slid open and a slender woman with a shaved head stepped out. "Let them be, Charles," she said.

"Sorry, Dr. Marx," Chuck said. "Just following policy."

Dr. Marx inclined her head for Grassal to follow her. Lilly started to walk too, but the doctor wagged a finger at her.

"Sorry, miss. Only Mr. Delgado. I'm sure he will fill you in on the details later."

Lilly scowled then cast a sour look at Chuck. "I'll wait outside."

"In the cold?" Grassal said, but by this point Lilly was already in the elevator.

The doctor strode back through the glass doors, and Grassal trailed her to an office with windows that provided a commanding view of a grey city covered in swirling slate clouds. Grassal sat on an angular burgundy leather chair across from Dr. Marx's steel desk. A few black-and-white photos hung on the wall. One was of Marie Curie, another of a long-haired Dr. Marx with the previous president. Both were smiling, and Grassal thought they could pass for sisters.

"First, Mr. Delgado, I want to be clear that, until anything is decided, everything we discuss here is off the record. My organization may need a couple days to come to a decision, and I may be forced to seek external support from those with fewer political scruples than myself. Now ... is a tenuous time for the administration."

"This could be a boon for the president," Grassal said. She arched an eyebrow and motioned with her hand for him to continue. "You have the opportunity to demonstrate both transparency, by acknowledging what is widely suspected, and magnanimity, by providing free and voluntary treatment. But it has to be free. This has to be inclusive."

"Who would want to be a guinea pig for something like this?"

"Trust me. If others have experienced what I have, then you're going to have to build a guinea pig corral."

"You want me to set up a clinic using an untried procedure that incorporates a foreign religious practice, and then offer it for free? The conservatives will be pissing their adult undergarments." Grassal took a deep breath and collected his thoughts.

"Three things. First, the religious aspect isn't important. De-emphasize that. Tell them that it's nondenominational, like ... exercise for the brain. Second, these people, myself included, are casualties of an attack on American soil, and our government has a responsibility to provide care for them, since it kind of let this happen. Third, if you'll accept the methodology of Suttani and Kongsampong, the trials are already complete. Safety and efficacy are assured."

"I know very well what meditation is, Mr. Delgado. I've practiced for years. What I want to know is, if meditation can alleviate symptoms of the affliction, then why do the procedure?" She stood from her desk, clasped her hands behind her back, and turned to gaze out the window. A light snow had begun to fall.

"If you're familiar with clinical data on meditation, then you know that it takes a long time to change the brain structure. That's the key to the Suttani Method. That's what we should call it. And I'm afraid that time is something people like me don't have. How much time have you actually spent talking to the afflicted?"

"I've read several anecdotal reports and examined the data you sent."

"But you've never talked to anyone who was afflicted?"

She frowned at him, shook her head, then lowered her voice.

"Just between you and me, Mr. Delgado, almost every senior-level official is holding their breath, waiting for heads to roll.

And, frankly, they should. The decisions of our leaders over the past two decades have prevented our military from doing the very thing the Constitution requires it to do: provide for the common defense.

"But I'm in a tight spot. The president says he wants to keep this business with the afflicted quiet, and I'm actually quite fond of my position here, so I intend to do what he wants. You might be right. This could be the thing he needs to restore some faith in his administration. But first, I need some time both to evaluate the research and examine the methodology. Then I'll have to research safety and contraindications."

"I can give you forty-eight hours," Grassal said. "But after that, there will be noise, whether you like it or not."

Dr. Marx waved him out of her office. Grassal found Lilly on the street smoking a cigarette.

"I've booked a hotel room for us, just down the street."

"You ... you didn't have to do that," Grassal said, but in truth he hadn't thought about where they would sleep.

"The room is comped. It took a couple tries, but I found a hotel manager sympathetic to our situation. We just have to, well ... they're going to use our images on their promotional material."

"I'll trade my use of my likeness for a free room."

As they walked to the hotel, a light snow fell on dark streets. Grassal called Annie and told her they would know something within forty-eight hours. She said he had done well, and Grassal's smile remained until well after the call ended.

Rather than wait patiently for Dr. Marx's call, they sought diversions. Over the next forty hours, using their free hotel room as a home base, between them they consumed seven liters of wine, four hamburgers, two kilograms of fried chicken, three kilograms of Korean barbeque, four spinach salads, and eleven apples. They played sixteen hands of rummy, visited three museums, and, while yelling drunken taunts out a taxi window at random pedestrians, insulted the sexual abilities of the governor of Ohio, who was out for a nightcap and a stroll with his mistress.

Forty-three hours after Grassal had made his offer, his phone rang and Dr. Marx's voice came on the line. Grassal wasn't sure, but he thought he detected the hint of a smile in her voice as she said that she had received not only approval but encouragement from the president himself.

"He shares your belief that this will help his poll numbers."

"What do you think?"

"The science isn't as rigorous as I would like. The nano-fabrication might take some time."

"But it's a go?"

"I had to make some compromises. The treatments will not be done at a hospital. None have the capacity or the tolerance for the potential liability issues."

"Good," Grassal said. "Hospitals are awful places anyway. So what will we do?"

"The GSA recently acquired a hotel called The Admiral. It's here in town, on Avenue E. Even better, it's still operating. I've secured funding to pay for both hotel and medical staff."

"Excellent. Let's hear it for surplus property." The doctor did not share his enthusiasm. Grassal waited for her to volunteer more, but there was only silence. "What else?"

"Oversight. I don't know the details on that yet. The committee is still forming committees to decide how this will be handled."

"You sound ..." he grasped for the right word, "despondent."

"Committees are where good policy goes to die. On the bright side, we can get started while the committee is forming, and maybe by the time the committee has formed all of its subcommittees and written its bylaws, we'll be finished. Are you on anyone's payroll right now?"

"No," Grassal said.

"Would you like to be? I'm sympathetic to your financial situation."

"I ... I'll be honest, my accounts are a little thin at the moment."

"Then consider yourself hired in an advisory capacity. You may employ one assistant, with the stipulation that if your assistant happens to be the daughter of a seditious, recently deceased cripple, you never breathe a word of this to anyone. Are we clear?"

"As machine oil. Can I let Annie break the story? She was kind of the reason we were able to visit Dr. Kongsampong."

"You can. Let her know that in about two hours we'll be issuing a press release calling for about fifty volunteers and that I'll be available for comment between now and then."

As soon as he finished that call, he dialed Annie and told her to call Dr. Marx as soon as possible. That task completed, Lilly suggested they go out for drinks to celebrate.

"I'd love to, truly I would, but my liver would kill me." He felt good, but his body needed time to recover. Between the travel, treatments, discussions, and the waiting, the past week had taken its toll. His plan was coming together, and hopefully, hopefully, he would finally make a meaningful contribution.

"Dr. Marx said I can hire an assistant."

"So hire an assistant."

"I was thinking that you ... I know you're busy trying to sell the bunker and all, but I couldn't have done any of this without your help."

"Me? Your assistant?" Lilly slapped her leg as she laughed. "I'll be your associate, but never your assistant." She lowered her voice and spoke in clipped tones, which Grassal assumed was her imitation of Dr. Marx. "And what would this job entail, Mr. Delgado? Hmm? Perhaps I can schedule meetings to discuss the scheduling of future meetings?" She reverted to her normal voice, a precise patter with the occasional, oddly placed inflection. "It's all semantics. I'll call you afflicted instead of infected if you'll call me your associate rather than your assistant. Deal?"

"Deal."

Two hours after his call to Annie, she sent him a text and told him to check the *Times of America Breaking* blog. He did. Within the past hour her initial six-sentence post and subsequent thousand-word interview had gained over eight hundred comments and several thousand shares. The CDC received so much web traffic they mistakenly stated that they had been the subject of a DDoS attack. Annie included this last detail later that evening in a feature-length piece that detailed Grassal and Lilly's work, their meeting with Dr. Kongsampong, and the eventual lottery system the CDC developed to cope with the overwhelming demand.

By the following afternoon, The Admiral was bustling with RNs, LPNs, cooks, and cleaners, mostly Veterans Administration employees who had signed up for voluntary overtime. Dr. Marx requested Grassal join her as she brought the facility online. With his associate at his side, he did so. He and Lilly helped prepare welcome kits, complete with drug literature, an instructional booklet for meditation and overall stress relief, and a note that read "toiletries and prophylactics available upon request." Nearby, a pharmacist was divvying up drug cocktails for each patient. On the third day, he and Lilly used a side entrance to avoid the crowd of treatment-seekers who had gathered out front, ignoring the center's repeated statements that treatment would be given based only on lottery results.

On the first day of admissions, five days after he first set foot in Dr. Marx's office, Grassal felt great. He had managed to increase his sitting time to almost fifteen minutes. For most of this, he maintained his focus. The effects of his meditation were staying with him. Only this morning, he had stubbed his big toe. Before, his normal reaction would have been to mutter a string of curses. This time, he only took a deep breath and observed the pain with dispassion as the throbbing subsided. The muscles around his broad shoulders felt loose and relaxed and his digestion was much improved, though this could've been a result of being able to afford quality food with his new salary.

Presently, Grassal stood in a receiving line to greet the lottery winners. With him stood Lilly, Dr. Marx, and a meditation instructor named Rumi Soon. The afflicted streamed in, hopeful and twitching. Some were alone. Others were accompanied by spouses. All carried a piece or two of luggage. All were ready to begin a treatment regimen at a place that one pundit had called a "combination of Club Med and New Vrindiban." With Grassal's face and name officially attached to the program, public support had grown, and the Delgado Initiative had become a popular, feel-good sidebar in the otherwise strange and dour annals of the Emergence. Most of the afflicted who walked through the doors of The Admiral gave Grassal a handshake and a word of thanks.

One man scowled at Dr. Marx from beneath bushy white eyebrows and asked why, if the only surgical procedure being done was the nano-injection, they would need to stay for a period of one to three weeks. Grassal had wondered the same thing, and Dr. Marx had promised to explain later.

"We feel that this will provide the highest likelihood of a positive health outcome. It's similar to lap-band surgery. You can't just do the surgery then expect individuals to change their behavior. You have to provide support and counseling." She lowered her green tortoise-rimmed glasses and looked at the plastic nametag he wore on a string around his neck. "In short, Mr. Davisson, we're not just going to give you an injection and then turn you out on the street. We want to ensure you have the ability to manage and control your affliction."

As the doctor spoke, the man's expression softened, and by the end he was smiling. "Well, you folks are my last hope. After my last episode, my wife took the kids to stay with her sister. I mean, I'm dangerous, but surely I'm not worse than Detroit, right?" He shook his head as he walked away.

"Um," Grassal said. "Maybe we could just tell them that the

manufacturing is behind schedule?" Dr. Marx scanned the room through narrowed eyes.

"Come with me." He followed her back into a wood-paneled office. An old metal clock ticked away the seconds. She closed the door behind them and sat down at the desk. Grassal found himself studying the access system on the wall. It was new; a plastic film still covered the LCD touch screen. "Please don't mention the delays. I'm trying to make a difficult situation better. Besides, according to Kongsampong's data, our patients will still benefit from learning the meditation practice and receiving the drugs. By the time the injections are ready, our patients will already be experiencing some benefits." Something about her eyes didn't strike Grassal as sincere, and he stroked his chin as he thought.

"Is that all? I know you said you made some compromises ..."

"That's all."

Grassal narrowed his eyes.

"Really?"

"Mr. Delgado, you are one of the most insistent, persistent, and infuriating people I know. Fine. You want to know the real reason we're having people here? Of course you do. But again, this doesn't leave this room. Remember, as a paid contract employee, you're bound to a nondisclosure agreement, which, if violated, could land you in a bottomless pit of shit from which you would never extricate yourself."

"It keeps getting better and better."

"I had to agree to conduct pretreatment observation. Some ... individuals want me to document the behavioral effects of the affliction both on individuals and groups. There are some pending legal cases, and I'm required to determine whether violence committed by the afflicted falls into the same category as that of the clinically insane."

"I can tell you it does."

"But I'm the expert, and they want my opinion along with some qualitative research."

"Is there anything else, Dr.?"

"There's always something else, Mr. Delgado, but for now it's all I can do to keep the jackals at bay."

15

On the first day of the Year of the Dragon, Amadeus sat on a bench outside the Hart Senate Office building and waited. He wore a wide hat like those that had come back in style over the past few years, gray slacks, a crisply pressed white oxford shirt, a suit jacket, and a gray-and-purple striped tie. A long black wool coat topped off the ensemble. The day was cold, though not as bad as last night, and winter clouds roiled. Last night's snow had been packed down by a thousand trudging feet, leaving the sidewalk icy and treacherous, but the bench had been dusted clear. When darkness fell over the city, the building's doors fluttered open and closed as a stream of workers left for the day. Amadeus held a flexscreen in front of his face as a shield. Earlier he had read about the flagging progress of H.R. 8005, but now Amadeus was running an app that made the screen a one-way mirror.

Amadeus saw his mark: Enzo Truman, the young man who had distributed the papers at the committee hearing. Janette had sent Amadeus a report that contained two useful pieces of information. One, Enzo Truman was a senior at West Virginia University interning as support staff for college credit. Two, he left his internship every day at five thirty, rode the red line north two stops, and walked to the apartment he shared with four other students. All their names were written down on a scrap of paper in Amadeus' pocket.

When he stepped outside, Enzo put on a pair of wireless ear buds and made his way toward L'Enfant Station. Amadeus followed him, keeping his head down as he melted into the crowd. Amadeus entered the station about a hundred meters behind Enzo, who discreetly picked his nose when he thought himself unobserved. The train arrived with a rumble and a hiss. Amadeus boarded three cars behind Enzo, since he knew where Enzo would get off. Packed shoulder-to-shoulder with the other office workers, Amadeus felt his heart racing, but not because he was afraid. He observed everything around him with great clarity. He heard individual conversations and noticed the way the fabric of his clothes felt against his skin. Stalking was an entirely new experience for him, and he tried to accept the disgust he felt when he realized he was enjoying himself.

At Enzo's stop, Amadeus hung back to give Enzo plenty of time to get out onto the street before he approached him. Given that whoever had murdered Jones appeared to have access to the security system in what should've been one of the most secure facilities in the country, Amadeus had thought it prudent to talk with Enzo far from any government buildings—even better to avoid being seen talking with Enzo on Metro surveillance altogether.

Outside, full dark had fallen, but to Amadeus the night street looked like the chamber of a firing furnace: every shop on Chinatown's H Street glowed red with neon. Red lanterns left over from the New Year's festivities swung from lampposts, and white lights affixed to metal poles covered the street like the paths of tracer bullets. Enzo stepped into a noodle shop with steamy windows. Amadeus waited outside.

When Enzo emerged, both arms laden with plastic takeout bags, Amadeus stepped in front of him and grinned. Enzo gaped at Amadeus for a moment, and when recognition came it started with a smile but quickly changed to a scowl.

"I shouldn't be talking to you," Enzo said, looking up then

down the street. "But I guess it's too late now." He raised one of the bags. "You like lo mein?"

Enzo's apartment consisted of a kitchen and a sparse living room, flanked on both sides by pairs of closed doors. The room smelled like unwashed socks, musk cologne, and stale beer. The furniture was old, mismatched, and scratched by cats. A hole in the wall had been poorly patched with plaster and left unpainted. Beside the hole was a bucolic thrift-store landscape painting upon which someone had drawn a crude class A demon. When he saw Amadeus' eyes looking around the apartment, Enzo said, "I just rent a bedroom." Amadeus sat on the couch while Enzo fetched two beers from the kitchen and sat cross-legged on the floor across from Amadeus.

"You should've seen my dorm room at UConn," Amadeus said. They started in on the lo mein, eating in silence. Amadeus wanted to make small talk but Gravity had previously counseled him to wait, to make Enzo ask why Amadeus had found him. Before Amadeus was halfway through his lo mein, Enzo asked.

"I think I know why you're here, but I can't help you. I really can't. I didn't choose to work in Payne's section, but that doesn't mean I don't want to do my job well."

"I'm just here to talk," Amadeus said, "and to make you an offer. I can help you. I have influential friends who can help you. But tell me, what do you mean by 'doing your job well?'"

Enzo's brown eyes flicked back and forth. Amadeus realized his presence, along with this conversation, was making him nervous.

"I mean that what happens at the office stays at the office."

Amadeus chuckled. "Like Vegas?"

"Like Vegas," Enzo said. That got a smile out of him.

"If it's like Vegas, then allow me to raise the stakes: full employment with a three-letter agency upon your graduation, provided you take a couple more classes and commit to a three-month paid internship." The last two provisions were included in case Enzo wanted to bargain.

"But I want to do development work," Enzo said.

"Then you'll do development work, but not with your transcripts, not on your own. I mean, a C in probability and statistics? An F in introductory calculus ... twice? *Intro*?" Amadeus had passed these classes with only a few minutes of study a day. "You'll do well to develop new ways to file papers in some gas company's administrative office."

"You've seen my transcripts?"

"I have influential friends. I can even make that drug charge go away. How could you possibly think giving Xanax to a teenage girl was a good idea? No, don't answer that." Enzo fidgeted in his place on the floor then looked down at his hands. "You want to work in the city, do the sexy government career thing, then you need a security clearance, and this is your ticket. Passing barbiturates to minors probably ruined any chances you might have otherwise. This is a once-in-a-lifetime opportunity, and I promise you it's the best deal you're going to get."

Enzo scowled, took a deep breath, and appeared to think the matter over. Amadeus sat back, ready to give him some time either to think or to pass out, but as soon as he exhaled, Enzo spoke.

"What do you want me to do?" Enzo said, wariness on the edge of his voice like condensation on their beer bottles.

"Listen. Be aware. Give me updates. And install a tiny piece of software."

"Hacking? No. Nope. No way. If they caught me—"

"Not hacking, and you won't get caught. Think of it like an application upgrade for the good of the overall governmental operating system."

"Leave," Enzo said. "This is so bad. I was making things right. You, Amadeus Brunmeier, of all people. You shouldn't have come to me. You've probably already ruined all that I worked for." He took a long swig of his beer, examined the bottle for a moment, then threw it at Amadeus' head. Amadeus leaned left and it sailed into the kitchen, where it shattered. Amadeus stood.

"Think about it, Enzo," he said as he walked out the apartment door. As he left, he heard footsteps clomping up the narrow stairwell. Amadeus couldn't go back in or pass, so he waited in the doorway. A man younger than himself stepped onto the landing.

"Amadeus Brunmeier?" he said. Amadeus smiled and said yes, he was Amadeus. "You know Enzo? That is so awesome."

"Sort of. What's your name?"

"Willard," Willard said, clearly excited to meet Amadeus Brunmeier, Hero of the Emergence.

"Good to meet you, Willard. Hey, I need a favor. Want to make a thousand bucks?" Willard's eyes lit up and a smile wrinkled his pink cherubic face. Amadeus wondered for a moment if he should do more to vet him, but this was an opportunity to act, and Amadeus wasn't going to give himself time to overthink it.

"Pop this into Enzo's computer." Willard gazed at the little USB drive Amadeus produced from his coat pocket. "A window will open. Click run. Remove the drive and hide it away. Assuming you're successful, I'll contact you tomorrow and we'll talk further."

"What's it for?"

"Something to help Enzo. But you need to understand that I'm paying you as much for your silence and discretion as I am for installing a program on a computer. Any schmuck can do that, but I need somebody I can trust. Can I trust you?"

"You can trust me. Keep it secret, keep it safe. Just like Gandalf said, Mr. Brunmeier."

"It's Amadeus."

"Don't you need my phone number?"

"I'll find you," Amadeus said, giving Willard a smile as wide as the Potomac. "Don't you worry about that. Good luck,

Willard."

Amadeus took a taxi across town, then made a circuitous route that led to an old apartment building eight floors tall. He entered the pass code on the door then took the elevator up to the movable HQ, an apartment with unpainted sheetrock walls, a scuffed wood floor, and furnished with outdated, utilitarian furniture. He checked the two bedrooms and found no one inside. On a whiteboard, a message scrawled in Gravity's handwriting read: *out for the evening.* That was fine with Amadeus; alone in a quiet apartment, he might be able to have a decent conversation with Lilly. So far she hadn't returned any of his calls or acknowledged any of his messages, but he had to keep trying. He dialed and reached her voicemail.

"Lilly, I wish you'd answer. I just wanted you to know that ... you should already know that I would never kill your father. But you don't believe me, so I'm working on something that will convince you otherwise. In the meantime, I hope you're taking good care of Grassal."

Amadeus tried Grassal, but he didn't answer either. Amadeus didn't leave a message.

With nothing better to do at the moment, he loaded Grassal's software, a modified Trojan with a key logger, and looked for the broadcast beacon. Willard had accomplished his task with surprising swiftness: Amadeus now had remote access to Enzo's computer. He cleared all the saved browser data. Once Enzo started logging in to sites, Amadeus would acquire the information he needed, and he would set his backup plan into motion.

Pleased with himself, Amadeus stretched out on a couch and shut his eyes. He jerked awake when the doors of the elevator opened. Gravity stepped through with Janette leaning on his arm. Gravity's stride was loose, his posture relaxed. Janette murmured something to Gravity and he replied with a low laugh. Amadeus coughed and muttered a hello, just in case they didn't realize he was there.

"Ah," Gravity said. "We were just celebrating the new dissent against H.R. 8005. Thanks to a few of our favorite pundits, this bill grew so toxic it contaminated its Senate counterpart. Its detractors framed the argument so that a vote for the bill was a vote against the military. Now, no politician with a sense of self-preservation, that being all of them, will touch it."

Amadeus nodded and smiled. Finally some good news. He told them about his progress with Enzo.

"The foot in the door," Gravity said, "is a much more subtle and effective technique. You should've gotten him to do some little thing for you first, then later he'd be far more willing to do a big thing—like compromise secure systems. But you're still just a pup. You're learning."

"I found a workaround." He told them about his deal with Enzo's roommate.

"Not bad, but next time," Gravity said, tapping the side of his head, "try to remember that honey beats vinegar, except when you're cleaning house."

The following day, Amadeus checked his keylogger and found the information he needed for his backup plan: Enzo's password and his student login information for West Virginia University. Amadeus first logged in to Enzo's student scheduling and enrollment page, where he viewed Enzo's transcripts. They were just as bad as the General's report suggested, a smattering of Cs and Ds with the occasional B thrown in. Enzo's only A was from his freshman year, an intro to psychology class.

Amadeus found Enzo's current course, a political science Practicum, and selected "Withdraw/Drop" from a dropdown menu. "Are you sure?" a dialog box asked. Amadeus hesitated for just a moment. This was wrong on so many levels, but it wasn't like Enzo's academic record could be much worse.

Amadeus clicked "yes."

Next, he navigated to the enrollment page and found the option that would withdraw Enzo entirely from the university. When prompted for the reason, Amadeus selected "personal" then pressed confirm. Enzo was no longer a student at West Virginia University.

Finally, he found the name and contact information for the professor over his internship and his faculty advisor and composed the following e-mail:

Dear Drs. Stewart and Whipple,

I'm sorry to inform you that I have to withdraw from the university for personal reasons that are too painful to discuss here. In the future I hope to complete the program but right now I need time to sort through these issues. I hope you understand.

Sincerely,

Enzo Truman

Amadeus sent the e-mail, added both Dr. Stewart's and Dr. Whipple's e-mail addresses to Enzo's spam filter, then deleted the sent message from Enzo's e-mail account.

Feeling slimy, Amadeus shut down the program and went for a walk. While he walked, he called Senator Payne's office. A secretary's warm, professional voice answered. Amadeus introduced himself to her, and something in her voice changed.

"You're probably wondering why I'm calling the senator's office." No response from the secretary. "I'd like to meet with the senator."

"She's booked until April."

"Surely she can take five minutes to meet with me and accept an olive branch? I'll make it worth her while. I expect she'll want to create a new version of the bill, and maybe I could help her with that." He wanted to start in about the security of the country, but something about the secretary's voice told him she wouldn't buy it.

"I'll get back to you," the secretary said. Amadeus thanked

her then made his way to a bank, purchased a thousand-dollar money order, then found a post office and mailed the money order to Willard.

Early the next morning, just after dawn, Amadeus' phone rang. Enzo's voice was high, fast, and breathy, like air whizzing from a crack in a pressurized tank. Amadeus greeted him and asked how he could help.

"You fucking dick," Enzo said. "You dirty, dirty dick. I know you did this. I just know it. Why? Why me? Why can't you harass someone else?" Amadeus was silent.

"I could just call my professor and the university and tell them that you hacked my information and withdrew me. I'm sure they would reinstate me."

"You could, but do you really think your university wants the controversy? There's a lot of research money going from my friends here in DC to Morgantown, and I expect your university would much rather keep that than, well, not exactly a star student."

"Take it back. You've got to fix this."

"Do you truly think your internship will continue if it's revealed that you've been a target for espionage? Look Enzo, I didn't want to do this to you, truly I didn't, but I needed your help in this, one way or another."

Enzo sighed. "I know. I knew that from the moment you came into my apartment. But I had to try. You're a fucking asshole. I hope you know that."

"I revel in it," Amadeus said. He had to appear confident. "For what it's worth, you'll be able to continue your internship, and once this is all over, I can help you get reinstated. I'm sure the university will understand." He tried to tell himself that in the long run Enzo would be better off, but for now Amadeus felt his own stomach clenching and souring. He caught himself tearing his post office receipt into easily balled-up strips. He reminded himself that he was doing this for Lilly, and he would pay whatever personal costs he had to in order to prove his innocence. Nobody, he thought, ever said redemption comes cheap.

"What do you want me to do?" Enzo asked. His voice was resigned, like a kid being asked to do additional chores. Amadeus heard air whooshing in the phone and imagined Enzo slack-jawed, breathing through his mouth because his brain was too occupied with what had happened to him.

"Just a minor server upgrade like we talked about before," Amadeus said. One hour later, Amadeus met Enzo just outside Farragut North and handed him a memory card loaded with Grassal's software.

Two days later, in a busy coffee shop at a Metro station four blocks from the movable HQ, Amadeus set up a virtual private network on a public Internet access point. He then used a Russian proxy to log in to Grassal's software. He couldn't afford to be detected in the task he was about to perform.

Once he opened Grassal's command window, he found information that would give a hactivist joygasms for a month: a short list of passwords and usernames used by the senator. Amadeus had no idea how many laws he was breaking, or had already broken, but when it came to Senator Amanda Payne, he didn't care.

He logged in to her e-mail account and searched for his name and that of his friends and enemies. This search yielded nothing, so he began to browse through her archived messages. Amadeus was concerned with finding out just who Senator Payne, cosponsor of H.R. 8005, was corresponding with.

Most messages were mundane: travel plans, administrative tasks for her assistants and interns, a long discussion with her ex-husband about where their children should attend high school. Some, however, were more directly relevant to Amadeus' interests. One long thread included a discussion with a state delegate named Devandra Cassidy about whether the subluminals were actually created by God, or part of Satan's plan to confound. Another message to a group of policy analysts discussed the finer details of H.R. 8005, such as whether approved contractors should have the discretion to quell protests and/or riots related to the Emergence. The senator believed they should.

After an hour of sifting through hundreds of recent messages, Amadeus went back to June of last year. There he started working his way through devotional chain e-mails, dirty jokes exchanged with her interns, and correspondence with her son regarding his high school preference. Nothing caught his interest until he arrived at the following message from Roland Jessup, the CEO of Securaux. The message was from September.

The Emergence was a tragic incident, but I think in the future we'll look back and see the subluminals were a boon to this country. Senator, the natural state of man is one of war, but modern man has no enemies except his own apathy. Struggle is to man what motherhood is to a woman: a rite of passage, a source of strength.

The subluminals gave the common man a ready enemy, one so vile and alien that even the bleedingest of hearts among us cannot sympathize. For every one man my company provided in defense of our homeland, ten more civilians were allowed the opportunity to engage the enemy, to experience the cleansing power of a total struggle against an enemy.

Senator, you've spoken at length about the moral decay of our country. I agree with you. But to overcome her decay, America must assert her strength by uniting against her enemy, and in my opinion she can most effectively unite under the public-private model we've discussed.

You'll receive credit both for cutting our bloated defense budget and increasing our security against future attacks (which my analysts believe are imminent). I can't judge whether or not

the rapture is at hand, but I expect if it is, you won't be here for
the tribulation. Rapture or not, at least you'll help strengthen
America's people and South Carolina's economy.

This was interesting, Amadeus thought. Here was the head
of a security company who made significant amounts of money
by killing subluminals predicting more subluminals ... and
ensuring his company would receive legislative approval to
exterminate them. He wasn't sure how this would benefit South
Carolina's economy. Maybe Securaux would locate their
headquarters there. Then there was the general fascist
sentiment of the message, which Amadeus attributed to Jessup
displaying awareness of his audience.

Overall, Amadeus was disappointed in his search. Besides
the unsurprising finding that a corporate CEO would lobby on
behalf of its company's interests, he had found nothing
inappropriate or incriminating in the senator's correspondence.
Nevertheless, he took a screen capture of the message before
logging out of everything. Perhaps General Janette Nguyen
would find this information useful.

Amadeus called Gravity and said, "I'd like to talk about
something. You know where to meet me." While he made his
circuitous route back to the apartment, Amadeus had a sense he
was being watched, but chalked it up to paranoia resulting from
his recent activities. After an hour, Gravity and Janette stepped
through the door of the movable HQ, bringing with them the
smell of cordite and winter. Amadeus sat with them at the table.
From her pocket, Janette pulled out her cloth bag of Scrabble
tiles and spread them out on the table.

"Well?" Gravity asked.

"I didn't find much," Amadeus said.

Amadeus handed a flexscreen to Gravity, upon which was
displayed the screenshot of Senator Payne's communication
with Roland Jessup. Gravity slid his finger across to scroll down.

The general fingered a tile, running it across the knuckles of her slender hand. A smile spread across Gravity's face as he looked from Amadeus, down to the flexscreen, and then back at Amadeus. "This is authentic? From the illustrious senator herself?"

Amadeus nodded.

"Well done," Gravity said.

"Remember the coffee jockey?"

Gravity and Janette nodded.

"I kind of destroyed his academic career but promised him a job in his field to make up for it. He wants to do development work."

"I'll find some gainful, comfortable, and not-particularly-difficult employment for the kid, maybe in the GSA," Gravity said as he slid the screen across the glass tabletop to Janette, who nodded as she read the message. When she was finished, her expression was that of someone who had just sniffed spoiled meat.

"I cannot fucking believe it. I knew somebody had put the senator up to this, but I didn't think it would be this guy. They're both fucking nut jobs. Do you know how much DoD paid Jessup's company to augment our forces?" Janette asked. Amadeus shook his head.

"Back in the aughts, private contractors cost about six times more than government meat," Gravity said.

"Just over half a trillion dollars," Janette said. "And they're still billing us. We've got people disputing some of the charges, but we practically wrote them a blank check. What could we do? Our hands were tied. I've got to hand it to them. They were fast to get guys on the ground."

The seed of an idea had been lying dormant in Amadeus' mind since he left the coffee shop, waiting for the right moment to germinate. Now that seed was ready to burst forth from Amadeus' mind-soil. A smile crossed his face. He decided to apply water and light in order to see what the seed might become.

"Are you talking 'special forces' fast? Or—and I'm just throwing this out there, pure speculation—like 'knowing where the demons are going to emerge' fast?"

"That's an interesting theory, A.B.," Janette said. Amadeus started to say something else, but she put up one finger, *shushed* him, furrowed her brow, and focused her attention on her Scrabble tiles. While she moved them around, she said, "I did my homework too. I didn't find much, though I did learn that this past summer a contract avionics manufacturer in South Carolina placed a large order for milling machinery capable of handling nanosteel. The machinery arrived, but the factory shut down because of disruptions in the status of the intellectual property agreements."

"Then ..." Amadeus said, trailing off. Gravity leaned back in his chair, putting his hands behind his head. Amadeus thought he looked smug, like the smart kid who knew the answer but was giving the slow kids a chance to respond.

"What?" Amadeus said. "I'm missing something. You're not saying ..."

Without saying a word, Janette used the Scrabble tiles to spell out the name *Roland A Jessup*. Once she was sure Amadeus had seen it, she began to rearrange them, starting with the "P" on the end. A smile spread slowly across Amadeus' face as General Janette Nguyen reconfigured the letters to spell *Pearl Sundajos*.

16

In the stone-and-hedge courtyard of The Admiral, six afflicted were building a snowman. Between the old slush that had melted and refrozen, and the new snow that had fallen in the five days since check-ins had begun, they had more than enough material to work with. Though no aboveground coal was to be found within a hundred miles of the capital city, the snow sculptors had made do. One of the patients, a young woman with hair the color of midnight, used a rock to crack the frozen surface of the goldfish pond. From it she retrieved two smooth, gray river stones. To ensure they stayed intact, she pushed them deep into the snowman's eye sockets. A carrot and a cantaloupe rind, presumably requisitioned from the kitchen, completed the face.

From his vantage point in the lobby, Grassal occasionally checked on their progress, giving the young woman extra attention, but today he was more interested in reading *One Hundred Years of Solitude*. For the first time in months, he had an excuse to lounge, read, and relax. Even before everything had gone to shit on Amadeus' graduation day, Grassal had had to hustle. Despite the financial aid and scholarships he had applied for and won (at Tommy Brunmeier's insistence), Grassal still had nasty student loan payments, the rent he paid on the little room in Harbor Point never got cheaper, and every time he commuted to the city his well-heeled info-security clients always invited him to dine with them in Midtown but never offered to pay. Bastards.

But now, with the immodest salary Dr. Marx was paying him, better even than what General Nguyen had offered him, Grassal felt the gnawing rat of the species *descentsus paupertatem* losing strength. After a couple months of this, he would not only be out of debt, he'd be able—for the first time in his life—to actually start saving money. Who knew? If all this worked out, he might get into the public health business.

As he ignored his novel and daydreamed about future careers and fat bank accounts, the alarm on his phone went off. Dr. Marx had insisted that Grassal attend the meditation classes taught by Rumi Soon, a silver-haired Californian formerly known as Eugene Wallace. He found the second-floor conference room nearly full of afflicted individuals sitting cross-legged and uncomfortable on pillows, or in chairs. Grassal took a spot on the burgundy carpet in the back and listened as Rumi invoked the Great Spirit, then asked if anyone there had ever attempted or studied meditation. A few raised their hands.

"As you know, in a few days you'll receive a treatment that will change the structure of your brain. The goal of the next few sessions is to build a foundation of proper meditative technique. The practice I will teach you is simple, yet incredibly difficult. However, I feel, and the research by Suttani and Kongsampong supports this, that some basic understanding is all you will need to succeed. I hope you've all reviewed your reading material; there will be a quiz later." This brought a round of polite laughter. "Let us begin."

For the next thirty minutes, Rumi Soon alternated between explanations of his technique, humorous anecdotes about the East Coast ("your mountains are so ... smooth, it's cute"), and restrained praise for his pupils. Grassal spent the first few minutes listening, but he soon closed his eyes, focused on his breath, and retreated into himself. When he opened them, the room was empty and darkness had fallen over the city. He had sat for almost four hours. Whatever Dr. Kongsampong had done to him was working. Grassal was afraid it might've worked too well, as his practice had caused him to miss a meal, and he hated to miss meals, even if he wasn't hungry.

The kitchen was closed, so he decided to hit a nearby restaurant. He didn't much want to eat alone, so he knocked on Lilly's door and announced his presence.

"It's open." Grassal pushed open the door to her room and walked in. She was leaning over a hotel desk, dressed in a loose gray blouse, jeans, and brown boots. Her hair was piled high on her head and secured with a leather band.

She put down the fountain pen she had been using. Grassal nodded to the papers on her desk and asked her about the book.

She sighed. "It's coming. Slow, but faster now. Being here is great, though. I love writing in hotel rooms. I've got a great view, and for the most part, I suffer no distractions." She gave him a half-smile.

"Sorry. I'll leave you alone."

"I'm joking, boy. Goodness." He asked her if she'd join him for supper, and she said she would.

Over a dinner of spicy *carnitas* and icy beer at a nearby Mexican restaurant, Lilly told him a rumor she had heard from one of the kitchen staff with whom she had smoked a cigarette. "There's a lot of sexy stuff going on at The Admiral. One woman caught her husband with another man in a linen closet. She said she was going to cut his other arm off. Another man, an un-afflicted spouse, left early because his wife had already coupled with two other dudes."

"Everyone here is an adult. Besides, sex is a great stress-reliever."

"For everyone else, but what about you? How do you do it, Grassal?"

"Do what? I don't do anything."

"Exactly. You're like a monk. You've never made a pass at me, or even that snowman-building chick who was talking to you. She was definitely easy on the eyes."

"Why would I? I mean ... you ... you and Amadeus. Plus, you're my assistant, associate, whatever, and the last thing I need is a sexual harassment lawsuit on my hands." At this he gave her a smile and she laughed. "But seriously, I'm still thinking about Lucretia ..." Just saying her name made him sad. She still hadn't returned any of his calls, e-mails, nor acknowledged the letter he had written her and adorned with treble-clef stamps. As for Lilly, Grassal had learned his lesson years ago after harmlessly flirting with Amadeus' sex-for-rare-books chick.

"Is it your testosterone? Maybe it's low? I mean, I know I'm not stacked or anything, but I'm no horse, either."

"I'm not sure if I should be insulted or not. How about you, are you insulted, long face?"

"No, of course not. Just making an observation. If I didn't know you better, or if I thought less of you ..."

"I'm not sure how to respond to that, but if you really want to know, I haven't had an erection since the thing with the pickle jar."

They finished their meal and, on their way back to The Admiral, laughed about how close they had come to having an awkward conversation. He liked how easy it was to talk to her. As soon as they strolled into the lobby of The Admiral, Dr. Marx found them.

"There's something you need to see," she said.

"Only if my ... associate can join me." Dr. Marx nodded, and they followed her into the back office. She entered a string of commands on a wall-mounted flexscreen. A series of side-by-side, top-view brain images appeared. The images in the column on the left were fairly uniform, with colorful plumes of red, orange, and purple that fanned out across both hemispheres. On the right, however, colors were a patchwork of splotches that varied from one to the next. The images reminded Grassal of a paintball shootout's aftermath.

"Before we look at brain porn, I'd like to share with you a little good news. Half of this first batch of patients received Dr. Suttani's drug preparation. The other half received a placebo."

"I thought it wasn't any good without the nano-injection," Lilly said.

"That's what I thought too, but I'm a scientist, and I like to design experiments. So I said, 'What can it hurt?' Well, the effect among the placebo group was null, but the experimental group improved even more than we'd hoped for. Of course, the improvement was still marginal; today we had two people from the EG enter *catatonia rigidus*. Another assaulted an LPN."

"Was she okay?" Grassal said.

"The LPN was a he, and he had nothing more than a bloodied nose. Anyway, on to the brains. The images on the right were retrieved from the files of patients who had CAT and functional MRI scans long before the Emergence and the onset of the affliction. Those on the left were taken about seven days after the same patients' initial contact and injury."

"The affliction affects the brain. That's not a surprise," Grassal said. "But how do you interpret it?"

"Look," Dr. Marx said. She entered another command, and a third column appeared. In this one, the scans were uniform with each other, but quite different from the others. "On the far left, this is what a healthy human brain should look like. These," she pointed to the far-right column, "were taken today. This similarity in activity patterns suggests that a kind of equilibrium is reached when afflicted individuals are grouped together."

"Are you saying that simply by getting the afflicted together there's some improvement?" Grassal asked.

"If you define improvement as creating a haven full of impulsive, overstimulated sex fiends, then yes, there's some improvement." The skin around Dr. Marx's temples twitched, and Grassal interpreted this as her ironic look.

"That explains the condoms in the welcome bags," Lilly said.

Grassal fought to suppress a laugh. "We were just talking about—"

"I suspect I have some idea about what you're about to tell me, Mr. Delgado, and I'd rather not hear it. The rumor mill is already running at full steam. Deniability is a beautiful thing. It's bad enough I've had to deal with Mr. Davisson standing on the hotel steps outside and providing a running commentary on his imaginings of the intimate anatomy of every female passerby over the age of fifteen."

"I suppose you've showed us all this for a reason?"

"I never said you weren't perceptive. Yes. And that reason is this: starting tomorrow, I'm implementing a policy that prohibits individuals from exiting the hotel."

"What?" Grassal said. "This is a voluntary treatment facility."

"Yes, and I have a thousand other potential volunteers practically beating down the doors to receive a treatment we won't be able to provide for at least another week. If anyone wants to leave, they can, but they'll be bumped to the end of the line. It's not like I'm barring the doors. Plus, we'll be organizing outside excursions for groups of four under the supervision of a nurse. But in the interest of public safety, operational security, and ..." She trailed off, as if searching for the word.

"And political expediency," Grassal said. Dr. Marx drummed her fingers on the table then nodded. Grassal heard something, but he wasn't sure what.

"That's why I'm paying you, Mr. Delgado. You might be an impertinent—"

She stood from her desk and was almost out the door before Grassal realized the sound he'd heard was women shouting. He and Lilly followed her to the lobby, where one woman was using her own prosthetic metal arm to beat another one, who defended herself with a plastic potted palm. Three men and two women watched with expressionless eyes. Grassal recognized them all as among the first afflicted who stepped through The Admiral's doors.

"You filthy, brazen hussy," the plant-woman said, stepping back to avoid the swinging arm. "You and your poof of a husband are trying to take away my man."

"You can keep him. We just wanted to play. It ain't my fault your man can't keep my man's cock out of his mouth."

"Go back to Grant County, you fucking hillbilly."

Dr. Marx slammed her hand down on the counter. Grassal felt the floor move beneath his feet. The old counter bell reverberated, filling the silence that fell over the room.

"Enough! Ladies, this stops now. You," she said, pointing to the woman with the plant, "are you afflicted?" She shook her head. "Then get out of my clinic."

"This is her fault." She stuck out her lower lip and pointed to the other woman. "And what about my husband?" One of the onlookers began to drum her fingers. Grassal looked closer and saw her eyes had glazed over. He pointed her out to Lilly.

"Dr. Marx?" Lilly said. Dr. Marx ignored her.

"He will stay if he wants to. He's a patient, but you're a guest. And you, drop the arm before I send you back to the trailer park."

"Drop it? Do you have any idea how much this thing cost me?"

"Then put it back on." She did so, placing the straps around her stump. The nanofiber electrodes snaked around the stump of her forearm and up into her blouse. Once they settled, she worked the thumb and flipper of her artificial hand. Grassal was impressed. His prosthetic employed only an admittedly comfortable suspension sleeve and liner.

All five of the onlookers were now visibly rigid. Two drummed their fingers on themselves. When Dr. Marx finally noticed them, she muttered a curse under her breath then turned her head to speak into an intercom on her collar. With Dr. Marx's attention elsewhere, the woman with the plant smashed it down onto her rival's head, and the fight resumed.

The onlookers began to mutter, their words a string of phonemic nonsense.

Grassal became aware of something tugging at his insides. The feeling was the same one he had experienced in the months after he quit smoking two years ago. He closed his eyes, focused on his breath, and the feeling passed. Thus centered, he moved in, put himself between the two women, and attempted to use his arms and overall girth to keep them apart. Despite the fact that their combined weight only nearly equaled his, this proved to be a mistake. Within seconds he had been punched, kicked, scratched, and would've suffered a bite to the cheek if Lilly and the LPN with a black eye hadn't grabbed the women and pulled them back. While he rubbed the worst of his injuries, something odd drew his gaze to the onlookers.

They had formed into a row and joined arms like a team of victorious athletes. The two on the end performed a rather impressive acrobatic maneuver, using one arm to brace themselves against their neighbor, then extending their bodies out to the side, parallel with the floor. As a unit, they marched toward the plant woman. She backed away and laughed nervously, as if unwilling to believe her eyes until now.

Lilly grabbed the plant woman's arm and ushered her out of the room. The unit attempted to move through the double doors that led to the conference rooms, but they maintained their formation and were unable to move forward. Both Grassal and Dr. Marx called to them in soothing tones, and for a moment Grassal believed it was working, but the unit was only regrouping. It swiveled around then began stepping toward them with grasping hands. Grassal and Dr. Marx kept trying to soothe the group as they backed toward the wide row of glass doors. When their backs were against the front door, Grassal pushed on the crash bar, but the door wouldn't open. He sidestepped and tried another one. Same result. He looked over at Dr. Marx.

"It's the new policy. It's for everyone's good."

"Except ours," Grassal said, muttering a string of expletives under his breath. Grassal thought for a moment. If the unit couldn't even figure out how to get through a door that was slightly too narrow, then they probably wouldn't have much luck going over objects. "You go left, I'll go right. Toward the stairs. Ready?"

Dr. Marx nodded, and after Grassal counted to three, they darted to either side of the unit. As they did so, one man released himself and sprang for Dr. Marx. In one fluid motion, she pulled a silver baton from beneath her white coat and pushed it into the man's gut like it was a saber. The man moaned and shuddered as electricity passed from the baton's end and through his body. Once she broke the contact and dashed for the stairs, the man remained standing, but instead of pursuing Dr. Marx further, he only gazed at the ceiling and muttered. The unit moved back toward him, and he rejoined it, threading his arms through those of an elderly woman.

Grassal and Dr. Marx barricaded the top of the stairs with a leather couch and a bookcase, then fortified their barricade with a heavy, brass-knobbed oaken cabinet. They finished with plenty of time to spare. The unit reached the top of the stairs but made no more effort to alter its surroundings than water does washing over river stones. After a moment spent trying to walk forward, the unit realized its path was obstructed and returned to the lobby.

Over the next hour, Dr. Marx and Grassal watched from the balcony as the unit moved aimlessly around the lobby. Eventually, the individuals who comprised the unit separated themselves from their fellows, lay down on the floor, and closed their eyes.

When the doctor judged it safe, she returned to the lobby with four nurses. Grassal's interest was drained. The thought of soaking in a tub, taking his drugs, and sprawling out on his bed proved an irresistible siren song.

"What happened here stays here," she said to Grassal before

he left. "I'm already catching enough flak for some of the happenings here. I don't need to make it appear we're hosting the psycho circus."

The following morning, the nurses distributed a notice paper that detailed Dr. Marx's new rules and procedures. Grassal and Lilly discussed them over a breakfast of fried eggs, toast, tangerines, and coffee. Grassal's body ached from yesterday's assault. A purple bruise darkened one of his eyes. The dining room was packed, so they spoke in hushed voices.

"At least she's set a definite timeframe for the rest of the therapy," Grassal said. The paper included a promise that injections would begin in two days' time. "That gives people hope."

"Sure. But this other stuff, no leaving without chaperones, locked doors ... it's starting to feel like a prison, or maybe a church camp. I can't decide which would be worse."

"Well, usually the sex at church camp is more discreet, so I'd say the former. But after what we saw last night, wouldn't you say she needed to do something? I mean, would you want to see something like that out on the street?"

"Hell no I wouldn't. But at least they're stupid and slow and I'd be able to run away."

"What if you couldn't run?"

"Then I'd have to do something to defend myself," Lilly said.

"Even though these people are sick?"

"Yes. Even if they're sick and innocent. Because, and I'm sure you won't argue with this, my right to defend myself is entirely independent of the mental state or intentions of my attacker. What matters is that I'm being attacked."

"Fair enough. But if that's the case, then we have an even bigger responsibility to ensure that no more situations like the one last night occur. Thus, the doctor's new rules."

Lilly sopped up some egg yolk with her toast and nodded. Her gaze was distracted, as if she were thinking this over.

"That's fair, I suppose—"

A murmur passed through the room. All heads turned toward the flexscreen on the wall. Someone shushed the crowd while another turned up the flexscreen's volume. Grassal nearly choked on his egg when he read the crawling headline: "Subluminals Overrun South Carolina Police Station. Dozens dead, more injured." He wondered why the news hadn't reached his phone. When he removed the slim device from his pocket, he found he had forgotten to turn it on this morning.

"Remember that feeling I had?" Lilly said.

Grassal said nothing. His first thought was that he ought to do something. He had experience dealing with these creatures. Perhaps he could offer some pointers to the local officials who had to deal with the problem. He shot off a text to Amadeus, though he suspected Amadeus was already aware of events. Just in case. Too much time had passed since they had last talked. He hoped Amadeus didn't think he was sore about the duct tape.

The description of the creatures and the attack were all-too familiar, with one exception: the multi-million-dollar Kipium Advanced Warning and Alert System had failed to detect any kipium interference. The state-of-the-art remote sensing technology had failed.

"I think things are going to get worse," Lilly said. She gingerly peeled a banana and took a bite.

"Going to? They already are. If they've got demon gates we can't detect, we've got problems."

"The trouble feels closer, more immediate. We need to think about leaving."

"Leave? Come on, Lilly. This is a federal program in the middle of the nation's capital. We're fine. Besides, we need to see this project through. It's the right thing to do."

"We are sitting on a powder keg. First, we had that little aberration last night, and then we get to watch this at breakfast?" She gestured at the screen. "You think your pal

Amadeus is going to ride in and save the day? No. He's a tinker who got lucky with his last contraption, but that won't happen again. Whoever is doing this has the money and resources to push the technology forward. It's an arms race, and as of this morning, the bad guys took the lead. Looks like Ross' asuras have started stirring up the milk sea again."

"But," Grassal looked around the room and lowered his voice, "you remember what your father told Amadeus about Ross."

"In the last year, my father's mouth proved to be like a stable: every time he opened his mouth, horseshit came spilling out." Lilly's eyes glistened in the morning light. She finished the banana and coffee.

"But horseshit has its uses, like fertilizer and compost."

"This fertilizer fed the murderous harvest in Amadeus' mind, and that harvest eventually got my father murdered. I think something that kills is the opposite of fertilizer."

"Lilly."

"No. Stop. I don't want to hear it. Amadeus killed him. And ... even if he didn't, which I doubt, he was complicit. He made it happen."

"You sound like you've changed your thinking."

"No. I still think he killed him." Folding a napkin and placing it on the table, Lilly pushed back her chair. "I'm going to write. Unless you're ready to leave, please leave me be." Grassal watched as she marched out of the room. Even her walk was pissed off.

Seeing his table was empty, a couple people moved to join Grassal. He shook his head and gave them a forlorn look. They sought out more jovial company. For a moment, Grassal thought about returning to bed and burying himself in a book for the day, but instead he called Amadeus, who answered on the first ring.

"You know I think Lilly's wrong about you. I know you didn't murder Jones."

"Thanks, buddy, that's good to hear," Amadeus said. "I guess you saw what happened this morning."

"What's your take on it?"

"I think a storm's coming on."

"Why do I suspect you're right in the middle of it?"

"Because you know me, that's why. Nice work with the clinic, by the way. I read a brief on it a couple days ago."

"We weren't official a couple days ago." Grassal smiled. "But I guess you've got that line. Take care, brother."

"Will do. You too."

Before riding the brass-walled elevator up to his room, Grassal stopped in to speak with Dr. Marx. She waved him in without looking up from the screen on her desk. "Sit down." Grassal sat. "What do you think about this morning's events?"

"I don't think they'll affect what we're doing here. South Carolina is pretty far away."

"I hope you're right, but I'm afraid it's closer than you think." She returned her attention to the screen.

"What do you mean?" he asked, but she ignored him. Grassal left, retrieved his novel from his room, and returned to the seat near the courtyard he had occupied yesterday. Someone had turned the cantaloupe rind upside down, giving the snowman a comically forlorn expression. Grassal read for awhile then dozed off, only to be awakened by a hand shaking his shoulder. He looked up to see Lilly standing over him, her cheeks flushed deep crimson.

"They've done it," she said.

"Done what?"

"Remember H.R. 8005? Take that bill, amend it with an insemination of Stalin's seed, then splice in some of the Kim family's crazier genes for good measure. That will give you a sense of what's in this bill. Finally, give it a new acronym; it's now called the KREATURE Act: Killing and Removing Emergent Atypical Threats Using Recommended Enterprises. It flew through Congress, and the president signed it an hour ago. Its backers used South Carolina as a justification. The fuckmonkeys didn't even debate it. I think maybe three or four senators voted against it. Those were probably the only ones who read it."

"What's in it? I mean, the PATRIOT Act was bad, but the world didn't end."

"First, a company recognized as a 'recommended enterprise' may take, and I quote, 'prudent measures to ensure the safety of the citizens regardless of the availability of local law enforcement.' With a single directive, they can quarantine and impose curfews on entire regions. They can suspend inter-state travel and detain individuals on public health grounds. Plus, the bill grants immunity to most crimes resulting from 'execution of the common defense.' These pricks could conceivably drop a bomb on a school in order to kill a single subluminal, and not only would they be immune from prosecution, but they'd be paid for their time and reimbursed for the bomb!"

Grassal took deep breaths, trying and failing to shake the fuzziness from his brain. He furrowed his brow and tapped his finger against his chin. "I suppose they've finally admitted the military can't defend the United States from the subluminals?"

"It means that a private military corporation can deploy anytime, anywhere in the US, to deal with almost anything related to the Emergence. Even better, there are citizenship exemptions for PMC employees. They can hire anyone from anywhere. Now, let's play paranoid for a minute and apply these facts to our present situation. What is the common thread that binds everyone here at The Admiral?"

Grassal was awake enough to catch her meaning. "It's not our physical symmetry. You don't really think ..."

"I think it's only a matter of time before we have a bunch of mercenaries guarding us as a 'prudent measure' to protect public safety."

"Surely not. We're not posing any threat to anyone, except maybe ourselves."

"Whether or not that's true is beside the point. I need to

know ... if the time comes to leave, are you with me, or are you with me?"

"With choices like that ..."

17

At the movable HQ, a flexscreen on the wall displayed four news feeds. An Army General conducted a conference call with her staff from an unfurnished bedroom. A former intelligence consultant gazed out the window at the sprawling District of Columbia. And a UConn valedictorian paced scuffed oaken floors. When General Janette Nguyen ended her call, her eyes were steely and her back erect. Amadeus thought she looked like someone about to face a firing squad with dignity and courage.

"Problem?" Gravity asked her.

"Word is they've just passed H.R. 8005 ... And, along with a dozen other generals, I've been relieved of my command for failing to coordinate an effective defense against future subluminal attacks. Never mind that all our plans were flatly rejected," Janette said. Her expression changed, and she looked at the phone with a mixture of disbelief and contempt.

"Now what?" Amadeus asked. Amadeus looked from Gravity to Janette.

"I'll do what I've always done. I'll fight my enemies with every weapon at my disposal. Officially or otherwise, I still have a great network of reliable and loyal friends. They'll support me if I need it. Trust me, I'll come through. I've faced situations far worse than this one."

"Okay," Amadeus said. He waited for her to continue, but she said nothing further. "So, as for the bill, maybe we could start by leaking this Sundajos thing to Annie."

"Not yet," Gravity said. "The source of this information would be obvious, and it's safe to say that nine kinds of brimstone will rain down on everyone involved, your aunt included. We're now in 'fucking with a multi-trillion-dollar business' territory. Things could get messy with a quickness."

"Right," Janette said. "As corrupt and reprehensible as this bill is, we've got nothing on Jessup but a recorded conversation with a dead man everyone hates and some illegally gained correspondence. Let's not shoot our load just yet. Plus, Amadeus here still can't prove to Lilly that he didn't murder her father."

"Not yet," Gravity said, "but from what I understand, he's not even considered a suspect. That, combined with what we now know, should be worth something."

"She's already made up her—" A text message notification cause Amadeus' phone to vibrate. He opened it. The message was from Enzo and contained only two words:

I'm sorry.

Amadeus ran a finger over his scar and puzzled over why Enzo would be apologizing to him. Showing the message to Gravity and Janette, Amadeus said, "That was the coffee jockey."

"He's giving you warning. He's compromised," Gravity said, shaking his head. "You really gave him your secure phone number?"

"He had to be able to contact me somehow. He's just a kid. I didn't think—"

"That's right. That's the problem. You didn't think." Gravity's eyes darted around the room. He began to clench and unclench his fist. "They'll come fast. Were you followed?"

Amadeus shook his head. "I don't think so."

Former General Janette Nguyen put her Scrabble tiles into their black velvet pouch. She then placed them in a satchel, from which she removed a semiautomatic pistol and two loaded magazines. From beneath the shabby couch, Gravity removed an aluminum case, entered a code, and opened the case to reveal a tactical shotgun. He began to load shells into a round magazine.

"Are we getting ready for a war?" Amadeus said.

"No, just a fast exit," Janette said.

"Just in case Jessup learned of our interest in his activities," Gravity said. He started packing up the laptops on the table. "With this afternoon's bill, with billions of dollars in contracts at stake, he has a hell of a lot to lose."

"But ... but ... how would they?"

"Come on, Amadeus," Gravity said, wrapping a cable around his arm. "Our interest alerted them, just like it did in Georgia. Maybe the Senate IT staff detected your little script on their network. Maybe Enzo confessed and they used digital forensics to learn about your interests. I think that's more likely. If the senator told Jessup, and I don't see why she wouldn't, then he would take action to shut us down."

"And since Enzo presumably gave them my phone number, they can determine my location," Amadeus said. He cursed under his breath, pulled his phone from his pocket, threw it on the floor, and stomped it under his heel.

"Nice gesture, but it's a little late for that," Gravity said. "We need to move."

"Damn it," Amadeus said as he pushed his shaggy hair back on his head and let out a sigh of exasperation. "This is the guy who ... who ... he could be the one behind everything! Why are we running? You used to be a three-star general, for fuck's sake."

"Securaux is very popular right now. If we don't have solid evidence, then I'd look like I'm attacking a political enemy. Please, trust me, Amadeus. I'm formulating a plan, but understand that this plan moves at the speed of government."

Footfalls came from the hallway, followed by a tinny clinking sound. Everyone froze then exchanged glances. Getting a nod from Janette, Gravity dashed from one window to the next, and then peered out to the streets below. Janette crept to the elevator door and looked through the peephole. Both made signs for "all clear."

"There's a fire escape out the window. Get ready to use it," Gravity said, pointing to the master bedroom. He trained the shotgun on the front door while Amadeus and Janette gathered the bags and scurried to the bedroom.

Outside the door a drill whined. Gravity put one finger to his lips. He listened, raised the shotgun, and readied to fire at the sound's source when the elevator doors opened. Gravity swung the barrel toward the door and looked for a target. No one was there. Tense seconds passed. Suddenly a hand appeared from behind the doorframe and tossed something toward them. The object flew in a slow, wobbling arc. Before it reached them, Gravity slammed the door then knocked Janette and Amadeus to the floor, covering them with his body.

An explosion jarred Amadeus' brain. The door exploded inward, knocking them all back. Flames licked through the shattered doorframe as splintered wood rained down. Amadeus' ears rang. He tried to stagger to his feet, but only fell backwards against the bed.

Amadeus saw Janette crawling toward Gravity, who was sprawled against a wall. Blood ran from his mouth, nose, and ears. A book-sized chunk of door shrapnel extruded from his chest, just over his heart. He gazed up at her then placed a shaking hand on her cheek.

"I'm done. But you two, go, damn it," Gravity said. "Take this." He pulled a key from a chain around his neck and tossed it to Amadeus. It landed in his lap. "A deposit box. Central Bank, E Street. Three seventeen." Gravity picked the shotgun up off the floor and fired two rounds toward the elevator door.

He wanted to stay with Gravity, but Janette was pulling him upwards. When Amadeus got to his feet, he caught a glimpse of a man in black tactical gear crouched and aiming a rifle at them. A second later, a burst of rifle shots rang out. The bedroom wall's sheetrock exploded in a constellation of bullet holes. Windows shattered. Gravity returned fire with his shotgun. Amadeus opened his eyes to see the man taking cover behind a couch. When he did, another man popped out. Gravity and Janette both fired. The man dropped.

"Go," Gravity said.

"Thank you," Amadeus said. "For everything." He locked eyes with Gravity, who gave him a half-smile and a nod then released a rhythmic volley of suppressing fire. Amadeus used the opportunity to step through the broken window and onto the platform outside. Janette was right behind him, pistol drawn. She scanned the fire escape's four floors, then nodded for Amadeus to start climbing down. The rungs were cold and slick with ice, but instinct and fear made him sure-footed. On the way down, he winced at each of the shotgun's explosions. Gravity's ammunition wouldn't hold out much longer.

They reached the street. Janette looked up toward the movable HQ, saluted in Gravity's direction, then grasped Amadeus' arm with her free hand and pulled him away.

"Come on, A.B. He did his duty," Janette said, more to herself than to Amadeus. "I've got a car in the garage." The shotgun blasts stopped. For a moment, the night was silent, save for sirens in the distance, until a rhythmic series of rifle shots rang out. Snow blew around them and the wind cut through Amadeus' thin black sweater, chilling his bones.

Just before they rounded the corner, Amadeus heard a clink and looked up to the fire escape to see two men heaving Gravity over the railing. Gravity tumbled head-over-heels through the billowing snow and landed on the sidewalk with a fleshy thud. A moment later, gunshots shattered the concrete sidewalk only meters in front of Amadeus.

He screamed and started toward Gravity's body, but Janette pulled him by his shirt, and that sensation brought him back to reality. His wide-eyed gaze settled on one of the riflemen standing on the balcony. He was taking aim at them. Two more were plodding down the stairs.

Amadeus ran away, hard and fast. Janette kept pace with Amadeus, despite running backwards so that she could fire at the rifleman. They rounded a corner, which provided a moment of cover and respite. But the momentary sense of relief disappeared quickly because, despite his rapid, shallow breathing and his stuffy nose, Amadeus caught a whiff of sulfur, putrid meat, damp ash, and wet dog. He tried to tell himself it was only trash moldering in the dumpsters of nearby restaurants, but the scent was too familiar and too engrained in his memory. The stench grew stronger as they neared the parking garage entrance. As they ran, Amadeus heard a man calling out to them. It was the other rifleman telling them to surrender, that their friend was dead. Amadeus would rather take his chances with whatever waited for them in the garage.

They ran down the curved drive into the parking garage, their footfalls echoing off concrete. The smell there was overpowering, and they both covered their noses with their shirts. Amadeus fought back the urge to vomit.

"Down one more level," Janette said.

"Of course," Amadeus said. They darted through the metal door and tromped down the stairwell just as more gunshots cracked and then they were on the lower floor and there it was: a class C quadruped subluminal, gray and panting, with muscles rippling and two columns of yellow eyes staring. The creature snarled when it saw them, then sniffed, stood up on two legs, and put both its arms over its head in a semicircle, exposing the pale flesh of its underbelly.

Amadeus and Janette froze while they watched this display. Janette switched out the pistol's magazines, and the empty one clattered on the concrete. Amadeus scanned for something he could use for a weapon and saw nothing but a fire extinguisher. The demon dropped back to all fours, spat something onto the concrete, then scraped one claw across the floor of the parking garage.

Amadeus.

Amadeus looked over at Janette, but she had not spoken, nor was the voice, with its windy, whispering quality, remotely close to her resonate alto. The hair on the back of his neck sprang to attention as he remembered the last time he had heard the voice: last summer, in the entrance to the compound, just before he and Grassal killed the behemoth class A. The creature again ran a claw over the floor, leaving a scar of broken concrete.

Fear me not, killer of Takun, the voice said. With that, the creature bolted toward them. Amadeus squared his shoulders and braced himself for the impact, readying himself to fight, no matter what the odds, but the attack never came. Instead, the creature darted between them and into the stairwell from which they had just come. Car keys dangled from Janette's fingers, jingling as her hand shook.

"I ... that," she said, but couldn't continue. A burst of gunfire was followed by the choked, guttural screams of men. Amadeus sniffed the air. Most of the demon smell had abated. He motioned for Janette to wait while, against his better judgment, he entered the stairwell and climbed. On the upper floor he saw two dismembered bodies, still dressed in black tactical gear. Their rifles lay on the ground, twenty yards away.

For a moment Amadeus considered going in to grab a rifle for himself, but a boot scuff alerted him to a third gunman who had entered the parking garage. Amadeus ducked behind a concrete pillar. In the reflection of a well-waxed Porsche, Amadeus watched the gunman as he made a tentative sweep of the room, his weapon level and ready.

A flicker of movement several cars away caught Amadeus' attention. The gunman was scanning the wrong side of the room through his rifle's iron sights. The creature moved silently toward the man like a stalking cat, despite its ursine gait, and crouched behind a car, waiting.

Amadeus hiccuped. The gunmen turned in his direction. Amadeus pressed his body against the car's wheel and clasped his hands over his mouth. A single gunshot shattered the Porsche's windshield. A man's gasp filled the silence that followed. Peering over the car, Amadeus saw the subluminal pounce upon the gunman like a lion taking down a wildebeest. Once it had the gunman on the ground, the subluminal tore out his spine and clenched it in its mouth like a bony noodle.

Amadeus shrieked, then ran back down the stairs. Bile forced its way from his stomach into his throat as he ran down to the lower level, where a tall, black SUV idled by the stairwell door. The passenger door flew open. Amadeus climbed in. Before he had closed the door, the SUV's tires squealed and they were on their way out. Amadeus rocked back and forth and tried to catch his breath. Without removing her eyes from the road, Janette pulled a handkerchief from the console and handed it to Amadeus. He hadn't noticed the tears streaming down his face.

They drove past the mutilated bodies of the men. Amadeus looked at them and wondered if they had children, or if they were only children themselves, hammered into soldiers and given a mission to kill, only to end up a bloody pile on the floor of a parking garage.

"Assassins, traitors, hired guns. Whatever you call them, they got what they deserve," she said. "This was no kill-or-capture mission. This was strictly an assassination attempt."

"I know. I'm glad they're dead. But this is my fault."

"You couldn't have known your actions would lead to this. No one could've predicted ..." Janette trailed off, and in the silence, Amadeus heard a *thump,* followed by the screech of rending metal as they left the garage and turned onto the street. Amadeus' heart leapt into his throat as he twisted around in the car, looking out each window. He saw nothing out of the ordinary. Janette said, "We can't stop." She scanned the mirrors, rolled down the windows, and sniffed the bitter cold air. Amadeus did the same, and when the reek of putrid meat hit his nose, he decided that the creature's scent had followed along with them.

When they turned onto the street, Amadeus scanned the road behind for cars that might be following them. Traffic was moving as it should. Nevertheless, Janette began a circuitous route, making left then right turns onto side streets, doubling back. Seen from the air, the route would look like the path of a forgetful rat trying to find its way out of a maze. The scent of the subluminal remained. After about ten turns Janette nodded, as if she was now sure no one was following them. Amadeus hoped their would-be assassins had not placed a GPS tracker on her car.

Janette said she was driving them to an HQ that wasn't as movable as the others. After that, neither spoke.

Amadeus was glad to be in motion, on his way away from that horrible place and on to somewhere else, anywhere else. The adrenaline had begun to drain from his body, replaced by a tension that was only partly relieved by movement. The leather seat felt firm and good beneath him, and he focused his attention on the sensation, to keep at bay the agony that threatened to explode from his chest. For several minutes, lights blurred past, and grief began to replace his fear. Just as he had done when his mother finally passed away, Amadeus moved himself to a place without thought or voice, a place of only physical sensation. There he would've stayed all night, were it not for a voice in his mind that said:

Fear me not, killer of Takun.

18

The morning after the passage of the KREATURE Act, Grassal and Lilly stood shoulder-to-shoulder in the stuffy, crowded meeting room. At the request of Dr. Marx, every sound-minded patient had assembled there. According to a nurse Grassal spoke with just before the meeting began, two individuals were missing and three were catatonic and under supervision.

Even with the extra sleep, he still felt drained from the previous day's events. When Grassal was stressed, he slept, and now he could've used a few more hours in bed. Sleep didn't always help, but it was the one surefire way to forget his troubles. To make matters worse, the snow falling outside triggered in him a subconscious reflex that made him want to nestle up in a bed.

Two male and two female nurses flanked Dr. Marx as she strode to the podium at the front of the room. A glistening sheen of sweat was visible on her freshly shaved head, and before she spoke, she glanced down at her phone. She wore her white lab coat.

"The past two days have been trying for everyone. Last night was a regrettable incident, and I take full responsibility for what happened. As for South Carolina, as of now all my sources tell me this was an isolated incident. We have no reason to expect this will end our mission here. However, the KREATURE Act may place upon us additional administrative requirements."

A murmur of discontent swept the crowd like the rumble of an approaching locomotive. Dr. Marx made a swiping gesture with one hand, and the murmur dissipated. Grassal understood now why she had donned the coat for this meeting.

"I assure you that treatments will go as planned. As of now, I expect we'll be able to administer at least five nano-injections starting tomorrow. From there, we'll deploy the injections as fast as our manufacturers can supply them. If everything goes well, we'll have most of you home to your families within the next two to three weeks.

Grassal bit his tongue. She still hadn't mentioned the brain images, or the fact that everyone there was a terminal patient, himself included, forever dependent on drugs.

"And who gets the injections?" a woman asked. "How will you decide that?"

"The same way we chose who to bring here: a lottery. We'll draw names tonight. In fact," she said, nodding to a male nurse, "Liam here has all your names in a jar, ready to go."

"This is bullshit," a man said, calling out above the din of the crowd. "Why don't you set up triage care? We know what happened last night. Why don't they get treatment first?"

"If your name is drawn, then you're perfectly welcome to offer your injection to someone else. You'll still receive yours, but it might be later."

"You don't know," another man said. He was skinny, blond, and had an Adam's apple the size of a golf ball. "You have no idea what causes this, or what's happening to us, do you?" Dr. Marx scanned the room and found the man's eyes. She cast him a withering look and held his gaze. He returned it. "Admit it."

"We never said we knew the exact details of what was happening."

"What do you know that you're not telling us?" the first woman said. "There's more, isn't there?"

"I have done my best to communicate, in layman's terms,

what is happening to you."

Lilly elbowed Grassal. He looked at her and shook his head. Lilly cupped her hands around her mouth. Grassal tried to grab them, but he was too late.

"Your brains have changed," Lilly said. "I saw some of your MRIs. They look different." The doctor's expression was stoic. The crowd grumbled and demanded more information.

"What she said is true," Dr. Marx said. "But you're all intelligent people, and I'm sure none of you—"

Shouting and slamming doors in the lobby interrupted Dr. Marx's flow, but she picked back up and continued in the same vein that was simultaneously reassuring and cajoling.

Grassal, however, slipped out of the room to investigate. When he discovered the source of the sound in the lobby, his fists clenched and heat rose to his face. Two paramilitary soldiers held the doors open while three more marched five people into the lobby of The Admiral. Black hoods shrouded their faces and plastic handcuffs bound their wrists. Grassal guessed the tall, Aztec-looking guy was the leader of the goon squad. As Grassal watched, the Aztec forced the people down onto their knees. Grassal heard at least one woman and one man crying.

Even before he noticed the scars and amputations, Grassal understood what was happening: they were using the medical list to round up the afflicted and bring them here. With the KREATURE Act in place, they were able to take advantage of the situation he had created. As a shudder of horror rippled through his big body, Grassal realized he had created an internment camp.

Dr. Marx flung open the double doors of the meeting room. Grassal watched as she looked from the newly arrived afflicted to the soldiers and comprehension spread across her face. She addressed the Aztec. He replied in Spanish that she would need to speak to his superior. Dr. Marx shook her head. Grassal translated for her, then shook his own head at her lack of Spanish.

"Who is your superior?" Grassal asked. The Aztec replied. At first Grassal thought he had misheard, but the Aztec repeated himself, and Grassal was sure he understood the Aztec's Nahuatl-accented Spanish. With certainty, he said to Dr. Marx, "Petunia. He says his supervisor's name is Petunia." Dr. Marx was nonplussed.

"Ask him what the fuck they're doing here, and under whose authority they're operating."

Grassal did so. The Aztec gave Grassal a wide grin, revealing three gold teeth, before answering. Grassal suspected he would find *San Malverde* inked somewhere beneath his black tactical clothing.

"We are employed by Securaux."

"Roland Jessup's Securaux?"

The little soldier nodded, pulled a bowie knife from its sheath, and cut the plastic handcuffs that bound the hooded, kneeling figure before him. The figure, dressed in only a T-shirt and tighty-whities, pulled off his hood, revealing a full head of mussed blond hair. A mass of scar tissue covered his forearm. His eyes darted around the room in search of danger. Finding none, he stood. After a moment's scrutiny, he settled his gaze on Grassal.

"You! This is your fault." His accusing finger was aimed at Grassal's face, and his well-exercised body was tense, as if ready to spring an attack on Grassal, who made a placating gesture with his hands and spoke in his best conciliatory tone.

"No, I had—I have nothing to do with them." He pointed to the paramilitaries who stood in front of the doors.

"They came to my house, broke down my door, and pulled me out of bed while my wife slept beside me. I applied for your study. That's how they found me."

Dr. Marx came to Grassal's defense. "No, they found you because of your hospital records. He has nothing to do with this." She turned down the corners of her mouth like someone examining roadkill. "When you went in for treatment during the Emergence, your information went into a database shared by the major health insurers."

The other individuals had removed their hoods and got to their feet. They examined the lobby with fearful eyes, like cats dropped at a kennel. One, a man with hair dyed red and parted viciously to one side, had no sooner stood than he began drumming his fingers on his leg. Grassal caught the doctor's eye and inclined his head in the man's direction. She nodded, spoke into her collar radio, and a pair of nurses appeared to take the man into isolation.

Their charges unbound, the soldiers stood around for a minute, examining the details of the room. One walked back into Dr. Marx's office. Dr. Marx yelled and started to follow him, but two soldiers stood with their feet shoulder-width apart. She cursed them all, then addressed a flushed-faced soldier who stood a head taller than even Grassal.

"Fucking brutes. I want to talk to Petunia. Where is she?"

"Petunia is a male, and he is busy now. You talk later," the tall soldier said. Grassal judged from his accent he hailed from the Balkans, or maybe Russia, but he wasn't sure. The soldier who had gone into the office returned and gave his comrades a thumbs-up.

"When is later?" Dr. Marx said.

"Later is soon. We come back. Bring more crazy infected people for you." He turned to his fellows. They chuckled as they pushed out the door.

"It's *afflicted*," Grassal said. He tried to follow them out as they left. The last soldier pulled the door closed. Grassal tried the door and found it locked. He turned to Dr. Marx.

"Until I know anything more, policy remains the same. I can't just turn these people out."

Night marched on. Grassal stood in the lobby with Dr. Marx and watched as a revolving cast of soldiers brought in more afflicted. Lilly had long ago retired to her room with two bottles of merlot smuggled out of the kitchen. Grassal had taken it upon himself to count the new "admissions." So far, he was up to one hundred and fifty. Almost all were in their bed clothes, and all their stories were similar: pulled from their beds while they slept, guns trained on their families. A few were given a chance to dress. Grassal did the math. The Admiral had three hundred rooms. With the initial fifty patients, about half of whom had brought spouses, and the staff of fifteen, they would soon need to devise some kind of room-sharing policies.

At half past one, while snow peppered the windows, the lobby doors opened and two men stepped through. One was a soldier, dressed like the other ones in black tactical clothing, but the other wore a white suit with a purple tie. Before Grassal could say anything, Roland Jessup had his arms spread wide. He wore a grin even louder than his tie.

"Dr. Marjorie Marx, your operation is even better than anything I could've devised. It's a real pleasure to have true professionals like you on my team." Grassal pointed from Dr. Marx, then to Roland Jessup, and back to Dr. Marx.

"This guy, really?" Grassal said. He didn't know much about this Jessup character, but Grassal remembered he was a royal dick at the congressional hearing.

"Sometimes you have to befriend one wolf to keep the others at bay," Dr. Marx said. "But this, Roland, this is not what we agreed to."

"You said you were flexible. Since no innuendo was intended, I assumed that your mission was to provide compassionate care for these sick folks. I also assumed an adequate level of protection for those outside who may be subject to their ... well, let's be diplomatic and say their 'rambunctious tendencies.'"

"I can't handle all these people. And the way they've been brought in, it's inhumane—it's despicable."

"That's right," Grassal said. "This is supposed to be a free, voluntary clinic."

"It's still quite free. And you, Mr. Delgado. I'm really glad you were able to get on Dr. Marx's payroll. Since my company will be providing security services, we're now on the same team. Co-workers."

"Fuck you, Jessup. Dr. Marx, if this guy is involved with the project, then I quit."

"Spoken like a true member of the underclass, though I must say you've done a fair job of pulling on those bootstraps of yours. I recognize you're quite the talented script kiddie."

"Script kiddies just copy and paste. I write my own scripts."

"Every subculture has their distinctions, but I'm too far out of the loop to recognize. Forgive my imprecision."

"Grassal, you're not allowed to quit," Dr. Marx said. "And Roland, this goes so far beyond what I discussed with the senator."

"The senator is somewhat preoccupied with an internal leak, so she gave me the authority to go do God's will. And right now, I think that God's will is that I ensure the public's safety against your patients. To think, it could've been any of us, or any of our loved ones ... at least for those who still have loved ones."

"Just because the senator says jump—" Dr. Marx said.

"I determine the height of my own jumps, thank you very much. As I'm sure you're aware, as of today I have the authority under the Act to jump just as high as I want, especially in matters related to the Emergence. Since I don't see the local police or *your* outfit doing this, I thought that I could serve the public good and provide this service. All of us here, we have an interest in serving the public, do we not? You want to keep them healthy, you want to see them cured, and I want to ensure an adequate level of public safety."

"And deliver maximum value to your shareholders," Grassal said. Roland Jessup turned to Grassal and gave him a wide smile.

"Should not a man be compensated for his labors? But now

isn't the time for such discussions. I'm due for a siesta." He turned to the tall soldier beside him. The man had a teardrop tattooed on the side of his face. "This is Petunia. I was told you wanted to speak with him."

"I've learned what I need to know," Dr. Marx said.

"Nevertheless, you might as well get familiar with him. He'll be staying here to supervise operations."

"Operations?" Dr. Marx asked.

"You can't just have a bunch of mentally unstable time bombs running amok in a hotel. Someone has to provide security."

"Just because they passed the KREATURE Act—" Grassal started.

Jessup cut him off. "This bill is a fine example of a public-private partnership that will strengthen America. We are the vanguard of mutual cooperation that is the bedrock of good public policy."

"All these people here, cooped up together, it's not a good idea."

Jessup ignored this. Even now, Grassal felt that gnawing tug, and he wondered if smoking some tobacco would alleviate the feeling. Grassal listened to the world around him and counted at least four different languages being spoken among the soldiers.

He asked Jessup, "Why are all your goons foreigners?"

"Why, Mr. Delgado, you of all people, a first-generation American, should appreciate opportunity when you see it. I'm giving these men a chance to earn citizenship, to show that America rewards the strong and deserving." Jessup leaned in close and whispered into Grassal's ear. "Besides, US citizens can't get diplomatic immunity for this work." Jessup cast a salute to Petunia and marched toward the door, accompanied by a cadre of six soldiers. Before the door closed behind him, he stuck his head back inside and said, "I highly recommend you do keep things light here, and cut it with the Buddhism crap. It makes the senator nervous."

When Jessup left, Petunia, the Aztec, and six well armed, war-torn citizens-in-waiting remained.

The first fight began that day just after dinner. Ten afflicted men, all of whom had been dragged out of their homes during the previous night, had organized themselves. They attempted to overtake the guards in the lobby, but the men, soft and paunchy from years of office work, were no match for the soldiers. All ten were beaten bloody and restrained with plastic handcuffs. By the time Grassal arrived, four were catatonic and muttering. Dr. Marx and two nurses were tending the injuries of those who would let them.

Now that the fight was over, the soldiers were leaning against the door, looking self-satisfied. Their number had increased during the day, and now Grassal counted twelve, but four of the original six were elsewhere. A couple of them smoked cigarettes, unconcerned about the twenty-year-old indoor-smoking ban. Petunia's high cheekbones were still flushed from the exertion, and his eyes glimmered in the morning light. Grassal thought he looked entirely within his element. But, so did Grassal, or at least he should have; this was the element he had created. These goons had no right to be here. It was bad enough they had dragged in these people. Grassal couldn't just let them beat the patients—his patients—like they were rioting inmates. Flexing his fists, Grassal caught Petunia's eye and held his gaze as he strode toward him.

"What the fuck was that?"

"The fuck was what?" Petunia said, smiling. Grassal shook his head and pointed to the injured.

"They threaten safety of everyone. They try to break down doors. They must be disciplined."

"Discipline them? My God, these people are sick," Grassal said. "You can't just assault them. This is a clinic, not a prison."

"They attack us first," Petunia said, his Slavic smile as wide as the Danube.

"You dragged them out of their goddamned beds in the middle of the night. I think you would do the same."

Petunia shrugged and stepped outside. Grassal wasn't done, but when he tried to follow him, two goons blocked his path. They shook their heads and nodded toward the batons they held in their gloved hands. Grassal spat at their feet and crouched down beside Dr. Marx, who was examining one man's eyes.

"Classes are still on for today?" he asked, acknowledging the injured man with as warm a smile as he could muster. The man regarded him with a vacant, confused look.

"I offered Rumi overtime to quadruple his workload. For now, he's willing to help, but ..."

"But we're on the precipice here. I recognize that. Dr., tell me, when are we going to see full delivery of the injections?"

"The schedule is the same. We should receive ten to fifteen today, and maybe an equal number tomorrow."

"So, weeks ... I don't think we have that much time before things go bad, not with these guys here. Look at what happened to these men."

"Grassal, we're doing the best we can with what we have. Now, if you don't mind, we will continue this conversation some other time." Grassal saw nothing to gain from pressing her, so he stood and headed straight for the two soldiers positioned in the doorway that led to the dining room. He maintained his stride as he approached them, and they stepped aside so that he could pass. Of course, he knew that given a reason they would just as soon crack his skull as share a coffee with him, but Grassal had to at least show himself that he wouldn't be intimidated by stick-carrying thugs.

In the hallway, the black-haired snowman girl caught his arm. Her slate eyes darted this way and that, and she looked over her shoulder before she spoke.

"Are they really rounding people up?" she asked.

Grassal pursed his lips and nodded.

"So what do you intend to do about it?"

"Do? We intend to help as many people as we can; that's what we intend to do."

"No, you personally. You own this. I only signed up for this treatment because your name was attached to it, but being in a prison with armed guards was definitely not what I signed up for. So what I want to know, Grassal Delgado, is what are you going to do about the situation you created?"

"I don't want them here either, but right now they have a legal mandate to do exactly what they're doing."

"I hope you'll figure out what to do. We're counting on you, Grassal. Is the lottery still on?"

"Two hours to go."

Minutes before the lottery began that evening, a courier arrived at the front doors with an aluminum box chained to his wrist. The soldiers permitted him to enter. Grassal watched as Dr. Marx examined the contents—twenty-five plastic hypodermic syringes—before signing for it and asking Grassal to lock them in her office.

The lottery was conducted in the meeting room and broadcast over The Admiral's internal television network. As she was judged the person least likely to inflame negative passions, Lilly was chosen to conduct the drawing of names. Dr. Marx, Grassal, and several self-selected patient representatives had debated whether or not to include the newly arrived in the lottery. Some said they should even receive priority as compensation for the degrading way in which they were brought here. In the end, they reached consensus: there would be two lotteries, one for the initial fifty, and one for the newly arrived. No one was entirely satisfied, but most agreed it was the fairest solution.

Minutes after the lottery concluded, Dr. Marx dispatched her nurses to the rooms of the winners. By dinner-time, the injections had been administered. Rumi Soon continued his breathing classes. A schedule was established and distributed for the next week. A handful of younger patients, led by the girl with slate eyes, built another snowman in the enclosed courtyard. Yet, despite the apparent return to routine, discontent had spread through The Admiral, and the patients had voiced their complaints to anyone outside who would listen. As a result, the story of The Admiral had spread. Reporters and throngs of protestors, the latter incensed by the passage of the KREATURE Act, had assembled outside The Admiral's doors. Inside, the patients taunted, shouted at, and even spit upon the soldiers, but the soldiers showed restraint and took action only when necessary to keep the patients away from the lobby doors and inside the hotel.

For his part, Grassal was happy to supply Annie with information about the roundups and the situation inside The Admiral, and on a call, he did just that. He told her how the soldiers had treated the afflicted. He explained how he and Dr. Marx had opposed any kind of mandated treatment or quarantine. He shared with her his general displeasure with the sight of armed individuals at his clinic. Annie said the anti-Brunmeier contingent was gaining more support each day, and a large minority of people now believed that a semi-permanent quarantine of the afflicted was in their best interest. Given the footage of the creepy human formation that had circulated, he supposed he could understand this sentiment. Before he ended the call, Grassal told Annie a story his *abuela* had told him about paramilitary roundups of dissidents in Medellin so many years ago. She said she'd try to work in a quote.

In the evening, while he and Lilly dined on fried eggs and buttered bread, Petunia's voice came on the PA. "I am sad to say that you must now have curfew. Everybody must be in room by eight o'clock." Disgruntled murmurs rippled through the crowd.

"That's five minutes from now," Grassal said. Lilly balled up her paper napkin and threw it on the table.

"Fuck them. They're going to have to drag me upstairs. I'm going to finish my dinner."

"Then they'll be dragging two of us."

"Thanks, Grassal." Lilly dabbed the corners of her mouth with the balled-up napkin. "But before we get dragged away, I'd like to see what's going on. Over the past few days, I've tried to ignore the worst of what's happening, as if that will make things any better, but you know what? I need to face this head on. Join me?" Grassal nodded.

With one minute remaining until Petunia's curfew, they walked toward the front lobby, now overrun by Securaux staff. Grassal counted at least twenty of them, including three women. Two soldiers stepped in front of Grassal when he tried to enter. Grassal tried again to push through, but they only shook their heads.

"I think you forget who I am," he said.

"Curfew is for all. Patients and staff."

At that moment, a door that led from the lobby to the conference room opened, and Grassal saw inside another formation of afflicted people. He recognized a few of them. He heard them, too; their rhythmic, muttered chants echoed across the black-and-white marble floor. Ignoring the nicotine craving and the soldiers who were telling him to leave, he craned his neck for a better view and caught a clearer glimpse of the scene. The afflicted were in a human cube formation. A blue arc of current crackled between a soldier's baton and the afflicted, and Grassal realized they were using shock batons on the cube people.

"You can't do that to them!" Grassal cried out. He sprinted forward and was rewarded with a shoulder-check from a big sub-Saharan African man.

"Go away. No more warnings," a female soldier said. She was a head taller than Grassal and just as stout.

"This is, no—" The female soldier drove a roundhouse kick into Grassal's side. Grassal stumbled. Lilly caught his arm.

Grassal regained himself and brushed off his clothes. Feigning a sheepish, apologetic smile, Grassal bent his knees in preparation for a lunge, but before he made contact, two metal rods touched his sides.

A needling pain followed by electric white heat sent him into convulsions as his body's fluids conducted the crackling current through his every afflicted cell. When a throbbing ache replaced the convulsions, he collapsed to the floor. A kick to the ribs kept him on his hands and knees. Grassal's blurry gaze leveled on Petunia, who smiled as he wagged a single finger at Grassal.

"You're not in charge here anymore. Now be good boy and go to your room. You too, little lady."

Grassal considered for a moment attempting to tackle Petunia, but he felt like he was coming out of sleep paralysis. While trying to stand, his right leg gave out and his face slammed against the floor.

"Fuck you, you mouth-breathing, sheep-fucking piece of donkey shit," Lilly said, her hands balled into fists.

"She is cute, no?" Petunia said. His soldiers, men and woman alike, rewarded him with approving nods. "Little lady, you have no idea what war can be like." A lurid smile spread across his cherubic face, forming wrinkles around his bright blue eyes, and he took a step toward Lilly.

Grassal's heart clenched.

"War? This isn't war, you damn meathead. This is a fucking clinic," Lilly said, stomping one foot. This brought another round of laughter. The tension in the room decreased a millimeter. Lilly appeared perplexed by Petunia's sudden conciliatory tones.

"We are here to prevent war, little lady. You do not believe me, so I tell you what war is like. When I was little boy during real war, rebels come to my house. First, they kill my father and brothers. Then they rape my mother. Then they kill her too. I was next, but government forces come and kill rebels. Now I am only one left."

Grassal reeled. Not what he had expected. The synapses in his head still tingled. He wondered if the combination of the electricity and the affliction was causing misfires in his mental firmware. Lilly was still, her eyes unreadable and fixed on Petunia as she listened to his story.

"They died because we were weak. My city, the police, the government. The rebels were idiots, but they were strong idiots. Because we had no way to match them, there was more suffering. You see, little lady, the people who deal with danger must be strong. These people are dangerous. Your government know this, and pay us because we are strong. If we are not strong, terrible things might happen. It is my hope that you can understand."

"I'm sorry for what happened to you, truly I am," Lilly said. "But look at yourself, Petunia. You're just repeating the cycle, pulling people out of their homes and locking them up."

"I admit this is unfortunate for tiny number, yes, but this way they no hurt themselves or their families. Would you rather we let a father beat his child into bloody paste? Or bring the father here for keeping safe?"

"That's not how this works and you know it."

"Nobody knows nothing. Except that these sick people are dangerous. They are dangerous because they get bit by subluminals. My job is to defend against subluminal attack. These are indirect type of subluminal attack."

Lilly's face darkened. "Attacks by proxy ... that's such bullshit." She turned on her heel and left the lobby. After casting one more suspicious glance toward the soldiers, Grassal followed her. Most of the feeling had returned to his right side, but between the remaining numbness and the challenge of walking on a prosthetic, Grassal's gait was still unsteady. Lilly didn't acknowledge him or his efforts to hobble alongside her, but that was only because she was muttering to herself. Grassal gave up trying to follow the disjointed thread of her self-conversation. In the elevator, he realized he had forgotten to take his morning dose, and he told Lilly he needed to go to his room.

"What?" Lilly said. Grassal repeated himself. "Oh, drugs, you need drugs. Got it." She ran two hands through her hair then looked up at Grassal. "I'll be by your room later. I have an idea."

19

Amadeus tried and failed to convince himself that the voice in his head was his own.

"Pull over. I think a subluminal is with us," Amadeus said. Janette gave him a wordless, affirmative nod and steered the SUV off the boulevard and onto the cracked pavement of a fuel station. As her eyes scanned rearview mirrors and the dark edges of the parking lot, she wrapped slender fingers around her pistol. By the time the SUV had come to a smooth stop, they were out of the car. Janette held a shotgun while Amadeus peered under the car.

Fear me not, Takun hunter, the voice said again. It sounded like a composite of several human voices carried on the wind, amorphous and flowing like water rushing over river stones. Amadeus couldn't tell if he was hearing the voice with his ears or his mind. He knew only that it came from outside himself.

"What is this, a Chinese fire drill?" a voice said. Three men emerged from the dim side of the gas station. One reached into his shirt, removed a revolver, and held it casually in his hand. They spread out, and Janette moved so that she could keep the one with the revolver in front of her and the SUV in her peripheral vision. The man with the revolver had the sunken cheeks and pocked skin of a meth addict. The other two, with their narrow-set eyes, neck tattoos inked in Old English script, and shaved heads, could've been twins. Janette looked them over and shook her head. The expression on her face was almost regretful.

They intend harm. Leave here now, the voice said. Amadeus looked around and realized no one else had heard it.

"That's an awful nice car you and your auntie got there," Meth said. "A little pea shooter, too. Why don't you two stick around for awhile and party with us? Or maybe just give us the keys."

Despite the danger his rational mind knew he was in, the events of this evening had drained Amadeus of anything other than sheer anger and defiance. Amadeus held Meth's gaze, took a step forward, and said, "Fuck off."

Meth's eyes widened, his nostrils flared, and he waved the pistol at Amadeus' face. Unflinching, unblinking, Amadeus looked at Meth and smiled.

Janette's pistol clicked as she turned off the safety and trained the gun on Meth. "Lower your weapon and back away," Janette said in her owning-the-room voice. "We're leaving now. Amadeus, get back in the car."

Meth hesitated. "Amadeus?" Meth said. "As in the hero fag-boy Amadeus Brunmeier? The one I saw on the news?"

"Did you not hear me?" Janette said. "Lower. Your. Weapon."

His companions looked at Meth, who narrowed his eyes. "I'm not scared to die. But maybe the little hero is. My gun is aimed at his face. You do anything, I smoke him, and my boy smokes you. But it don't have to be like that. We'll settle for your vehicle. Charlie." One of the twins pulled a revolver from the back of his pants, albeit reluctantly, and aimed it at Janette.

She ignored him. Her hand was as steady as stone.

The pistol shook in Charlie's hand.

"Looks like we've got ourselves a Mexican standoff," Meth said. "Gimme the keys."

"You really don't want that car," Amadeus said. "It smells

awful. It's better if you just walk away from here."

"Actually, they can have it. It's just a government car. We'll walk, Amadeus. I'm sure these men need it and its contents more than we do," Janette said. She lowered her weapon. Amadeus wanted to protest that they were probably going to kill them anyway, but he held his tongue.

"Yeah, it's our tax dollars, bitch," Meth said. He spat, ground it under his heel, and smacked his chest. "Our money."

"If that's a government car," Charlie said, "then you know they're tracking that shit."

Amadeus looked at Janette, who said, "Probably."

He suddenly understood her angle. It was dangerous, and it might not work ...

The voice Amadeus now attributed to the creature whispered, *I will help.* Amadeus wondered if his sanity had grown wings and flown off into the night.

"That's not quite right," he said. "Excuse me for contradicting you, but there is *definitely* a tracker installed. I, for one, should know about trackers."

"What's so funny?" Meth said. He wagged the gun at Amadeus like someone flicking water from a spoon. "Stop fucking smiling. You think this is a fucking joke?" Amadeus forced his smile down. Meth's eyes flicked to the weaponless twin, then he nodded toward Amadeus. The weaponless twin took two steps forward and punched Amadeus with a machine-fast jab. Amadeus moved his head just fast enough so that the punch missed his nose and caught his cheekbone. He reeled but kept his balance.

The world went white for a moment, then he was adrift in the ocean. A voice in the distance said, "The tracker, that fucking tracker. Where is it?" Amadeus gestured in the general direction of the SUV then mustered his focus and croaked out a reply.

"The back, it's in the back," Amadeus said.

"Give me the keys. Let's see what's in there," Meth said.

Amadeus caught Janette's eye. She still had her finger on the trigger. He thought he saw the tiniest hint of excitement in her eyes. She nodded toward the driver's side door.

"The keys are up front," she said. Meth opened the driver's door, reached inside with one arm, and pulled the jingling keys from the ignition, never allowing the pistol in his other hand to waver from Amadeus, who had hoped to see the creature's silhouette darting behind tinted glass but was disappointed.

"What the fuck are you ... it smells like a fucking corpse in there. I'll have to buy a bunch of those fucking pine trees and shit."

"Government cars," Janette said for explanation.

"The remote keychain for the back doesn't work," Amadeus said. "You'll have to use the key. It's the little one."

"I know which one it is," Meth said. He handed his gun to the twin who had punched Amadeus. He aimed it at Amadeus with far more confidence than Charlie, who was blinking like he was trying to expel a dust mote from his eyes.

Meth smiled at his companions, slid the key into the lock, and lifted the back hatch. His eyes grew wide and he put one hand over his mouth. A flash of gray shot from the trunk and knocked Meth to the ground. He screamed until the creature tore open his throat with its mouth. With its back legs, it tore open Meth's chest cavity and sent bloody viscera flying. The twins had turned to run before Meth's guts hit the ground. Janette trained her weapon on the creature. Amadeus put his hand up, motioning for her to hold, and examined the subluminal.

Gray, brown, and green hexagonal patterns covered its smooth, salamander-like skin. At the end of each of its slender, triple-jointed legs were manipulators that looked like a cloven hoof grafted onto the back of a hawk's talon. The creature's neckless head was shaped like that of a mantis. Yellow, green, and violet eyes stuffed close together like caviar covered the base of its neck like a collar. From there, the eyes extended up to the crown of its head, where they converged around a throbbing, lumpy gray and black blob the size of cantaloupe.

When it finished tearing Meth's head and torso apart, a long, black tongue lolled from its wide, lipless mouth filled with gray, pinpoint teeth. Chunks of flesh and bone were strewn in every direction. Only Meth's arms and legs remained. The demon shuddered and turned toward Amadeus, making tuneless sounds like a birdsong or a child's whistling. Janette took a step toward the car but maintained her aim.

"Don't shoot it," Amadeus said.

"How did you know what it would do?"

"I know it sounds crazy, but ... it talked to me."

The creature drew itself up on two legs, raised its forelegs over its many-eyed head in a U shape, and then leaned back like a person stretching. It turned to Janette and repeated the gesture. She regarded it without expression.

All you see is all I am, the creature's voice said, and Amadeus remembered where he had heard it. This was the same voice he and Grassal had heard back at the Jones compound.

"Did you hear it?" Amadeus asked Janette. She shook her head without taking her aim off the creature.

Our interests align. A few moments passed. A siren's wail drew closer.

"What do you want?" Amadeus said aloud. He put his hands to his temples and shook his head. Gravity was dead, and he was talking to a subluminal. This thing shouldn't be able to communicate. But it shouldn't have helped him either, and Gravity shouldn't be dead.

Travel from here. Now move quickly. More talk later.

"Did it answer you?"

Amadeus knew his face was white. He nodded. "It ... it wants to go with us. It says our interests align."

"Tell it to get in the back." Before Amadeus said anything, the creature leapt into the cargo area and pulled the hatch shut behind it. The movement was no louder than a finger scraping wet sand.

"I wasn't expecting that," Amadeus said.

Janette tossed the keys to Amadeus. "Sometimes your best allies are the most unlikely ones. But that doesn't mean I won't kill it if I have to."

Inside the vehicle, Amadeus started the engine and adjusted his mirrors to keep an eye on the back of the SUV. Janette sat facing the rear of the vehicle, pistol ready.

"What are you?" Amadeus said to the creature.

I am Vaskulo, the demon said. *I am Takun.*

"Ask it how our interests align," Janette said. Amadeus started to speak, but the voice began before he could form the words.

Against our will, Takun arrived here. We desire return.

"And why come to me?" Amadeus said.

We fear you. We embrace fear. We respect you. You killed Takun. We understand why. You were ignorant. Now you know: Takun have souls. You have guilt. Lover suspects you. You seek redemption.

"How do you know that?" Amadeus said. The thought of something so vile and alien peering into his mind and knowing his troubles ... He clenched the steering wheel. A tractor-trailer blew past them. Its gust made the vehicle shake. Amadeus repeated his question, but the creature said nothing for several minutes. Janette only blinked and stared at the back of the SUV. If the subluminals, the Takun, had consciousness, then all those that were killed ...

Leave the highway.

"It says to get off the road," Amadeus said to Janette.

"Then do it. There's an exit ramp just over this rise."

As Amadeus left the highway, he saw the flashing lights of a roadblock a kilometer on down the interstate. The ramp was clear.

"The fuck?" Amadeus said under his breath.

I see far. Trust me, seeker.

"Why should I trust a demon?" Amadeus said.

Unfortunate signifier choice. Takun aren't demons. We are manifestations, assembled from dreams, birthed from imagination. My true body exists in elsewhere. Turn left now.

Amadeus did as he was told. His stomach twisted when he realized he was taking orders from a demon. The buildings along the avenue changed gradually from brown brick row houses and apartment blocks to sprawling retail towers illuminated by yellow sodium lights. The texture of their walls reminded Amadeus of the inside of a cave. Traffic thinned and he had the road to himself.

"Where are we going?" Amadeus said.

You seek truth. For your lover. I provide truth. You grant trust. Cooperation flowers here. Marshall Hathaway's home. We go there. He has information. You know him. Black-eyed man. He will help. Turn right now.

"It's telling me that the black-eyed man will help us," Amadeus said, not believing the words coming out of his mouth.

"Depends on how you define *help*. There are ways to facilitate information collection," Janette said, "but they're not pretty."

"Vaskulo," Amadeus said, "how do you know this?"

Takun share eyes. Takun share ears. Takun trade whispers.

"I don't know about this, but if it's right ... Janette, you said you still have a network of people available. Could you send a team in there?"

"I could arrange something. It might take a few hours."

This is undesirable. Hathaway departs soon. Time is short.

"I don't know if you know this or not, but we've just—"

Hathaway plans killings. Today's plan killed your friend Owens. The creature growled. Amadeus felt the floorboards rumble. *Visit him now.*

"Fuck," Amadeus said. "Fuck. Fuck. It says we need to go to Hathaway's right now. I think that's what these directions are. I don't ... we only have one pistol between us."

"That's not exactly right." Janette leaned behind her and

pulled the middle seat forward. Amadeus heard latches unfastening and a metal case opening. "We're actually pretty well equipped. At this point, do we have any better options?"

Silence filled the SUV as Vaskulo directed them into a housing development called Piney Woods. Amadeus pulled to a stop in front of a split-level brick house where a silver van sat in the driveway. A tarp covered another vehicle Amadeus couldn't identify.

He is inside.

From the case, Janette retrieved a sawed-off shotgun with a pistol grip. She handed it to Amadeus.

You want revenge.

Amadeus wasn't sure if this was a question or a statement. He rubbed his thumb over his scar in a circular motion.

"Yes, but we need information more. Did this man kill Jones?"

This remains unclear. Proximity yields understanding.

Amadeus scanned the yard and the house. Light bled from a basement window. "I think he's downstairs."

"Exfiltration," former General Janette Nguyen said, "is always dangerous, especially if this is the same black-eyed man you know and love. But if that thing's right, it could be the break we both need. Are you ready, A.B.?"

"As I'll ever be."

20

That night, from his room on the twelfth floor of The Admiral, Grassal gazed out at long rows of apartment towers arranged like dominoes. A floating billboard bobbed beneath a waxing crescent moon and implored residents to "try Solvolenta, New Columbia's premier solution to fatigue and general malaise." The air in the room was stale, so Grassal started toward the window with the intention of allowing in fresh air, but Lilly grabbed his shirt, shoved him into the bathroom, and turned the bathtub's handle. He felt himself stiffen. As steam began rolling from the shower, she pulled him close and whispered into his ear.

"It's for bugs," Lilly said. Her gaze darted around the tiny bathroom. "We set off a fire alarm."

"That's your plan?" He thought this was a horrible plan.

"Yes, and it'll work, too. When the alarm goes off, the doors will disengage, and everyone will leave at once. They can stop a few people, but they don't have enough guards to keep everyone inside, and with all the people outside, all the escapees will be able to blend right in."

"I think that's a bad idea. What if they override the locks and we end up with a bunch of panicked afflicted in the lobby?"

"Grassal, we've got to try. No one has the right to keep people here like this—I don't care how fucked up they are. And as for me, I will not be a prisoner again."

"I'm not fucked up," Grassal said, then thought about the past week and frowned. "Okay, maybe I am. And what do you intend to do with your Mauser? I know you brought it. Open fire on the soldiers? Or afflicted?"

"No, no, no. The first would be suicide, the second would be murder. I brought it with me because it's something I'd rather have and not need than need and not have. Besides, I'm not about to leave it here. I do know how to use it, but I hope I never have to."

"I hope you don't either."

"Grassal, this is all beside the point. What matters is that we have to show them they can't do this. I mean, think what would happen if a real fire broke out. We'd be trapped. We'd burn alive," Lilly said, patting Grassal's shoulder before shutting off the shower and walking out of the bathroom.

"I still think it's dangerous."

"It's only a drill. You have any better ideas?"

Grassal slouched and shook his head.

Lilly smiled at Grassal as she ran her fingers over the fire alarm's red plastic housing. She asked if he was ready. He lifted the handle of his brown canvas backpack, and looked at her own bag. He hoped no one would notice that he was packed and ready for travel. He further hoped that no one would realize or suspect Lilly was carrying a pistol and ten rounds of ammunition.

To save time, they had skipped lunch, but in his backpack Grassal had packed some salami, cheese, and apples he had liberated from the kitchen that morning. He would have time to eat soon enough.

Lilly pulled the alarm's white handle. Nothing happened. She tried again, lifting the handle up and down as if trying to draw water from a pump. Grassal scanned both directions of the hallway. He half-expected some authority figure to throw open a door, place a hand on his shoulder, and ask them just what they thought they were doing.

"Let's go, Lilly. Come on. We can't stay here. There might be a silent alarm." Lilly nodded. They ducked into the stairwell and climbed two flights back to their floor. Just outside the stairwell door, he saw another fire alarm lever. He pulled it for the sheer hell of pulling it. The sudden cry of the alarm made him jump and shake his hand as if he had touched something hot.

"Shit," Grassal said. They returned to the stairs and started making their way down. Others joined them. By the time they reached the lobby, people crushed against them. Some mumbled to themselves, others surveyed the room with nervous, darting eyes. In the lobby, a row of guards stood in front of the doors, electric batons held before them. Petunia climbed onto the wooden counter and addressed the crowd.

"There is no fire. This is child's prank. Everybody please return to your rooms." Grassal tried and failed to locate Dr. Marx.

While Petunia repeated his announcement, Rumi Soon pushed his way forward and beseeched Petunia with both hands. "You do not have the right to hold us here. No one consented to this."

"Your elected representatives did. If I am understanding your system correctly, government exists with the consent of the governed, no?"

"What if this was a real fire?" Rumi said. "In a prison there's a yard. We don't even have that. Are we less important than convicted criminals?"

"This is no prison, so is safe. We stay inside. We maintain operational integrity."

Rumi's face was red despite his placid expression. "We are indeed prisoners here. This confirms it." He took a step toward Petunia and assumed a martial arts stance.

The same soldier who had fought with Grassal now strode

toward Rumi and swung the baton at his neck. Rumi batted it away and countered with a low kick, which she rolled beneath. As she sprang to her feet behind him, she slammed the baton into the base of his spine. His arms flailed and he collapsed to the floor. Blood dripped from his mouth. The snowman girl knelt beside Rumi and held his head.

"Shame on you," she said to the soldier, who regarded her with an iron expression. The alarm kept wailing. The snowman girl pointed to two men. "You two, help me get him out of here." They rushed forward and carried Rumi from the lobby.

Someone yelled that they smelled smoke. A murmur passed through the crowd. A woman in a pantsuit began to make guttural noises that sounded like a cross between a sputtering engine and a vomiting dog. The crowd took a collective step backwards, creating a circle around her. She gazed at the ceiling with yellow eyes. Her dilated opal pupils were the size of quarters.

"I repeat. There is no fire," Petunia said. "Go back to your rooms before we use force."

"She's spacing," a man's voice said. The woman clenched and unclenched her fists. A man outside the circle dropped to his knees and emitted a single tone like a low-pitched test frequency. The woman switched to a single note, and together, their voices blended like two cello strings coming into tune. Once they achieved sympathetic resonation, their voices became a droning mutter of nonsense phonemes.

People around Grassal pushed and jostled, and Grassal felt himself being moved backwards. Grassal grabbed Lilly's hand and pulled himself closer to her. She squeezed his palm. He saw fear in her eyes, but something else as well. The snowman girl appeared on the balcony overlooking the lobby. She held a wet towel over her face. After she had caught and held Grassal's gaze, the snowman girl leaned over the oak banister and addressed the crowd.

"The fire's on the second floor. First, they round us up, and then they try to burn us alive. Remind you of anything?" Grassal heard a few "amens" and murmurs of agreement. "We need to move. We can't let them hold us here like this. Fight them!" The crowd roared with something close to righteous bloodlust.

Grassal saw a group of men fall on two or three soldiers. The remaining eight soldiers maintained a perimeter in front of the door, holding their crackling batons before them like obsessed, harpoon-wielding whalers awaiting their cetacean nemeses. For the moment, most of the crowd was holding back, but Grassal noticed a plastic potted palm being passed from hand to hand over their collective heads. A few individuals grasped steel chairs with clenched fists.

"Shit," Lilly said. "Shit, shit, shit. This is not what I had in mind." She scanned the room for a better position. "Over there, let's get against the wall. This is about to get ugly." Four men and a woman dashed forward toward the guards. All were hit with shock batons. All dropped to the floor and began to writhe. The blond man who had been dragged in wearing only tighty-whities was the first to get back to his feet.

Though the soldiers had repelled them easily enough, they tightened their formation and closed ranks, leaving the pair of doors nearest the desk unguarded. Someone threw the plastic potted palm at the unguarded door. Palm and pot bounced off the door.

A few people cursed, then an obese woman in biker leather dashed forward and attempted to bludgeon the Aztec with a chair. A pair of guards jammed their batons into her flesh. Her muscles seized and she dropped. The chair clattered to the floor. Three men responded by charging the guards who had attacked the big woman. Three others tackled the Aztec. Two men held him on the floor while the third kicked his sides. The other guards reacted by shocking first the three and then everyone else in their immediate vicinity. More people joined the melee. In moments, all the soldiers were trying to fend off two or three people each. A couple soldiers had lost their batons to the crowd.

With the soldiers distracted and a second pair of doors clear, the remainder of the crowd charged forward. Their bodies pressed against the locked doors, a human flood assaulting a glass and steel levee. A woman in a red knit sweater was using the leather-clad woman's chair to pummel the doors. She could work at it all day, but Grassal knew it wouldn't shatter. The glass was too thick.

Lilly and Grassal stayed back. Lilly yelled to him, but Grassal couldn't hear her over the alarm and the cries of the crowd. He shrugged, and she pointed to the stairwell. Thick pillows of smoke tumbled down the stairs. The fire was consuming the floors above them. They had only minutes until it reached the lobby.

In the back of the crowd, the number of people spacing had grown to about ten. Most of their voices matched the utterances of the first two, and Grassal heard even more cello strings coming into tune. Grassal felt the nicotine-craving pull, took a deep breath, felt calm return, and devised a plan.

Two pairs of thick, rectangular glass doors ten meters on either side flanked a revolving door in the center. Grassal scanned for an emergency release button, lever, latch, battery, or something, but he'd be damned if he saw one. Neither latch, lock, nor keyhole was apparent. Only unpainted steel U-braces a hand long and attached to hinges held the glass in place. The U-braces probably held an armature, with a fail-secure electromagnetic lock built into the doorframe. Given a current, the armature would break the electromagnet's hold.

Grassal remembered the screen he had seen on the wall in Dr. Marx's office. He tugged Lilly's coat and pointed to the desk. The journey through the shoulder-to-shoulder crowd would be measured in millimeters, and along the way they'd have to pass through the spacers. With one hand, Grassal pushed through, parting the dense crowd. With the other, he held on to Lilly's. Nobody noticed or cared when he jostled them. If they weren't spacing, they were too focused on the drama unfolding around them.

Upstairs, something snapped and crashed. Smoke slipped from the cracks of a doorframe and out across the ceiling, creating a thick cloud a full head high. Lilly had pulled up her shirt to cover her face from the fire's chemical smell.

Something slammed into Grassal's neck and he cried out in pain. The spacers in the crowd began to thrash and claw at Grassal, ignoring Lilly. Grassal drew them sideways, away from Lilly, and covered his head with his backpack, not that it did much good. Punches, kicks, and slaps came from every direction.

Grassal's legs began to quiver and twitch. If he lost his footing, he'd be trampled. He needed to make a path. He swung a fist into a man's vacant face, and the man tumbled to the floor. Grassal gained a meter but immediately lost it when a hand yanked him backward by the shirt. Stumbling, he saw an old man pulling on his prosthetic. Grassal twisted and stomped the man's forearm with his natural leg.

Ignored by the hostile spacers, Lilly had almost reached the desk. The snowman girl was also there. She was squatting on the counter, fending off a pair of spacers with a shock baton.

Hands, first one, then two, then three, grasped Grassal's backpack. With a series of well-placed head butts and groin kicks, he wrested it free. The attack was unrelenting, but it lacked any cunning, and Grassal thought he would be able to hold against it for some time. At least, that's what he thought until a plastic potted palm smashed against his head, his knees buckled, his backpack was pulled from his hands, and the room filled with white.

Grassal opened his eyes to see Lilly's hands locked over his belly and four pairs of clenched fists pummeling his chest like a chest-side Swedish massage from hell. He felt himself being hit, but he no longer felt any pain. As Lilly shoved him ahead, Grassal understood she was using him as a combination plow and shield. Snowman girl was assisting Lilly by clearing her path with the shock baton. Their task was made easier because the initial press that had been attacking them had dwindled. Most of their earlier attackers were now fully, squarely in spacing mode. Grassal tried to bring his arms up to provide for their common defense from the remaining attackers, but his synapses were still misfiring, and his arms only flapped and jerked like a marionette's.

"You've got stones, girl," Grassal said to the snowman girl. "Well done." His tongue was thick but he got the words out. She winked at him.

From somewhere over their heads came the sound of splintering, rending wood. Two of the attackers stopped punching them and entered full-spacing mode. Lilly kicked one of their remaining attackers in the knee. He dropped. Though Grassal felt as uncoordinated as poor Amadeus, he still had girth, and this he used to body check the last attacker, an athletic teenage boy whose head crashed against the long mahogany check-in desk. The boy wheezed, curled into a ball on the floor, and began to seethe.

Now that Grassal had room to breathe and move, he surveyed the room. Bedlam. About half the patients were spacing while the other half were fighting with the guards or pounding on the clear glass doors. Grassal heard the crackling of electricity and occasionally saw a flickering blue electric arc. Some people gazed in from the street outside, but because of the angle, the reflections, and the blowing snow, Grassal couldn't tell if they were Securaux guards or civilians. Flames licked from two of the vents, the room smelled of burned plastic, and Grassal was sure he had felt the floor beneath him rumble and shudder.

Lilly had just pulled herself up into a sitting position on the desk when a gunshot drew the attention of everyone with conscious awareness. The fighting stopped and the shouting died down.

The spacers' monotonous mutterings were the only sound in the room. Dr. Marjorie Marx stood on the balcony overlooking the lobby. She held a snub-nosed revolver in her hand, her eyes a controlled burn. The Aztec was dead at her feet.

"As a representative of the agency overseeing this operation, I demand you open the doors." She strode across the balcony, down the stairs, and toward Petunia. At the bottom, the members of the crowd who were still cognizant parted for her. "If you want to stay and die in order to maintain operational integrity, you may do so."

"And let this outside?" Petunia said. He had one hand wrapped around a man's throat. Another lay crumpled and unconscious at his feet. "This is not possible. The sprinklers will work soon."

Dr. Marx fired another shot into the ceiling then leveled her pistol at Petunia.

"I said open these doors so that I may evacuate my patients. I'm not asking again."

"We are in control here, not you. We will stay here until there are—"

Dr. Marx squeezed the trigger. A spiderweb crack blossomed in the door glass just above Petunia's head. He didn't flinch. Part of the ceiling over the balcony opened and a flaming tangle of wires tumbled free. Dr. Marx frowned, and she made eye contact with Grassal just before Petunia pulled a semiautomatic pistol from his waistband and shot her in the chest. She fell to the ground in a heap. An anguished cry escaped Grassal's mouth, the room emitted a collective scream of anger, and a large group rushed first Petunia and then the door where the crack had appeared. In a matter of seconds, Petunia was on the floor amid a mass of thrashing, flailing legs and arms. Snowman girl fell on him with her baton.

Grassal didn't care about Petunia's fate, but poor Dr. Marx ...

He had to do right by her now. With Lilly's help, he climbed over the counter, knocking a brochure rack to the floor. Behind the desk, he found a dummy terminal, but it only contained the reservation system. A young woman cowered at the end of the desk closest to the doors. Grassal walked over to her while Lilly ran back to check the office door. She wore an Admiral nametag that read, "Stephanie."

"Office is locked," Lilly said.

"Stephanie, can you unlock the doors?" Grassal said. "Can you do it?" Stephanie stared at him with wide eyes and held a balled fist in front of her face. Grassal repeated himself.

"I don't know. No. I'm new. I started just before they closed the hotel. I ... I only did check-ins. They told me I had to come back or they'd cut off my unemployment."

"Okay, girl, think. What about the manager's office? Can you get in there?" Grassal said. The woman said nothing. Grassal crouched so that he could be eye level with her.

"Everything was always unlocked when I was here. God, I don't want to die."

"Nobody's going to die, but you have to help me. How about an office key?"

"Um ... um ... I don't know." Lilly pushed Grassal aside and stood over the girl.

"Listen, you sniveling, whimpering little child," Lilly said. "Do you want to die in here?" Stephanie said nothing. "Because you will. If you don't come up with something, we're all going to die." The woman began to cry. "But you won't die like the rest of us. You won't make it that long. Because I will strangle you."

"Lilly, please!" Grassal said. "She's scared. You're not helping. Stop." Lilly narrowed her eyes, shot a glance at the girl, and nodded. She put two fingers to her temples and took a deep breath. Grassal wiped sweat from his brow.

"The drawer. On the end," Stephanie said, pointing toward Lilly. "Where your crazy friend is. There's a key ring in there." Lilly pulled open the nearest drawer and dumped out the contents. Tape, paper clips, receipts, and restaurant coupons fell to the floor. "No, the one next to it." Lilly opened that drawer and pulled out something that looked like a teenager's charm bracelet.

"There are a hundred keys here!" Lilly said.

"I ... I think it's got a rectangular head," Stephanie said. Lilly tried a few keys, cursed, then threw the whole jingling ring at Stephanie. Grassal thought he heard a siren, but with all the other sounds filling his head, he couldn't be sure.

"Find it," Lilly said.

Stephanie began thumbing through the keys. Grassal stood up while she looked. He opened a door that led down a hallway, then turned as another chunk of the lobby ceiling collapsed. A girder pinned one of the spacers to the ground. Lilly pushed Grassal into the hallway. Four doors, two on either side, lined the hallway. Grassal tried all of them. All locked. Stephanie called out to them from in front of a now-open office door. Grassal raised his eyebrows and congratulated her.

"I picked the one that was worn from use."

"First-class thinking. Sorry about her," Grassal said. Lilly scowled at him. Stephanie scurried away from them.

Dr. Marx's setup had been augmented by an array of monitors, which displayed input from cameras situated around the hotel. Several of the screens showed static. Others showed flames climbing up the walls.

Grassal ran his fingers across the control panel and the screen came to life. All the buttons were digital and ... Grassal squinted ... in some other language. Not English. Farsi? Dari, maybe? He slapped the wall in frustration then looked closer. At the bottom was an icon of a British flag, half the size of his fingernail. He pressed it. The letters on the screen switched to English. He set to work, ignoring the sound of something crashing down on a floor above him and the screams that rose from the lobby.

The main screen was a row of commands for system control keys. He hit the button that said global. The screen changed to a

3D schematic of the hotel. On the left was a menu with G, 1, 2. He pressed G. The layout for the first floor opened. The schematic showed each window and door. The outline was green, with certain sections in red. Grassal studied the image for a moment then got his bearings. The red represented locked doors. He ran his finger over them. Nothing happened. He tried again. Same result.

"Is that it?" Lilly said.

"I think so. I'm trying to figure it out."

"Well, look for something that says, 'lock!'"

"Because I wasn't doing that before. Jesus Christ on a cracker, Lilly." Grassal said. He'd never seen her like this, but he'd never been trapped in a burning building with her, either.

Along the top of the screen, a row of buttons read HVAC, FS, water, security, additional services. He pressed the button for security. The screen returned a text spreadsheet, a series of numbers. Grassal read the first line: "Main doors. 0534. Status: inactive." A little lock icon appeared. He pressed the icon. The status changed to disengaged.

"I think I've got it," Grassal said. He pressed each of the locks. "Go check." Lilly ran out to the lobby. While he waited, Grassal reactivated the fire system, but the security cameras showed no change in the blaze. When she returned, her eyes were red, and smoke rolled across the ceiling of the room. She shook her head.

"The building is falling apart. There's a hole in the ceiling of the lobby. It's bad. You've got to hurry."

Grassal scrolled down the list, several screens long. He pressed the lock/unlock icon for one several times. He listened for a sound but heard nothing. Another crash came from the lobby. Grassal tried to reason it out. According to the control system, the doors should be unlocked, but the fault must exist between the control system and the doors. Fail-secure systems usually have a backup battery, but if the battery is disconnected, the electromagnet stays in the lock position. He could try a shock baton, but its current would fry the 12-volt security system. He looked around the room until his eyes settled on a small metal cabinet above the door, three meters from the floor.

"In there. I need up there," Grassal said. Together they pushed the desk to just below the cabinet. Monitors, mugs, and papers fell to the floor as Lilly cleared its surface. Grassal could almost see inside. Lilly passed him the wheeled office chair. He climbed on while she held it steady. Inside the cabinet, he found the battery backup. The positive wire had been cut. He stretched, stripped the plastic casing away with his teeth, and twisted the wire around the lead post. As soon as he did so, he heard a cheer rise up from the crowd in the lobby.

"That did it. Let's go," Grassal said. They left the office and saw people streaming out the doors. The lobby had almost cleared—and just in time. Orange, blue, and green flames engulfed the back wall. About twenty spacers remained, oblivious to the thick smoke around them. About half of them were climbing all over each other in an attempt to do ... something. A few were on the floor. No one helped them. Stephanie was on her hands and knees behind the counter, coughing and swaying. With Grassal's help, Lilly lifted Stephanie over the counter. On the other side, Lilly threw the woman's arm over her shoulder, but she fell to the floor.

"Consider this my apology," Lilly said as she tried and failed to lift Stephanie. Grassal came to her aid, and together they carried Stephanie out the open doors and into the sweet, chilly outside air.

After he finished coughing, Grassal ran back inside.

21

Amadeus and Janette stepped out of the SUV and onto the suburban street. Clouds hid the crescent moon, making the night dark. A few houses down, a dog barked. Cars raced down the highway that skirted the edges of the development. Otherwise, all was quiet. Amadeus took one look back at the SUV, half-expecting to see the creature that called itself Vaskulo peering through the glass, but the vehicle appeared empty.

"This might get ugly," Janette said.

"I can handle it."

"Don't be so sure. You never know what you'll see in situations like this. All I'm saying is prepare yourself to do what needs to be done to get our man. If that thing is right, this might make everything worth it." She closed her eyes and shook her head. "Well, almost everything."

They crept up along the side of the split-level house. Amadeus looked around for any motion, or anyone watching from the warmth of their own homes, but saw nothing. Everyone had closed their blinds to the winter outside. Frost-covered grass crunched beneath his feet, and the shotgun's metal barrel was cold against his hand.

Behind the house, a deck overlooked a yard. A grill sat under a vinyl cover. Downspouts ran from the gutters into big white water collection tanks. In the middle of the yard sat a rusty metal swing set with weeds growing beneath it. Amadeus hoped it belonged to a neighbor. Janette peered in the back door, blocking out the night's light with her hands, and tried the doorknob. It turned. She flipped her head for Amadeus to follow her.

Amadeus glanced over at the swing set and hesitated. A thought began to form in his mind, a suspicion that he was repeating a cycle—or just doing unto others what had been done to him. He pushed that thought out of his mind as Janette stepped inside, pistol in hand. Careful not to slip on the icy deck, Amadeus followed her in.

He stepped into a kitchen lit by only a streetlight. Keeping the shotgun's barrel pointed at the ceiling, he held his breath while Janette peered around the corner into a dark living room. A laugh track punctuated the night, and Amadeus nearly let out a yelp.

"Downstairs," Janette said, her voice a whisper, her eyes wide.

"He'll hear us on the stairs."

"We sneak. I'll go first." Amadeus regarded Janette and thought, for the first time, that she might not be completely sane. Amadeus looked down the stairs that led to the basement. They would remain unseen until they reached the bottom ... unless he heard them. He wanted to convince Janette to turn around, to find another way, but she was already descending. He expected to hear the stairwell creak and groan, but it was silent. Well-built, he decided.

Two steps from the bottom, Janette lingered behind the wall and motioned for the shotgun. Amadeus handed it to her and took her pistol in exchange. She ran her hands over the stock and, barrel then took the last two steps down, the gun aimed at the room ahead of her. Amadeus followed, the unfamiliar pistol in his hand.

The black-eyed man sat on the couch, awash in the glow of a

wall-sized screen. Amadeus instantly recognized his highcheek bones and long hair. A little girl—Amadeus guessed she was five or six years old—was asleep on his chest. She wore Tinkerbell footie pajamas. Amadeus wanted to vomit. Janette made eye contact with the black-eyed man and put a finger to her lips. She motioned for Amadeus to look around.

The basement was one large, open room. A few empty beer bottles sat on the coffee table. Shelves stocked with canned food lined the wall closest to the street. A map of the Western Hemisphere hung along the back wall. Red, blue, and yellow pins were stuck in various locations across North and South America. Amadeus realized the placement of the pins corresponded to the location of either a demon gate or, in the case of the yellow ones, his own locations. There was New York, Colorado, San Francisco, and Portland. Arrows pointed across the Atlantic and Pacific Oceans. Looking over his shoulder, Amadeus saw Janette and the black-eyed man staring at each other, motionless. The girl still slept.

Amadeus picked up a flexscreen from the workbench, folded it, and put it in his pocket, though he doubted it held any useful data. He also pocketed a phone, but not before using it to take a photo of the map. Beside the workbench was a desk covered in unopened mail. Amadeus examined a piece of it in the flexscreen's glow. The name read "Marshall Hathaway." Vaskulo was right.

Marshall Hathaway now had both of his hands up. Janette was whispering something to him. When she finished, he looked down at his little girl then nodded at Janette.

"It was right," Amadeus said in a voice breathless and quavering. "That's him."

"Get your gun on him," Janette said. Amadeus aimed at Marshall's head and hoped no one would have to fire. Marshall tried to slide from beneath the girl without waking her. The girl stirred. Amadeus held his breath. By the time the black-eyed man was on his feet, the girl was rubbing her eyes. Marshall took several steps away from the child.

"Go," Janette said in a sharp whisper as she motioned toward the stairs with the shotgun. Marshall stood with his back to the mirrors, motionless. The girl opened her eyes and began to shriek.

"Stay right there, pumpkin," Marshall said, but made no move to silence the child.

"Upstairs and out the door. You're no stranger to this kind of thing," Janette said, her voice carrying over the girl's high-pitched screams. She lowered her voice to a growl. "Try anything and I'll kill you. It's been a while." The girl stopped for air, and in the moment of silence Amadeus heard footsteps upstairs.

"Janette?" Amadeus said, looking up. Marshall smiled. Janette positioned herself so that her back was to the shelf-covered wall rather than the basement door. The footsteps stopped. The girl's shrieks changed to gasping sobs. A light flicked on at the top of the stairwell, then someone padded down the stairs. A woman stepped through the door. The little girl dashed across the room and threw her arms around the woman's legs. The woman scowled at Marshall and stroked the child's head.

"I warned you. I warned you, Marshall."

"Honey," Marshall said. He pointed at Amadeus then Janette. "These two—"

"What are they going to do to Daddy?" the child said, looking up at her mother.

"We're just going to talk here for a little bit," Marshall said. "Go upstairs with your mother, pumpkin."

"I want you all out of my house," the woman said, then to Marshall, "and that includes you."

She turned and led the girl from the room. Amadeus wanted to call out to the girl, to say her mother was right, and they were only going to talk for a few minutes and then everything would be fine. But he stood as motionless as Marshall, who wore the forlorn expression of one left behind on a sinking ship.

"You heard her, Papa Bear. Let's go. Unless you'd like your daughter to see her father eviscerated. Don't think I won't, either. I've done worse, far worse. I am terror. I am your nightmare. But you have a choice. Decide quickly." Janette's face was hard and controlled as she stepped behind Marshall and jabbed his back with the shotgun. "You know as well as I do what happens if the police arrive. Either way, this doesn't end well for you. You have ten seconds. Nine. Eight." Her finger stroked the trigger. When she reached two, Marshall took his first step, and within a minute, they were outside.

In the backseat, Janette had her finger on the trigger of a shotgun aimed at Marshall Hathaway. Amadeus knew him as the black-eyed man, though the black in his eyes had faded, just as Amadeus' had. This supported Amadeus' hypothesis that the ocular darkening that had plagued him occurred as a result of kipium exposure.

Janette placed a black hood over his head, and Marshall Hathaway was silent. Amadeus thought about Vaskulo in the back, what it was learning, what it wanted. He felt guilty and sick with himself, no better than the people who had broken into his father's house. Now he was driving some kid's father off to be ... what? Tortured? Murdered?

"Amadeus, pull over, open the glove box, and hand me the knife," Janette said. Amadeus pulled over, this time in a well-lit Übermart parking lot. He opened the glove box and found a bowie knife, which he unsheathed and passed to Janette. Marshall tensed.

"Where is it?" Janette asked.

"Where is what?" Marshall said.

"You know what. Your meat tag."

"I'm not ..."

"You are somebody's asset, somebody's dog, and no self-respecting paramilitary outfit fails to put a leash on their attack dogs. I suggest you tell me where it is *before* I start cutting." She dragged the tip of the knife from his cheek, down the side of his neck, and across his chest.

"Fuck. Fine. On my right forearm. Up, closer to the crook of my arm, warmer, warmer. Fuck." Amadeus glanced back to see her flexing her fingers around the hilt. "There." Janette drove the knife into his arm and twisted. Marshall screamed and Amadeus winced as Janette dug around in the tissue with the knife's tip. Marshall took rapid, shallow breaths through clenched teeth while she worked. Finally, she raised the bloody knife.

"There it is," Janette said. She held up a pea-sized chunk of gray metal before flicking it out the window. "Remote ID implant. I'd rather we not have any surprise visitors." Janette wrapped a rag around his forearm to ensure he wouldn't bleed to death, but Amadeus wondered what they would do with Marshall after they were done with him.

Amadeus returned to the highway and followed Janette's directions until they were out of the city, through a suburb, and pulling into the parking lot of a sprawling storage facility. A sign proudly advertised twenty-four hour access. "Go down that row there, just past the boats. Drive until I say stop." Amadeus nodded.

At a garage door near the end, he stopped. Janette stepped out of the car and opened the garage door. Amadeus pulled into the cramped storage space. After closing the door behind them, Janette punched some numbers on a control panel on the wall. The floor lurched beneath them and the walls began to rise. That wasn't right. Amadeus shook his head and realized the walls weren't rising—they were descending.

When the elevator ended its descent, Amadeus looked out into a long hallway carved out of sandstone and lit by fluorescent light bars. Not what he'd expected at all. Janette rolled aside the cage-like gate. She saw Amadeus looking around and said, "Mr. Jones inspired this iteration of the movable HQ. Once we're inside, I've got Marshall, and you're in charge of the creep." Amadeus nodded as Janette opened the door and pulled Marshall out by his shirt.

Shotgun in hand, Amadeus cracked the back hatch to release the creature. A tiny part of him expected Vaskulo to spring from the back and tear out his throat. Instead, Vaskulo hopped onto the floor and began to stretch, moving its body in fluid motion as if it were a spring. Amadeus eyed the creature with suspicion. It had been right about Marshall, but that didn't mean he had to trust it. Done with its stretching, it turned to regard Amadeus with its hundred eyes.

Fear me not. I foreswear revenge. You were ignorant, as were others.

Amadeus shuddered. He wasn't sure if he should be relieved or frightened.

Janette said, "Let's go. Just down the hall, there's an area designed for discussions. Marshall, you want to leave here alive, you'll ensure we have a productive discussion." She pushed Marshall and they started toward the room at the end of the hallway.

Amadeus heard Marshall sniffing the air from beneath his hood and wondered if he knew a subluminal was with them. He wondered if Marshall would talk, and if not, if Amadeus would watch this man die. He shuddered when he realized the thought pleased him, but he told himself it didn't matter, that they were only doing the will of the universe in fast-forward. On a long enough scale, everyone had to die sometime. Some people just deserved to die sooner than others ... and this man was one of them.

22

Inside the lobby of The Admiral, the spacers who had yet to succumb to the smoke had arranged themselves into a messy rectangle two persons deep and five wide. Their arms interlocked and their chanting had unified. Several bodies were sprawled on the tile floor. Three or four were spacing, but the remaining five were very dead. Three of these were soldiers, and two of these soldiers Grassal identified as Petunia and the Aztec. The former had been pummeled until his face was a barely recognizable, meaty pulp. The latter had a knife protruding from his jugular vein.

Grassal ran around behind the group. He tried to ignore the pulling sensation in his own mind. In the back row, a wide man with silver hair and a sport coat was closest to the flame. Grassal tried to pull him free of the rectangle, to make him walk, but he wouldn't budge. Grassal tried again, but the man swatted at him as if he were a fly.

Grassal's backside tingled from the heat, his lungs ached and stung, but he pulled harder on the man's locked arm. The elbow gave, and the man toppled over, stiff as a fencepost. Even on the floor, he never stopped muttering. Grassal grabbed him by the coat and dragged him across the floor. The effort winded him, his deep breaths filled his lungs with smoke, and his body spasmed in a fit of coughing. After he recovered, he dragged the man outside.

His vision was blurry and his eyes stung. He called out for Lilly and received no response. He could hear the crowd and just make out its form. He spoke as loudly as he could without coughing.

"Come on, goddamn it! There are still people inside. Help me!"

Grassal didn't wait for an answer. He dashed back inside, but instead of choosing to free the person nearest the flaming wall— an old man with a walrus moustache—he played favorites and focused his attention on the snowman girl. She was between the old man and a middle-aged woman. When he pulled her arms free, she punched him in the stomach. Grassal took the blow then carried her rigid body into the cool night.

After spending a moment outside to recover, his vision cleared and he saw why no one was moving. Soldiers in ventilation masks stood behind waist-high metal barricades in a semicircle around the entrance. The soldiers held shock batons, and a few held shotguns. A fire truck was parked half a block away, and two firefighters were arguing with some of the soldiers.

"Please." Grassal waved his arms in wide, crazy arcs as he yelled for someone, anyone, to come and help him remove the people still inside. Four firefighters scaled the barricades. Some were shocked, others shot with what Grassal realized were beanbag rounds. Grassal cursed. One of the soldiers aimed a shotgun at Grassal and shot him in the chest.

The impact knocked him backwards onto his ass and his head hit the concrete. He thought his brain was jarred loose from its housing. Disgruntled shouting rose from the crowd. Instinctively, Grassal touched the spot where he had been shot. There was no blood, only a burning throb, like being stung by a thousand bees. A small bean bag was on the ground beside him. Grassal pocketed the bean bag and got to his feet.

At least eight people remained inside, trapped in their own

bodies and left to burn to death while soldiers not only looked on, but prevented anyone else from helping. No, not real soldiers. Securaux soldiers. Even from here, Grassal could hear the command to keep everyone back being shouted in at least four languages.

Grassal's ears began to ring, the edges of his vision grew white, and he saw darkness rush across the crowd like a shadow cast by fast-moving clouds. He felt a hundred lines of energy emanate from his head. Over the darkness of the crowd they looked like shimmering silver threads or spider silk covered in morning dew. Some of his silver threads extended inside the building, while others wrapped around the heads of others. After a moment, he realized everyone extending or receiving threads was an afflicted person from The Admiral. The nicotine pull had grown stronger. He felt his consciousness becoming dislodged from his body, but he called upon the limited training he had received, focused his mind, breathed deep, and felt himself become whole again. The silver threads retreated from his vision.

The fight between the firefighters and the soldiers had spread. The firefighters were winning due to sheer numbers, and people were now crossing the barricades. Grassal cried out for volunteers. Within a moment, he was back in the lobby with three women and a man.

They worked in teams of two to carry the spacers outside. When Grassal and the man were on their way back in, the lobby ceiling broke open. The backdraft sent long fingers of searing yellow flame and smoke out the open doors. The flames washed over the man and singed Grassal's eyebrows. The man collapsed, his clothes melted and aflame. Grassal removed his jacket and beat the flames out. He was joined by three others. When the man's clothes were extinguished, his skin was a thousand shades of red and all his body hair was burned away, but he was alive. A man and a woman pulled him toward one of the waiting ambulances across the street.

From inside, Grassal thought he heard screams, but flame-shrouded girders blocked the doorways. Still, he moved closer, holding his shirt over his face to protect himself from the smoke. He wanted to go closer, to at least try, but he felt hands on his shoulders pulling him backwards. Grassal looked up to see streaming arcs of water. Smoke rolled from every window of the hotel.

The brawl had grown. He couldn't tell who was fighting whom. Grassal was dizzy and his eyes stung, but he looked for Lilly, called for her. She was nowhere to be seen. He wondered where she had gone ... and why. He reached for his phone but remembered he had left it in his backpack inside.

A kick landed on his hip. He turned to face a woman with wide-pupiled yellow eyes and a sinister grin. She was one of the people he had dragged out. Instead of becoming a rigid statue once she managed to pull herself up, she'd become fully mobile and poised to attack Grassal. A quick scan of the sidewalk confirmed that several of the brawl participants were spacers. Some were fighting amongst themselves, while others were fighting with the crowd. Everyone had gone bat-shit crazy. No wonder Lilly had left. He needed to do the same.

As The Admiral burned and the street exploded into violence, Grassal ran, surrendering his will to this most basic human movement. He took advantage of the extra elastic energy provided by his prosthetic's springy carbon fiber. As he ran, he pushed thoughts of Dr. Marx, of the snowman girl, of Stephanie out of his mind. For now, he decided to focus on his own sanity and survival. Three minutes later, wheezing forced him to stop at the red base of Chinatown's dragon-flanked gate.

His lungs burned and he choked down air. He was sure the smoke and heat had seared his bronchial tubes. His mouth was pasty, and his stomach ached with hunger. He lacked drugs, wallet, food, and phone. These items had been in his backpack, which now burned with The Admiral.

Grassal tried to be positive. He knew he could get the

necessary drugs from a sketchy pharmacist, or maybe even a hospital—though he'd almost rather become a spacer than go to a hospital. Money and communication would have to sort themselves out. But a pharmacist would need to know his prescription. Grassal tried to remember the drugs and dosages and realized he could not. The drug list had been saved on his phone, and all the extra drugs had been in The Admiral. In fact, Dr. Marx had allocated almost all her resources to The Admiral ... except one: Chuck the secretary. Chuck would have access to a copy of Dr. Kongsampong's research as well as some of Dr. Marx's records. Grassal smiled as he thought of the cherubic bastard, and decided he would contact him shortly. If that didn't work, he could try Annie. She wouldn't have all the documentation, but she should at least have a drug list. Now, though, he needed water.

Grassal peered in shop windows, looking for a water fountain, and found a bubbling cooler with little paper cups in the Mai Ping market. The market was warm and he gulped cup after cup. As he drank, an old man came out, his tanned, lined face covered in liver spots. He looked at Grassal then spoke.

"Thirsty?" He scowled at Grassal from beneath big gray eyebrows that looked like used erasers.

"I'm sorry. There was a fire, and my friend is gone, and ..." The man's face broke into a wide grin.

"It's okay. I'm only joking. Drink all you want. Maybe you're not so sorry as you think." The old man tottered back to his stool behind the counter. Grassal drank more, and while he did so, his eyes searched the room and settled on a landline phone behind the desk. Grassal gestured to the phone.

"Could I use your phone? I'm ill, it's a local call, and ..."

"What? A young man without a hand phone?"

"I lost it. "

"You could use my shop phone, but the lines are down. Maybe because of that big fire a couple blocks away. I don't know." Grassal asked him about pharmacies.

"You think a pharmacy is going to stay open on a night like this? You're crazy."

Grassal smiled, saw the silver threads flowing out of his head and around the market, and thought the man might be right.

Grassal decided to go to the downtown CDC offices, the same ones he had visited with Lilly what seemed so long ago. He hoped to call Chuck for the drug list, but if there were drugs on site, maybe he could get the drugs and a hard copy of the drug list in one trip.

Once he had made his decision, the billowing silver threads stretched out from his head and in the direction he intended to walk. As an experiment, he turned a corner and began heading away from the CDC offices. Some of the threads twisted around themselves, became knotted, and an uneasy feeling raced through his veins and settled on his heart. When Grassal returned to his original direction, the threads untangled and the feeling dissipated.

Traffic filled all four lanes, but the sidewalks were nearly empty. Grassal jogged with his hands in his pockets, wary of frozen patches hidden by the fresh, new layer of snow that continued to accumulate. Cabs passed by on the street, and he berated himself for losing his wallet. The one time in his life he could afford to splurge on a two-kilometer cab ride, and he didn't have any way to pay for it. Two blocks ahead, a bearded middle-aged man dashed through a crosswalk. Horns blared and brake lights flashed. He pumped one fist in the air, and Grassal was sure the man was crying out the name of the late Dr. Marjorie Marx.

A few more minutes of jogging brought him closer to his goal. Along the way, he looked for pay phones, a hotel, another open store, or something, but saw only closed businesses behind metal gates and locked apartment entrances. In a park in the middle of a traffic circle, three white teenagers dressed in watch caps and heavy coats were having a snowball fight. Grassal crossed the street onto the circle and hailed them with a wave. They stared at him while he asked if could use one of their phones to make a call. Grassal's silver threads first flowed over then away from their bodies, leaving a border an arm-length long.

"It's an emergency."

The teenagers all exchanged glances. One of them threw a snowball at him. Grassal dodged it, but the other two launched snowballs that hit him in the chest and head. They laughed as Grassal ran away. As he ran, Grassal smelled burned plastic and felt his muscles stiffening. He stopped to breathe and felt sorry for the teenagers, for the people attacked by the spacers, for people trapped in their rooms when the fire started. Grassal tried not to think about how it started, or the fact that it had probably started just after he pulled the alarm.

He heard the roaring crowd several blocks south, toward the White House. Tens of thousands of people had converged on the green space from Lafayette Square down to the Washington Monument. They chanted and waved signs. Occasionally, he heard crackling explosions like small-arms fire, but that could've been fireworks left over from Lunar New Year celebrations.

Grassal decided to stay well north of the protest, but the closer he came to the CDC, the thicker the crowd grew. By the time he could see the CDC's glass-and-steel exterior, he realized he would never get through the crowd. While he considered his options, a guy with a curly mop of red hair bumped hard into him. As the man started to apologize, recognition crossed his face, and he broke into a wide smile.

"Grassal Delgado. So good to meet you." Grassal looked down and saw he carried a hand-painted cardboard sign. Big red letters read, "Repeal the bill!"

"Is this ... What's going on?" Grassal didn't want to presume anything.

"Everything, dude. First we get the demons running all over the place. The government starts giving out fat contracts to kill them, and lo and be-fucking-hold, once it's clear there's money to be made, more demons show up. Scumbag Congress passes the KREATURE Act, and within a couple days Securaux overruns The Admiral and tries to burn everyone inside. But I don't need to tell you that, do I ... Grassal? You're a fucking hero!" The man placed both hands on Grassal's shoulders and shook him with excitement.

"Damn," Grassal said. He blinked and let all that sink in. The guy gave Grassal time to process the information. Finally, Grassal said, "I meant all these people here. Is it because of—"

"It was The Admiral, dude. That did it. It was the needle that broke the camel's butthole."

"So why protest the CDC? We ... they were trying to help."

"Who knows? It's not like Securaux has any offices downtown, or anywhere else. That's just where it started when a few people told their friends, their friends told their other friends, and the fire of fury spread into a self-organizing protest. Last I checked, the general consensus was to move everyone down to the Mall."

"Huh ... weird question, but can I use your phone?"

Grassal searched, found, and dialed the number to Dr. Marx's office. Chuck answered on the first ring.

"Chuck, it's Grassal Delgado. I need your help. I need the drug list ... and the drugs if you've got them." Grassal shielded the phone's receiver from the bitter wind.

"You will have nothing of the sort, you terrible, dangerous man," Chuck said, enunciating every syllable. "I'm trapped inside, Dr. Marx is dead for nothing, and everything, every last shred of everything that's happening right now is your fault. I should never, never have let you speak to her." Grassal imagined Chuck moving the handset away from his head and toward its base.

"Please, wait, Chuck, please. Maybe you're right, that I'm to blame, but no one could've predicted this. And just so you know, Dr. Marx died a hero. She stood up to them."

"If we had followed the old policy, none of this would've happened."

"And what policy was that?"

"Deny everything." Chuck sniffed. "You hyper-alpha ape. I hope you catch drug-resistant gonorrhea, Mr. Delgado."

Deny everything. Grassal thought that this policy couldn't be any more wrong. Denial accomplished nothing except to help the powerful save face. Grassal needed to do the opposite, to tell everything he knew in a very public way. The treatment. Their plan. And the way Securaux had annihilated what he and Dr. Marx had built. Grassal thought of the snowman girl, how her words had motivated a group of individuals to take collective action. If it weren't for her, they all could've died in there ... and for what? Grassal pushed the thought from his mind and decided to call Annie.

"Two more calls?" Grassal asked. His silver threads had mostly faded, but the few that remained wove around and over the redheaded guy's chest.

"Sure, dude. Happy to help."

Grassal didn't know anyone's phone number, but he kept a master list of contact information online. He accessed this, found Annie's, and dialed.

"Annie, it's Grassal, and I'm in a fix ..." After reassuring her he was okay, Annie said she'd e-mail him the drug list. Before he ended the call, Annie warned him that the protest could become dangerous, especially if Metro police decided to ask for help. Several private military corporations had already offered their assistance in this Emergence-related matter. Grassal cursed and wished her all the best.

Finally, Grassal tried calling Lilly. After the fourth unanswered call, he settled for leaving a voicemail message: "If you get this message in the next hour or two, please wait for me at Jackson's statue in Lafayette Square. I've got to find a pharmacy." Message left, Grassal returned the phone to the guy, who gave him a good-natured slap on the bicep as he started away.

"Gotta go, dude. Good luck. And just so you know, the chant is, 'Remember Dr. Marjorie Marx, murdered by Securaux.'"

Moments after Grassal had begun his search for a pharmacy, or at least some free food, a thousand silver threads grew from his head like time-lapse footage of seedlings. A few shot north, away from the protest, but most wove themselves together in a shimmering tube. The tube corkscrewed into the air like the snaking body of a Chinese dragon and arced downward to a point on the ground about a kilometer away. Grassal turned his head. The tube remained stationary on its distant end point, east of the Washington Monument, toward the Mall, and right in the middle of that teeming, chanting crowd.

Grassal wanted to go anywhere but there. He thought he had seen a pharmacy just a couple blocks up an avenue he had passed earlier. But when he took his first step, every nerve ending in his skin began to itch. Involuntarily, he turned around. The itching ceased as fast as it had begun. He started off in a different direction. The sensation returned. Resigned to his fate, Grassal started toward the tube's end point on the other side of the crowd.

Halfway to the end point, when he stood shoulder to shoulder in a crowd thicker than the one back at The Admiral, the tube partially dissipated. The freed threads began to pass over, around, or into the people around him. Grassal thought the threads looked like the output from a very powerful Tesla coil ... only the behavior of the threads appeared too deliberate to be considered plasma-like.

All around him, people chanted, "Remember Dr. Marjorie Marx, murdered by Securaux." Hundreds held signs scrawled on cardboard boxes or poster boards. Individuals and groups shouted other slogans. Nearby, a group of about twenty people kneeled in a circle and sang hymns. They held flickering candles in their clasped hands. The crowd maintained a respectful distance.

Grassal moved at a rate of about ten meters per minute. After five minutes, he saw that the silver tube ended on a local television news van, and once the van registered in his mind, the tube dissipated and the silver threads branched out in every direction.

The van was parked near the edge of the crowd on a street only partially blocked by protestors. A man with a mustache was talking to a woman in a vest. She held a camera at her side. He tried to make eye contact with the man, but something occupied their attention. When Grassal drew closer, he saw they were smoking cannabis from a colorful glass pipe. Grassal waved as he approached them, but they still paid him no attention.

"Hey, excuse me, are you with," he said, pointing to the big blue number "6" on the van's side, "Channel Six News?"

"No, channel fifteen," the man said. Smoke and fog rolled from his mouth while he spoke. "We just beat up their anchors and stole their van." The woman tittered. Grassal frowned at them. "Just fucking with you. Yeah, we're channel six. What's up?"

"He looks familiar," the woman said. "Reminds me of one of those mass shooter types."

"Turn sideways for us," the man said. "Let's see you in profile." Grassal scowled at them. He almost turned away. "Wait a second. I remember now. You're the guy who was with Amadeus Brunmeier when he gave that speech. You were on crutches. Gutierrez, Gonzales, Garcia ..."

"Delgado. Grassal Delgado."

"Ellis, this guy was at The Admiral," the woman said. "An expert witness who could give us a first-hand account of events." Grassal watched as ambition and interest spread across their faces like an oil spill. He had them.

"Okay, okay," the man named Ellis said to the woman. To Grassal, he said, "Would you be willing to tell us about it?"

"I will, but you have to help me find a pharmacy ... and buy me lunch."

The woman introduced herself as Samantha and pointed Grassal to a cooler full of food in the van. Grassal gorged himself on spiced tofurkey loaf, tangerines, potato chips, and a liter of milk. As he ate, the silver threads faded and he began to feel human again. Afterwards, speaking directly into Samantha's camera, he told them everything, ending with the snowman girl's speech, the rescue of the spacers, and the street brawl. Most of it was public knowledge, but because he was going on record, he wanted to be thorough.

After he was finished, Ellis twisted one end of his mustache and said, "Roland Jessup. Isn't that the same guy who made like a billion off the Emergence?"

"That's the one," Grassal said.

"Technically, though, what he did was perfectly legal under the KREATURE Act," Ellis said, gesturing to Samantha to turn off the camera. "Grassal, I know you were instrumental in making all this happen, but now I have to ask: what the fuck were you thinking?"

"We had a safe and effective cure we were working to provide to every afflicted individual who needed treatment. And we would've been successful, except for Securaux and that goddamned bill."

"You're infected, aren't you?" Samantha said.

"Afflicted. But, yeah," Grassal said. "I am."

"I'm sorry," Samantha said.

"Can you get us access to Amadeus? I'm sure he'd like to comment on this," Ellis said.

"No. Maybe. Probably not," Grassal said. "He's been off doing, eh, other things."

"What kind of other things?" Ellis said.

"I'm not sure, to be honest. I haven't talked to him in some time," Grassal said. He thought about the duct tape and smiled.

He missed his neurotic little friend.

"There's a rumor that Amadeus' father is still alive and that Amadeus is out looking for him. Is that true?" Samantha said. Grassal looked at her and considered the question. For a moment, he was tempted to let it all out, but he shook his head.

"No. This is incorrect. I would know. I'm close to Amadeus. I was with him through everything. I saw the goon squad. I heard the shots that killed his father."

"What about his personality?" Ellis said. "Some people say he's developed quite the attitude. I mean, he did punch a reporter awhile back."

"PTSD," Grassal said. "Or is it PESD? I don't remember. Come on, Ellis, you've got to admit that reporter was out of line."

"Would you punch a reporter?" Samantha said.

"He called Tommy Brunmeier a psychotic terrorist. I would've punched him for that too." This conversation had gone way too far off course. Grassal decided to bring it back.

"I've been out of touch for a few hours." He didn't want to ask the next question, but he had to know. "Do they have a count? From The Admiral?"

"Fifty-four, estimated," Ellis said.

Grassal moaned like he had been punched. Fifty-four people. And *he* had pulled the fire alarm. He had given someone the opportunity to start that fire. He was responsible for all this. Grassal placed a hand over his mouth and struggled to keep down his milk and tofurkey. No, not just him. Securaux. The politicians. They were all elements in this reaction. He was just the catalyst.

"Look." Samantha stretched a flexscreen and handed it to him. On screen was a grainy surveillance photo showing Grassal and Lilly. His hand was on the fire alarm. "There's a photo circulating of you and the woman. That's Lilly Jones, right?" Grassal clenched his fists.

"I didn't start that fire, and I didn't lock those people in there. I did, however, pull the fire alarm, but someone had to demonstrate how dangerous the situation was." Grassal didn't mention it was Lilly's idea. "I'll not run from this."

Samantha pulled up an article from the Tops News Agency; whoever had written it hinted that Grassal himself had started the fire. No mention of Securaux, the locked doors, or even the round ups. Biased fucks, but given the source he shouldn't be surprised.

"Are there other articles like this?"

"Some," Ellis said. "Right now it's mostly the kooky fringe saying this, but give the PR suits enough time, and you'll be our next bin Laden."

"People have got to know what really happened." Grassal looked at the crowd outside. They were angry, confused, and maybe just a little bloodthirsty. He could work them. Amadeus wasn't the only one who could give a speech. Grassal had coached him, after all. Looking from Ellis to Samantha, Grassal said, "Do you have a PA system on this thing?"

When Grassal climbed to the top of the van with the microphone in his hand and Samantha's camera aimed at him, he was just a crazy dude climbing on a van with a microphone. However, the first people who saw him recognized him. They called to others in the crowd. Tens then hundreds of pairs of expectant eyes fell upon him. Grassal channeled his inner snowman girl.

"Ladies and gentlemen. My name is Grassal Delgado." His voice boomed out over the din and the chants. A handful of people held their phones up to record him. That was better. He continued, "You might know me as Amadeus Brunmeier's gimpy-yet-dapper sidekick." This brought a few polite chuckles. "Today, at The Admiral, we suffered a terrible tragedy that was completely avoidable." His words echoed far, and more people turned to listen. "Most of you know I was involved in setting up this clinic, but I would like to set the record straight with some confessions."

"I confess that I am afflicted with the subluminal disease. I lost my foot during the Emergence, and like so many others in The Admiral and around the world, I still carry a lingering part of the creatures with me.

"I confess that it was my idea to provide treatment to the afflicted. I acted out of self-interest and ambition. You see, I learned about the Suttani Technique and Dr. Kongsampong's cure thanks to a writer named Lewis Braxton. I thought, 'Damn, something should be done,' so I pestered poor Dr. Marx until she agreed to help me. And I happily lent my good name to this project."

He stopped to breathe and looked toward Lafayette Square. He didn't see Lilly.

"I confess that when conditions first started to deteriorate, I at first did nothing because I did not believe they would get any worse. Later, when the situation became dangerous and untenable, I pulled that fire alarm, because I saw no other possible remedy. Someone within had to sound the alarm, because no help came from without.

"And finally, I confess that I thought our government could be a force for good ... but I was wrong, because the KREATURE Act is now law. We have been hijacked by dangerous extremists who place profit and ideology above public safety. The KREATURE Act isn't about protecting people. It's about profit, and it wouldn't even be thinkable if we hadn't used our military for wars of choice over the past two decades."

His crowd of listeners now easily surpassed a thousand, and they stood, rapt, while they watched him. No one chanted. Grassal remained in the flow, in the rhythm of his speech. He noticed four Metro police officers dressed in full riot gear watching him from beneath raised helmets. The oldest one, a trim man who appeared in his fifties, spoke on a phone while he looked up at Grassal.

"My friends, I ask you, what could cause a corruption to

occur with such speed? Is this the work of a common man?" He raised his eyebrows and held the mic out to the crowd. A few people shouted, "No!" Grassal smiled and repeated his question. This time a hundred voices provided a response.

"Is this the work of compassionate people?"

"No!"

"Do we lock up our ill and maimed?"

"No!"

"Is this acceptable?"

"No!"

"Then listen to me, ladies and gentlemen, listen to me with your minds open, for I am going to reveal the real enemy. The real enemy—" An explosion shook the ground. The crowd dropped for cover, falling down as if their legs had turned to jelly.

The older police officer called out to Grassal. "Get down from the van!"

"I'm not finished."

"Two hundred Securaux troops and a pair of Abrams tanks rolling down E Street say you're finished. They're coming to break up this crowd. Tell these people they've got to leave," the officer said. "Please. You can save a lot of lives."

Grassal cursed then drew a deep breath.

"Everyone." He knew his voice would be drowned out by the sound of the crowd, but he had to try. The officer had reached the top of the van but kept his distance. "Everyone, please listen to me. It is Securaux. Securaux is the enemy, and they're coming here. You need to leave. Go somewhere safe." The officer gave Grassal a satisfied nod.

"Let them come," someone yelled. "They'll make martyrs out of us."

"We're taking them down," one person shouted. He looked like an accountant who had just left his desk.

"We're sick of this shit," a woman in hospital scrubs said.

"Killing their own citizens," another voice said.

"When will it stop?"

"Who will stop it?"

"If not us, then who?"

"No ... no ..." Grassal said. "Don't be martyrs. Too much blood has already been spilled today. Please."

The officer grasped Grassal's bicep. His blue eyes blazed with ... something. Anger. Fear. Respect. Grassal felt the hair on his neck rise at being so close to a cop. Grassal expected the worst, but instead of throwing him to the ground, the officer said, "I lost a cousin in that fire today. I know you were trying to do the right thing." He looked toward E Street and shook his head. "I just got off the phone with the chief. She told me the mayor wants us to push the bastards back." Grassal smiled. "Well, what are you waiting for? Tell these people Metro police will oppose Securaux."

Grassal raised the mic to his mouth and spoke. "Metro police are on your side, and they—"

Another explosion, followed by small-arms fire, sent a murmur of fear through the crowd. Grassal and the officer crouched down. He realized he was atop a van, holding a microphone, before a crowd he had brought to the precipice of violent opposition. The nature of his situation became apparent. His self-preservation instinct kicked in, and he hurried back to the ground. More shots cracked. The officer followed him down, shook Grassal's hand, and returned to his fellows. Ellis patted Grassal on the back.

"Well done. You want to ride with us? I can't promise it's safe, but it's sure to be interesting."

"You're not leaving, then?" Grassal said.

"We're ambitious local journalists in the middle of the biggest story since the Emergence, and we have a direct participant along with us for commentary," Ellis said as he started the van and backed up. The van bumped into a car then peeled out, driving along the periphery of the crowd. "Do you think we're crazy?"

Grassal, sitting in the back among the monitors and computers, didn't say a word. Today, his standard for crazy had reached an entirely new level.

"Are you in or out, Delgado?" Samantha said. Her green eyes gleamed, and her stoned smile unnerved Grassal. Something in that look told him he was about to head straight into a situation he would probably regret. Still high from his speech and believing the pharmacy could wait, he gave her a wide smile.

"I'm in. Of course I'm in."

Ellis drove the van down the avenue, along a side street, and turned onto E Street. Eight blocks distant, taking up both lanes, rolled a paramilitary convoy: four personnel trucks and about fifty soldiers marched alongside two tanks. Some troops rode motorcycles.

"That's so fucking wrong," Ellis said. "I never thought I'd see the day ... Sam, get a shot of that, some close-ups. We need to get these guys on camera."

"Right, boss," Samantha said. Ellis turned the van so that the passenger window faced the approaching convoy. Samantha held the camera on her shoulder and panned the scene. The monitor in the back of the van displayed Samantha's camera feed. Grassal saw the soldiers wore black flak jackets and helmets, while some wore black suits and face shields. A beehive had been stenciled on the sides of the vehicles. Ellis provided commentary, saying this was like the force that had helped Huntington during the Emergence, all foreign mercenaries, only now there were no subluminals to fight.

Ellis drove the van a block closer. A motorcycle rode out and met them. The driver motioned for them to turn around. Ellis shook his head and pointed to the camera. The driver pulled a pistol and aimed it at them.

"Are you getting this?" Ellis said.

"Yeah," Sam said.

"You in the back, don't let him see you, just in case," Ellis said to Grassal, who wasn't going to argue. Ellis drummed his hands on the steering wheel. Through the monitor, Grassal watched the motorcyclist raise the pistol over his head and fire. Ellis, Samantha, and Grassal all flinched.

"Okay, Ellis, I got that, but let's find another place to film."

"Best idea I've heard all day," Ellis said. He turned the van around and sped off. "Just tell me where to go, ideally out of the way of those fucking tanks." Ellis turned back to Grassal, oblivious to the road and the traffic before him. "Can you believe this shit? Tanks in downtown DC. This is the kind of shit that used to happen in red China."

"Got it," Samantha said. "You need to turn left, drive five blocks, then make a right on Howard. There's an apartment building with a public roof. We can take the stairs and get a great view of the Mall."

"How does she do it?" Ellis said, mostly to himself.

"Rooftop gardening forums," Samantha said.

From the roof of the Sawtooth Apartment complex, they had a clear view of the National Mall, which had almost filled with protestors. Grassal had missed the window for meeting Lilly. He tried and failed to reach her with Samantha's phone. Instead, he sent her a text: *Get out of downtown.*

By the time he finished, the convoy had grown. Grassal now counted four tanks, six personnel trucks, ten jeeps, an equal number of urban assault vehicles, and a lot of men on foot. Through the zoom lens of the camera, Grassal could see they carried all kinds of weapons—not just beanbag guns and tasers. The Securaux beehive logo was stenciled on most of the vehicles.

The crowd had formed several distinct groups, each clustered around some central person, as if each person were a network node and those surrounding them output devices, though Grassal couldn't be sure what that output was. Unable to hear specific words, Grassal occasionally caught the chant:

"Remember Dr. Marjorie Marx, murdered by Securaux."

"Everything good to go?" Ellis asked.

Samantha said she was ready.

"Right now I want you to pan across the entire crowd, then zoom in on the convoy as it rolls in. A paramilitary convoy in downtown DC—it's still blowing my mind. I simply cannot believe this is happening. My God, think of it ... So, we'll just let it roll. It could be a standoff, this situation could last for hours, or it could explode before our faces. Whatever."

As they started setting up, another burst of gunshots cracked in the air. The crowd emitted a few screams, but Grassal saw no injuries. He decided it was another warning shot. Ellis held the camera and paced around the roof while Samantha set up another tripod and AV gear.

"Here," Ellis said to Grassal, "you hold this while she sets up. Ever operated a professional camera before?" Grassal said he had not. "It'll be on the tripod so it won't shake. Just pan back and forth between the tanks and the people, and if there's blood, zoom in."

Grassal took over for him. The camera reminded him of a coin-operated viewing binocular at a scenic overlook, and he thought of the only family vacation he'd ever taken with his mother and stepfather, a trip to the White Mountains. She was fresh out of rehab, he was fresh out of jail, and they kept talking about a fresh start. Grassal, age eleven, had hopped on a bus and tried to run away. The police returned him to his parents that night. He began the next day with a broken nose and two cracked ribs. Happy memories.

While Grassal panned the camera across the scene and looked for Lilly, his silver threads reached into the sky like the tentacles of a jellyfish.

23

The hallway ended in a room the size of two tractor-trailers. Computer monitors, a shortwave receiver, a frequency scanner, and a telephone sat on a workbench against the wall. Loose wires for power and communications hung from pegs drilled into the scraped sandstone walls. Fluorescent lights hung from the ceiling. A camera on a tripod faced a chair, and nylon straps hung from its arms, legs, and back. An oriental rug covered the floor. Amadeus thought the room had a nice, homey, torture-chambery feel.

Janette guided Marshall to the chair and fastened the nylon straps around his wrists, legs, and waist. The chair creaked under Marshall's thick frame as he squirmed to test the secure bindings. After turning on the camera, Janette retrieved a first-aid kit and tended to the gory wound she had inflicted on Marshall's arm, giving Amadeus hope that she didn't intend to kill him after all.

Finished, she twisted her head to pop her neck, stretched out her shoulders, and drove a fist into Marshall's face. Unprepared for the blow, his head flopped back at an odd angle. For a breath Amadeus thought she might've broken his neck, but Marshall moved his head back and forth while muttering curses.

"That's for the bullshit I've had to put up with since this started." She dropped another punch into his chest. He wheezed. "That's for Claudius." Finally, she punched him in the groin. "That's for me having to make your poor wife a widower. Unless, of course, you decide to talk with us."

"We both know torture gives you shitty information," Marshall said. "Especially when you have an innocent man." Amadeus thought he detected a hint of amusement in his voice.

"That doesn't mean it doesn't feel good," Janette said. "You deserve to be beaten to death."

Vaskulo crept around the edge of the room. His claws clicked on stone as he walked, soft and foreboding. Surely Marshall heard the sound. If he had any experience with living subluminals, and Amadeus was sure that he had, he had already figured it out. After a few moments of looking at the creature, Amadeus heard its voice say, *This man caused her father's death.* He nodded. Everything else it had said had been right so far. If this was true, this might be worth it.

"Marshall," Amadeus said, "I have video that you were present immediately following the murder of every member of Captain Carl's Mobile Extravaganza. The local cops called it a meth lab explosion, but I'm sure if the FBI learned the details, they'd want to pursue terrorism charges."

"And should you survive to face those charges, your cooperation would certainly be noted," Janette said. She nodded to Amadeus, who continued.

"But that's only the beginning. We have a source who claims you were responsible for the attack on our apartment that killed Claudius Owens. Another links you with the murder of Holden Jones. And let's not forget all the joy you've brought to my life."

"You know damn well your father is alive," Marshall said. "I told you as much in San Francisco, you ungrateful little fuck."

Amadeus did not respond to this. Instead, he said, "I chose not to kill you before when I had the chance, and even right now, I don't want to kill you." Amadeus saw Janette shaking her head.

"But I do," Janette said. "So it's better for you and your little family if you talk with us."

"Roland Jessup, the man we believe is your employer, threatens the stability of this country. Tell us about your employer." Amadeus reached for the hood on Marshall's face, but before removing it, he nodded for Vaskulo to move to the darkened hallway. The Takun understood his meaning and crept off into the shadows. "You have a chance to make things right. Talk to us, and things might go well for you. First, who killed Holden Jones?"

"You did, of course. With poison." Marshall's face was red and swollen in places, but his eyes, no longer black but hazel and a little bloodshot, showed pleasure. He smiled, displaying a couple chipped teeth.

Amadeus shook his head. "We both know that's incorrect. How about another question? Tell me about Roland Jessup."

"Who is Roland Jessup?" Marshall said. His smile had grown wider. Amadeus nodded and looked over at Janette, who paced a circle around Marshall before speaking.

"Cut the bullshit, Hathaway, or we'll have to go back to your house and bring a couple guests to this party," Janette said. Marshall scrutinized her, clearly trying to gauge whether she was serious or not. Something in his face softened, and Amadeus thought they might be able to persuade him after all. Even if he didn't like the method, Amadeus needed the information.

"Because what daughter wouldn't want to watch her father break down, denounce her, and pull the trigger on her mother?" Janette said. Amadeus felt sick.

"You wouldn't," Marshall said. Amadeus wanted to agree with Marshall, but something about Janette's expression made him question this assessment.

"Marshall, you've taken lives from others," Janette said. "Isn't it only fair we take yours?"

Marshall was silent.

"Let's give him some time to think about this," Janette said.

"Put the hood back on him. I'm tired of looking at the ugly bastard." Amadeus did so, cinching the string around the bottom so that Marshall's neck was just a little constricted.

While Amadeus completed this task, Janette read news from a laptop. Her expression darkened, and she motioned Amadeus over. He read the article and put his hand to his mouth. The Admiral. Grassal and Lilly had been there. He immediately checked the list of known dead, then the list of survivors, and felt tears of relief when he saw that they'd both made it out ... but out into what? The rest of the news included accounts of violent protests, tanks and foreign soldiers downtown, clashes between city police and paramilitary goons, and the KREATURE Act. Amadeus tried and failed to wrap his brain around everything he had just read.

He looked to Janette, and they both looked across the room to Marshall. Janette motioned for Amadeus to follow her to the other end of the hall, out of earshot.

"This changes nothing," Janette said. "We'll make no mention of this as we continue our discussion with the prisoner."

"Prisoner," Amadeus said, turning the word over in his mouth.

24

Grassal gazed through the viewfinder at the convoy, now less than two blocks away from the main mass of the crowd. He panned back and forth. Samantha frantically tried to finish hooking up the AV equipment. Ellis held a pocket mirror in front of him, combing his wiry blond hair straight back over his head.

The convoy had come to a stop a block away from the crowd that filled the Mall. A line of Metro police officers four deep and eighty meters wide stood between the convoy and the crowd. Several blocks away, a dozen Metro police cars en route to provide support for the line were blocked by the teeming crowd.

A sputtering round of gunfire caused another cry to pass through the crowd, but no one fell. From the convoy, a voice began booming from unseen speakers and echoed off the buildings surrounding the Capitol area.

"Disperse from here immediately. You are ordered to return home," a man's accented voice said. "Metro police, we have the situation under control."

Grassal zoomed in, trying to pinpoint the source of the voice, and he saw, in the middle of the convoy, flanked by two urban assault vehicles, a black van with solid black windows. Grassal guessed whoever was commanding this convoy was inside, and he wondered whether Roland Jessup was a boots-on-the-ground or a command-from-the-hill kind of guy. Though Jessup had made an appearance at The Admiral, Grassal suspected Jessup was the latter.

He panned across the convoy and focused the camera on eight box trucks. They looked like military toy haulers, maybe for Jeeps or urban assault vehicles. A tiny voice in his mind suggested they could also be packed full of subluminals. Grassal shook this thought out of his head and attributed it to lingering paranoia.

"Grassal, will you be joining me on camera?" Ellis asked. Grassal shook his head and said he'd already been on camera too much today.

"Okay, I'm all ready to go," Samantha said, standing up and dusting the bits of roof gravel from the knees of her slacks. "Ready, Ellis?"

Ellis took one last glance in the mirror and nodded. Grassal handed the camera to Samantha. She unfolded a cylindrical metal object to create a parabolic dish, put a microphone inside it, and attached it to a long boom.

"Hold this just over my head," Samantha said, giving Grassal the boom. "Okay, boys, here we go."

"This is Ellis Arbaugh with Channel Six News, and we are coming to you live from downtown Washington, DC. Earlier today, the death of fifty-four people in the fire at The Admiral Hotel sparked protests at the CDC, which have spread to the National Mall. Sources tell me that these protests began as a result of The Admiral deaths, which some attribute to the excessive security put in place there after passage of the KREATURE Act. Now, however, protestors are making themselves heard. Concerns range from civil rights abuses, the growing power of private military corporations, and suspicion of the motives behind the KREATURE Act's passage."

A phone buzzed. From the corner of his eye, Grassal saw Samantha check it. Her eyes grew wide and she waved the phone at Ellis, who gave her an almost imperceptible nod.

"I have some new information coming in, so for the moment we're going to cut to the protests below. I'll be right back with more commentary."

Grassal listened to Ellis and Samantha's conversation. He overheard only snippets, but he was sure he heard the words "death", "agent," and "leak." While they spoke, Samantha fitted Ellis with an earpiece. On the ground below, a circle had formed around two men who held red signal flares. Those around them had moved back to avoid being doused in a shower of sparks. Samantha fed information to Ellis by reading off the flexscreen.

"Ellis Arbaugh back with you. I have just received word that the *Times of America* received a cache of classified documents related to the ongoing investigation into the Emergence. These documents were leaked only hours ago, apparently as a result of the death of an as-yet unnamed intelligence agent. This agent was directly involved in the Emergence and recently played a pivotal role in the capture and interrogation of Holden Jones."

Grassal shuddered. Gravity was dead. Grassal was sure of it. It had to be. He hung his head and mouthed a silent prayer for the old man.

"The *Times* states that, according to the documents, there is considerable dissent within the intelligence over the actors involved in the Emergence, and ..." Samantha spoke into a small mic, and Ellis looked up at her. "My God. I've been told that the documents also contain evidence that the group responsible for the Emergence was one of the companies who profited from cleanup and removal operations. Remember, though, this is an uncorroborated statement and does not mean ..."

Ellis turned and looked out to the crowd. Here and there, throughout the crowd, people were reading the very same news on their phones. Grassal's stomach clenched. Ellis shook his head and looked back at the camera with a level, fiery gaze.

"Given the events of the past few days, this is a truly

terrifying interpretation, but I urge you to remember this is just that, an interpretation. If true, though, this amounts to nothing less than an act of war."

Ellis ended his segment with a long look at the camera, then Samantha returned the camera to the protesters. Ellis used the break to read more reports, muttering to himself as he did so. Grassal borrowed Samantha's phone again, but he couldn't get any calls through. He sent e-mail messages to Lilly, Amadeus, and Annie. In each one, he included Samantha's phone number on the odd chance they could get through.

25

An hour passed, then another. Marshall had volunteered nothing. At Janette's insistence, they waited. While they did so, Janette informed him that no outside communication signals could penetrate the walls of this room, but they had a landline and wired Internet, which she used to make a series of calls. During one of the calls, Janette asked for someone to research how to start her own company. During another, Amadeus thought he heard her asking for approval for some kind of plan from a senator. While she spoke on the phone, Janette kept the shotgun in her hand and her eye on Vaskulo, who had curled into a meditative ball in the hallway.

After she returned her attention to the prisoner, Amadeus checked his e-mail and found a message from Grassal that read:

Downtown is a mess. Securaux goons have moved in. It's the KREATURE Act. I'm with a news crew, but I'm not sure for how long. Is it true about Gravity? Also, I've lost Lilly. Call me if you can.

The message ended with a phone number he didn't recognize. KREATURE Act? Lost Lilly?

Amadeus tried the number on the landline once, twice, thrice, but couldn't get a call through. He responded to

Grassal's message and told him Gravity was dead, but he omitted the details and said he would keep trying to call. While he waited, he filled himself in on the details: subluminals in South Carolina, the emergency KREATURE Act passage, and the leaked documents that were causing an uproar. That last sounded like something Gravity would do. Amadeus smiled and sniffed back a tear. He closed his eyes and allowed himself to process the information. He realized that if nothing had detected the kipium in South Carolina, then someone had devised a way to mask the kipium frequencies. His Gate Crashers were now obsolete, and the demon gate technology had taken another step forward. Fucking Moore's Law, Amadeus thought.

He dialed Grassal again. This time his call went through, and Amadeus fought to restrain his excitement at hearing his friend's voice, though he had to encourage Grassal to speak up, for he could barely hear his friend over the crowd noise.

"On the roof," Grassal said. "Overlooking the National Mall. There are Securaux guys everywhere."

"That doesn't surprise me. Just in case we get cut off, write this number down," Amadeus said. He heard Grassal request pen and paper from his companions.

"Gravity's leaked documents," Grassal said, "do you really think it was Securaux, not Ross?"

"For the demon gates, I can't say for sure, though we're pretty certain Roland Jessup was involved in Jones' death. But don't tell Lilly that, not yet. I'm still gathering information there. What about you? Are you okay?"

"I had some killer drugs, but I'm out now. I'm with the news crew, and they were going to help me find a pharmacy, but reporting on the convoy kind of took precedence. What's happening with you and the general?"

"I think we're on the verge of getting some vital information and ..." Amadeus started to tell him about Vaskulo but thought better of it. Instead, he said, "Let's just say the information is coming from an unlikely source."

Grassal said nothing.

"You take care of yourself. I'm sorry I can't be there to help you. If you see Lilly, just tell her to be patient, and to give me—"

Grassal gasped, then said, "Oh shit. I've got to call you back. I think I just found her."

Amadeus heard a click, and the line went dead.

26

"Oh shit. I've got to call you back. I think I just found her," Grassal said. He passed Samantha's phone back to her and stuck Amadeus' number in his jacket pocket. Grassal had been watching the camera's output on screen while he spoke with Amadeus, and a figure with brick-red hair and a familiar gait had caught his eye. He lost her though, and cursed himself for not paying more attention.

"Grassal," Samantha said, "I just remembered there's a pharmacy about three blocks from here. It's a tiny place, but it's open twenty-four hours. I used to go there when I worked Capitol beat."

"Later, later," Grassal said. In truth, a part of him wanted to run down the stairs right now and have his prescription filled, but that would take time, and he couldn't risk losing the girl who may or may not be Lilly. Instead, he squinted and surveyed the scene. Paramilitaries in riot gear had set up metal barriers and pushed back the crowd. At first Grassal thought they were trying to make a path, but they were pushing the wrong way. Grassal fought the urge to scratch his head. He couldn't make sense of what they were doing. The trucks had spread out, which to Grassal didn't seem like a good strategy, but he observed just a little longer, and when two more long metal barriers had gone up, he realized they weren't so much pushing people out as fencing them in.

A flash drew his eye to a tank. A pillar of fire rose from its black metal armor. Grassal zoomed with the camera and saw something else fly in and ignite. Molotov cocktails. The flames burned themselves out, but not before the side gunners had opened fire on the crowd immediately surrounding the tank. Some people dropped, but others fired back. Hundreds streamed away from the tank, save for a few pockets of people who chose, for whatever reason, to fight back. The Metro police maintained their formation, moving only to permit the fleeing crowd to pass through them.

"This is getting—" Grassal began, but stopped as the barrel of the tank swung around, aiming away from the line of police and toward a group of stationary protestors. The barrel flashed orange a nanosecond before he heard the booming report. The shot cut a line through the crowd like a finger dragged over a dusty tabletop. The police raised their guns but held their fire. A cry rose from the crowd.

"They've fired on United States citizens!" Ellis screamed. His calm, professional demeanor was gone. He put his palms to his temples. "Jesus, Mary, and Joseph." He looked back at Samantha. "I'm sorry, but this ... get the camera on that."

Samantha zoomed in on a few who stood their ground, flanking the line of police. On screen Grassal could see their expressions: angry and defiant and terrified. She panned over the Securaux soldiers lined up behind the tanks and urban assault vehicles, then to the police, who had only ballistic shields for cover.

"MPDC, you will stand down," a voice boomed, the same one as before, only louder. "We have authority here to clear this crowd using any necessary means. Which includes force." The voice paused, as if considering, then said, "Everyone must disperse now. Go to your homes and no one else dies."

For a moment, the only sound was the rumble of engines, then a solitary female figure stepped forward. A thousand silver threads flowed from Grassal's head, across the crowd, and surrounded her like a shield. He squinted and felt a rush of dread wash over him. He guided Samantha's camera and aimed it at the figure. It was Lilly.

She strode out into the space between the Securaux soldiers and the police lines, her arms out in front of her, accenting her points with angry gestures. She reached the middle and faced the convoy. She still wore her backpack. One of the tanks tracked her with its barrel. After putting the parabolic dish on the mic and increasing the gain, Grassal was able to make out her words.

"You cowards. You fucking pricks. These people are not your enemy. They're just like you, except they didn't choose to become spineless jellyfish mercenaries. You're pussies, each and every one of you. You're murderers and fascists and mobsters enforcing the patriarchal, authoritarian power structure. Power mongers. You are the lowest of the low. You want to kill me? You want to kill me? I've lost everything, and it's because of people like you! I'm through with you. I'm through."

"The FCC is going to kill us," Samantha said. Ellis shushed her. The police made no move to remove her from the situation. Grassal gripped the balustrade around the roof while the edges of his vision went white. All this time focusing on his own problems had just created more problems for everyone else. Now Lilly was about to get herself killed, and he had to get her out of there. Without his drugs, doing so might cost him his sanity or his life, but it was the right thing to do, and he was sure the silver threads had somehow directed him here just for this purpose.

"I have to leave," he said to Ellis and Samantha. "Thanks for the food."

"Grassal, what about the pharmacy?" Samantha said, but Grassal's legs were already carrying him down the stairs, out of the apartment building, and onto the street.

The moment he stepped through the door, a gunshot made

him duck. He rose and sprinted to the metal barricade. Only a hundred meters ahead of him, Lilly still berated the tanks. Someone fired a warning shot. She didn't even flinch. Grassal ran toward her and called out, trying to catch her ear, but she was as imperturbable as a pro basketball player on the foul line. More shots exploded and pieces of the Mall's snowy lawn flew up around Lilly like exploding dust. Only warning shots ... for now. Grassal was halfway there. Lilly hadn't moved or flinched.

Grassal smelled cucumbers and charcoal and burned plastic then felt a tingling sensation. All around him, the edges of things shifted, bled into those around them, and shot a million brilliant rainbow lines into the night. His own threads merged with these lines, and they all pulled him toward Lilly like a thousand tiny gusts of wind, iron filings heading toward a magnet. The world slowed to a crawl. He leapt over a barricade and was in the open space between her and the tanks when she turned to him and said, "Grassal?"

Grassal had almost reached her when an explosion shook the world. His mind registered a bullet tunneling through the air toward her. He cried out, and all the nearby rainbow lines and silver threads converged on the bullet, changing its trajectory so that it flew harmlessly up into the night sky.

When he was upon her, Grassal scooped her up with one big arm and threw her over his shoulder. He dashed through the space between the forces. The crowd on the periphery parted for him, and he ran away, far away. Lilly pounded on Grassal's back and demanded he put her down. Grassal neither heard nor cared. He was now only a physical computer with one function: remove Lilly from danger.

He carried her another twenty blocks before he tripped over a curb. Lilly flew from his shoulders and landed on her butt. She barely managed not to hit her head. Grassal lay on his side, his legs still pumping like a dog in a dream.

"Grassal? What the fuck?" Lilly said, but Grassal didn't hear her. The words went into his mind and curled up, like a bear preparing for hibernation. The lines of color were now spinning all around him and flowering up into the sky in a flowing, luminescent pillar of light.

Grassal became aware of himself long enough to realize that Lilly, now standing on her own two feet, was safe. Relief flooded his veins. His consciousness separated from his body, then washed over and through Lilly. A force pulled him toward the pillar, but he remained tethered to the Earth.

He felt himself being pulled apart, as if drawn and quartered, and Grassal knew he had only one choice. In his mind, he envisioned a knife in his hand. The knife appeared. With one shimmering, translucent hand, he severed the thread that connected him to his body, and the pillar of light carried Grassal Delgado out of the world.

27

A shiver passed through Lilly moments after she pulled herself up from the pavement. A car horn blared as its driver swerved around them. The smell of her own sweat filled her nostrils. She started to tighten her coat, but the shiver passed as quickly as it had begun. Kneeling over Grassal's body, she placed two fingers to the rough, unshaven skin of his neck. Her sensitive fingers detected a weak pulse. His face looked so peaceful, like he was sleeping, and his body was rigid, like a soldier standing at attention. She ran her hand over his cheek. His skin was cool and clammy despite his recent exertion. Leaning over his face, she found his breath smelled like shaved aluminum.

"Oh, Grassal. What have you done?" She grabbed his jacket and strained as she tried to pull him off the street. Two buttons popped off his jacket, but Grassal remained in place. She cursed. Lilly knew she could accomplish many things on her own, but moving Grassal's big body was not one of them. He needed medicine, care, and warmth, and she could help with all of that, but none of it mattered if she couldn't get him out of traffic.

Suddenly, two faces peeped from behind a nearby dumpster. One of them said something to the other then they both stepped out.

"You okay, lady?" a voice said. A child's voice. Lilly was glad it was a child, but she wasn't sure why.

"Can you boys please help me with him?" She looked from one to the other. They both had bright brown eyes and curly mops of black hair. She guessed they were around ten years old.

"A car come through, that'd be it for the fat boy," the shorter boy said. Lilly sniffed back something she hadn't realized had come on.

"He would hate it if you called him that," Lilly said, but she smiled, and with their help, she managed to drag Grassal off the patched street and onto a cracked sidewalk.

"We saw all that," the taller boy said.

"Saw what?" Lilly said.

"The lights. It was like a concert or a video game."

"There weren't any lights," Lilly said, though she heard the doubt in her voice. Both boys scowled at her. Definitely brothers. Just because she hadn't seen anything didn't mean they hadn't. For Lilly Jones, truth had taken on a more flexible quality, pliant like clay, its form changeable, moldable to fit different situations. They had seen lights. Why argue?

"I must've missed them."

"He's gone," the other boy said, pointing to Grassal's sleeping form. "Up to heaven. God took him. Up and away."

"Don't you say that," Lilly growled at the boy. The boy shrugged and said he knew what he saw. "Sorry, it's just, I've had a long day. Thank you."

The boys brushed their hands off on their jeans in the exaggerated way only children can and then ran off for places unknown without another word.

Grassal was out of traffic, but that was about it. She couldn't just sit here and wait for more help. Calling 911 would be a waste of time, and it's not like she could move Grassal. She checked his pockets, hoping for a liquid form of his drugs, or keys to a car, a cigarette, or even cab fare. The only thing she found was a phone number. Not sure what good it would do, she dialed the number, and a familiar voice, the voice of a man she had once loved, a man who had betrayed her, answered.

Cursing, Lilly held her own phone away from her head as if it were a piece of spoiled meat but, after a moment, returned the handset to her ear said to Amadeus, "I need your help."

Moments after she ended the call, she heard a group of people screaming only a few blocks away. At that, she removed the Mauser from her bag, attached the shoulder stock, and hoped ten rounds would be enough.

28

After Amadeus hung up, he beckoned Janette over to him. Speaking in a whisper, he told her why he had to go but said he'd like to use his absence for another reason. She pointed toward a radio receiver on the shelf. An old-style microphone sat beside it, and a black nylon bag was stuffed beneath it. From the bag, Janette fished out an ancient two-way radio the size of Amadeus' hand.

"Remember, cell service can't penetrate these walls, but there's a shortwave antennae topside. If shit hits the fan, let me know. Officially, I'm a civilian, but I think it's time I started my own private military corporation."

Amadeus nodded. He felt better knowing he would have some kind of backup, even if he hoped not to have to use it. Amadeus familiarized himself with the radio while Janette returned her attention to the prisoner. Vaskulo paced a circle around Marshall's hooded frame. Janette still kept an eye on the Takun, but she now seemed more relaxed in its presence.

"You haven't said anything, Marshall," Janette said, nodding to Amadeus, who picked up the thread.

"And we're running out of time. We've given you plenty of opportunities to work with us, but you'd rather be stubborn. I think I'm going to pay a visit to some people who are very important to you, though I can't promise I'll bring them here."

"You will do nothing," Marshall said. His voice remained steady.

"They may not come with me, so I might have to film it. I'm sure you'd like to watch that, over and over. Though, if you can tell me who killed Jones, I might hold off on your daughter," Amadeus said. As the words left his mouth, he hated himself, but he had to get Marshall to confess. From the dark recesses of the hallway that led to the elevator, Amadeus saw motion, then heard Vaskulo's voice in his mind.

I'll feed nightmares to this man. He will think ... talking is better. You want this?

Amadeus' hand shook. As of today, he had threatened to kill a man's family and schemed with a Takun. Sure, Vaskulo had only helped them, but still ... it was a *creature*. Yes, a sentient creature, but the same kind of creature that had killed so many innocent people. Amadeus was at the elevator door before he answered.

"Do it," Amadeus said before he punched the button that would take him to the top.

Though the smell had nearly faded from the SUV, Amadeus still had to roll down the windows before he programmed Lilly's location into the GPS. The traffic heading away from the District was heavy and conspired to keep him in the storage facility's parking lot. When he nosed out, some drivers shook their head at him, as if trying to warn him away. A couple times he started to pull out, and drivers sped up and flashed their lights to keep him in.

He saw a small hole in the traffic, slammed the accelerator, and made it through, but no sooner had he straightened out the SUV than a horn blared. Out of instinct, Amadeus looked behind him. He saw only open, snow-covered road. When he turned, he saw a pair of headlights sliding toward him. He felt the impact before he heard the screaming metal. For a lingering moment, the world shook and then was still. Amadeus looked down at himself. Both he and his ride were reasonably intact, but outside, smoke billowed up from the little red hatchback that had hit him. Amadeus drove on and hoped everyone was safe. Someone else would have to help them.

While he had escaped the crash without any injuries, his vehicle wasn't so lucky. At around forty kilometers per hour, everything shook. Driving in a straight line required so much attention that Amadeus almost missed the pack of creatures that were streaming from an open bay of an Übermart distribution warehouse beside the highway.

With the luxury of distance and an open road, Amadeus stopped to examine them. They were different, almost humanoid, except they walked on all fours and had long, turtle-like necks that terminated in featureless heads. Some were covered in needlelike spines.

Amadeus shuddered.

After several moments of rubbernecking, he realized the distance between the creatures and himself had shrunk. He thought he heard tormented shrieks of pain, and he sped away— as much as he could in his wounded vehicle. As the swarm of creatures faded into his rearview, he held the shaking steering wheel with both hands and tried to slow his racing heart.

His path was still clear, but in the other lane were all those people sitting in their cars, trapped … He tried not to think about it. Lilly and Grassal were his priorities, no one else. He grasped the handheld radio and tried to reach Janette. No luck. When he looked down to ensure it was on, a window shattered.

One of the creatures was trying to pull itself inside. With one clawed hand it slashed at the back of Amadeus' seat. Holding the wheel with one hand, he jammed the handheld's antenna into one of the creature's six big yellow eyes and pulled it out. The creature thrashed at the driver's side window. Amadeus swerved toward the concrete barricades that lined the highway. The window glass spidered just before the SUV grated against the concrete, crushing the creature. It released its grip and collapsed on the highway, mangled and writhing.

Amadeus followed the instructions of his GPS and left the Beltway. After a couple kilometers, he was in the Columbia Heights business district. On the street ahead of him, people laden with office equipment and store fixtures swarmed into and out of the broken glass of storefronts. Outside a franchise computer retailer, police had parked their cruisers in front of the door, guarding the store from the crowds. Amadeus saw the same thing farther down: a dozen police had formed a semicircle in front of every bank on the street.

On a corner, at the end of a row of overturned cars, a small mob was kicking a man who was huddled into a ball on the sidewalk. Several police officers watched from across the street, unwilling to abandon their defense of a neighborhood branch of a Union Global Bank. As Amadeus drove past, one man stopped kicking the man and regarded Amadeus with a hostile stare, mouthed his name, and flipped him off. Amadeus returned the gesture and drove on. Occasionally gunfire crackled in the distance.

One roadblock, two small mobs, and one stray Class B subluminal later, he arrived at the intersection where Lilly and Grassal should've been, but when he stepped out of the battered SUV, they weren't there. Amadeus got out and yelled for Lilly.

Everything fell quiet. The distant hum of traffic and crowds faded. Amadeus heard only the wind rustling the branches and snow falling upon itself. Three blocks north, something caught his eye: a group of people marching down the street in lock-step. Amadeus squinted and cupped his hands to his ears. They were like the woman at the airport, or Grassal, only ... no, they weren't marching as a group of individuals would march. They were moving as a single entity. He counted about twenty of them. Their bodies were tangled together, arm around torso over head under legs. The entity emitted a collective moan, and while he watched, the people began climbing over themselves. Within thirty seconds, they had arranged themselves into a shape that resembled a buckyball ... or a hollowed-out virus. Once constituted, the human virus started toward the entrance of the cul-de-sac between two office towers, propelled by hands, arms, elbows, and knees, its speed that of an elderly jogger.

A gun fired. The virus stopped. A single body tumbled out of the virus and to the ground. Other bodies shifted and filled its place. A familiar female voice yelled taunts and insults. Amadeus sprinted to a spot behind the virus. At the end of the cul-de-sac, he saw Lilly crouched behind a truck. She held an oddly shaped pistol in her hand. When she saw Amadeus, she put one finger to her lips. Grassal lay beneath the truck. Even from this distance, Amadeus could tell he was stiff.

"Lilly!" It felt good to say her name, and he called again. Only then did he realize she was trying to shush him. The virus turned its attention to him. Amadeus began to wave his arm and call out her name, "Lilly, Lilly, Lilly!" He had vague plans to draw the virus far enough away from his friends that he could drive his vehicle around them, pile everyone in, and get the hell away.

The nonsense chant of the human virus was closer, the sound throbbing, pulsing in and out as if breathing. He heard other voices as well, angry shouts and whooping calls. He rounded the corner to the street where he had parked, and he saw a group of nearly fifty people.

The small mob he had seen before had grown, and they were moving toward his vehicle. A few held makeshift torches. One man held a shovel above his head. Amadeus looked for pitchforks but was disappointed. A line of overturned and flaming cars stretched out behind them. They needed only a few seconds to flip his SUV. Setting it ablaze took a little longer, but they succeed in this as well before moving on to the next car. Behind him, the virus had rounded the corner.

Halfway between an angry mob and a human buckyball, a new plan struck Amadeus with the force of the New Empire Builder he had ridden so long ago. He faced the cell and waved to attract its attention. If he could lure it toward the mob ...

Four more gunshots cracked, and Amadeus was close enough to watch as a teenage boy's chest exploded. He went limp but was kept in formation by the arms and legs around him. The shots, however, drew the attention of the mob, which turned its attention to him.

"It's that Brunmeier fucker," a man's voice cried.

Another said, "He's the one. He's responsible for all this."

The mob charged toward him. Amadeus looked from the virus to the mob and back. Both would be on him in under a minute. Unconsciously, Amadeus fished a crumpled receipt from his pocket and stuffed it into his mouth. When he realized what he was doing, he spit out the paper.

The virus was only a few car lengths away from him when he saw his exit: an alley between a coffee shop and a Korean barbecue restaurant. The alley intersected with another alley after only a block. He chose this direction, running past parked cars, dumpsters, mounds of black snow, and buckets of hot coals. By the time he was six car lengths in, the virus had become stuck in the alley's opening, like a cork in a bottleneck. For now, this prevented the mob from following him.

He reached the intersection, looked in both directions, and saw two dead ends. Amadeus was trapped. He looked for a ladder, a back door propped open, a fire escape, but there was nothing. Another gunshot took out part of the virus, but it was rearranging itself to fit into the alley.

For the moment, the virus and the mob were keeping each other occupied, but he knew that wouldn't last. With no way to fight and no exit in sight, Amadeus started pulling on car doors in search of an unlocked vehicle. After setting off two alarms, he found the back hatch of an old Honda unlocked and crawled inside.

The interior was window-deep in discarded fast food bags. Everything smelled like mold, body odor, and cigarette smoke, but with its tinted windows and parking spot behind a full-length dumpster, Amadeus couldn't have asked for a better hiding place. He lay down on the rear floorboard and piled bag after wrapper after bag upon himself for camouflage. Unable to see anything, covered in trash, and nearly choking from the smell, Amadeus turned on his handheld and called for help.

29

With the attention of the ball thing turned to Amadeus, Lilly used the opportunity to drag Grassal back into a restaurant's trash alcove. As damp and dirty as it was, at least it provided cover and was out of the snow. She didn't think Grassal would mind, but she let out an exasperated sigh. Amadeus showed up, and the mob followed right behind him.

She'd had her plan, and he ruined it. Somehow, he always managed to make things worse, and if he escaped from his current predicament, and she from hers, she would have to berate him for it. As it was, her options for escape were constrained. She could get away on foot, but she wouldn't leave Grassal, even if his self-absorbed, one-legged Hispanic ass had thought he was "saving" her. But now she was once again stuck, responsible for caring for a sick man grown sicker.

For the moment, she had some cover, but only enough to avoid an inattentive glance or two. That creepy human ball thing could roll back at any moment. The mob probably hadn't seen her yet. And she had a few rounds left in her Mauser. One good thing about living in rural Colorado: she'd had the time and space to become an excellent markswoman.

She put a hand on Grassal's neck; he was still cool and stiff but not showing any visible signs of pain. For this, she was grateful. At least she wasn't making his situation worse.

"Grassal, what have you gotten us into?" Lilly asked him.

She left the alcove then the cul-de-sac and peered around the corner, first toward the fighting, which was bottlenecked in the alley where Amadeus cowered, then down the street. One of the overturned vehicles was a courier box truck. On its side a slogan read, "Big packages are our little specialty." She thought this was a dumbass slogan, but it gave her an idea.

Confident that Grassal would be okay alone for a few moments, Lilly moved to the side of the street opposite the fighting. She darted from one car to the next for cover as she made her way toward the truck. The back door was locked. Using the undercarriage as a ladder, she climbed the truck, tried the passenger door, and found it locked. She knocked out the window glass with her pistol's butt and dropped down inside. In the back, she found exactly what she was looking for: a heavy-duty hand truck. She tried the back door. It unlocked from the inside. Lilly then took the hand truck, along with several rubber tie-downs, back to Grassal.

As stiff as he was, he was still hard to load onto the cart. She ended up rolling him onto his side, taking care not to let the concrete scrape his face too bad, aligning the cart so that it spooned him, then wrapping the tie-downs around his body. When she was sure Grassal was secure, she strained and strained to lift the cart. When she managed to get him off the ground and began wheeling him along, she found the hardest part was avoiding the ruts and potholes of the alley.

Finally, she was out of the alley and pushing the cart onto the sidewalk, grateful for the handicap ramps on every curb. Save for the people fighting with the creepy ball thing, the sidewalks were nearly empty. She moved away from the madness and toward the only thing that mattered: shelter for the sick.

On a side street two blocks away, she found an open door. Only the streetlight illuminating the bare shelves told her this was a stockroom. It smelled of disuse and piss. With no other discernible entrances besides the one she had used, Lilly decided this was as safe a place as any for Grassal to shelter. Kneeling, she planted a dry kiss on his cheek and pulled the door closed. With Grassal safe, she knew she had to figure out some way to help Amadeus. Murderer or not, she had brought him here, after all.

Resuming her previous vantage point, she saw that the ball thing was contining to work in Amadeus' favor. The alley entrance was a drain, and the ball thing was a tenacious clump of hair even a mob couldn't remove. Lilly looked for a way in. Metal doors covered all the storefronts. The buildings on either side of the alley rose over four floors, and she took a moment to search out vertical paths. Colorado had been great for rock climbing as well as shooting, but no suitable paths presented themselves to her ... until her gaze returned to the street and settled on the steel grate beneath her feet. Some wires and machinery were visible, along with a tunnel that quickly descended into darkness.

After making sure she remained unseen, she slipped beneath the grate and lowered herself down the ladder. Closing her eyes, she visualized the layout of the tunnel before her and guessed how many steps she should take after she made her turn. Before leaving the light of the street, she double-checked the rounds in her clip. After all the shots at the ball thing, she had four rounds remaining ... none of which she hoped to use.

With a hand on the wall, she felt her way down into pitch black. She hoped the stink was only a leaky sewer line. The drone of the ball thing's chant mingled with the raucous shouts and occasional cries of the mob, but as she proceeded, this sound was replaced with that of trickling water and the thrum of machinery. Her footsteps echoed all around her, and she wished she had spent more time on echolocation. One week two summers ago with Tim just wasn't enough time. Yet even enveloped by darkness, the walls she could feel around her body and over her head gave her a feeling of security. She attributed the feeling to too much time living underground. One day, she would have a high-rise apartment.

Soon the wall ended and she reached the intersection at the alley's entrance. Lilly was almost—but not entirely—certain she was going in the proper direction. On down the tunnel, a few slivers of light cut through the blackness beneath where she estimated Amadeus would be. She took a tentative, probing step in that direction, found solid ground, took another step, and felt confident she could move forward.

From the distance, a howl echoed off the concrete walls around her. Lilly froze. Every fine hair on her body stood up. The sound reminded her of a whale's mating call combined with fingers dragging across a chalkboard. She quickened her pace and fought the urge to break into a run. If she ran, she would risk kissing the concrete or twisting an ankle. The bellow repeated, closer this time. Lilly turned off the safety and stroked the curved trigger.

When she was almost to the light, a familiar, putrid odor entered her airways. She choked back a gag. The smell was the one she remembered from the days when she and Amadeus had made their daily topside checks to see if those filthy creatures continued to inhabit her bunker. It still infuriated her that she'd been forced to huddle underground for so long, when, for the first time in her life, she would've otherwise had the freedom to do as she pleased.

The anger sharpened her senses. She became aware of the texture of her clothing against her skin. The seams that ran down the sides of her jeans. The constriction of the bra around her chest. The elastic band that held her hair back in a tight bun. Down the corridor, something scraped against metal.

She reached the light, which entered the tunnel through a grate. Above her, she could see the soles of the mob's feet. She hadn't gone far enough, but even if she had, and even if no mob were above her, it wouldn't matter, because no ladder rose to the street. She kept moving.

The creatures were closer, but she was almost where she

needed to be. In her mind, she could see the two groups above her head, and as she crept along, she saw herself passing beneath them and getting closer to where Amadeus hid.

Finally, she felt metal rungs protruding from the wall. Streetlight entered through three coin-sized openings on the ceiling. Lilly guessed this was a manhole cover. But as soon as she grabbed a lower rung, she heard something scuttling nearby, followed by hissing, wheezing breath.

For the second time today, she chose to stand her ground. This time, nothing and no one would prevent her from doing so. Letting go of the rungs, she put the pistol's stock against her shoulder and aimed in the direction of the sound. The gun was powerful and her aim good, but the hallway was dark. Until the creature reached the light beneath the grate, her ears would help her more than her eyes. She took a step back, into the shadows. Thinking helped nothing, so she silenced her mind and waited.

The scuttling grew louder. Her heart beat against her chest. She heard flesh rubbing concrete. She tapped the trigger, ready.

The creature announced itself with a howl.

Lilly fired in the direction of the sound. Three rounds remaining. The creature bellowed. She fired two blind shots before the creature stepped into the light beneath the grate. It was almost human in shape but it walked on all fours. Spindles of hard tissue protruded from its back, and for just a moment, it stopped and regarded her with watery black eyes.

Lilly aimed between its eyes and squeezed the trigger. Black liquid bloomed on its forehead, and the creature dropped. She couldn't hear anything but the ringing in her ears. Lowering the gun, she started to climb when something grabbed her foot and pulled. She screamed and bludgeoned the creature's claw with her pistol. It released her just as the manhole cover above her opened. Amadeus extended a hand to her. She handed him the pistol and scrambled up the ladder. Once on the street, she forced herself to wipe away the smile on her face while he replaced the cover.

Crouching, she surveyed their surroundings. The alley's entrance was still crammed with fighting bodies. She pointed to where the alley intersected a back street. Amadeus saw her gaze and shook his head, a gesture so forlorn she almost felt sorry for him. "Dead ends," he said. She scanned for other exits and found none. A cynical smile rose to her lips as she realized she had once again gotten herself trapped as a result of trying to help someone. At least this would be the last time she made this mistake.

"I didn't kill your father, Lilly."

Lilly ignored this and pretended to scan the buildings for climbing routes.

"What about Grassal?" A greasy restaurant receipt was stuck to the front of his shirt. She pulled it off and flicked it away, lest he be tempted to eat it.

"Back that way." Lilly pointed in the direction she had come. "He's safe for now, but he's catatonic. I haven't been able to find any drugs for him."

"What's down there?"

"Things. But they're different. I killed one. They look ... almost ..."

"I think I know which ones you're talking about."

"... almost intelligent."

Amadeus raised an eyebrow and started to say something to this, but a cacophony of hoots and shrieks from below cut him off. Without waiting to be told, Amadeus shoved the manhole cover fully back into place. Unclipping a black device from his pocket, he extended an antenna and spoke into it. He listened, nodded a few times, and put it back on his belt.

"I doubt that'll hold them, and once they see the dead one, they'll start climbing," Amadeus said. "But that's okay."

"Okay? Okay? Are you such a stupid fucking romantic that you want to die with me by your side? Or are you just fucking stupid? There is nothing okay about this particular situation. If you weren't such a fucking ... how you got yourself into this," Lilly pointed to the mass of fighting bodies, "is beyond me. You possess a level of quixotic chutzpah combined with across-the-board stupidity that makes you a rare breed among men, and I don't mean that in a good way. You—"

"Lilly. Chill. There's—" The ground shook beneath them. It reminded Lilly of a ship's engines under power. They both looked down at the manhole cover. "Car. Help me." Before she could say anything, Amadeus was on his feet and leaning into an open car door.

Lilly understood what he was doing and started to help him. He had put the car in neutral and was pushing from the front. With his back to the crowd, Amadeus couldn't see the man who had broken free of the fray and was limping toward him. Lilly raised her gun, but the man kept coming, baseball bat in hand. She yelled for him to stop. He ignored her. Amadeus strained and pushed to move the car, but he was too scrawny to push even an old Honda. She needed to help him, but this fucking guy ...

She heard a clink, and the manhole cover moved. Lilly had to act. She made her decision. To the man, she said, "Last warning. Turn back now or I will kill you." He ignored her. Lilly pulled the trigger and the man fell backwards. Two more broke free from fighting with the ball thing and started toward them. That was it. The gun was empty. Amadeus grunted with exertion, but the Honda still hadn't moved the mere meter it needed to cover the manhole.

She dropped her pistol and helped Amadeus. Just before the car's rear wheel blocked the manhole, the metal cover flew off. One of the creatures started to pull itself out. The Honda crushed its arm as its tire dropped into the open hole. Amadeus slumped as if at rest. After picking up her gun, Lilly pulled him back by the shirt, away from the two men.

"You saw what happened to your friend," Lilly said, nodding to the man she had killed. Her voice sounded more confident than she felt. She took aim. "This is your last warning."

They hesitated.

"You created all of this," one man said, pointing first at Amadeus, then around the alley. "My wife is one of *them* now." He wore gold-rimmed glasses and a torn black peacoat.

"I'm sorry for your wife. I really am. But I tried to *stop* this. You think I wanted all this? I didn't want anything but ..." He looked at Lilly, and she gave him a nod of support. "But it doesn't matter what I say, or what I want. People like you don't want to be convinced."

The other man spoke. "I think you and your father planned this together, some kind of convoluted scheme for fame or money or something."

Something crashed behind them, their eyes widened, and without another word they turned on their heels and ran back toward the fighting mass. For a second, Lilly was relieved, but then she saw the Honda being pushed up by several pairs of black, spindly arms. Amadeus grabbed her hand and ran with her to the very end of the alley.

The creatures had nearly turned over the Honda, and on the other side of the ball thing, the creatures were streaming out of the grate. They'd soon be overrun, either by the creatures coming out of the manhole, or by those breaking through the bottleneck. This was it—her stupid, final demise, and Amadeus was smiling. Smiling!

"What could you possibly be so happy about?" His grin grew bigger, and she had to restrain herself from dragging her fingernails across his face. Then she heard it, a whooping sound, faint at first, but growing louder. A shadow fell across the alley, and a black helicopter appeared, blotting out the sky above them. The Honda flipped over, and creatures began to pour out of the manhole. A rope ladder hit the ground in front of them. Amadeus handed it to Lilly, and she realized that she, too, was smiling.

As the first of the creatures pulled itself from the manhole and the others overran the ball thing, Lilly Jones and Amadeus Brunmeier held onto the rope ladder and each other. Snow swirled around them as the helicopter lifted them into the air, high above a city that was tearing itself apart.

30

With a winch and a stretcher, Amadeus and Lilly pulled Grassal onto the roof and loaded him into the cramped confines of the Lakota Eurocopter. Marshall's wrists and feet were strapped to a seat frame in the back. His skin was pale and a bloody white bandage covered one of his eyes. Snow continued to fall.

Vaskulo was curled up behind a storage case. Lilly hadn't seen him yet, and Amadeus ushered her away from the helicopter to the edge of the roof. In the distance, human and Takun battled. Even over the rotor's buzz, Amadeus heard pops of gunfire.

"There's something, someone ... let's just say we have an unlikely ally," Amadeus said. "And I want to prepare you to meet him—it." The indefinite gender pronoun gave it away. A look of disgust spread across her face, then she smiled and opened her eyes wide.

"No. Nuh uh. Nope. No way. This is, you ... your sense of humor is one of the things I really hate about you," Lilly said, shaking her head. "That's not even funny. And what's with—"

Before she could ask about Marshall, Vaskulo sprang from the helicopter. Lilly screamed and took a step back. Vaskulo put its long arms over its head in a semicircle. Amadeus put a hand on her shoulder.

"It's really, really weird, I know, but it's not a threat to us. Quite the opposite, in fact."

"This is fucked," Lilly said, putting both hands over her mouth. Amadeus followed her gaze first to Vaskulo, then to her gun, and finally to Janette Nguyen, who was stepping down from the helicopter. The former general's presence and nonchalance toward the subluminal seemed to calm Lilly down. Janette strode over to Amadeus and Lilly and threw one arm around each of them.

"These are strange times, my friends," Janette said, flicking her hand at the creature. Vaskulo did two backwards somersaults, landed in the helicopter, and returned with a flexscreen in its outstretched hand.

"You'll like this," Janette said to Amadeus. With a tentative hand, Lilly took the flexscreen from Vaskulo and stretched it out to magazine size. Amadeus stood beside her. The video showed Marshall strapped to a chair at the storage facility. He gazed at the camera with one eye. Blood drained from the other eye socket, and a gooey red blob that had been his eye lay on the floor by his feet. In a tremulous voice, he stated his full name and confessed to the assassinations of both Holden Jones and Claudius Owens. This clip was followed by grainy security camera footage of a man pumping something from a canister into a metal air duct. Lilly paused the video and zoomed in until she could see Marshall's face. Janette tapped the flexscreen.

"The coroner's report stated your father died of asphyxiation," Janette said. "One of my sources informed me they found traces of sarin gas in the ventilation system. Two other prisoners were exposed as well, but they recovered. Your father wasn't exactly in the best of health, and the gas was too much for him. We don't know how Marshall got into the facility, but this should be sufficient to demonstrate we've found your father's killer."

Lilly dropped the flexscreen and started for Marshall. Janette stepped in front of her, put a gentle hand on her chest, and spoke in soothing tones.

"Let me kill him," Lilly said.

"No can do, Lilly," Janette said. "I made an arrangement with him that isn't yet settled. Besides, did you want to murder Amadeus when you believed he was responsible for your father's death?" Lilly shook her head. Amadeus watched Lilly and waited ... just a few more moments before she realized ...

"Oh fuck," Lilly said, turning to Amadeus. "I am so fucking sorry." She nuzzled against his shoulder, repeating, "I'm sorry, I'm sorry," over and over. Her tears seeped through his shirt and chilled his shoulder. As he held her, Amadeus looked around. Janette averted her eyes from them, Vaskulo returned to the cockpit, and Grassal was stone still on his stretcher. In the distance, plumes of black smoke rose toward the sky. Amadeus caught a glimpse of a big class A subluminal lumbering down one of the diagonal lettered streets. As much as Amadeus wanted her to stay close, he clasped Lilly by the shoulders and looked into her moist, bloodshot eyes.

"You risked everything for me. And as bad as I treated you, you still came when I needed you."

"Of course. And I'd do it again, and again. Nobody ever said redemption came cheap."

She said, "I was so damn wrong about you. Can you forgive me?"

To the south, a building collapsed into dust. Amadeus hesitated. "Lilly, I need to understand. How could you think I would do something like that?"

"He was my father. I was devastated. Whoever sent those pictures, they must've known me well enough to know I would jump to a conclusion ... I had to blame someone, and there you were, looking so guilty."

"But who sent the pictures?"

"It doesn't matter. What matters is that you risked your life to prove your innocence to me and that you're still here, still holding me, after the way I treated you. Amadeus, can you ever forgive me?"

Amadeus took her hands and nodded.

"You're so fucking weird," she said. She sniffed back tears, but she was smiling. Amadeus nodded and released her hands. Lilly turned toward the former general, who faced the city, her hands folded behind her back, her feet shoulder-width apart. "How?" Lilly asked, gesturing with the flexscreen to Marshall. Amadeus explained everything up to the point he left to find her, but he left out the part about Vaskulo offering to plant nightmares in the man's mind.

"We made a deal," Janette said. "He gave me the two confessions, and I let him keep one eye." Amadeus shuddered. "However, a man in his predicament would say anything, so I asked for some corroborating evidence. Marshall delivered in the form of an encryption key. DoD security videos are undeletable and have mirrors of mirrors, none of which remain in the same place for very long. This should have helped us figure out who killed Jones, but Marshall was smart enough to have someone tap the video feed and encrypt the data while it was being recorded. Now we're on to the second phase of negotiations." Janette beamed in victory.

"Which include?" Amadeus said.

"Well, in addition to letting him keep an eye for his confession, I promised to get his family out of Washington. But before I do that, I think he'll need to sweeten the deal and tell us a little more about Roland Jessup." Janette surveyed the city as she spoke, her gaze occasionally settling on a faraway gunfight or fire. "I know just the thing that will do that."

She intends harm to his family.

"Amadeus, see about setting up a camera. I want to make sure we get his confession on tape." Amadeus nodded and, following Janette's lead, piled back into the helicopter.

"Where did you get a helicopter?" Lilly said, testing her headset radio. She was in the copilot's seat. Janette pushed the yoke forward and the helicopter lifted into the air.

"It's good to have friends." As the former general looked out over the city, a wide grin spread across her face.

31

Two hundred meters above the District, while snow fell around them, Amadeus attached a video camera to a rack with two plastic cable ties. The camera faced Marshall, who now wore a headset microphone. He was handcuffed to the jumpseat's metal frame. Finished, Amadeus strapped himself in across from Marshall, who had tracked his every movement with his single eye. Amadeus wasn't sure whether to feel fear, loathing, or pity for the man.

Below, new Takun. Angry, confused, mournful.

In his mind, Amadeus said, "Mournful? Why?"

In their minds, this is the City of Night. Humans are jailors. Human blood earns them passage back to the Luminance.

"Tell me more."

We are prisoners of these bodies. This is reality. Simplified for you.

A few minutes passed. He looked out at the city below, got his bearings, and realized that Vaskulo was again right: they were en route to Marshall's house. He hoped the man's wife would be smart enough to leave that house. When they were closer, Amadeus noticed Marshall clenching and unclenching his fists, like someone working out tight muscles. He knew where they were going. Amadeus gave no indication he saw this and instead chose to wait. This would give Marshall's mind more time to imagine what they were capable of. And just what, Amadeus wondered, were they capable of?

The helicopter descended, and even from the air, Amadeus recognized Marshall's house, with its overgrown bushes and Zen garden, complete with a frozen koi pond. So far, this section of the city appeared untouched, though traffic clogged the nearby highway and fires burned only a kilometer away.

Janette directed Amadeus' attention to a screen mounted in the cockpit. She flipped some switches, and a video feed of the ground below appeared on the screen. Using a joystick to adjust the camera angle, she eventually aimed the camera at Marshall's house. She typed some commands on the screen, and the live video was replaced with a thermal image showing two bodies huddled together, one significantly smaller than the other.

"A man's fortress can become a prison ... or a target," Janette said. Amadeus nodded. He didn't like this. "Turn on the camera." Amadeus did so. Janette descended until the helicopter was less than a hundred meters off the ground and they faced the back of the house.

Amadeus heard Vaskulo. *Takun are nearby. They are new. They heed me.*

"You know where we're at, don't you, Marshall? You know who the people on the thermal are," Janette said. Marshall was silent. She flipped two red toggle switches on the console, then opened a red cover on the yoke and placed her finger on a red button. "Well? Nothing?" Marshall was silent. Janette shrugged, and the helicopter shook as she fired round after round into Marshall's backyard. Fragments of the little red pagoda now littered the yard.

"I despise Zen gardens," Janette said. "Grow some goddamned pumpkins. Now, do you have anything to say?"Amadeus studied the helicopter's control system. The safety appeared to be two red switches in the center.

"You wouldn't," Marshall said.

"You said the same thing about your impromptu eye surgery."

"They're innocents. They have nothing to do with this."

"A lot of innocents are going to die today. That doesn't seem to bother you. But you have a choice."

He is sincere, Vaskulo said. *He believes they will die by his employer if he talks.*

"Then tell him differently," Amadeus thought.

"You would kill a woman and child?" Marshall said.

"Would you like to test me? I promise you, I've done worse. A woman like me doesn't become a general by being compassionate." On the ground two hundred meters away, a dozen new Takun stalked through the streets. "Nothing? Okay, then."

Janette depressed the firing button and strafed the upper floor of Marshall's home, from one side to the other, shooting out every window and leaving a neat line of bullet holes in the brick. By the time she had finished, Amadeus' entire body itched. Marshall closed his eyes and hung his head. He looked like a man saying a prayer or collecting his thoughts.

"Talk to us, Marshall." On the targeting screen, the crosshairs settled over the bodies of the woman and child. Amadeus fought back vomit. She was going to do it.

"Just kill me," Marshall said. "Please, leave them alone."

"No can do, Mr. Hathaway. That'd be a waste. You have too much information. I'd rather kill everything you love while you watch."

"I ... I cannot." Marshall said.

I promised safety for his family.

"That's unfortunate," Janette said. Just as her thumb brushed the firing button, Amadeus stretched forward and grabbed the yoke. The helicopter lurched and the guns fired over the house's roof. Cursing, Janette peeled his fingers from the yoke and pushed him back as she used both hands to correct the helicopter's pitch and yaw. When Amadeus was back in his seat, Marshall stared at him with one pale eye, his expression unreadable.

From Janette, he heard, "A.B., you're only prolonging this ugly business." But her voice held no malice for him. "Marshall, I can prom—"

"Contracts," Marshall said, hanging his head. "We did it for government contracts, at least partially. And strength. To rebuild the strength of a once-great country made weak and flaccid by its own success."

"'We' being ...?" Janette said. Marshall was silent. Amadeus pointed out the window. Hundreds of Takun were now streaming toward the house. Marshall grimaced when he saw them.

"Securaux, of course. Do you have any idea how much money can be made by fighting an enemy that you yourself create? Complete vertical integration. The government-military-industrial-prison complex has been doing it for decades, and my employer found a great way to get in on the action. It's beautiful, really. I could've retired in three years."

"Roland Jessup is our man, then?" Janette said. Marshall pursed his lips then nodded. "I nailed it. Please, Mr. Hathaway, say that for the camera."

Marshall looked into the camera with his one eye and said, "Roland Jessup is responsible for the Emergence."

"Good boy," Janette said. "Now, explain to me one more thing. Why in the name of fuck would you let this many creatures out? I know the stats on Securaux, and there's no way they'll be able to handle this. You could've just been happy with your little KREATURE Act, occasionally released a flock of demongulls, swooped in to clean up shit, billed our Uncle Sam for your troubles, and fattened your offshore accounts. But it looks to me like things got out of hand, you murdering fuck."

"There were ... design complications."

"What do you mean?" Amadeus said.

"I mean that we rushed the design. Sometimes the gates don't power down fast enough, the creatures kill the operators, and the creatures keep coming out. Is that enough for you? Can we please get my family out now?"

"One more thing, and I think you know what it'll be," Janette said. "Roland Jessup. Where is he? How can we find him?"

"I don't know."

He is lying.

"He's lying," Amadeus said to Janette. After he spoke, he grabbed Marshall's hair and pressed his face against the helicopter's window. "Look. Look. Do you see them? I might've saved your family from the general, but this is your doing, your retirement plan. And if you don't tell us where we can find Jessup, I'll let this play out because their blood will be on your hands. Will you save your family from your own actions, Marshall Hathaway?"

"God damn you all," Marshall said. "Forty-two by fifteen by twenty-three. In the middle of the Chesapeake Bay. There's an offshore operations center. In a situation like this, that's where you'll find him."

"Thank you," Janette said. With that, she turned to Amadeus. "Ready for a little rescue mission?"

32

Lilly lowered the cable and watched Amadeus descend to the ground. The creatures had formed a circle around the house, but they seemed in no hurry to attack. She cast an uneasy look toward that horrible, fascinating creature Amadeus called Vaskulo. She knew he was communicating with it somehow, and she suspected it was communicating with the other creatures, but the thought unsettled her, almost as much as the idea that Amadeus would allow subluminals to ravish an innocent family. She looked down at Grassal and wished he were awake to provide her with some advice or insight.

Janette Nguyen handed a headset to Lilly and motioned for her to put it on. Lilly obliged, and Janette Nguyen said, "I saw what you did with the tanks. Not many young people would do what you did."

"I didn't really think about it," Lilly said. "To tell you the truth, I kind of lost control."

"Girl, I've never seen anybody more in control. Word from the Metro police is that you rattled some of the operators. A few even laid down their guns."

Lilly shook her head. She hadn't expected that, though what she had expected, she wasn't sure. Instead, she wondered about the future. "Where will we go after this?"

"We'll take his family to safety, probably somewhere west.

After that, I need to get somewhere to coordinate a counter attack, probably Andrews, and get him into custody. He may still be useful."

Lilly felt a tug on the cable. Down below, Amadeus stood behind the house with a woman and a little girl. Lilly wondered why, after having a helicopter shoot up their house, they would consider boarding said helicopter. When he tried to affix the harness to the woman and the girl, the girl tried to run away, but the woman pulled her back by her shirt. Amadeus harnessed them and waved to Lilly. She pressed the button on the winch, and they began to rise.

Marshall beamed and pressed his face against the window as they rose. When they were about three-quarters of the way up, the girl saw her father. The fear on her face was replaced with excitement, and she squirmed in her harness, causing the helicopter to shake.

When she saw the girl's reaction, Lilly felt something constrict in her throat. Maybe when the girl was older, when she understood just who and what her father was, her reaction would be different. For now, however, it pleased her that the little girl still got excited when she saw her father ... even if it was more than her father deserved.

The woman, who Lilly assumed was Marshall's wife, gasped when she saw her husband. Though Lilly hadn't seen him since Prague, she assumed he wouldn't normally be covered in bruises, handcuffed, and missing an eye. Nevertheless, the woman and child fell on him before Amadeus even removed their harnesses. Marshall assured them everything would be all right, and together the three of them wept.

Forty-five minutes later, the former general landed the helicopter near an apple orchard in rural West Virginia and told them to get out. "You can't just leave us here," the woman said, yelling to be heard over the buzz of the helicopter's rotors. She motioned to the deserted brown woods that surrounded them. "This is ... it's ... dirty. It's deliverance country."

"Welcome to West Virginia. There's a town with a hotel a couple miles down that road," Janette said, pointing to a two-lane track nearby. "And it's not like you can't afford it. Roland Jessup compensates his creatures very well." Janette watched the woman for a reaction, but she gave no indication the name meant anything to her.

The helicopter's rotors swirled dead leaves around them. Several deer darted across the orchard and disappeared behind some trees. Lilly helped the woman and the girl out of the helicopter.

"Why did you hurt my daddy?" the girl asked. Lilly squatted so that she could look her in the eye.

"Your daddy made some bad choices, and those bad choices put a lot of people in danger." This troubled her more, so Lilly continued. "My daddy also made some bad choices. One day ..." Lilly had to stop as her throat had constricted. She looked at Vaskulo and was able to continue. "One day, maybe we can forgive our daddies for what they've done. Until then, just remember not to blame yourself. Okay, sugar?" The little girl had a dumb, vacant look on her face. Lilly hoped only that she would remember this conversation in the years to come. With that, she and Amadeus returned to the helicopter, and he slid the door closed behind them.

The woman and the girl shielded their eyes from the helicopter's wind as they took off. While Janette piloted them toward their destination, she spoke with someone on the radio. Lilly could only overhear bits and pieces of the conversation, but she was sure the former general was talking with a senator about starting a company.

33

Janette landed on the helipad near the control tower at Andrews Air Force Base. Firemen, mechanics, and airmen readied planes with frantic energy. During their brief descent, a quartet of jets had taken off only seconds apart.

A limousine sped across the tarmac, stopped behind a transport aircraft, and deposited several well-dressed people. Eight rifle-carrying soldiers dressed in desert fatigues formed a perimeter around them. Amadeus squinted and saw Senator Payne and Enzo among them.

"The rats are abandoning ship," Janette said as Amadeus threw open the helicopter door. He clenched and unclenched his fist as he closed the distance between himself and the man who had cost Gravity his life.

When Enzo saw Amadeus, his eyes grew wide and he took a reflexive step behind Senator Payne. She glared at Amadeus then said to the soldiers, "Stop that man."

With some reluctance, two soldiers stepped into his path. Without breaking his stride, Amadeus pushed through the soldiers, stepped around Senator Payne, and slammed his fist into Enzo's temple. Enzo staggered and fell to the ground. Senator Payne was screaming for the soldiers to arrest Amadeus. They ignored her at Janette's command.

Satisfied, Amadeus returned to his companions. Two airmen

came to attention and saluted Janette. Amadeus couldn't hear them over the roar of accelerating jets, but the former general's face had darkened. Janette nodded and inclined her head toward the group of soldiers around the senator. They nodded as she addressed them. She then started toward the politicians. Amadeus and one of the airmen followed her. The other ran off while speaking into a phone. Even though her gray wool skirt and black leather jacket gave no indication of her former rank, the soldiers escorting the politicians came to attention when she approached. Senator Payne's eyes were wide.

"You will stand down, Nguyen," Payne said. "You know I'm a ranking member—"

"Senator Amanda Payne, you're under arrest for violation of US code title eighteen, section two thousand, three hundred and eighty-one." The senator gaped at her. "This is the citation for treason, in case you forgot. We have you on the record as giving aid and comfort to Securaux, an organization we can now prove is an enemy of the United States."

"Treason? You've got no authority here, and you should be ashamed of yourself. I'm a senator, and you're ... you're not even a real American, let alone a general."

"As of this moment, you're a former senator, and I am now head of the newly formed Joint Defense Services Corporation. I'm sure you remember that section thirteen of the KREATURE Act authorizes new companies to begin operations during Emergence-related emergencies?"

"You just ... you can't ... who approved you?" Payne said.

"Senators Fielding and Graythorpe both signed off on my proposed defense consultancy. Thanks to your bill, I didn't have to go through all that pesky red tape." She pointed to the soldiers who had failed to block Amadeus' path. "You two. You're responsible for accompanying the prisoner onto the transport. Her assistant may accompany her, if he wishes." She produced the memory card from the camera which contained Marshall's confession. "Give this to your commanding officer.

Tell him it's from me. These airmen told me you'll see him in Dayton."

"Yes, ma'am," they said in unison. They descended on Amanda Payne and led the former senator onto the transport plane. She walked with her head hung. Enzo looked around. His eyes met Amadeus' before scurrying along after them. The other politicians had already slunk away and boarded the plane.

Takun converge here. Some follow orders. Others seek you.

Amadeus looked back to the helicopter and asked for clarification, but the creature was silent. Janette told the remaining six soldiers to accompany her. They did, and she spoke to them as they walked. More jets took off in quick succession.

"Janette," Amadeus said, but she ignored him.

Janette stopped three-quarters of the way to the helicopter and surveyed the little squad. A couple smiled, but an equal number stood with mouths agape. "You're all Army men, so you should know me and my record. If you don't, you shouldn't be wearing that uniform. That said, here's what you need to know right now: we are in possession of a very novel intelligence asset. Even though I was initially loath to do so, I can now vouch for ... it. I am placing my trust in you to trust in my own professional judgment."

One of the soldiers, a man in his mid-forties, stepped forward. "Thank you, ma'am. Men, you heard the general. Er, former general. But, if I may be so bold, ma'am, what is this 'it'?"

As if on cue, Vaskulo jumped from the helicopter's cargo bay and surveyed the scene. The soldiers trained their rifles on it.

"That's it. It is a Takun, and it is sentient. At ease, soldiers," Janette said. The soldiers looked around, unsure. "This creature helped us locate a certain scumbag you'll find inside the helicopter. You may lower your weapons." All but one soldier did so. He looked to his sergeant.

"Sergeant?" the hesitant soldier said. His voice's register was somewhere between wariness and a whine. His rifle shook in his hands, and his eyes darted from Vaskulo to Janette and back.

"Lower your weapon, PFC Stone," the sergeant said.

PFC Stone shook his head. He was muttering something. Amadeus strained his ears and heard he was repeating the phrase, "All enemies, foreign and domestic."

"Sergeant, do your men wear body armor?" Janette said. She stood shoulder-to-shoulder with the sergeant. He nodded and gave her a perplexed look. "Good." Before the sergeant or anyone else realized what was happening, Janette had removed the sergeant's sidearm from its holster and shot PFC Stone in the chest. The impact knocked him onto his back. His rifle clattered onto the tarmac. He screamed and put his hands to his chest. She stuffed the pistol into her waistband.

"Does anyone else have any objections to my professional judgment of what constitutes an appropriate intelligence asset?" No one spoke, but Amadeus noticed a faint smirk at the edges of the sergeant's mouth. PFC Stone was back on his feet, but unsteady.

Moments after the transport plane took off, the airman she had spoken with earlier returned in a Jeep.

"Nothing there, ma'am," he said.

"They're sure?"

"They swept everything within fifty kilometers of the coordinates provided. There's nothing there but a garbage patch."

Janette Nguyen pursed her lips then walked to the helicopter, released Marshall's handcuffs, and yanked him out by this shirt. He tumbled to the ground, and she planted a kick in his ribs. Amadeus winced then glanced over at Lilly. She was in the helicopter, leaning over Grassal.

"This creature gave us wrong information. He wasted our time and resources." Marshall looked up at Janette—and grinned. Blood streamed from his mouth, his one eye was bloodshot, yet he appeared to be enjoying himself, like a child who misbehaves for attention. Janette aimed the pistol at

Marshall's head. "Would you like one last try?"

A siren began to scream. One of the hangar doors swung open. Four armored Humvees and a tank drove out and rolled toward the northern perimeter of the base.

"What's happening?" Janette said.

"Entities approaching from all directions, ma'am," the airman said, screaming to be heard over the sirens. The squad exchanged looks, and some double-checked their weapons. Marshall tittered. Janette kicked him again, and he wheezed.

"Tell me where to find Jessup."

"Even if my brain contained that information, I wouldn't divulge it to you."

"Then you've outlived your usefulness." She raised her gun. Before Amadeus could stop himself, he stepped between Janette Nguyen's weapon and Marshall Hathaway. He put his hands out in a pleading gesture.

"Janette, please. This man is the worst sort of human being. It's a shame we have to breathe the same air as him. He's a first-class shithead. But if you execute him now, and I just stand here and watch, then I'll be complicit, and I'll always ask myself what kind of man I'd become."

"Treason is punishable by death, Amadeus."

"But are we executioners? Look out there, General. Look at what's coming. Instead of executing him, why not just leave him to his fate?"

Janette put a hand to her chin and gave a thoughtful nod. "I like it. Your suggestion has a perverse kind of justice that appeals to me." She scanned the horizon then pulled Marshall to his feet.

"You heard him. Is there anything else you'd like to say before I tell you to run?"

Marshall spat a gob of blood at Amadeus' feet. "Why don't you just kill me now?"

"Because refusing redemption is punishment enough," Amadeus said. "Good luck, Marshall Hathaway."

Marshall looked from Amadeus to Janette then to the open runaway ahead of him. And then he ran.

34

Spared from execution by Amadeus, Marshall was halfway to the north end of the runway when about twenty creatures clambered over the chainlink fence that ran around the perimeter. Marshall saw them and changed course. Moments after he did so, two jets flew overhead and dropped something on the creatures. Pillars of brown smoke and debris geysered into the air, and the blast sent Marshall staggering. Four creatures emerged from the blast and bounded toward him. He tried to run, but they closed the distance in seconds and fell upon him.

Lilly looked on as inter-dimensional demons tore her father's murderer to ribbons. It didn't feel like closure, but she supposed it was the next best thing. While she watched, Janette Nguyen spoke into her radio, saying, "Is there space in the nest?" She nodded then turned on her heels. "Right. Great. I'm sending some kids up to you. The Brunmeier boy is with them, as well as a subluminal with them ... yes, a fucking subluminal. You're not paid to ask questions."

Pointing to the control tower, Janette said to Lilly, "Take your friend up there, wait until this is clear—about thirty minutes—then get the hell out of here. Word is things are going to get hot later. I'd love to fly you out, but I need to coordinate operations down—" A trio of jets flew overhead, and flames engulfed a stand of trees in the distance. "—here. I can't promise you'll be safe, but at least you'll be out of the line of fire."

A wave of creatures streamed out of the flames and onto the tarmac. Grassal was still strapped to the stretcher, and Lilly bent to check the straps. When she did, she found them tighter than they had been. She pushed on his chest, and he seemed to bob like a boat. Lilly attributed this to her lack of sleep. Amadeus was staring at the subluminals that were tearing apart Marshall's corpse and made no move to help her. Lilly waved a hand in front of Amadeus' face. He snapped his head up like a student waking from a nap.

"Sorry," he said. Vaskulo scuttled to a point a few meters away, positioning himself between them and the oncoming tide of creatures. "It's weird. I just sent a man to his death, but I don't feel anything."

"You shouldn't. He brought it on himself. Let's get Grassal out of here," Lilly said. They lifted their friend. He felt so light. Before they left, Janette cleared her throat, causing Lilly and Amadeus to turn around. Snow blew around her, and the wind tousled her hair. She quickly shook their hands, and before they parted, she said, "I wish I had more kids like you two. It's been an honor. Good luck. You're going to need it."

35

Hundreds of class Cs and hominid-types had begun to converge on Andrews Air Force Base. Other, as-yet-unclassified kinds of subluminals joined them. One creature had several horse heads growing from an arachnid body structure and towered four meters off the ground. Near it rolled a spiny mass of pulsating black flesh. Another creature's body was an eyeless ovoid the size of a farm tractor that waddled along on two flat feet. A hundred anemone-like tentacles grew from its sides. Several plantlike creatures with an indeterminate shape achieved locomotion by planting and uprooting writhing tendrils.

"This looks like my nightmares took a puke," Lilly said.

Amadeus took all this in as they ran toward the control tower, carrying Grassal between them. Vaskulo trailed behind them, chirping and whistling while it ran. They were only fifty meters from the door, but the creatures were coming so fast from all directions. Some crawled on the buildings that surrounded the tower. Machine-gun fire erupted nearby in the air and was answered with a chorus of bellows like a whale's song amplified in an echo chamber.

"I don't think we're going to make it," Lilly said.

"Don't say that, we—" Amadeus stopped as Grassal gasped and moaned. His stiff body strained against the straps ... only he wasn't moving, and the burden of the stretcher had suddenly become much lighter. Amadeus looked at Lilly to make sure he wasn't hallucinating. She nodded. She felt it too. Something was making Grassal lighter, but he wasn't going to float away like a balloon. The phenomenon was more like pushing the north poles of two magnets together. Vaskulo paced a perimeter around them. A formation of four small aircraft passed over them and released a barrage of rockets into an area near the highway. After a moment, Amadeus realized they were drones.

Thirty meters from the door, a pack of eyeless, mouthless hominid-types swarmed down from the roof and bounded toward them. This was it. Even if they had weapons, there were too many of them coming too fast. Amadeus' heart sank. He looked at Lilly and knew she had reached the same conclusion. Gently, he released his grip on the stretcher. Lilly did the same, and Grassal floated a meter above the ground. Amadeus took his friend's hand in his, leaned over to his ear, and said, "I got back up, Grassal, and I'm going out on my feet. You've been a first-class friend." He kissed Grassal's unshaven cheek before he strode over to Lilly. He held himself tall and kept his eyes locked on hers as the creatures approached. Snow blew all around them.

"Will you forgive me?" Lilly asked. Snowflakes clung to her hair and coat.

"I never stopped loving you, Lilly Jones. Of course I forgive you." Tears welled in Amadeus' eyes as he thought about the life they hadn't yet spent together.

"Ami ... I love you, too."

Her body felt good against his. Amadeus blinked back tears and gazed into her spruce-green eyes as the scuttling pack descended upon them.

36

When the claws failed to take her down, Lilly looked up to see Vaskulo stretched to his full height. His mouth was wide open, releasing what looked like heat waves. The creatures moved past them like water flowing around a river stone. "Amadeus," Lilly said, and Amadeus' eyes grew wide when he saw what she saw. She listened and heard a warbling, atonal melody. The creature was singing, though the timbre was like a violin bow dragged across a single strand of human hair.

Amadeus and Lilly began to laugh, a sound wild and maniacal. They held tight to each other and Grassal while the swarm passed over them. When it was done, Vaskulo dropped back down and started for the door at the base of the control tower. Amadeus grabbed the stretcher and told her to follow them.

"Vaskulo said it can't stop them all," Amadeus said. Lilly looked back to where they had last seen Janette Nguyen and she regretted it: billowing flames and black smoke roiled over the place they had been only minutes ago.

Amadeus must've seen the expression on her face because he said, "If anyone can take care of herself, she can. Come on."

The steel double doors to the control tower were locked, but when Amadeus pounded on them, a man's voice said, "Are you human?"

"Last time I checked," Amadeus said in reply. The door opened. A man with silver hair and gold-rimmed spectacles peered out. Lilly saw a group of uniformed schoolchildren—they looked to be around fourth or fifth graders—huddled under some plastic benches in the lobby. She and her companions stepped inside, but when the old man saw Vaskulo his eyes grew wide and he began backing away. Amadeus put out two conciliatory hands.

Lilly tried to soothe the man. "Easy, easy. This individual's name is Vaskulo, and it just saved our lives."

The man worked his mouth but no sounds came out.

Amadeus said, "How many children are here?"

"Thirteen, including me. I'm their teacher. I brought them on a field trip, and ... that thing! I can't let the children near it."

"It's fine. I promise you," Amadeus said. A sound like a beaver's tail slapping water sent about half the children into fits of crying and wailing. The subluminals had begun to throw themselves against the windows that looked out to the runway.

"The glass won't hold," Amadeus said. "We need to get to the control tower. It's not much, but at least we'll have the fire doors behind us."

The teacher's expression changed. He took a step closer to Amadeus, took off his glasses, and his face broke into a grin.

"I thought I recognized you," the teacher said. He clapped Amadeus on the shoulder. "You're a good kid."

"If you believe that, then you'll have to trust me about Vaskulo. Will you trust me?"

"I don't think I have much choice." The teacher took a deep breath, then said, "Students, follow this man, single file, but keep away from the creature."

37

The empty control tower was large, bright, and warm, but thirteen children, four adults—one of which was on a stretcher —and one inter-dimensional creature made for a tight fit. The children kept their distance from the creature, preferring to huddle against themselves rather than risk coming within arm's reach of it. From their vantage point, Amadeus could see in every direction, and what he saw made him wonder whether they would be able to leave. Creatures continued converging on the snowy airfield from every direction. The military was outnumbered by at least fifty to one. Amadeus watched as one group of Humvees formed a circle to protect a .50-caliber machine gun mounted on a trailer. For a few minutes, the formation worked, and the machine gun tore some of the creatures to shreds, but soon the creatures simply covered the trucks like a snowdrift. Drones occasionally swooped in, releasing payloads of rockets or white phosphorous, but this only eliminated small pockets of the creatures.

Lilly grabbed Amadeus' shoulder and pointed east. He squinted and saw a herd of five class As emerging from the whiteout. They resembled the creature that had pursued Grassal and him out of San Francisco.

"Everyone down," Amadeus said. "If those things see us, they'll tear up the tower." As soon as the words were out of his mouth, he realized their futility. The creatures stood at least ten meters taller than the tower, and they would surely see them huddled inside. Scanning the distance, he selected a couple potential routes through the suburbs that might work for his group, but the area was crawling with creatures. Without weapons or cover, going out there would be the death of them all, but if he could get those drones to lay down suppressing fire along their route, they might have a chance.

Through everything, Amadeus had managed to hold onto the radio, and the radio still had a charge. Amadeus turned it on and spoke.

"This is Amadeus Brunmeier. I am in the control tower at Andrews with over a dozen children. We need a way out of here." He received no response, so he repeated this message over twenty different frequencies. Static was his reward. He looked out over the airfield. The approaching class As were just as ugly as the one he had killed before, the only difference being these had spindly quills the size of flagpoles jutting from their backs.

Finally, the radio squawked. Relief filled him when Janette Nguyen's voice came on.

"It's good to hear your voice," Amadeus said. "I thought you'd been overrun."

"And I thought you'd already escaped. God damn it, A.B."

"What do you mean?"

"This place is twenty minutes away from looking like Dresden on the thirteenth of February, nineteen forty-five."

"They wouldn't."

"Not they, me, and yes, I would. I have to, Amadeus. I've got no choice."

"Did you get out?"

"Hell no. I'm in the mobile command center in hangar D, right in the middle of this shit. I thought we could fight our way out, but there are too many, and if they finish us here, there's nothing to keep them from overrunning downtown. You know what that would do to this country?"

"Janette, please, there are a dozen kids here with me. We can't just let them die."

"Shit, shit, shit," she said. Amadeus started to speak, but Janette cut him off. "Let me think." She yelled something to some subordinates whose answer was inaudible.

"Look, I've got some Humvees equipped with surface-to-air missiles here in the hangar. Between those and the drones, we might be able to blast a path out of here for you."

"That's assuming we can get out of here. But if you open the hangar doors ... your command center—"

"There's nothing left to command. You get out of the control tower, and I'll get you off the airfield. I've already made my decision. I'm done, one way or another. What'll it be, A.B?"

Amadeus answered immediately. "Do it."

"Good. Get everybody downstairs and ready. You move in three minutes. The fireworks begin in about eighteen."

Amadeus tried to speak, but his voice croaked. Janette waited, and finally Amadeus was able to say, "Thank you, Janette."

"Thank me by burying Roland Jessup in an unmarked grave. Good luck, A.B.. Janette Nguyen, head of the Joint Defense Services Corporation, signing off." The radio clicked, and then there was silence. Amadeus looked from Lilly to the children, who sat cross-legged on the floor. About half of them were crying. Some held little navy-blue backpacks over their heads.

"You heard her," Amadeus said, fighting to keep his eyes dry. Within a minute, the drone formation began firing along a direct path northeast, creating a flaming corridor between the control tower and the freeway. Subluminals lined the edges of the corridor. The teacher began to usher the kids to the door, but Amadeus stopped him. "Not yet. We wait."

"Wait? You heard the woman. She's going to bomb this place."

"Two minutes."

Down on the tarmac, the doors of hangar D slid open. A tight row of four desert-brown tanks rolled into the subluminal swarm, secondary guns blazing. They released a simultaneous volley from their main guns, which bought them some breathing room. Two Humvees followed close behind. When the Humvees had cleared the doors, they aimed their turrets toward the class As and released a volley of missiles. The missiles streamed low across the ground and exploded against three of the class As. One dropped. The other two staggered. Black fluid sprayed from their wounds. The remaining four made toward the source of the missiles.

Amadeus looked at the clock: just over a minute until they needed to leave. He needed to make sure they had an exit.

"I'm going to check downstairs," Amadeus said. To Lilly, he whispered, "If I don't make it back, if you hear anything but me outside, do not open that door. Okay?" Lilly nodded, grabbed him by the collar, and kissed him. Amadeus put a hand to her cheek and started down the stairs. By the time he was halfway to the bottom, he could hear grunts, howls, and snorts from the ground-floor observation lobby.

At the base of the stairs, Amadeus put his ear to the door to listen. Something slammed against the metal door. Amadeus jumped back. A dent appeared, followed by another one. A chill ran up Amadeus' spine. He looked around the base of the stairwell for another exit and found none. After sticking his head in the elevator, he confirmed that no lower floors were available.

Amadeus ran back up the stairs and pounded on the door. Lilly opened it for him, her eyes relieved. Just before Amadeus pulled it closed, he heard the ground-floor door crash open. He ascended the six steps inside the control tower and tried to catch his breath. All eyes were on him. He shook his head.

"Blocked. That way," he pointed downstairs, "is no good."

"What do you mean, no good?" the teacher said. Amadeus gave him a forlorn look.

"Children, we've got to brace that door."

The children stared at him.

"I need whatever's not nailed down in front of the door."

"You heard him," the teacher said. "Get to it. Quickly now!" The children piled chairs, computers, and communications gear on the little landing in front of the door.

Amadeus tried to reach Janette on the radio. After several unsuccessful attempts, he dropped the radio and slumped into a chair. Yesterday's newspaper sat beside a transmitter. Amadeus picked it up, tore a strip from the Life section, and crumpled it between his fingers. Lilly plucked the paper from his hand and threw it to the floor. Something scratched against the door. The children screamed.

"Any ideas?" Amadeus said.

"I don't have any, but it's up to something." She nodded to Vaskulo, who had its arms spread wide and its head cocked back toward the sky. Amadeus listened but heard nothing other than the fighting outside, shouts from the radio, and the sniffles of terrified children. Since his encounter with the creature at his house in Stamford, his hearing hadn't quite been the same.

Outside, the tanks released another volley from their primary guns. Another class A dropped to the tarmac, its torso cratered with tank rounds. Three class As and thousands of smaller subluminals remained. The first class A reached the tanks. With a single swipe, it knocked one tank back fifty meters. The tank continued to fire with its secondary guns while aiming its barrel at the class A. Before it had a chance to fire, the class A took two long bounds and crushed the tank underfoot as if it were a soda can. The Humvees retaliated with missile fire, and the class A dropped.

The teacher grabbed Amadeus' arm and pointed. Another wave of creatures had emerged from the wooded area on the north end of the runway. Instead of going toward the fray, however, they began streaming onto the still-smoking path cleared by the drones.

"We wouldn't have made it anyway," the teacher said.

Vaskulo made a series of quick chirps and then leapt up onto a radar screen. After a moment, one of the remaining two class As broke off from the fighting and raced toward their position. The six-legged creature was jet black and stood taller than the control tower. Twenty yellow eyes covered the top of its spade-shaped head. A long, black tongue lolled from the creature's mouth while it walked. Misshapen muscles bulged and flexed with every step. Red spines like a hundred flagpoles swayed on its back.

"That ... that thing is leading the demon to us!" the teacher said. The children screamed and dropped to the ground. The teacher started for Vaskulo. Amadeus grabbed his sweater and held him back. The teacher swatted at his hand, but Amadeus wouldn't let go. Instead, he smiled at the teacher.

"I think this is a good thing."

"A good thing? You have got—"

"Watch," Amadeus said. The teacher stopped struggling and watched.

The creature was only meters away from the glass, but instead of attacking the tower, it began swatting away the subluminals nearby as if they were ants. With one swipe, it sent a dozen smaller subluminals flying across the runway. The creature continued working on the remaining nearby subluminals, alternately crushing, smashing, and shredding them. After less than a minute, only a handful of subluminals remained near the tower. These displayed their sense of self-preservation by running away toward the larger group of creatures gathered in the middle of the airfield, where two tanks and one Humvee remained. Subluminals surrounded them on all sides.

Less than ten meters of open air separated them and the big subluminal. Vaskulo faced the creature and raised both his arms above his head in a semicircle. The big creature did the same, casting a shadow over them as it drew itself up to its full height.

Amadeus and Lilly exchanged a look. From their vantage point, the movement exposed its belly to them. The creature then dropped back to all sixes, causing the ground to shake beneath their feet. Vaskulo did a backwards somersault and landed on the floor beside Amadeus. The big creature extended a claw toward the control tower.

Glass will rain.

"Everyone, get down," Amadeus said. The children threw themselves to the floor. The teacher put his coat over a couple of his smaller charges. Amadeus covered Grassal with his body. Lying across him felt like holding onto a pool float.

The windows exploded and glass crashed around them. Icy outside air filled the room. Amadeus looked up to see the creature removing a big gray claw from the tower's interior. The children whimpered as a thousand shards sprinkled down over everything. The creature peered in with its tire-sized yellow eyes, then repositioned itself so that its spindly back lined up with the glassless window and pushed its body against the tower. Vaskulo bounded through the window frame and onto the creature's back, eventually settling in the depression where the creature's shoulder blades met.

Amadeus looked at the clock. They had just under ten minutes. The creatures continued to press against the door, and the barricade was beginning to move under the pressure.

"Help me with him," Amadeus said to Lilly as he grabbed Grassal's stretcher. Lilly shook her head. Amadeus saw the doubt in her eyes, put a finger to her lips, and leaned in close to her ear.

"This is our only way out of here. If we don't go with Vaskulo, no one else will either, and you know what that means. I trust Vaskulo, and I need you to trust me—with every ounce of your being. Will you do that for me, Lilly?"

"This feels wrong. It's so weird ... but yes, I'll trust you." Amadeus smiled and replied with a sharp nod. Together they negotiated Grassal's stretcher through the window and onto the creature's back. The red and orange spines made Amadeus think of a bamboo forest on some alien world. Lilly stayed with Grassal, and Amadeus returned to the window's edge. Several of the children were ready to follow their lead, but the teacher was yelling at them to back away from the window.

"You can't seriously believe that these ... demons are trying to help us," he said. "Children, do not go near that thing. I was wrong about you, Mr. Brunmeier."

"Ride a demon or die by fire. The choice is yours," Amadeus said.

The old man furrowed his brow and harrumphed.

"Do you have any better ideas? Perhaps you think the ground route is preferable." Amadeus pointed to the place where the vehicles had been. Only a mountain of shredded scrap metal remained. His throat constricted and he looked away. Something cracked in the barricade. "And that's assuming you can get down the stairs. I'm sure that would end well. The main benefit is that you wouldn't have to live very long with your mistake."

"But they're monsters," he said. "They kill people."

"As of today, I'm a monster as well, and so is my friend. We both sent men to their deaths. People become monsters when it's in their best interest. And right now, it's in everyone's best interest but ours to fire bomb this place and destroy these creatures before they head downtown. You and I, we can't stop that. So we have to choose: trust a monster or die defiant, and allow the innocent to die with us. What'll it be?" The teacher stroked the skin waddle beneath his chin, muttered a curse, then began to shout.

"Children, it's time to go. Grab a spine and hold on!"

Together, Amadeus and the teacher helped the children from the floor to the instrument panel and onto the subluminal's back. A few children were hesitant, but with some encouragement and cajoling from the teacher and Amadeus, all the children made the transition safely. Amadeus was the last on. No sooner had he put both feet down on the creature than the creature began bounding away from the airfield and along the charred path the drones had cleared. As the chaos faded behind them, Amadeus directed a salute in the direction of Janette Nguyen's twisted metal grave.

38

Lilly never saw the jets, only the results of their work: a thousand angry fingers of flames and roiling black smoke that reached into the winter sky. Even from their distance of about a kilometer away, she felt the heat of the flames, and realized if they had been any closer to the blast zone, they would all have wicked sunburns. She wondered if today's events would be filed under "brilliant strategic decisions" or "modern pyrrhic victories."

The creature carried them north on the Beltway. Where they were going, Lilly wasn't sure. She knew only that the creature was more nimble than she had imagined, gracefully wending its way over stalled traffic. Its footsteps were light, and it seemed to be making a special effort not to crush any vehicles below.

They approached a military convoy and small-arms fire erupted. Amadeus began shouting into his radio. Within seconds, the gunfire stopped, and they continued unmolested. Lilly looked down to the convoy to see twenty pairs of eyes staring up at them in disbelief. Lilly waved down at them. No one waved back.

Behind them, black smoke rose and spread across the sky like ink dropped in water. Before them spread the outlying suburbs. Occasionally she heard random bursts of gunfire, but either the creature was unfazed by the shots or the shooters had terrible aim.

Their pace remained constant until they reached a football field. The creature cast a shadow from the goal to the fifty-yard line. The teacher's eyes were wide and his expression perplexed. In the middle of the field, the creature kneeled, stretched out its legs, and exhaled rancid air from its lungs. This made the distance between the turf and the creature's back only a couple meters. Some of the children were laughing while they slid down the creature's smooth side.

The teacher said to Amadeus, "This is their school. How did it know?" Amadeus shrugged and shook his head. The teacher accepted this non-answer and stuck out one hand. Amadeus took it, and they shook.

"I owe you an apology, Mr. Brunmeier."

"Not necessary, but accepted."

The teacher climbed down from the creature and ushered the children toward their school. The creature returned to its feet, and Lilly pulled Grassal's still-floating stretcher behind her as she moved closer to Amadeus. Twenty meters above the ground, she wrapped an arm around his waist and looked into his eyes. He smiled at her, but the smile concealed something—sadness maybe, as well as determination.

"We're never going to have a normal life, are we, Amadeus?" Amadeus chuckled and shook his head.

"Gravity and Janette Nguyen are dead. My best friend is catatonic and floating. My father is hiding out with a wealthy madman. My inter-dimensional demon pal Vaskulo tells me the presence of these subluminals threatens the very existence of our world. And somehow, I have to find a way to make everything right. This is my normal. Do you want to be a part of it? Are you all in?"

As the DC suburbs passed below them, Lilly's heart skipped a beat as she realized what he was asking. She responded with a breathless, "Yes."

"I mean totally in. I promise to love you, to treat you right, to give you what you need, but I need you to trust me, no matter what happens, or what the world tries to throw at us. May I have your trust?"

A tremble raced through her body. She touched his face and said, "It's yours. I promise."

"Then," a sly smile crept onto his face, "will you marry me, Lilly Jones?"

"Yes, Amadeus Brunmeier, I would love to marry you."

Amadeus' face broke into a wide smile. He pulled a brightly colored ring from his pocket. She thought the stone was opal, but it could've been plastic. It didn't matter. She smiled, and he slipped it over her finger. As the sun set behind them and snow clung to their clothes, they kissed and held each other against the rising dark of another winter's night.

Epilogue

Everything was falling apart, despite the successes.

"God motherfucking damn it," the administrator said. Snow fell from grey skies into the choppy Atlantic waters. The sun had just dropped below the horizon. He paced the deck of his ship, occasionally slapping his hand against the steel handrail.

The administrator looked at his assistant, a scrawny Iraqi boy related to poor Abdullah by blood or marriage or some opaque tribal affiliation.

"How many gates are left?"

"Three of the four in the metro DC area, as far as we know, and all seven up and down the coast. We've dispatched teams to destroy them. The gates should be out of commission within the next twenty-four hours."

He'd been too ambitious, and now he had to clean up his own mess. "How many nasty Ts are we looking at?"

The assistant typed some commands into his phone. "At last count, twelve thousand, three hundred and forty six, all varieties, plus twenty-five class As."

"That's twenty more class As than we needed. Do you know how fucking hard those things are to kill? No, don't answer that."

The administrator left the deck and walked down the stairs to his command center, his assistant trailing behind him. Inside, two technicians sat at workstations. They hunkered down when they saw the administrator. A screen hanging on the wall showed a list of key assets. Alpha team was still tangled up downtown. This was going to make cleanup significantly more difficult. Eight more screens flicked among video feeds from up and down the coast. DC, Baltimore, and Atlantic City were FUBARed. The gates down in the Carolinas and Georgia were shitting out subluminals, but at least down there everybody and their grandmother owned a couple rifles for killing animals. Only, the administrator knew better than anyone that the nasty Ts were anything but animals.

"Where is that fucking engineer?"

"Which one, sir?

"'Which one, sir?' Come on, kid. Use that noggin. The one who signed off on the new design. Go find him." The assistant scurried out of the room.

The administrator put his hands to his temples and expelled a long sigh. He never wanted this. Just a couple hundred of them popping here and there would've kept him and his boys flush in work for the next several months, but he'd gotten too ambitious. Seven gates were too many. It wasn't like he needed to convince anyone of the necessity of his services. Washington knew they needed him. They'd passed the KREATURE Act for him. One gate, maybe two, would've been plenty—*plenty*—but no. He had to sign off on seven gates, seven *defective* gates, all of which lacked a properly functioning inter-dimensional sphincter. Worse, his theory had been wrong, too. Americans hadn't grown stronger and more unified through struggle. They'd just gotten bitchier.

The engineer, Abdullah's replacement, appeared in the door, all frail and pigeon-toed.

"You wanted to see me, Mr. Jessup?"

The administrator stood up from his seat, grabbed the engineer by his comb over, and turned his face toward a screen that showed flames rising from the Capitol building.

"Look at what your sloppy work has done. I told you to check, double-check, and triple-check for bugs. I told you we couldn't afford any mistakes. I told you the future of our organization depended on the quality of your work. And what did you say? You said, 'It's good, Mr. Jessup. I've got this. I'm a Six Sigma black belt.' Black belt, my fucking ass. Do us all a favor and go throw yourself overboard."

The administrator gave the engineer a good push, and he scampered out of the room. As soon as the engineer left, the president stepped into the command center. With his thumbs hooked in the belt loops of his jeans, he scanned the room. The two technicians got to their feet to greet him. The president flashed the technicians a smile, then inclined his head toward the door. They took the hint and left.

"Good afternoon, Mr. President."

"Roland, Roland, Roland," the president said, placing a familiar hand on the administrator's shoulder. "All these years, you've been great. Truly, you have. From your work in Iraq to the Narco Wars, to the cleanup, you've been the most effective operator a politician could ask for. But this time ... this time, you fucked up, kid. You've overplayed your hand, over-farmed your field, shot your wad, *et cetera, et cetera*. Your operation's done jumped the shark, and ... you follow me?"

The administrator nodded but made no attempt to look contrite. "I take full responsibility, Mr. President."

"Then you'll figure out a way to clean this up. This is far, far beyond what we talked about. You were supposed to call just enough of those things to affirm the inherent *rightness* of the KREATURE Act. But ..." He pointed to the screens, which spoke for themselves and finished his thought. "So put those damn gates in reverse, reverse the polarity, flip the orientation, whatever the hell it is you do. You think I wanted to put this contingency plan into action?"

"It doesn't work like that, sir," the administrator said.

"Then how about a virus, like in *War of the Worlds*? Or a

food allergy? Everybody's got those damn things nowadays. My chief of staff says he's allergic to water unless it's got alcohol in it. The bastard stays drunk all afternoon."

"I'll take that into consideration, Mr. President."

The president gazed at a feed showing the smoking ruins of an airfield.

"Can you believe that crazy bitch? Blew up Andrews. Man, I never thought I'd see anything like that. Glad I was already on my way down when that happened."

"I respect her sense of duty, Mr. President."

"You stiff son of a bitch. Cut it with that 'Mr. President' shit. Technically, it's your fault I'm dead," he said, using his fingers to put air quotes around the word "dead." "It's an unwritten rule that when you kill a man, you can dispense with formal titles. As of today, the VP's taking over. Official word is I died taking potshots at subluminals from the Truman Balcony. I'm gone like the breeze, obsolete like Betamax, and out like the fat bitch in dodgeball. With all this shit going down, I'm happy to become a nobody, and I look forward to spending my golden years boozing and whoring in tropical environs. I feel bad for leaving the job to Darlene, but she knew what she was signing up for." The president turned on his heel and started for the exit. Before leaving, he turned to the administrator. "And Roland? Kill that Brunmeier kid, will you? I was wrong: that little fucker and his pals *were* right in the middle of this."

"I thought you—"

"He was good for numbers, but my numbers don't matter much now, only my Wikipedia entry. My God, this is going to keep the conspiracy theorists busy for decades." The president chuckled to himself as he left.

"Yes, sir."

Alone, the administrator sat down and put his head in his hands. Maybe there was another way. The president was full of shit—they both knew it—but maybe he could convince Big Ugly to call them off.

Deep in the ship's hold, outside the door to the containment pens, a guard opened the door for the administrator. Everything smelled of rotten meat, ozone, and ammonia, and the administrator had that sick feeling in his stomach, just as he always did when he saw these fucking things.

He reached his destination and peered through the polycarbonate wall of the creature's pen. Big Ugly was eating from a pile of ammonia-drenched fish and kelp. The Takun twitched and looked up from its meal. Its body was long and sleek, like an amphibious reptile, but its insectile head was covered with yellow and purple eyes, all of which now stared at the administrator.

You seek counsel. For you, human, I have none.

"Come on, now, Big Ugly. Your brethren, or whatever the hell you call them, are having a great party. And these new ones, the humanoid ones, I hear they're *especially* effective, given their sheer creep-factor."

The administrator took a step forward and pulled his shirt up over his nose.

You create them only to die. Takun as fodder. For your money.

"Aw, that's not true. Eventually, things will settle down, and we'll all coexist, one big happy family. But until then, yes, some will die. But isn't it better than life as a fungus?"

Nonbeing was everything. The Luminance was our souls' home. Existence is pain. Our song is a mourner's lament.

"They're birthing pains. It's nothing to worry about. For most of human history, birthing new life was a dangerous business."

Takun were pulled here without choice.

"Ah, the teenager's complaint: I didn't choose to be born. Well, fella, you're all here now, and pretty soon we're going to have to learn to get along. Don't get into one of those depressive moods of yours. Besides, killing them's no big deal. You said so yourself: all the dead Takun simply return to the Luminance, so no harm done. Right?"

They are you. You are us. You made us from your memory. You harm yourself every time we die.

The subluminal's rump twitched, and it flung itself against the glass walls of its containment pen. Its grotesque face smooshed against the polycarbonate, and the administrator would've laughed if he hadn't nearly pissed himself. The creature slammed its powerful claws against the glass once, twice, and a third time. The floor beneath the administrator shook. Then the creature crouched, and a sense of discomfort washed over the administrator. He closed his eyes.

When he opened them, he was in his childhood bedroom. He looked down and saw a book that contained illustrations of monsters in his small hands. The present page showed scaly and ferocious European and Asian dragons. Even though nearly forty years had passed since he'd thought about that book, he remembered its familiar weight and the slick feel of its pages. He flipped to the next page. As soon as he did so, he closed the book, but he took control of the memory and opened it back up. There, in full color, were illustrations of grotesque creatures with mottled skin and heads covered in eyes attached to squat, powerful frames.

The administrator dropped the book and backed away, knocking over a table where several Little League participation trophies sat. The administrator curled up into a ball and covered his face with his hands as the familiar hiss of a subway car's brakes replaced the quiet of his bedroom. He lay on brown, hexagonal tile. Warm liquid flowed from his body. He knew this scene too well, but he uncovered his face anyway. Twenty feet away lay Alyssa and Kaylee. Blood pooled around their still bodies.

Squeezing his eyes shut, the administrator willed the vision to end. Normally, his recollection of this scene would segue to the hospital room in which he had awakened a man robbed of everything he loved.

Not now.

The administrator groped on the floor until his fingers

touched something cool and heavy—a long-barreled revolver. Grabbing the gun, he felt a rush of strength, and the administrator got to his feet. He looked around for the shooter, but the platform was empty, no one else but himself and his dead family. Inside the revolver's cylinder, a single bullet was missing. No one else. No one else ...

The revolver slipped from his fingers. When it hit the floor, the subway car's doors opened and a thousand Takun streamed out, filling the platform with their corruption. They swarmed first over the bodies of his wife and child before enveloping him. The administrator put his arms over his face and screamed until he realized he was not being torn apart.

When he uncovered his face, he saw he was still standing before the thick glass of Big Ugly's cage. Letting his arms drop, the administrator began taking deep, slow breaths in an attempt to bring his heart rate down and control his shaking limbs.

"Shit like that is why you can't come up and play with the big kids ... because after driving us insane, I'm pretty sure you'd rip out our hearts and eat them, just for fun."

The Takun turned his back on the administrator, and the administrator was glad. He knew his eyes were puffy and red. He'd need a few minutes to compose himself, lest his people get any ideas about what really went on during his conversations with his communicator.

A few minutes passed, and the administrator returned to his cabin. There, he poured himself three fingers of bourbon, took a drink, and set the glass on an end table. Collapsing into his chair, the administrator adjusted the familiar shape of the doll until it sat just so between his left hip and the chair's leather arms. The bourbon sloshed in its glass as the ship hit rough water.

"It's going to be a long, long night, baby girl."

Afterword

Thank you for reading this latest installment in the *Emergence* series. Find out what happens next in *Reunion: The Emergence, Book 3*, which is now available.

If you enjoyed this book—and I sincerely hope that you did— please take a moment to leave a quick review on Amazon or Goodreads. Even better, pass a copy of this work along to your friends. By doing so, you'll support my little writing career and help new readers discover my work.

You can learn more about my current and upcoming books at www.sethmbaker.com. While you're there, please join my mailing list and I'll keep you up to date about new releases.

As always, I appreciate your time and patronage.

Seth M. Baker

Acknowledgements

Thanks to Chris Enix, Stacey Buckner, and my ever-patient wife Tiffany for slogging through earlier versions of this work and pointing out all that was illogical, nonsensical, and/or downright rotten. Special thanks also go to Deranged Doctor Design for the fantastic cover, to Sharon Honeycutt for her sharp-eyed editorial services, and to Stephanie Diaz and Celestian Rince for proofreading this work.

About the author

Seth M. Baker has worked as a software engineer, international English teacher, freelance writer, and pizza delivery driver. He's been making up stories since he was a kid.

He grew up in West Virginia, USA and has traveled extensively. His earliest memory is of a wildfire consuming the hill behind his house.

He lives in a misty Appalachian valley with his wife and sons.